The Footsteps That Stopped

A Chief Inspector Pointer Mystery

By A. E. Fielding

Originally published in 1933

The Footsteps That Stopped

© 2014 Resurrected Press
www.ResurrectedPress.com

Published by Intrepid Ink, LLC

Intrepid Ink, LLC provides full publishing services to authors of fiction and non-fiction books, eBooks and websites. From editing to formatting, to publishing, to marketing, Intrepid Ink gets your creative works into the hands of the people who want to read them.
Find out more at www.IntrepidInk.com.

ISBN 13: 978-1-937022-75-4

Printed in the United States of America

Other Resurrected Press Books in *The Chief Inspector Pointer Mystery* Series

The Eames-Erskine Case
The Footsteps that Stopped
The Clifford Affair
The Cluny Problem
The Craig Poisoning Mystery
The Tall House Mystery
Tragedy at Beechcroft
The Case of the Two Pearl Necklaces
Mystery at the Rectory
Scarecrow

RESURRECTED PRESS CLASSIC MYSTERY CATALOGUE

J. S. Fletcher
The Herapath Property
The Rayner-Slade Amalgamation
The Chestermarke Instinct
The Paradise Mystery
Dead Men's Money
The Middle of Things
Ravensdene Court
Scarhaven Keep
The Orange-Yellow Diamond
The Middle Temple Murder
The Tallyrand Maxim
The Borough Treasurer
In the Mayor's Parlour
The Saftey Pin

R. Austin Freeman
The Mystery of 31 New Inn from the Dr. Thorndyke Series
John Thorndyke's Cases from the Dr. Thorndyke Series
The Red Thumb Mark from The Dr. Thorndyke Series
The Eye of Osiris from The Dr. Thorndyke Series
A Silent Witness from the Dr. John Thorndyke Series
The Cat's Eye from the Dr. John Thorndyke Series
Helen Vardon's Confession: A Dr. John Thorndyke Story
As a Thief in the Night: A Dr. John Thorndyke Story
Mr. Pottermack's Oversight: A Dr. John Thorndyke Story
Dr. Thorndyke Intervenes: A Dr. John Thorndyke Story
The Singing Bone: The Adventures of Dr. Thorndyke
The Stoneware Monkey: A Dr. John Thorndyke Story
The Great Portrait Mystery, and Other Stories: A Collection of Dr. John Thorndyke and Other Stories
The Penrose Mystery: A Dr. John Thorndyke Story

The Uttermost Farthing: A Savant's Vendetta

Arthur Griffiths
The Passenger From Calais
The Rome Express

Fergus Hume
The Mystery of a Hansom Cab
The Green Mummy
The Silent House
The Secret Passage

Edgar Jepson
The Loudwater Mystery

A. E. W. Mason
At the Villa Rose

A. A. Milne
The Red House Mystery

Baroness Emma Orczy
The Old Man in the Corner

Edgar Allan Poe
The Detective Stories of Edgar Allan Poe

Arthur J. Rees
The Hampstead Mystery
The Shrieking Pit
The Hand In The Dark
The Moon Rock
The Mystery of the Downs

Mary Roberts Rinehart
Sight Unseen and The Confession

Dorothy L. Sayers

Whose Body?

Sir William Magnay
The Hunt Ball Mystery

Mabel and Paul Thorne
The Sheridan Road Mystery

Louis Tracy
The Strange Case of Mortimer Fenley
The Albert Gate Mystery
The Bartlett Mystery
The Postmaster's Daughter
The House of Peril
The Sandling Case: What Would You Have Done?

Charles Edmonds Walk
The Paternoster Ruby

John R. Watson
The Mystery of the Downs
The Hampstead Mystery

Edgar Wallace
The Daffodil Mystery
The Crimson Circle

Carolyn Wells
Vicky Van
The Man Who Fell Through the Earth
In the Onyx Lobby
Raspberry Jam
The Clue
The Room with the Tassels
The Vanishing of Betty Varian
The Mystery Girl
The White Alley
The Curved Blades

Anybody but Anne
The Bride of a Moment
Faulkner's Folly
The Diamond Pin
The Gold Bag
The Mystery of the Sycamore
The Come Back

Raoul Whitfield
Death in a Bowl

And much more!
Visit ResurrectedPress.com
for our complete catalogue

FOREWORD

The period between the First and Second World Wars has rightly been called the "Golden Age of British Mysteries." It was during this period that Agatha Christie, Dorothy L. Sayers, and Margery Allingham first turned their pens to crime. On the male side, the era saw such writers as Anthony Berkeley, John Dickson Carr, and Freeman Wills Crofts join the ranks of writers of detective fiction. The genre was immensely popular at the time on both sides of the Atlantic, and by the end of the 1930's one out of every four novels published in Britain was a mystery.

While Agatha Christie and a few of her peers have remained popular and in print to this day, the same cannot be said of all the authors of this era. With so many mysteries published in the period, it is inevitable that many of them would become obscure or worse, forgotten, often with no justification than changing public tastes. The case of Archibald Fielding is one such, an author, who though popular enough to have a career spanning two decades and more than two dozen mysteries has become such a cipher that his, or as seems more likely, her real identity has become as much a mystery as the books themselves.

While the identity of the author may forever remain an unsolved puzzle, there are some facts that may be inferred from the texts. It is likely that the author had an upbringing and education typical of the British upper middle class in the period before the Great War with all that implies; a familiarity with the classics, the arts, and music, a working knowledge of French, an appreciation of the finer things in life. The author has also traveled abroad, primarily in the south of France, but probably to Belgium, Spain, and Italy as well, as portions of several of the books are set in those locales.

The books attributed to Archibald Fielding, A. E. Fielding, or Archibald E. Fielding, are quintessential Golden Age British mysteries. They include all the attributes, the country houses, the tangled webs of relationships, the somewhat feckless cast of characters who seem to have nothing better to do with themselves than to murder or be murdered. Their focus is on a middle class and upper class struggling to find themselves in the new realities of the post war era while still trying to live the lifestyle of the Edwardian era. Things are never as they seem, red herrings are distributed liberally through the pages as are the clues that will ultimately lead to the solution of "the puzzle," for the British mysteries of this period are centered on the puzzle element which both the reader and the detective must solve before the last page.

A majority of the Fielding mysteries involve the character of Chief Inspector Pointer. Unlike the eccentric Belgian Hercule Poirot, the flamboyant Lord Peter Wimsey, or the somewhat mysterious Albert Campion, Pointer is merely a competent, sometimes clever, occasionally intuitive policeman. And unlike the Inspector French stories of Freeman Wills Croft, the emphasis is on the mystery itself, not the process of detection.

Pointer is nearly as much of a mystery as the author. Very little of his personal life is revealed in the books. He is described as being vaguely of Scottish ancestry. He is well read and educated, though his duties at Scotland Yard prevent him from enjoying those pursuits. He is fluent in French and familiar with that country. He is, at least in the first book, unmarried, sharing lodgings with a bookbinder named O'Connor, in much the manner of Holmes and Watson, though O'Connor disappears in the subsequent volumes.

While the early books fall plainly in the "humdrum" school with Pointer appearing almost immediately and much of story revolving on the business of tracking down various clues, the later novels are much more concerned with the lives of the characters surrounding the mystery. Pointer is much less center stage, often arriving instead at mid-book to clean up the pieces and insure that the guilty do not escape justice. It is, perhaps, this lack of focus on the detective, which has caused the works of Fielding to fade away while the likes of Poirot seem to attract the interest of each new generation.

One intriguing feature of the Pointer mysteries is that they all involve an unexpected twist at the end, wherein the mystery finally solved is not the mystery invoked at the beginning of the book. I leave it to the reader to judge whether Fielding is "playing by the rules" in this, but it does keep the books interesting up to the last chapter.

The Footsteps That Stopped is the third mystery in the series involving Chief Inspector Pointer. It begins in a fairly conventional manner with the death of Mrs. Tangye, the wife of a man of business. The death has the appearance of either suicide or an accident, but of course Pointer suspects murder. Clues implicate various suspects including her husband, the nephew of an earlier husband, her companion and so on, yet until he can determine *how* the murder was committed, the chief inspector can't even prove that a crime *has* been committed. All seems to rest on the mysterious footsteps one of the maids claims to have heard just before the death, footsteps that stopped. *The Footsteps That Stopped* is a delightful period mystery that will keep the reader guessing until the final chapter.

Despite their obscurity, the mysteries of Archibald Fielding, whoever he or she might have been, are well written, well crafted examples of the form, worthy of the interest of the fans of the genre. It is with pleasure, then, that Resurrected Press presents this new edition of *The*

Footsteps That Stopped and others in the series to its readers.

About the Author

The identity of the author is as much a mystery as the plots of the novels. Two dozen novels were published from 1924 to 1944 as by Archibald Fielding, A. E. Fielding, or Archibald E. Fielding, yet the only clue as to the real author is a comment by the American publishers, H.C. Kinsey Co. that A. E. Fielding was in reality a "middle-aged English woman by the name of Dorothy Feilding whose peacetime address is Sheffield Terrace, Kensington, London, and who enjoys gardening." Research on the part of John Herrington has uncovered a person by that name living at 2 Sheffield Terrace from 1932-1936. She appears to have moved to Islington in 1937 after which she disappears. To complicate things, some have attributed the authorship to Lady Dorothy Mary Evelyn Moore nee Feilding (1889-1935), however, a grandson of Lady Dorothy denied any family knowledge of such authorship. The archivist at Collins, the British publisher, reports that any records of A. Fielding were presumably lost during WWII. Birthdates have been given variously as 1884, 1889, and 1900. Unless new information comes to light, it would appear that the real authorship must remain a mystery.

Greg Fowlkes
Editor-In-Chief
Resurrected Press
www.ResurrectedPress.com

CHAPTER ONE

"I THINK I'll go on up to Riverview." Chief Inspector Pointer, one of the Big Five of New Scotland Yard, laid down the report which he was reading. "Yes, I think I'd like to see the house where yesterday the mistress was found shot, the companion seems to've been endowed with second sight, and where a caller apparently dissolved into air."

Superintendent Haviland stared at him blankly, and then around his own Twickenham police station.

"The coroner's verdict was 'Death by misadventure,'" he said finally, glancing at the clock as though to assure himself that that was only half an hour ago. "Of course, as I was just saying to Mr. Wilmot here, the verdict's all wrong, but it was the only possible one according to the witnesses. Perhaps it's just as well. It sounds better than 'suicide,' for the relatives."

They were talking of the death of Mrs. Tangye who had been found, yesterday afternoon, sitting dead beside her tea-table, with a service-revolver lying on the floor beside her, and a bullet from it through her heart. The Webley was a souvenir of her days as an officer in the Waacs during the last year of the war, and was kept on a bracket in the room. Her husband had explained to the Coroner that his wife had recently spoken of having her initials engraved on it. He suggested that she must have been looking it over with that in her mind when she had met with her fatal accident. The Coroner thought this sounded highly probable. There was no question at the inquest, or before it, of foul play. To say that there was no sign of a struggle, hardly did justice to the ordered neatness of the room and the dead woman. She wore at neck and wrist fine lace frills which would have torn at a touch. The very material of her new gray velvet frock was as spotless and smooth as when she had slipped into it after lunch. The bullet fitted the revolver. The only finger-prints on the butt were those of the dead woman. Apart from these facts, Mrs. Tangye was the last person to sit tamely in a chair and let any one press a weapon against her breast, as the blackened frock, as well as the autopsy, showed must have been done. She was a good shot. She had once in France put a bullet through a drunken Annamite's foot with most unrattled precision.

The chair on which she was found was a fragile, gilt affair which she favoured for making tea. Any struggle, and over it would have gone. It was not so much as scratched. Behind her stood a none too firmly placed electric stand-lamp. It too would have crashed very easily. On the table beside her lay a china bell-push. The bell was in perfect order, and had not been rung.

Nothing was reported missing. Her purse lay in her handbag with over five pounds in it on a chair in the room. The French windows were said to have been found locked from the inside. The servants were certain that no one could have entered the house unnoticed between four, the hour when Florence, the parlour-maid, had brought in the tea-things and seen her mistress alive, and six, when she had made the terrible discovery.

No sound of a shot had been heard, and yet the revolver bore no marks of a silencer. It was thought that it must have gone off when some noisy vehicle was passing.

All the friends of Mrs. Tangye with whom the police had been able to get into touch agreed that she had seemed in the best of spirits, and that the suicide was out of the question.

She was thirty-five, and even the gossipy circle could not hint at any entanglement on her part.

Yet Haviland, the Twickenham police Superintendent, did believe that it had been a case of suicide. For on the day before her death Mrs. Tangye had sent off a large trunk of clothes to the Salvation Army leaving out for herself only the garment she was wearing. And yesterday, the fatal day, she had spent some hours destroying all her private papers.

"What on earth do you mean, Pointer?" Wilmot, the third man, asked curiously. "I've seldom listened to duller evidence. But I suppose I'm prejudiced. Naturally, as a newspaper man, I had hoped for something more worth while, more–"

The door flew open. A young man dashed in. Nodded to Wilmot and Haviland. Shot a discreet glance at Pointer. Seated himself in front of a battered typewriter in one corner, and began a spirited imitation of a machine-gun in action.

Pointer looked at him.

It was a pleasant glance, and Newnes was one of the youngest reporters on the Staff of the *Daily Courier*, but he interpreted it correctly.

"Let me see to-morrow's sun rise!" he pleaded. "I was the first person called in by Mrs. Tangye's maid, you know. And this is my last will and testament concerning her. You needn't caution me to print nothing without permission. I'm more than discreet. I'm dull."

The men laughed.

"Perhaps you wouldn't mind telling your story again. I wasn't at the inquest." Pointer settled himself in a chair.

Newnes, like all his craft, minded nothing but exclusion. He began at once:

"Yesterday afternoon, about six, I had just strolled over Richmond Bridge, when a maid rushed out of one of the big houses screaming, 'A doctor! Help! Help! She's dead!'

"Behind her in the doorway stood another woman, who called to the first to 'Come back, Florence! Come back at once!'

"I thought if 'she' was dead, I couldn't do much harm. So I said 'Hold on. I'm half a doctor. Let's see what's wrong.'

" 'She's killed herself. Oh, she's dead! Come in and see what you can do for her, sir. Oh, the poor mistress!'

"I took her by the arm and walked her back to the door again, where the other woman, who turned out to be Mrs. Tangye's companion, was still standing. I explained that I had been a medical student (I didn't add that it was only for two months) and that perhaps I could do as well as anybody. 'Quite as well.' She said as coolly as you please: 'There's been an accident. Mrs. Tangye has shot herself. I think no one ought to go in till I've telephoned to the police. Better give that hysterical girl something to quiet her meanwhile.'

"I pointed out that as she and the maid had both been in the room, I might be permitted a look at the lady. Possibly something could be done after all. She nodded towards a door. I opened it, and stepped in. I heard her ring up the police station as I did so. There, beside a tea-table in a deep recess, sat a handsome, well-dressed woman with her head sunk on her breast. She looked about thirty. She was quite dead. Her cheek, which I took care to do no more than touch, was icy. A revolver. . . ." He proceeded to describe what he had seen:

"While I was making my notes, the Superintendent arrived. He--"

"Many thanks." Pointer held out his hand. "If anything turns up that the papers can be usefully told, you shall have the first hint. And now—sorry, you know, but police-routine—"

Newnes made no protest. In a large town, a man is a reporter, not by the grace of God, but of the police.

Wilmot came under quite another heading. His discretion, like his position, was not a mere promise, but a well established fact. For several years, he and his articles had been the helpers of the law. For Wilmot was that much abused definition, a criminologist. And a great one.

"The ploughman homewards plods his weary way." He watched from the window Newnes' reluctant turning of the corner. "And now, may merely mortal man inquire what has brought one of the Big Four of the New Scotland Yard upon the scene?"

Pointer drew out his pipe. "When there's anything odd about the actions of three people connected with a case in town which ends in a death, or rather begins in one, some man from the Yard is sure to drop in sooner or later. Merely as a matter of routine."

"Odd about *three* people, sir?" Haviland repeated aghast.

"Let me see," Wilmot murmured. He loved riddles. "There's Mrs. Tangye for one of course. She didn't shoot herself every day to be sure. But the other two?"

"There's her companion," Pointer said tranquilly.

"Whom you credit with occult powers! A fashionable but quite unexpected attitude."

"How else was this Miss Saunders able to tell so quickly, and so certainly that her employer was dead?" The Chief Inspector filled his pipe, while Haviland listened spellbound. "As the evidence stands, Miss Saunders says that she had barely got back, and was taking off her things in her room upstairs when she heard the maid call out. That, mind you, is the first sign she had that anything was wrong in the house. Now, the parlour-maid says that after one shriek—when she found her mistress sitting cold and still in her chair—she darted from the house in a blind panic. Your Mr. Newnes, who strikes me as an accurate observer, and is, of course, trained to notice carefully, says that he saw Miss Saunders standing in the doorway—already certain, that Mrs. Tangye is dead—when the maid rushes towards him. The maid screams for help. She's natural, however incoherent. The companion composedly tells him there's nothing to be done. If she really only came out of her room when she heard the girl below, it's not easy to understand how she could have been so positive, from one hurried glance, that Mrs. Tangye was past all aid. It looks as though she knows more than we do, about the whole affair. As if, supposing her to have been out at all, she had gone into the room where Mrs. Tangye was, immediately on her return, and found her dead, before going on upstairs."

"What! Without saying a word to any one!" Superintendent Haviland was a married man. Pointer was not. The police officer thought that this was a bachelor's idea of feminine powers.

"And the visitor who vanished into thin air," Haviland went on, "do you mean Mrs. Cranbourn, sir, for your third person? The lady whose coming at six led to the discovery of the body?"

"Just so. Mrs. Cranbourn. But for her having been expected—that point only came out just now at the inquest—"

"No, sir. As a matter of fact I mentioned her name here, in the report I sent in last night." Haviland bent over the sheets.

"It's not the visitor's name. It's the fact that she was *expected*. Known to be coming. . . ."

"Coming by a boat-train," Pointer spoke slowly, with a curious look in his eyes, "so the parlour-maid says she was told by her mistress. No boat-train could get in in time enough to let Mrs. Cranbourn have four o'clock tea with Mrs. Tangye at Riverview. Then why was it ordered at four? And Florence was not to bother to come in again until Mrs. Cranbourn should come." Pointer looked down at his boot-tips meditatively.

"Getting into touch with Mrs. Cranbourn should clear up many difficulties! But even as it is, what became of her?"

"Florence—that's the parlourmaid—thinks she hurried off without waiting, when she saw what had happened. Natural enough under the circumstances." Haviland spoke rather stubbornly.

"But where to? Which way did she go? Straight on up to Heaven? Remember, Newnes saw only the running maid, the standing Miss Saunders, and no one else. You arrived before he left, and found no sign of her."

"When you put it like that, it sounds odd, for a fact." Haviland bit his lip.

The caller had not been seen since. It was believed that she must have slipped away in the general confusion. The Coroner, though he regretted her absence, did not think that her evidence would have been of more use than that of the numerous other friends available. For she had not found Mrs. Tangye alive. Mrs. Cranbourn was a barrister's widow, living in Malaga, and was unknown to the maid by sight. The police had had a cable from the consul there, saying that the lady had left the town a week ago.

"Her visit seems a big trump in Tangye's hand—it certainly points to accident rather than suicide," Wilmot murmured.

Haviland grunted, non-committally.

"Why don't you believe Mrs. Tangye's death an accident, Haviland?" Pointer asked.

"How could it have been one, sir? Apart from the fact of the trigger working uncommon stiff, the safety-bolt acts perfectly, and Mrs. Tangye was used to that particular revolver. Then look at the tearing up of her papers, and the packing off of her duds."

"Tangye explained that, you know," Wilmot reminded him.

"But Mrs. Tangye wasn't going abroad for another month. And why not leave her papers? To my mind, her desk and her wardrobe were as good as a signed confession that she had made away with herself."

There was a short silence.

"Personally my belief hasn't been changed by the verdict," Haviland murmured after a pause, "though it ends the case as far as we are concerned."

"Unless, of course you, sir—" he turned to Pointer and

left the sentence unfinished.

"Any special reason you know of which isn't given in the reports for her to've killed herself?" was his only answer.

"Well, there's Mrs. Bligh. She's just left for Cannes this morning. Colonel's widow. Lives in Cadogan Square. Belongs to a very smart set. She and Mr. Tangye. . . ." Haviland's tone was full of meaning. "The fact is, though there's nothing to prove it, I think Mrs. Tangye got wind of the affair, and got fed up. Lost her grip of things, and decided to end it all."

"If every woman whose husband goes off the rails at times were to shoot herself, the surplus of females over males in the British Isles would soon be a thing of the past," Wilmot pointed out dryly. Haviland grinned, but stuck to his guns.

"I don't pretend I mayn't be wrong. As a matter of fact, I've got two headings in my notebook, same as you say you have in your head, Mr. Wilmot, and I enter things accordingly. Most of 'em, so far, go on both pages. I can't think you'll want me to add another headline, sir."

Haviland finished with his eyes on Pointer. The Chief Inspector was skimming through the life story of the dead woman.

"Mable Headly. Only child of the Rev. Charles Headly, rector of Over Wallop for twenty years, and Nether Wallop for thirty," he read out.

"Sounds peaceful!" murmured Wilmot. Haviland took up the tale:

"Miss Headly taught at the Holland Park High School till war broke out. Then went to France as an officer in the Waacs. She married Clive Branscombe, the architect. He built the Chelsea war memorial, I think?"

Haviland turned to Wilmot.

"May he rest in peace, in spite of that and other crimes of a like nature," breathed the newspaper man.

"They lived in Cheyne Walk for some five years. A year after he died, she married Tangye. That was three years ago now."

"Any children?"

"None all round, sir," was the comprehensive reply.

There followed another short silence.

"Only one will known," Pointer mused aloud, "leaving everything to her husband. Made on her marriage to him. Contents familiar to every one. How much did she have to leave?"

"She had nothing when she married Branscombe, but he left her ten thousand in cash, which she promptly invested in Tangye's firm. There's a belief in some quarters in fact, that that was why he married her. The sum came in very handy just then, they do say. And besides that ten, she had some nice bits of property here and there in Worcestershire that were rated for death duties at another ten thousand. Of course, I don't know how much of the land she's sold. You see, she'd destroyed all her memos."

Pointer stood up.

"I'd like to see the revolver."

Haviland brought it from the safe. It would have to be returned within an hour or two to Tangye anyway, he thought. Pointer lifted out the weapon on its slung carrier, puffed some bright coloured powder over it, and blowing gently, studied the result intently with his glass.

"Seems to've taken the marks of her grip very well."

"It has for a fact. The poor soul had been having buttered crumpets for tea."

"Have the Tangye's a dog?"

"No, sir." Haviland looked puzzled.

"Is there a cat in the house?"

"No, sir." Haviland wondered how many more animals would be suggested, but he looked with wrinkled brows at Pointer.

"Those scratches seem recent. What made them?"

"Tangye thinks they must have happened in France. The revolver was always kept in its box at Riverview. You'll notice her fingerprints are over the scratches, so the latter can't mean anything, sir."

Pointer noticed more than that. He gave the weapon another long look before he straightened up.

"I should like the usual photographs and enlargements of that made at once, please." Then the Chief Inspector turned away. "It's a problem!" he said, studying his boot tips.

"You mean the explanation as to whether it was suicide or accident? I can't make up my own mind definitely." Wilmot spoke in a surprised tone. It was true that he was not often afflicted with doubt.

"No. I mean the explanation of the facts."

Haviland pricked up his ears.

"Why, sir, even the fact, which had first seemed puzzling, that, though Mrs. Tangye was considered right-handed like most of the world, the weapon lay beneath her left hand, and carries its finger-prints, was explained by an old friend. Mrs. Tangye had been left-handed in her girlhood, and though she had trained herself out of the habit, yet in moments of great excitement she was liable to 'revert.' Inquiries made in her father's parish—he's been dead these fifteen years nearly—corroborated this. To my mind, there's no question but that it was either suicide or accident. Judging by the facts, that is."

Superintendent Haviland always judged by what he considered facts. And by them alone. "Those finger-prints on her revolver, sir. They're Mrs. Tangye's right enough. It isn't as if there were any reason to suspect they're faked. They're uncommonly clear ones."

"They're uncommon from more points of view than one," the Chief Inspector murmured, with that air of detachment that was so marked a characteristic of his, and so deceptive.

"What in the world are you driving at, Pointer?" Wilmot asked curiously. "Quite apart from her finger-prints, foul play seems an absolute impossibility. Surely no woman would have sat still and let herself be shot down like a mad dog, without a struggle. Without ringing that bell beneath her very fingers!"

"As a matter of fact, sir,"—Haviland was so bewildered that he had some difficulty in finding his voice,—"I very carefully looked even at the cushion on which her feet were resting. I photographed it specially, though it doesn't come out well. Those marks on it could only have been made by a pair of resting feet. She hadn't pressed them in, or tried to rise. Her slippers were a bit dampish from that stroll in the garden which she'd taken just before tea. Yet they hadn't done more than dust the velvet with sand, as you might say."

"How does the woman's death strike you, Wilmot?" Pointer asked abruptly. He was a great admirer of the newspaper man's articles.

"Like Haviland, I think, on the whole, that it was suicide. Though since hearing the evidence just now, I shouldn't be amazed if the husband were right, and it turned out an accident. Certainly the effect of tranquillity in Mrs. Tangye's face and pose struck me very much when I was taken to see her yesterday. I think it was more marked in reality than it is in the photographs of the scene. What intrigues me most in the case, I confess, is that Chief Inspector Pointer should have thought it worth his while to come down about it."

Haviland wondered too.

Pointer did not explain.

"As I said, I'll go on up to Riverview with you, after lunch, Superintendent, if that time will suit you. I want to ask a few questions. The answers may clear up some of the items that puzzle me."

"You interest me tremendously, Pointer. By Jove, you *do* interest me!" Wilmot was not flattering the other. He really was glad now that Newnes had caught him— Wilmot—yesterday. The whole affair was exceptional as far as he was concerned. Newnes had dragged him out of the evening boat-train at Victoria, where he had been on the point of dashing across the Narrows with three other newspapermen of his own standing to investigate a rumour. A rumour which had only reached well-informed circles as yet, and which very guardedly hinted at regicide. It came from a state where such incidents do occasionally lend a mediaeval touch to court life. The special correspondents were all keen as so many unhooded falcons, but Newnes, breathless, dashing up with the effect of long legs floating behind him, had seized Wilmot by the arm.

"Couldn't find you—wanted—stay—Vibart—letter." He gasped. While well-meaning porters draped themselves hastily upon him.

Wilmot, snatching up a bag from between his feet, had sprung out as the wheels began to turn. The two other men were half inclined to follow. If the great Wilmot found it well to stay, where lay the point of their going on? But they thought better of it. Even newspaper men may once in their lives, have relations. It was possible that W. W. had been fetched home for some overwhelming family disaster.

Newnes had handed the man beside him a letter. Tearing it open, Wilmot—in a vile temper—for he had had to make a dash to catch that train, had read:

"DEAR WILMOT,—Rumour unfounded. H. M. was merely having a private week-end. Want you to ring me up on the 'phone immediately.
"Yours, VIBART."

Within five minutes Wilmot was connected with his temporary Chief, editor and permanent friend, Lord Vibart, the owner of the *Daily Courier*. To him the other spake winged words. Since the affair which Wilmot had been commissioned to undertake had fizzled out, Vibart had another suggestion to make. It seemed that the *Courier's* youngest reporter had just had a stroke of beginner's luck by being the first outsider to find a Mrs. Tangye, wife of a member of a well-known county family, sitting dead beside her afternoon tea-table. The police thought it was suicide. Would Wilmot take a look at the case, and send along one of his special articles.

"Of course, I quite understand, my dear chap, that you're above any suicides except royal ones," Vibart said dryly (Wilmot's high opinion of himself was well known) "but I particularly want the spot light to play on Twickenham just now."

Wilmot knew that, and knew why. Vibart was backing a new helicopter, and the trials were to be staged there next month. But he failed to see why he should alter his plans for the sake of the other's pocket.

"It's not in my line," he said unyieldingly. Nor was it. Outside of the realms of politics, murders, difficult and involved, were Wilmot's province. He had no superior in laying bare the psychology of the criminal. And he did it, not with the scalpel, but with the pitying touch of one who saw something beautiful dragged through the mire, something fine blunted. No man living could surpass him in investing the most sordid crime with a touch of the Inner, of the Noble. He was a master in the art of suggestion. Like some marvellous chemist Wilmot could extract 'atmosphere' from a poker and a bottle of stout.

"Anything's in your line, if you'll undertake it," Vibart said placatingly. "Look here, there's no other chap can handle it as you can. Stir up the public to run a special bus out to see the house where it happened."

Vibart had the soul of a tradesman.

"But the arrangements for my holiday are already made," Wilmot protested truthfully enough. As the other affair had fallen through, he did not see why he should not put the clock forward. In fancy he was already basking in a green, sunny nook between Lequectico and San Sebastian, where little black pigs curled their tails in the orchards, and the trout were only waiting to rise to anything with blue Andalusian cock-hackles on it.

"Well, my dear chap, forgive the remark, but he who pays the piper—you know. You stood out for a pirate's ransom before you promised to go to Gretonia. I think we must get our money back somehow. I don't see you returning that cheque." Vibart thought plain-speaking might avail.

It did. Wilmot capitulated. He had gone out with Newnes to Twickenham. To the handsome old house near Richmond Bridge, had sent in an article of "The Hollowness of the Solid," which was a little masterpiece in its own *morne* line, and was prepared to send in one last, on the blood-lust that crowds inquests. Neither article was in the least what Yibart wanted, but Wilmot was apt to take his own line.

Haviland turned away from the safe.

"I've finished now, sir. But I can take you up to Riverview after lunch if that would suit you better."

Wilmot reached for his hat. "I'm off for my deferred holiday in Spain." He spoke with an anticipatory smile. "Otherwise I should have enjoyed hearing how it all flattened out into a most ordinary affair."

"Why not wait a day or two," Haviland urged, "it won't take long either way. I mean, until we find out for certain. The Tangyes like the Branscombes had lived here, or near here, all their lives. We know all about them."

"That's why I'm off," Wilmot tossed a match away. "People whom you know all about, Haviland, aren't in my line at all."

"Don't you believe it, Superintendent, and waste a fond farewell." Pointer scoffed: "We shall see Mr. Wilmot again at Riverview this afternoon, depend on it. And very welcome you'll be," he finished, turning to the newspaper man. "You, and any help you can give us."

"Help? What in?" Wilmot opened his eyes till they looked like round marbles. "Oh—you mean in putting the room to rights after you've had the carpet up, and the wallpaper down, and taken the furniture to pieces. I know your airy methods. But possibly I may drop in on my way to the boat-train for the last time. Possibly I may."

"Very possibly," Pointer agreed. Wilmot, with an answering smile, walked briskly down the steps of the police station.

A hand touched his shoulder, it was Cheale, a solicitor, and the claims investigator to the Company in which the dead woman had been insured.

"I've been combing the streets for you since I lost you after the inquest. Come and have lunch with me."

"This is Twickenham," Wilmot pointed out sadly, "yonder is Bushey Park. Do people lunch hereabouts? If so, prithee where? In Richmond tea-gardens?"

"They take a seat in a friend's car," Cheale steered him towards it, "and let themselves be whirled away to Picadilly."

"Cold grouse? Moselle?" Wilmot bargained, his foot on the step.

"We'll split a bird and a bottle," Cheale answered handsomely. Like the car the lunch was his Company's.

He chose a safe corner, and in guarded voices they discussed the inquest.

"It's a clear and simple case of suicide," Cheale began.

"Clear and simple!" repeated Wilmot. "Is anything ever quite limpid?"

"You think it's suicide," Cheale looked at him with certainty. "What about your article in to-day's *Courier?*"

Wilmot met his gaze with a faint, deprecatory smile. "I'm a newspaper man. When it's a case of two alternatives I naturally choose the more spectacular, or the more dramatic. Whichever word you prefer."

"But speaking as man to man?"

"There you go again," complained Wilmot. The two were old friends. "As what man to what man? As a journalist to the consultant of an insurance company that bars suicides from payments, of course I back suicide. If I were Tangye's friend, and speaking to him, I should equally agree with him as to his wife's death being undoubtedly an accident."

"Turncoat!" the other muttered reproachfully.

"Backslider!"

"I'm a broken reed," Wilmot confessed. "Don't lean on me. I change sides as often as a Chinese regiment—or a lateen sail.

"Singing with the wind;
Veering with the current."

Cheale looked pointedly at the grouse, the wine, and then at the man opposite him. Wilmot and he laughed.

"Our directors read that article of yours this morning. They want you to investigate this case for us, if you will. For, as you say, we have a suicide clause in all our policies. Of course the Company doesn't want to contest an honest claim, as you know well. Not that I mean that Tangye would put forward a dishonest one— "

"But you think so!"

"Well—no. I wouldn't go as far as that, either. Other people too can sit on both sides of the fence. But Tangye struck me as over-keen this morning in the court-room about the death being an accident. Ram it down your throat— dare-you-to-disbelieve-it tone and manner, that I thought a little odd. Though he looks a bit of a blusterer. Also the evidence itself seems to me to point as much to suicide as to a slip. But I must go over to Dublin at once on a complicated investigation that may need time. Will you take the case on? Prove for us that Mrs. Tangye's death, was, what I believe it was, a suicide?"

"How do you prove a suicide?" Wilmot asked captiously. He was known to his conferes as Wilful Willie. "Isn't it rather like proving something to be a ghost? I can see how you prove a murder, but a negative?"

He inhaled the bouquet of the wine. Fragrant. Hinting at far-off violets.

"Yet, quibbling apart, you think it's one? Come, out with the truth! You were better than the best detective in the Brice Revenue Frauds. And in the Tomkins murder, you were right again as to where the murderer would be found. I heard that you prophesied before any one else how the Palking diamond theft would turn out."

"Some song, Caedmon!" Wilmot murmured approvingly, with closed eyes and a fatuous smile. "Sing on, Minstrel! Sing on the Works of Wilmot the Wonder. The Wizardly Winner!"

Cheale took no notice.

"Well then," the Special Correspondent laid aside his chaff. "To my mind, on the evidence as so far known, I— the veritable I—hover between a suicide and an accident. Now inclining strongly to the one, now to the other conviction. When did Mrs. Tangye insure with you?"

"She and her husband both took out policies in favour of each other, instead of settlements, when they married."

"Big ones?"

"Ten thousand pounds apiece."

Wilmot pursed his lips.

"Who pays the premiums?"

"Tangye pays both according to the agreement."

"Supposed to be fairly well-to-do, isn't he?"

"Used to be. Very much so. But the firm has never recovered from that Mesopotamian crash in oils just before he married. And we happen to have private information, that a big Irish broker with whom he has large commitments, won't be able to weather settlement. That's day after to-morrow. Hit by the fall in the franc. If so, Tangye too, may have to go under. I shall be able to get more definite information tomorrow on the spot. Now, what's your answer? Will you look into the case for us? Sift any claims that Tangye may make? As I told you, he's already thundering for the insurance money."

"The river always gives me rheumatism," objected Wilmot.

The other mentioned what sounded like an excellent plaster in Bank of England notes, and Wilmot did not consider himself a wealthy man.

"You'll take your own line, of course." Cheale lit a cigarette. "Had it been any one but you, I intended to suggest looking up Mrs. Tangye's past as a first step."

"Mrs. Tangye's past! Mr. Tangye's present is very much more to the point, believe me, if you hope to prove a suicide."

"That's our platform obviously. The idea of domestic trouble. But you haven't given me an answer yet. Will you take the case on for us?"

"For the truth—yes," Wilmot corrected him quickly. And to do Mr. Cheale and his Company justice, that was what he wanted. They settled it at that. Cheale went into particulars.

His lunch over, Wilmot telephoned his new interest in the case to the Chiswick Police Superintendent, who was just finishing a modest midday meal with the Chief Inspector. Pointer in particular welcomed the news most cordially, for, as he explained to Wilmot, it would greatly help his own inquiries.

"If you'll slip me in under your cloak, and let me ask some questions ostensibly to help you make up your mind I'll be greatly obliged. Otherwise, I should be rather put to it to get the information I need, without arousing suspicion that suspicion was aroused."

As Wilmot taxied out to the two officers, he ran over in his mind the questions he wanted to put. He had not troubled to do so before. Wilmot was not a detective. He had carefully abstained from probing the Hinterland of the Tangye's married life yesterday. All he had sought then was sufficient material for his dreamy, gloomy sketch of the quicksands under the smiling ripple.

Arrived at the station, he hastily skimmed through Haviland's report.

Besides the servants, the household at Riverview only consisted of Mr. and Mrs. Tangye, and Miss Saunders, the companion. It was Miss Saunders who, after telephoning to the police, had rung up Mr. Tangye's offices in the city. The head clerk, who took the message, told her that Mr. Tangye had already started for home. He had reached Riverview in a quarter of an hour to be met by the sympathetic Superintendent with the news of the tragedy.

Questioned about the way in which the rest of the day had been spent by Mrs. Tangye, the maids had had nothing out of the way to report. Nor did the diary which the police had reconstructed with great care of the days before yesterday, the fateful Tuesday, show anything noteworthy.

On Saturday the husband had gone off for a week-end in the country. Mrs. Tangye often shared these, but this time it was a man's shooting party in Norfolk, and she had remained at home. On Sunday morning, however, she had telephoned to a local garage for a car, and had driven down to an orchid-show which was being held at Tunbridge Wells.

She had left home in the car about twelve in the morning, after arranging over the telephone to lunch with a friend in that town. The telephone messages sounded as though both ideas had been suddenly taken. Mrs. Tangye had let her three servants go off duty until six. Returning at that hour, Florence found her mistress had just got back with a headache, and wished dinner cancelled. Next day, Mrs. Tangye had seemed quite herself again.

Most of the morning she had spent at the hair-dresser's. In the early afternoon she had sent Florence, who acted more or less as her maid, with a note to Jay's. It concerned an evening frock which they were making for the woman who was not to live to wear it.

As he read the note aloud which Florence had taken to the firm in question, the Coroner had agreed with the husband that it did not sound as though Mrs. Tangye were weary of life. She had asked for something younger-looking in the way of trimmings to be sent her for selection.

Florence had got back by five, in time to serve tea as usual. Mr. Tangye had returned by then from his week-end. He had only stayed a short time before returning to his office on some very pressing business, which Mrs.

Tangye had told Florence would detain him in London overnight, and possibly for a few days.

The husband explained that the business in town which had taken him away on this last, complete, day of his wife's life, was only an accumulation of letters. There was nothing whatever in the nature of business worries to call him from home.

In the additional notes which the Chief Inspector put at his command, Wilmot learnt a few other items about the husband. Pointer was known to keep his papers always up to time, with suggested work blocked in, and to lock them daily in his safe at Scotland Yard, so that should anything happen to him, the case would not be hampered.

Wilmot read that the firm of Latimer and Tangye was one of the most respected on the London Stock Exchange, and though it had suffered severe losses a couple of years back, yet, by moving from an expensive house in Chelsea to Riverview, and cutting down their household to its present modest proportions, the Tangyes seemed to lead a very comfortable, care-free existence.

Latimer was long dead. Tangye was in sole command.

CHAPTER TWO

THE afternoon was very still with the misty stillness of a day in late November. To Wilmot, the Thames, running so softly beside them as they walked up from the police-station, seemed like the river of life. Enigmatic. Uncertain. Never the same for more than a minute. Now an unbroken stretch of shadows leaden and hopeless. Now a fairy stream, all silver and glitter.

Much hung on their errand. One word from the tall young man swinging ahead in front, and some life now at ease would become a hunted thing. Wanted by the police. The life itself wanted. Forfeit to law. It must be a strange feeling. He had sometimes thought that criminals enjoyed their peril with an awful joy. The exultation of wit pitted against wit. But would that word be spoken here? The Special Correspondent had found nothing yesterday to justify it. He was looking forward keenly to seeing the Chief Inspector at work.

Wilmot had never been accused of a lack of belief in his own very considerable powers. It was therefore, perhaps, characteristic that the possibility of a man entering a room with him, or after him, looking it over, and discovering clues where he could see absolutely nothing, should seem to, him a marvellous feat. He remembered Pointer's words about the dead woman's finger-prints on her revolver. Uncommon in more ways than one, the Scotland Yard expert called them. Yet they had looked all right to Haviland. And they had looked all right to him. They were Mrs. Tangye's without a doubt. What then was odd about them?

Wilmot had never been of the French school which ranks reasoning higher than observation. To him, the bushman's gift of reading a spoor was one of the most entertaining exercises of intelligence still left to a humdrum world.

Twickenham has some fine old houses. Riverview was one of these. Wilmot, looking up at it, thought, as he had thought yesterday when Newnes had taken him to it, that a less likely setting for a tragedy it were difficult to imagine. Every brick spoke of security. Of comfort. Of calm. The garden that surrounded it was an overcrowded, cluttered-up affair where one acre had been made to carry the trees, and shrubberies, and herbaceous borders of three.

Florence, the parlourmaid, opened the door. A constable who had followed took up an unostentatious seat in the hall. Pointer was never eavesdropped.

"Shall I show you to the room, sir?" Florence evidently thought that the house held but the one. Haviland still had the key in his pocket from the inquest. "Miss Saunders is out for the moment, but she'll be back soon."

The three men stepped into a large room which had a little windowless extension jutting out towards the river, forming a snug, draught-proof retreat, where stood a tall lamp, a square double-tiered tea-table, a couple of comfortable armchairs, and the high, slender, little, occasional affair on which Mrs. Tangye had been found seated.

The room itself opened into the garden by a couple of long windows which fastened with a patent catch impossible to open from the outside.

Wilmot looked about him with interest. He had not had time before, or rather, his mind had been too occupied with other things, to let him sense the atmosphere then. Gazing around him now, he tried to reconstruct the dead woman's personality from what he could see, as might a man fresh come, knowing nothing of the tragedy. He was planning a little article on "Hidden Forces" for one of his impressionist sketches.

It was a pleasant room. Dark brown, with covers and

hangings in vivid wall-flower tints ranging from red to clearest amber. It was a comfortable room. Even the castors were well oiled. Symbolic this last, Wilmot thought. Life too, for Mrs. Tangye had evidently been well oiled. It was not in the least a subtle room. Yet the dead woman had obviously cared for music, for, on the two pianos the parts of Stravinsky's own reduction of his latest concerto were still open.

Wilmot flicked the pages shut with a contemptuous finger, murmuring something about "watered Bach." Then he seated himself on a chair by the wall, and folding his arms, stared around him inch by inch. He could see nothing, however small, that looked even odd, let alone suspicious. Evidently neither could Haviland. Though his eyes flew along the walls—the ceilings—the windows— with the speed of a new fighting plane doing stunts at a review. The gaze of both men came to a standstill on Pointer, who was sauntering around the room with his swift, unhurried, step.

He stopped at the tea-table first. On a used plate the handles of a little gilt knife and fork detained him. Then he stooped to the undershelf. Only one cup and plate showed signs of use.

"You found no finger-prints in the room, except those of the people in the house?"

"Just so, sir."

"Those on the bolts of the French windows inside the room were Miss Saunders's?"

Haviland nodded assent.

"Correct, sir. She says she tried them to make sure they were fast. They were."

"She claims to've been away from the house changing a book for Mrs. Tangye at the circulating library from four to nearly six. How about it?"

"I couldn't verify it at the library itself, sir. But she was seen in some tea-room close by about that time. I confess I haven't tested her alibi, for her evidence seemed all right— I mean, the case seemed quite straightforward, in fact. I mean—" Haviland pulled up. What he really meant was that he thought the case was not one that required investigations of that kind.

Pointer had passed on to the fireplace, where Haviland had had the ashes kept. Pointer picked up a newspaper and gently fanned them.

"Only paper ashes. Mrs. Tangye seems to've burnt her letters out on the hearth. Piece by piece. No marks of stirring on the tiles. But what about the fire itself?" Pointer asked.

"Must have been lit late. Just a couple of smouldering logs were all I found, sir. I had them taken away, but the ashes haven't been touched."

"Wasn't the room cold?" was the next question.

"Not to notice. At least ... I had my great coat on ..."

Haviland flushed. Had he overlooked something? But Pointer turned away immediately.

"Now, Superintendent, you saw, when you first came in here yesterday?"

Haviland was secretly impatient.

A lot of work was waiting for him back at his station. He had been here on the day before, and had gone over the room very thoroughly. A detective from the Yard had been here. The Coroner had been here. It seemed hardly likely that any late comer could find anything worth while, even if that late comer was the youngest Chief Inspector at the Yard. Mrs. Tangye's death was either suicide or accident, a quite ordinary affair. Merely imperfectly docketed at the inquest. But he obediently explained to his superior how the room had looked when he had entered it.

"That clothing over there is what she was wearing when found, I suppose?" he asked when Haviland had done.

"Correct, sir. I had them brought in here for the jury to look at this morning." Top of all was the velvet frock with the powder blackened breast, and the scorched hole.

"You can see, pressed into the pile, the very ring the autornatic made." Haviland pointed to a little circle. "At least, a part of it. Along this burnt bit here."

You could see a mark. But was it made by her revolver? It looked a very thin line to Pointer.

He turned away, and seated himself at Mrs. Tangye's writing bureau. Haviland watched him with the air of a man about to be completely and entirely justified. He felt certain that he would yet leave the room without a stain upon his official character. He had found nothing amiss because there was nothing amiss to be found.

"You say in your report, that, not finding her keys, you opened the desk with a pass-key. How about it?" Pointer asked on rising.

"They're mislaid somewhere. I only looked through this one room for them of course."

Pointer made no comment, but asked to see the body.

They found Newnes in the upstairs room, putting the last touches to a sketch. Pointer signed to him to finish.

"If she did it intentionally, I wonder if she's glad now or sorry." Newnes hoped to start a little debate which would enable him to slide into the official circle. No one answered.

"Has she changed her lot for the better?" he mused, with one eye on Pointer.

"She certainly has for good," Wilmot said dryly, pulling up the blind to its fullest extent.

Death is not the brother of sleep. Nor does it look it. Sleep is active. As active as waking. The subconscious is in full control. The work of repairing, rebuilding, is going on full speed ahead. But death—for what lies before us, is the actual end. Nothing now but a return to its component parts await the wonderful machine which has been definitely scrapped by its owner. To Wilmot indeed, all that there ever could be, or ever had been, to Mable Tangye lay before them.

As for the two police officers, the point of greatest interest for the moment was not why, but how.

Newnes took another reluctant departure. Then only did Pointer go up to the coffin. He gazed very searchingly at the face inside.

Suicide demands an unusual temperament. Pointer saw no signs of it here. To him these were the last features to associate with the voluntary pushing open of that door which we call death. Mrs. Tangye looked a handsome, upstanding, hot-tempered, rather selfish woman of around thirty. One who would put up a good fight for all her possessions, including life. There was pluck in her face, as well as resolution. He would expect this woman to have found a way to cut her losses, supposing she had them, not allow them to swamp her. Yet equally certainly she was a woman who would not have gone against the accepted order of things. Respectability was stamped on her. Conventionality engraved on every line. Even around the corners of the mouth where an impulsive temper lurked as well.

Pointer studied her hands carefully.

"Come on anything, sir?" Haviland asked, after a pause.

"They have been washed, of course. But on her left hand under her two wedding rings are traces, of what will prove to be butter, I fancy—" He pushed a tiny wad of sterilised cotton beneath them and then put it away in a corked bottle which he swiftly labelled, "—as you'd expect from the greasiness of her finger-prints on that revolver. That's why I asked about a cat or a dog. I thought she might have been feeding one. Yet apparently only a quarter of a crumpet was eaten, and that with a knife and fork, on whose very smooth and polished handles she left no finger-prints whatever. Odd!"

"Shall I tell you what I think is odd?" Wilmot, giving up all idea of spectacular developments, lit a cigarette, and, as usual prepared to take the centre of the stage. It was his favourite stance.

"The oddest thing about this affair that I can see, is the, reason that made Miss Saunders have Miss Tangye's body put in this shabby room at the end of the corridor. Why not in her own bedroom?"

"Because of Mr. Tangye, I suppose," Haviland suggested. He liked commonplace explanations. He found them generally the right ones.

"Why not shift him? There's a well-furnished spareroom nearer the stairs. Why stick her away in this boxroom? It's little more," the newspaper man insisted.

"Well, that's a fact," muttered Haviland, "that's a fact."

Pointer led the way downstairs. In the hall they met Tangye. When he heard that Wilmot was acting for the Insurance Company, his jaw tightened. After a second's pause, he asked all three into his study which was opposite the room where the tragedy had occurred.

The stockbroker was an unusually handsome man. So well dressed, that he was only saved from being over-dressed by a certain ease of carriage. He had rather full, dark eyes. A pleasant manner when he chose. And a very pleasant voice at all times.

As he was one of those people who cannot imagine a talk without a drink, he unlocked a tantalus at once.

Pointer declined a cocktail, and so, after a moment, did Haviland. He could not see what the Chief Inspector had to go on, or even whether he were going on, but should this prove a "case" then Tangye obviously might be in it, and the rules of the Force forbade a drink with a possible arrest, unless for the purpose of getting at the truth.

"You sent me a note, I think," Tangye returned to the Chief Inspector, "asking me some question or other about my wife's friend, Mrs. Cranbourn. I've just had a cable from her from Marseilles. Would you care to see it?"

The stockbroker handed him a slip of paper on which Pointer read:

"*S.S. Reina Hermosa.*
"Read of your dear wife's tragic death in paper.

Terribly grieved. Maid mistaken in my name as visitor. Mable knew I am away Mediterranean cruise. Started week ago. Could not possibly have been England yesterday. Only reached Marseilles this morning. Leaving to-day. Next stop Piraeus. Letter follows."

"Must have been another lady of the same name who was coming," Tangye explained. "There seems to be some sort of a muddle. Not that it's of any consequence except in so far as that the mere fact of a caller coming, renders the idea of suicide absolutely preposterous. Some imprudent gesture on my wife's part—she handled that revolver very recklessly —I don't pretend to explain it. But there was no cause, none whatever, for her to take her own life. The very supposition was monstrous." And he glared at the Superintendent.

"Nothing is missing, I understand?" Pointer asked.

"Nothing whatever."

"How about her keys?"

Just for a second Tangye hesitated. Then he said casually, "I don't call them lost; mislaid, possibly. Nor are they of any importance."

"Had she no latch-key?"

"I suppose she had. But they're sure to be somewhere in the house."

"There's a safe in your bedroom, I think?"

"Always open. We never used it. It was in the house originally. My wife had no valuables. She didn't care for jewellery."

"Mrs. Tangye had a cousin," Pointer began, after a leisurely glance around the room, "who was brought up with her from childhood. About the same age too, I believe."

"Oliver Headly?" Tangye nodded. "Quite so."

"Was she in communication with him at all?"

"Not as far as I know. He's not been heard of for years."

"I suppose he's been notified of her death?"

"No one knows his address."

"He's her only living relative, I understand?"

Tangye nodded once more. "Supposing him to be alive. He hasn't given a sign of life for ten years or more."

Pointer was looking out of the window.

"There's no way down to the river from the house, is there?"

"Oh, Lord, no! None needed. River at the bottom of the garden, always means garden at the bottom of the river,"

Tangye spoke with feeling.

"But you fish?"

"Dace or roach, which?" scoffed their host.

"Oh, come now, sir," Pointer eyed the expensive double outfit on a side wall. Split cane, and spliced salmon rods hung to one side of trout rods, and a couple of serviceable hickories such as he himself used. Tangye's gaze followed his.

"Oh, those! I do a bit now and then, when away. But my wife could land a salmon with the best of them on the Tay."

Pointer continued to stroll around the room in a negligent way. Then he glanced at Haviland, who rose thankfully.

"Can we look over your bedroom, sir?"

Tangye said by all means, and chatted on to Wilmot.

Pointer found that, unlike Tangye with the river, Haviland had not overstated the case in his notes. Mrs. Tangye had cleared out practically everything in the way of clothes but those in which she had been found dead.

"She hadn't packed anything for herself," Haviland pointed out, "didn't even have her dressing-case taken down off the wardrobe. The fact was, she'd finished with clothes. That's what I think."

He watched Pointer draw aside a strip of tapestry which hung between the beds. Behind it was a safe. Haviland talked on.

"Tangye's a cool chap! His wife's not buried yet, but here he is chatting away about Mayflies as lightly as though he were one himself. In fact, to listen to him, you'd think, now the inquest is over, that he hadn't a care in the world!"

"No." Pointer said reflectively, looking along the door of the safe. "No. I wouldn't make that mistake. Tangye has at least one care left. And that is to direct as much as possible of his conversation to Wilmot, less to you, and as little as possible to me. But he's not a cold-blooded man. I take it he's been very highly keyed-up, and the let-down is coming along a bit fast for his nerves. Just send a puff of finger-print powder over this door, will you. You have your bag with you."

The yellow powder discovered no marks, not even on the handle-knob. Pointer and Haviland tried the other metal objects in the room. All showed the usual signs of handling.

"That's funny, for a fact." Haviland peered through a glass at the immaculate surface of the safe door. Pointer sniffed at the hinges.

"Been recently cleaned with ether. Unlike the handles of the little knife and fork in the morning-room, which were clean, but not cleaned."

Pointer led the way downstairs, and asked for a room in which the claims investigator could put a few questions to the household—or have them asked—ostensibly for his benefit.

Regina Saunders, who had just returned, was the first called. She came in so quietly that Wilmot did not hear her. He looked at her attentively as she seated herself. Yesterday he had barely known that she existed.

Walking up to the house just now, he had wondered whether the explanation of the discrepancies in her statements which had puzzled Pointer was going to turn out one of those sordid, triangular affairs called usual, because they are the exception. She did not look like a charmer. But you never could tell. Never. At a first glance she seemed to consist chiefly of negatives. She was not old. Neither did she suggest youth. Without being pretty, she was not bad-looking. Apparently she had no marked characteristics of any kind, unless it were those of the perfect background. She seemed a type of "Ye Discrete Companioun." Silent. Dark. Attentive.

Gazing at her intently, Wilmot put her age, correctly, as close on forty. For the first time focussing his mind on her as she sat composedly facing Haviland,—Pointer was casually glancing through the morning paper,—noting her down-dropped lids, her pale, tight lips, Wilmot felt as though he were standing in front of a house with drawn blinds and closed doors, behind which were wild doings.

It was one of his intuitive, telepathic impressions which, so far, had never let him down.

"I should like to run through the facts of yesterday again, with you," Haviland explained, "for the benefit of Mr. Wilmot who is looking into Mrs. Tangye's death. He has asked the Chief Inspector and me to put a few more questions."

She said nothing.

"How long have you been with Mrs. Tangye?"

"Three years." The little dark eyes looked up for a second. Something in the glance told Wilmot that the time had seemed long to this woman; very long.

"And before that?"

"I was mother's help to a Mrs. Wren. She will be quite willing to answer any questions. I was with her five years, and left of my own choice."

"May I ask why Mrs. Tangye wanted a companion originally?" Pointer asked.

"Chiefly for music. She had a good voice also, she was extremely fond of duets."

"Were you ever a nurse?" the Chief Inspector continued.

She looked surprised. "Never."

"Was Mrs. Wren's husband a doctor? Was your father anything connected with medicine?"

She was obviously puzzled. "Mr. Wren was a vicar. My father was an organist. I've never had anything whatever to do with nursing, or medicine, or illness, or anything of that sort. Why do you ask?"

"Only part of our regular routine," Pointer said reassuringly. He rose and, followed by Haviland, stepped out through the French windows to look over the garden. They had agreed that Wilmot should be left alone with her to do some of the questioning.

"Now, between ourselves, Miss Saunders, what sort of a woman was Mrs. Tangye?" Wilmot spoke confidentially. It was a tone that had helped him more than once. It was wasted on Miss Saunders.

"Do you think there's much difference in women?" she asked indifferently. "Much real difference?"

"The Colonel's lady, and Judy O'Grady," he quoted with a smile.

"Quite so. Though there's no case of Judy here," she spoke sharply. "Mrs. Tangye is dead, poor soul. Dead." She repeated the word, lingering on it. To Wilmot's acute ear there was something approaching unction in her voice. "I, for one, would rather say nothing against her."

And with that she gave a most illuminating character sketch of her late employer. Envy, hatred, malice, and all uncharitableness were in every sentence. According to her, Mrs. Tangye had been a selfish virago.

"Yet you stuck it here for three years," Wilmot said thoughtfully.

"The pay was good."

Pointer and the Superintendent returned from their inspection of the garden.

"All seems in order. Now, Miss Saunders, about Mrs. Tangye's last days—"

But when it came to Monday, Regina Saunders was of no help. Once a month she had that day off in addition to her free Sundays. As she had explained at the inquest, this last Monday had been her own, and been spent away from Riverview.

"And when did you decide to leave here?" Pointer asked.

"You could hardly expect me to stop on after Mrs. Tangye's death," she said coldly.

"It's a censorious world," Pointer agreed, "still—you left —when?"

"About seven, I think."

"I see. Now, as we explained to you, this gentleman," Pointer turned to Wilmot, "is investigating the death on behalf of the Insurance Society, and we want to give him all the aid we can. Would you object to occupying your old room again for a few days? It would be a help to be able to turn to you at any time."

"I am here all day. I am staying on to superintend the household for a little while—at Mr. Tangye's request. But I prefer to go home to my sister's at night."

"But to oblige us? Just for a night or two?" Pointer wheedled. "Something might turn up after you had left here?"

Miss Saunders looked impatient.

"I never go back on a decision. Once I have made up my mind, I stick to it."

"Admirable trait," Wilmot murmured in mock admiration.

"We should, of course, expect the Insurance Society to pay for the convenience," Pointer went on, "a pound a night is the usual thing, I believe, in a case of this kind, where it's done merely to help the investigation, and is only a question of two, or at most three nights." He turned to Wilmot.

"Quite so; a pound a night," Wilmot agreed.

Miss Saunders pondered the proposal for the first time. Evidently Pointer's improvised tariff appealed to her. But after a minute she shook her head. "I prefer to go to my sister's, as I have arranged."

There was a pause.

"Did any one see you leave the house yesterday when you went to the circulating library?" Haviland asked.

"I don't know. But at any rate the person who served me with tea in the Japanese tea-room next door might remember me. She knows me by sight quite well." Miss Saunders spoke indifferently.

"Did Mrs. Tangye want any particular book brought back, or leave it to you?" Pointer asked.

"She left it to me. I found nothing that she would care for, so I brought home the book she had given me. She had not quite finished it I knew."

"Did you ask the librarian for any book?"

"No."

"You didn't change any book whatever there?"

"No."

Pointer glanced at Wilmot.

"Now going back to the cause of Mrs. Tangye's death," the newspaper man began, "which is what I want to establish, you feel sure that she didn't shoot herself intentionally?"

"Quite sure. Why should she shoot herself? She had everything in the world that she wanted, hadn't she?" the last words came with a rush.

"Do you mean Mr. Tangye?" Wilmot asked so blankly that Haviland bit his lip.

"I mean everything." But Miss Saunders spoke more guardedly. "Mrs. Tangye wasn't used to the kind of life he gave her. A motor, and maids, and that. She told me herself once that she had known what it was to be bitterly poor."

The stipend of the Reverend Charles Headly having been under three hundred a year, out of which he had to pay a curate, the men thought that that was quite likely.

"Then you think she was happy?" persisted Wilmot.

"As much as her temperament would let her, I do. She was one of those women who always want what they haven't got. She was always contrasting Mr. Tangye with Mr. Branscombe's perfections."

"That doesn't sound to me a happy life," Haviland murmured.

Miss Saunders flashed him an ironic glance.

"You mean in fact that they quarrelled?" he persisted.

"They led the usual married life," she said dryly. Wilmot laughed, while Haviland, who was a very happy man in his home, looked at her with marked distaste.

"Mr. Tangye says you were the last person to see Mrs. Tangye's keys. Could you tell us when that was?" Pointer asked suddenly.

Her eyes were on his as he spoke. Far back in them a spark glowed suddenly. The question had obviously come as a complete surprise. And all three men thought that the surprise was not the only emotion stirred. There was anger. And there was something that for a second suggested dismay. But she looked down her nose immediately, and said with perfect composure, "I can't think that he would say such a thing!" This was true enough.

"My mistake doubtless," Pointer said easily, and changed the subject to the visitor, the supposed Mrs. Cranbourn, Miss Saunders said that she saw no one as she ran down the stairs. She thought that the caller must have stepped into the drawing-room and let herself out later on.

"But the reporter who came back with the maid said that you remained in the hall till the police came."

"That's quite true." Miss Saunders looked puzzled. "But perhaps she left after the police arrived. We were all in the morning-room together for a time then."

"Impossible. I had a man posted at both doors. Front and back." Haviland was very certain of this.

"I hadn't thought of it before. What *did* become of her?" Miss Saunders looked uneasy.

"Leaving her on one side for the moment, how did you first learn that Mrs. Tangye was dead?"

Miss Saunders repeated what she had told Haviland, and the Coroner.

"You came immediately Florence screamed?" Pointer's tone suggested a delay. A suspicious delay.

"Certainly."

"At her first scream?" Pointer persisted. As though he

intended to prove that in some way the companion had been dilatory.

"I ran down immediately. She only screamed the once. I glanced in at the open morning-room door, and hurried after her to try and stop her making a scene in the street." Miss Saunders spoke contemptuously.

"But Mrs. Tangye was not sitting where you could see her from the door."

Miss Saunders made a movement with the edge of her cupped hand, as though brushing off some imaginary crumbs from the table top beside her.

The room was very still.

"I may have gone in far enough to see her sitting in her chair," she said finally.

"And by merely glancing at her from a distance, you—without any medical knowledge—were able to tell the reporter who met the maid that no help was wanted? That he need not go into the room where Mrs. Tangye was?" Pointer spoke gravely. "You took that formidable responsibility on yourself after one look?"

"Didn't you try to do something for her?" Wilmot burst out. Both he and Haviland were watching the woman intently, at whom Pointer seemed barely to glance. She looked quite unruffled. But again her hand swept the table top, with a slow, considering movement.

"I suppose I must have run up to her," she said meditatively. "As to helping her—" there was something repressed in Miss Saunders level tones, "of course, I didn't want to touch her till the police came."

Haviland nodded official approval of that eminently correct attitude. But Pointer looked very wooden.

"Why? Did you think a crime had been committed?"

She passed a furtive tongue over her thin lips.

"Such an absurd idea never entered my mind."

"Any more than the equally absurd one of trying to see if you could do something for the poor lady," Wilmot retorted.

She did not shift her eyes from Pointer, though she

answered the comment.

"One does not need to be the king's physician, nor yet a gifted detective," her gaze was mocking, "to know what a bullet wound over a heart means, with a dropped revolver on the floor by the body's side."

"To go back to what happened after Florence screamed," Pointer continued; "you still maintain that you were able to run down the stairs, get across the whole of the morning-room to the recess, make certain that Mrs. Tangye was dead, get out of the room again, and be seen standing in the front door before Florence had more than left the house? The reporter said that as the door opened, and she rushed out, you stepped into the open doorway behind her."

"It all happened so swiftly," Regina Saunders muttered.

"Still, human beings take some time to move from one spot to another, you know."

"This cross-examination is ridiculous," she snapped defiantly. "It tells nothing."

"On the contrary! It tells much," Pointer's voice was very hard. "It tells us that you didn't run into the morning-room at all when Florence called out. You went straight down the stairs to the front door, reaching it just as the maid flung it wide. In other words you knew, without going in, what was in the morning-room. You knew because you had already been in there. Don't try to mislead us!"

Pointer turned on the woman with something very forbidding in his stern face. He towered over her. He stood six feet three. She paled. But her eyes remained watchful and ready. Again she swept the table beside her, her gaze now following the motion of her hand.

"You're right," she said suddenly, speaking in a pleasant, conversational voice. "You're quite right. When I got back from the library, or rather from the tea-room a little before six, I went in to the morning-room to tell Mrs. Tangye about not bringing her any book. I found her—

dead! Just as Florence did a little later. I was so horrified. ... It was such a shock. I managed to get to my rooms. But once there—I think I fainted. I had just pulled myself together when I heard Florence scream, and ran down to the front door. As you guessed. Frankly, I cannot see what is wrong in my not saying that I saw poor Mrs. Tangye a moment before the maid did. And lost my nerve in consequence for a few seconds."

Pointer made no comment on this amended account.

A question put by him as to whether she had ever met Mrs. Tangye's cousin Oliver was answered in the negative. She did not even know, she said, that Mrs. Tangye had a relative alive.

Florence came in next. She was very nervous, but Haviland soon put her at her ease.

Pointer, apparently for Wilmot's sake—seemed much interested in Mrs. Tangye's directions about her expected visitor. Especially in her order that she was definitely, and distinctly "not at home," to any other caller. No matter whom.

"She told me that I wasn't to worry if Mrs. Cranbourn was late. Very late. As the boat train was often hours behind time."

"Worry?" Pointer echoed, "what did she mean by that?"

"I suppose that I wasn't to worry her," Florence suggested shrewdly, "the mistress couldn't abide fuss. Never liked me to go in and out much. Oh, I had to make my head save my heels with Mrs. Tangye, I assure you, sir. I think she spoke as she did to stop my bothering her with more hot water, or freshly-toasted cakes."

"That was quite usual, was it?"

It was. Florence repeated that there had been nothing in the least unusual, or out of the way, in her mistress's manner or directions yesterday, and also that nothing however trifling had happened then, or before, which she had not already told.

"How was it that the police only found a couple of logs

alight in the morning-room fireplace when they were here
yesterday evening? Was the fire only lit very late?"
Pointer asked casually.

"Oh, that fire!" Florence clasped tragic hands.

She told them that the chimney was always
uncertain, but that yesterday it had distinguished itself.
Nothing the maids could do would make it burn, let alone
blaze. From before breakfast until the hour set for tea it
had smoked sullenly.

"I wonder that Mrs. Tangye didn't use another room,"
Pointer mused.

"You'd have wondered more, sir, if you'd seen how
thick it was in there. Fit to kipper a haddock, it was
really."

Florence went on to tell how she had urged her
mistress   let her bring the tea-things into the drawing-
room, as on other occasions when the morning-room
chimney had been tiresome; but Mrs. Tangye would not
hear of it.

"The wind changed after four, I noticed when I opened
the door at six that the fire was behaving itself—all
things considered—better than I'd hoped."

The fireplace was in the main part of the room.

"Wasn't the room cold?"

"Not so bad when the windows were shut, for the
kitchen chimney warms it then, but it was bitter when I
brought in the tea-things. Mrs. Tangye had to keep the
windows open because of the smoke. She must have shut
them later on when the fire began to blaze up.

Florence was as certain as she had been at the
inquest that the windows were tightly fastened when she
caught sight of her dead mistress.

"Tell us once more about the visitor, what did she look
like?" Wilmot asked, on Pointer glancing at him.

"Mrs. Cranbourn, sir? Sort of stout and all muffled up
in a fur coat with a large collar up to her eyes. Very
wheezy voice. I couldn't notice much, for she stepped past
me at once, saying, 'I'm most frightfully late, I'm afraid.'

She was talking and moving all in one breath. I opened the morning-door and went forward saying, 'Mrs. Cranbourn to see you'm. But when I got to the alcove—" The rest they knew.

She had no idea what had become of the caller. "I suppose she caught sight over my shoulder of Mrs. Tangye. At any rate I didn't see her no more. But when I think of the poor mistress sitting there—"

"Did the visitor step towards the morning-room as though she knew the house?" Pointer asked.

"She did. Mrs. Tangye always has tea in there in winter."

"Then the lady must have been to Riverview before?"

"Very likely. But not in my time. I've only been here a year. Mrs. Cranbourn must have known the house from before then."

"Are you sure it was Mrs. Cranbourn?" Pointer asked quietly.

"Why, who else could it be, sir? At that hour, and all bundled up from a journey?" Florence stared at the Chief Inspector as though he must be strangely dense not to see this for himself.

"That's true. She was very agitated, you said, I think?"

"She was in a frightful rush, sir. She almost shoved past me. But there! We little know! The next moment I must have pushed past her to get out of the room!"

Florence could not amplify her account of the caller. The shock of finding Mrs. Tangye dead had wiped away all clear remembrance of the woman whose arrival had led to the discovery.

Pointer turned the subject.

"Mrs. Tangye's dress looks to me rather handsome. All that fur and silver embroidery. Isn't it more elaborate than she usually wore of an afternoon?"

"Oh, yes, sir. Mrs. Tangye dressed very quiet. That frock was going to be worn at a wedding next week."

"Had she had it on before?"

"Once. This last Monday."

"Ah yes, the day she sent you to Jay's."

Pointer went over the Monday too, very carefully with Florence. He learnt nothing fresh.

Coming again to Tuesday, and to the missing keys, Florence said she was sure that she had seen them lying on the top of her mistress's writing bureau when she was in the room at four.

Pointer glanced at Wilmot.

"You look a clever girl," Wilmot said flatteringly, "what's your opinion of this sad affair? Your honest opinion as between friends. The inquest is over now."

"Oh, sir, of course it was an accident! She didn't kill herself! Not she! Why, there's that evening-dress. She'd only just ordered it. You don't throw away sixty pounds for nothing, do you? At least Mrs. Tangye didn't. And those shoes that were being made to match. Oh no, sir. It was an accident. Mrs. Tangye did something careless-like with that Webley of hers, and that was that!"

"As a matter of fact, have you ever see her handling the revolver when you were in the room?" Haviland asked.

"I shouldn't have been in the room long, if I had, you bet." Florence spoke with a vigour that made the men smile.

"And when did you last see it in its box?" asked Pointer.

"Monday morning it was there all right. I know by the weight. But it wasn't in it yesterday morning."

The inquest had elicited the fact—from Tangye—that his wife had spoken of putting it in a drawer in her bureau to help her to remember about the initials.

"Can you suggest any reason why Mrs. Tangye went through her papers so thoroughly yesterday morning?" Pointer was now questioning her. She could not.

"And about Miss Saunders—did she start her packing on Monday or only yesterday morning?"

"Yesterday morning, sir."

Haviland inwardly opened his eyes.

"Ah yes! After that quarrel she and Mrs Tangye had." Pointer was bluffing.

"You mean their talk after breakfast, sir? Oh, they weren't quarrelling. The mistress's voice was quite low and soft. And she always raised it when she was angry. Always. It sounded to me more like it was Miss Saunders who was huffed. I heard her say, 'It's not the money. It's how it looks. I insist on staying till at least the end of the week.' That was the first thing after breakfast, that was."

"Ah yes," mused Pointer again, "the quarrel came after lunch, I think."

"It couldn't have, sir. The mistress went out directly lunch was over, and there was no trouble when they were at table. There hadn't been no quarrel or the mistress would never have talked to her as she did. Talked quite a lot for Mrs. Tangye."

"Where were they when you heard Miss Saunders speak of leaving?"

"In the morning-room, sir. Miss Saunders said that and walked out."

"Did she look vexed?"

"Well no, sir. But that goes for nothing. Miss Saunders never shows when she's angry. But she pays you back for it just the same."

"You don't like Miss Saunders?"

Florence did not. But servants rarely like companions.

Pointer harked back to yesterday afternoon, and tried his last cast:

"You said at the inquest that your mistress came in from the garden as you brought in the tea-tray?"

"Yes. Five minutes to the hour that was."

"Did she often go out in the garden after dark? On such a day as we had yesterday?" Pointer was doing all the questioning now.

"Well no, sir. Now I come to think of it she doesn't— didn't."

"Did you see her in the garden at all?"

"I couldn't have. You see, sir, in this house the back garden is all at the side. Except just a little bit that's in front."

Wilmot laughed outright.

"She was alone in the garden, I suppose?" Pointer went on.

"Oh yes, sir. Quite alone."

"How do you know, if you couldn't see her?" Pointer persisted, half-smiling.

"Well, sir, I should have heard voices, shouldn't I? The window of my pantry—it's too high up to see out of, but it gives on to that side." She stopped suddenly, as though remembering something. A rather startled look spread over her face.

"Yes?" cooed Pointer persuasively.

"Well, sir, that's funny! Talking of her being alone, my sister Olive, she said to me as we were giving the silver a rub-up before bringing in the tray, she said that she thought she heard a crunch-crunch on the gravel behind the mistress. But then Olive—" she hesitated, "my sister hears things. She's not normal, the doctor tells us." She announced the fact with some pride. "She's taken on something cruel at Mrs. Tangye's death. Says she felt it coming, and ought to've warned her. But there, Olive is that way! It's not being normal does it."

"What did she hear out of the pantry window?"

"Something like steps coming after the mistress over the gravel, sir. Very soft-like and cautious. I switched on the electric to have a look—we was working by the fire—and at that the steps stopped dead. Not Mrs. Tangye's. The other ones I mean."

"You heard them, too?"

"Quite clear for just a moment before they stopped."

"Footsteps that stopped when you switched on the light," Pointer looked at his boot tips. "I'll look at your pantry in a minute. Did you or Olive hear the steps again?"

They had not.

"Some butcher's boy coming for orders," Wiltnot's tone was dryly amused.

"At that hour of an afternoon, sir!" It was Florence's turn to be diverted.

"Oh, well—missed the tradesman's entrance in the dark, and hoped to be directed to it."

"Then why did the steps stop, sir?"

"Were they peculiar footsteps?"

"In a way. They seemed to have a sort of kink to them every now and then. Sort of a catch, if you know what I mean." She tried to illustrate her meaning, and did a Highland fling which failed to convince.

Olive was next summoned. She was a slender, pale, young woman with over-large eyes, and a timid smile.

"We're still uncertain about this affair," Wilmot began on a sign from Pointer, "now what do you think about it? You ought to have formed your own opinion, living in the same house. Do you think that Mrs. Tangye meant to shoot herself, or was it a genuine accident? Come now, as between ourselves."

"Well, sir, I don't know what to think. Florence, she thinks—"

"We know what your sister thinks," Pointer assured her pleasantly, "but you now?"

"Well, sir, cook thinks—"

"We shall learn in good time what Cook thinks, but what about you? Mr. Wilmot wants to hear your opinion."

Olive grew desperate.

"Well, sir, I can't help thinking the mistress *did* do it. But was drove to it like. She was all of a twitter that last day. Yesterday. I think she did it in a fit of passion, half wild about something. I felt it coming along, sir. Oh, I felt it creeping on her."

"Just what do you mean by that?" Wilmot spoke gently, but with obvious curiosity.

"I feel things beforehand, sir. I knew when father was going to die weeks and weeks before the crane broke. I felt the same feeling come on me again a couple of days ago. Sunday morning it was I got up with it. And it's never left me since."

"Surely it's left you by now," Haviland suggested in his hearty, healthy, beefy voice.

"Not to notice, sir." A cryptic reply that made his lips twitch.

But she, too, had heard no sound yesterday afternoon that could possibly have been a shot.

"Now, about Mrs. Tangye, did you see her by chance in the garden before tea?" Pointer asked, as though nothing had been said on the subject.

"I heard her walking up and down on the path that runs past the morning-room windows. It's been freshly gravelled."

"Was Mrs. Tangye alone?"

"I—don't—know." Olive spoke slowly. "I have wonderful hearing, sir. That's what makes it seem so funny I heard no shot. No blind man can hear better than me. I heard footsteps creep up behind the mistress. Getting nearer and nearer. They weren't more than a yard behind her when Flo turned up the light, and they stopped. Flo heard them too, just then."

"But I thought you said you weren't sure if Mrs. Tangye was alone in the garden." Wilmot spoke in some perplexity.

"But you can hear things sometimes that you couldn't see." Olive spoke under her breath with a quick dilation of her pupils. "I know you won't believe me, sir. Flo doesn't in her heart. She thinks its because of what happened after. But I knew then those steps meant harm to the mistress."

"Were they peculiar footsteps?" probed Wilmot again.

"Not in the way you mean, sir, though they had a sort of stumble to them. But I pray God never to hear 'em no more."

Haviland thought the atmosphere was getting a bit tense.

"You spoke of Mrs. Tangye having killed herself," he

began, "why should she do that? Come now, Olive, just
you hold on to facts. Don't think of spooky things any
more." Olive looked rather hesitatingly at the police-
officer.

"Well, Mr. Superintendent, now it can't harm nobody,
now that the inquest's over, I don't mind saying that I
saw her myself going through the master's over-coat
pockets. This last Saturday, just before dinner. He had
left his top-coat behind that he usually wears down to his
office. And Mrs. Tangye pulled out a letter and stood
reading it. Short note it was. She folded it up, and stood
tapping the floor with her foot before she put it into her
handbag and went on into the dining-room with a toss of
her head that as good as said she had made up her mind
to something—" Olive stopped, as though she had said too
much.

No pressing could get her to supply the name of any
woman from whom the letter might have come. Obviously
she did not know it. And to the rest of the questions put
her, she could only bear out what her sister had already
told them. She too had never heard Mrs Tangye refer to
any living member of her family.

Miss Saunders stepped in to say that the undertakers'
men were coming, and that Mr. Tangye would be obliged
if they need not know that the police were in the house.
They would be some time. Half an hour probably. Pointer
turned ostentatiously to Wilmot.

"Let's go for a stroll," that figure-head suggested. "We
can come back and finish afterwards."

CHAPTER THREE

THE three men walked towards the river in silence for some minutes. A soft, sibilant murmur came from the water which had lost its lights now, and lay hidden in mist. It seemed to Pointer to be chanting "Accident—Suicide—Murder? Accident—Suicide—Murder?" under its breath.

Any of the three might still be the word that would fit the puzzle which the Chief Inspector intended to solve.

Haviland turned to the newspaper man.

"Well, whether accident or suicide, we hand it over to you now, Mr. Wilmot. Unless the Chief Inspector thinks otherwise, of course. I suppose the case is closed, as far as the police are concerned? Olive seems to've got hold of the right tip. That letter that she saw Mrs. Tangye reading must have been the last straw. As a matter of fact, I said we should find that something of that kind had happened."

Pointer lit his pipe.

"The footsteps that stopped," he spoke the words as though they pleased his ear. "Sounds like one of your own articles, Wilmot."

Wilmot turned a meditative eye on the Chief Inspector, "Nice head-line. But I make a point of never misleading my public."

This time it was Pointer who looked his question.

"Well, even if they ever existed, which I very much doubt. Tangye may have run down from town hoping to make his peace with his wife. Say that there was a row on Monday which made him skip dinner at home." Both Wilmot's listeners nodded. Each had already said that to himself. "He may have gone into the garden after her. It would cost me my reputation to raise hopes of a dramatic development, and then have it fizzle out into father's list slippers."

"You think it will?"

Wilmot did not reply for a second. Had they found anything which suggested foul play? Honestly, as far as he could see, they had not. But what about Pointer? His were the eyes that counted in this search.

"What does the Counsel for the Prosecution say?" Wilmot asked instead of replying.

"That when you talk of suicide—"

"Or accident. I'm afraid I think that's only too possible," Wilmot said pensively.

"Or accident. You forget the butter under Mrs. Tangye's wedding rings," Pointer spoke very seriously.

"You overwhelm me with confusion, so I had!" Wilmot spoke in mock consternation. "Is this the sort of rock on which a police inquiry is built? I've no idea how that mysterious process begins. Do you inventory the butter on her finger solemnly under the heading of 'Clues of which the Police are in Possession'?"

"No, no!" Haviland laughed in his turn. "The fact is, we haven't found even the ghost of such a thing as a clue which points to a crime, have we, sir?"

"And where there's no clue there's no crime?" Wilmot queried.

"Whose steps stopped in the garden?" Pointer asked. "Tangye would have come on in, if they had been his. At least, so it seems to me. Why was her left hand so buttery that it left such clear prints on her revolver and yet none on her fork?"

Haviland turned to him quickly.

"You spoke before of her prints on the Webley as being odd, sir? In what way, in fact?"

"I can tell better when I have studied the enlargements," was the evasive reply.

There was a short silence. This was different from theorising beforehand. The Chief Inspector was looking over the fields. Was the *Hark, Hallo!* coming? It all lay with the young man leaning with folded arms on the low parapet of the bridge and staring straight before him with level, quiet eyes.

Haviland fidgetted with a cigar. "Of course," he said dubiously, "it's a question of finding out what's essential and what isn't. . . ."

Wilmot gave a short laugh. "Be able to do that, Haviland, and you'll be a god, not a policeman."

"Still, as a matter of fact," Haviland went on doggedly, "that is what has to be done."

"And pray what is the essential fact or facts here?" Wilmot asked indulgently.

Pointer answered for the Superintendent, "The most essential thing in. this case is to find out exactly what happened on Sunday. When the break occurred."

"Break?"

"Between the old Mrs. Tangye and the new Mrs. Tangye. Between the woman who went on as always, and the woman who apparently changed her habits so much."

"She seems to've quarrelled with Tangye on Monday as usual," Wilmot reminded him.

"True," Pointer had to smile at the other's tone. "Yet she first began then to prepare for her coming departure."

"Safe word that. We can all meet on it," Wilmot murmured approvingly.

"Apparently, only apparently, of course," Pointer went on, "she seems to've been her usual self till Sunday morning."

"Till that letter she read," Haviland breathed.

"Until she went to Tunbridge Wells at any rate. Possibly that decision itself marked the beginning of the change. For when she gets back she goes to bed. She starts next day weeding out her wardrobe; the day after she tears up her private papers. It looks to me as if something had happened down at that flower-show."

"Sunday," Wilmot repeated meditatively. "I don't follow you there, Pointer. The break, as you call it—the breaking-point would be nearer the mark, I think—

occurred in my judgment, not between two Mrs. Tangyes, but between her and her husband, and took place Monday afternoon. You say she had changed by Monday. I can't see any change before that talk or quarrel, with her husband about five in the afternoon. On Monday morning she had had her hair waved says Florence. We know that in the afternoon, she took a vivid interest in her new evening-dress. Those preparations on which we all lay so much store, though we read them differently, only began after she had seen and talked with her husband at tea-time."

"No, not quite," Haviland corrected, "as a matter of fact she went out and left word before five with Carter Patterson to take her trunk to the Salvation Army's old clothes department. *Before* her husband got home from his weekend."

Wilmot did not know this. It altered his argument as he at once said.

"And you think what happened on Sunday when she was away from home so important, do you sir?" Haviland asked, "More so, in fact, than the letter itself, which sent her down there?"

"We may be able to guess the letter from what took place. But not the other way round. Was the show the sort of thing that would get into the papers, Wilmot? London papers?"

"You mean would any reporters be sent down to Tunbridge who might be able to help us? Not one." Wilmot explained that orchid shows in country towns, even big ones like this affair, would never get beyond a line or two, and those would be telegraphed up by some local amateur enthusiast, who would also, in all certainty, write the articles in the more important country papers. The exhibition firms supplying the smaller ones with data.

"The show on Sunday is one essential then, sir. Are there any others?" Haviland had been meditating on the Chief Inspector's words.

But Pointer did not answer directly. He seemed to be thinking aloud, "Monday afternoon, when Miss Saunders is absent, Florence is sent off too on an errand, and Olive is told that Mrs. Tangye's not at home to any one before five o'clock, and is given a stiff bit of mending to do. In other words, Mrs. Tangye secures herself from interruption Monday afternoon. Then next day, yesterday, Miss Saunders is sent out. She's the only one in the house who can come and go as she likes, remember. She generally has tea with Mrs. Tangye of course—"

"And Mrs. Tangye gives particular orders for an uninterrupted chat with her special friend." Wilmot spoke impatiently. "My dear fellow, no one could accuse you of swallowing camels, but you certainly do go for any gnat in sight."

"Doesn't Mrs. Tangye's partiality for having tea in an impossible room strike you as peculiar?" Pointer countered.

Haviland stared. Wilmot permitted himself to look puzzled.

"Senseless whim," he murmured, "but not necessarily criminal, I should have thought."

"Not necessarily senseless," Pointer replied with a faint smile.

"You think the smoky fire—but would that weigh much, in fact, with a desperate woman—sick of life?" groped Haviland.

"It would weigh heavily with a woman expecting a visitor," Pointer reminded him. Haviland stepped away to let a perambulator come up and pass them.

"In the plan which the Superintendent drew of Riverview," Pointer went on in his absence, "Haviland's an excellent officer, very thorough along his own lines. He has a quick eye."

"He has—for a fact," Wilmot laughed, and Haviland, catching the last word, grinned.

"I'm an Essex man," he said in excuse, as he turned to Pointer when the bridge was empty again, "you were saying, sir?"

"That in your plan the morning-room shows as the only one in the house which can be entered directly from the garden, without having to pass any other window. Now, adding this interesting detail to the unusual fondness of Mrs. Tangye for a smoky room yesterday, and you get quite an intriguing little sum."

"You might, if they belonged together," Wilmot agreed cautiously, "but if you add the density of the atmosphere to the distance from the earth to the moon, your result's not likely to be of much practical use."

"That's what I thought when I learnt from the evidence at the inquest that Mrs. Tangye had been *expecting* a visitor. An expected caller drew a straight line through my sum. This cable of Mrs. Cranbourn's, however, reverses that. Or rather, what seems like a stroke through the whole, becomes one of it's most important items."

"Are we at last to be permitted to glimpse your meaning— to fathom the mysterious depths with which you credit that fact?" Wilmot screwed up his eyes. A sign of close attention.

"Remember the situation of the morning-room. Mrs. Tangye's sticking to it in spite of discomfort, and add the new fact that very definite instructions were given by her that she was not at home yesterday, except to a certain, very carefully specified lady, who quite positively couldn't come. I maintain that my sum total's worth thinking over. Especially if you add a few other extras floating around."

Wilmot pondered for some minutes.

"You mean?" he repeated cautiously.

"This: Mr. Tangye never gets back on Tuesdays from his office until half-past six at the earliest. Mrs. Tangye sends her companion off just before four to change a novel for her at the circulating library and tells her to have tea out. The library is about half an hour away. It doesn't close till seven. Tea at Riverview was ordered at four; one would have thought that Miss Saunders could have had it before going for the book. The maid, after bringing in the tea-things, always leaves her mistress undisturbed until she clears away at six. That is a rule of the house, we learnt. Now, if in addition, Mrs. Tangye tells her that on no account will she be at home to anybody except to some one who isn't—can't be— coming, then, in this way she both has an excuse for ordering, as she does, a very ample tea, and also insures in every possible way that she can count on being undisturbed for two hours. Four to six."

"But the caller of later on? The woman who came and said she was frightfully overdue," Haviland protested, "aren't you forgetting her? Her name may have been Cranbourn too, as Tangye suggested."

"Sort of gratuitous little muddle that's quite to be expected," Pointer agreed."

"Yes," Wilmot said slowly, thinking over Pointer's words, "you can't get around the fact that some woman came. And on an appointment, you know."

"I don't know," Pointer put up his pipe with a sigh, "I must leave her on one side for the moment. Her coming doesn't explain anything—nor hang together with anything."

"She made a bee-line for the morning-room," Haviland pointed out.

"True; but I can't see why Mrs. Tangye should stick to that particular room in spite of smoke, and bitter cold, for the sake of some one who could come to the front door, and therefore could have been shown into any other room. At least as far as we yet know to the contrary."

"Then for what reason did she stick to it?" Wilmot asked irritably. He never liked asking for solutions.

"There's just a possibility that Mrs. Tangye gave some one an appointment in that room. Some one who was not to come to the front door. It was this bare possibility which brought me down to Twickenham in the first place. Only that expected visit—that bluff—about Mrs. Cranbourn—put my theory all out, for the moment."

"Um-m. Seems to me a very heavy scaffolding to build around one smoky chimney," Wilmot temporised. Had he been the one to originate it, he would have hailed it with joy.

"Oh, there are other things. Why did Mrs. Tangye walk up and down outside that window, while the maid brought in tea? Unless it were to be on the lookout lest this 'some one' should blunder into the room while the girl was still there? It was hardly an afternoon to select for a turn in the garden. The open window would send its ray of light far out as a beacon, a guide, remember."

"You think Mrs. Tangye had given some one a rendezvous, a secret appointment yesterday afternoon?" Wilmot cocked his head on one side. "Is that where that cousin of hers comes in? The one you questioned Tangye about? Your interest in any one is rarely to their credit. Who is he?"

"He seems a bit of a dark horse. Distinguished himself at Oxford. So much so that the authorities thought one half term quite sufficient. I haven't got all the notes on him yet. Apparently, as Tangye said, he dropped out of sight some dozen years ago."

"But Mrs. Tangye was Mrs. Grundy's twin sister. Nothing romantic. Nothing of the heart could make the lady we looked at just now step one inch off the beaten track. Take that from me."

Pointer took it. Took it very seriously. Wilmot's judgments on men and events were not to be lightly passed over. He had a famous knack of winning by a head. His own head, as Fleet Street put it.

"Nevertheless, the fact remains," Pointer continued, "that on the two days following last Sunday, Mrs. Tangye takes very similar measures to safeguard herself from interruption for at least a part of the afternoon."

"There's that vanished cousin of hers," Haviland put in, "he might fit the idea you have about that morning-room. Supposing he's done something and couldn't show his face, in fact."

"Just so. He might. Though I don't necessarily think that it was a man who came. As I said before, I only call the criminal 'him' for the sake of brevity. Also women don't commit murder as often as men do."

"Not enough courage," Wilmot was no lover of the fair sex. "But even if you're right about Mrs. Tangye's reason for speaking as though she expected Mrs. Cranbourn, I hold that it would only be to gain time for the last, fatal step. That at least is how I read the story. Sorry. But it seems to me the only reading—so far. I see no possibility of that bullet having been fired by any othgr hand but Mrs. Tangye's.

"I maintain," he said again, after turning Pointer's suggestion carefully over in his mind, "that Mrs. Tangye stuck to that room because it was, or rather had been, her favourite. She had spent many happy hours there. The room tells that. She wanted to say good-bye to life in its friendly atmosphere."

"And the order for a larger tea than usual?"

"More bluff. To have the room to herself. Remember you yourself suggested that reason for the minute directions about admitting any one but Miss Eden."

Pointer shook his head.

"I can't see that Mrs. Tangye's actions yesterday play any part in the theory of a suicide. In mine they do. In mine each is vital. They're unintelligent in any other light. Mrs. Tangye could have shot herself much better in bed."

"The fact is, that's what's been bothering me," Haviland broke in, "but I think she may have meant to be found by Tangye. Or even by her caller."

"Anything's possible." Was all Pointer would allow that shot, by way of marks. "But so far, no new facts shake my theory. And when a theory's not shaken by closer inspection, it's strengthened."

"Nice little pile of chance sweepings is all I can see," Wiljnot sighed.

"Naturally."

Pointer and Haviland both smiled.

"It's all very well," Wilmot admitted grudgingly, "but your theory doesn't hold the late caller."

"I don't know yet if it's necessary that it should," Pointer said equably. "Mrs. Tangye's own actions don't seem to have included her either. The order to the maid might have been to exclude her. Time will show where she belongs. Outside or inside. But the idea of suicide makes the whole series of things incomprehensible to me."

"And you think in your theory they become translucent? Comprehensible? Come, as a favour to me, expound them in that light."

Wilmot was quite in his element. He always enjoyed a discussion of theories. He obviously meant what he said Pointer was never keen on holding forth, but Wilmot pressed him again.

"I really should like to know how the facts look in this new light to your Scotland Yard mind. If you'll excuse me calling it that. I mean it as a compliment. And after your unkind references to my biased point of view—" he laughed and settled his elbows more comfortably on the coping of the bridge.

"Well, looking on Mrs. Tangye's death as a crime. Always bearing in mind that that's only a hypothesis as yet—"

"Oh, I do!"

"The first thing that strikes one is the way she was killed. A bullet rather suggests, other things being equal, that the murderer was not a member of her household. Poison is their usual weapon, in a premeditated crime. Next—there's been no effort to mislead the police, or delay the finding out of the dead woman's identity."

"Granted," Wilmot said at once; "identity evidently plays no part in this sinister affair."

"It may play a part just the same," Pointer demurred. "Its part may be that the sooner it's known that she's dead, the better."

"You mean the Insurance claim Tangye sent in by the eight o'clock evening post yesterday?" Wilmot raised an eyebrow reflectively. "'Pon my word, Pointer, almost thou persuadest me. . . ."

"The visitor was apparently not one of whom Mrs. Tangye was frightened. She sends Miss Saunders out on Tuesday. She had sent Florence out on Monday, the day when, I think. the caller came the first time. The crime, if I'm right, and there was one, was too well executed for it to have been planned without a very careful inspection of the premises. But to continue with Tuesday, the husband is away from home. Judging by the preparations, the secret caller is some one Mrs. Tangye is prepared to welcome. The ample tea and so on. Of course they may merely represent so many attempts at propitiation. But Mrs. Tangye doesn't look to me like a woman who would bend easily under pressure."

"It all sounds to me like her cousin," Haviland mused again.

"But her smart frock?" the Chief Inspector queried, "her dressed hair? But whether Cousin Oliver or some one else, obviously the relationship, or tie, between them is not one that Mrs. Tangye cares to acknowledge. The visitor is to come and go unseen."

"Supposing—just for the moment—that such a being exists, wouldn't any murderer have taken care to trump up some specious need for secrecy?" Wilmot pointed out.

"Possibly. But unless the need were real, and affected both, I should have expected, since she was perfectly mistress of her own time—that she would have arranged to meet him elsewhere. But obviously that might not suit the murderer. One place would be very unlike another place to him."

"Then the secrecy was more important to her than to him, in your fascinating, but to me, quite impossible melodrama?"

Pointer thought not.

"As a rule, when it's only to one person's interest that

so much trouble be taken, the other person, the one not so vitally concerned, makes some slip, that gives the whole show away. None has been made here. On either side. Mrs. Tangye seems to've taken as much care beforehand that nothing should be known about a caller coming in by the garden, as he takes afterwards to be sure that he's left no trace."

"There wasn't a mark of finger-print in that room that didn't belong there," Haviland said earnestly.

Pointer felt sure of this.

"The visitor whom I'm imagining," Pointer went on, "came in the day-time. On a Tuesday. Though in winter Mrs. Tangye's generally alone over the week-ends. Choosing the day-time looks to me as though he were either married, or lived in chambers, or at an hotel, or some place where his comings and goings at night might be noticed. As to the day of the week, that looks as if time pressed, and he couldn't wait till the next week-end."

"What about the past week-end?" Wilmot asked, "and even if it were any one in the house—mind, I don't believe for a moment in your theory—they might well be too shrewd to choose the night. Rather a home-made look about a job done then."

Wilmot had a wide experience of murder cases. Wider even than Pointer's. For Wilmot was only called in to take or make—*causes celebres.*

"They could have faked a burglary," Haviland suggested.

"Good faking is an art not acquired in one night," Wilmot pointed out.

"Suppose we say that hole is halved," Pointer suggested. "But was it Mrs. Tangye, or this mysterious visitor of hers that made her leave nothing among her papers bearing on her own affairs? Or is their absence unconnected with her death?" He was asking himself the question. "At any rate her visitor belongs, or came into her life, before she went to France. Before she corrected herself of being left-handed. Apparently he has not seen her in the meantime, since she's trained herself out of it. Offhand one would say some old lover cropped up. . . . And that, I think, is as far as mere deduction takes us."

"It could scarcely carry you much further unless you assisted it with a crystal ball, and a Ouija board," Wilmot murmured.

"Except," Pointer was impervious to sarcasm when he chose, "that no sounds whatever were heard from the morning-room. Which looks as though there had been no unexpected entrance of still another person, a third party, who was not in the secret."

"Of course, Tangye being out, Miss Saunders out, and the servants having their own tea shut away in their quarters, that doesn't mean much in fact," Haviland murmured. "But the room, and Mrs. Tangye herself—no, sir! There was no sign of any sort of trouble to be seen."

"Just so. We may take it that there was only one visitor. Some one whom she thought a friend. But who was not. Some one who profited by her death. For it was a deliberate crime—if a crime."

"You should write novels," Wilmot scoffed.

"Ah, I said this was only theory—speculation. Like some of your articles."

"Quite so. But I live by my fancies, whereas I thought you at the Yard depended on footing the solid earth for your daily bread. And once again, what about the woman who came at six, and said she was frightfully late? It looks as though in your solution of the problem A and B would have to meet 'Which is absurd.' According to your own premises, I maintain that there was only one caller at Riverview yesterday. The woman whom Florence showed in. Or do you suggest that Mrs. Tangye was playing the part of Providence to a young couple? And the gentleman arriving first, shoots her as a lesson not to meddle?"

"I don't think Mrs. Tangye would have put herself out to such an extent for any mere friend. For anything but sheer necessity."

"Then your theory exonerates Tangye—I mean, if it's a fact that there's a criminal here?" Haviland asked. "Though, as a matter of fact, there can't be, sir! You must excuse me, but I can't see it your way."

"So much the better! If I'm right you'll come round, both of you. If I'm wrong, there's only one misled. As to Tangye—it could have been an accomplice of his. Though I see no reason for that thought, and many objections. Still, it could have been."

"And where's Miss Saunders in this most bewildering dream of your's?" Pointer laughed; he knew Wilmot would ask that.

"She's outside. Not inside."

"Really? Like the late caller, eh? Forgive the question, but are *all* the facts of the case going to be outside your theory?"

Pointer only made a good-humoured gesture of not being able to tell yet.

"You'll have to keep her outside," Wilmot warned him in mock anxiety, "because otherwise she blows it sky-high."

"She does," Pointer agreed. "My theory presupposes no inside helper except Mrs. Tangye herself."

"Well, a suicide verdict doesn't fall to pieces because of the companion," Wilmot murmured in high good humour, "personally, I welcome her as a human note. So you call a 'theory' something that begins in smoke and ends in mythical steps heard by a couple of hysterical maids?"

"They struck me as very truthful young women. Don't run down the only corroboration I've got so far as to the existence of that unknown visitor! As I see it," Pointer watched the river as though he did see "it," and only "it" in the running water, "some one came into that morning-room by the long windows yesterday just after four. Came in, after having been to the house the day before, and laid his plans. Came in after having possibly followed her about in the garden until the flash of light from Florence's pantry warned him that he might be seen.

Very likely he had overlooked that little slit high up in the ivy. But afterwards—after he came in—" Pointer fell silent.

"It sounds most alluring. Most dramatic! But no, no! I can't see," Wilmot prodded the air with his cigarette to accentuate each word, "no, I cannot see how there's the possibility of foul play here. Mrs. Tangye in her own home—a good shot—the bell to her hand—her maids within call —her finger-prints on her revolver—"

There was a pause. "And Miss Saunders, . . ." Pointer said again, "is she shielding some one? If the latter, what is the motive? Love?"

"Of lying," Wilmot finished cynically.

Pointer laughed, but refused to believe that here they had an example of art for art's sake.

"I had thought when I read about that visitor in the reports on the inquest that Miss Saunders might be shielding her, but assuming her ignorance about the lady's departure to be honest, and I do, it looks as though she might be shielding Tangye. And that fits in with another impression left by her evidence. An impression as though she had been more guarded when Haviland first tackled her yesterday than she was this morning, or at the inquest."

"And that's a fact," Haviland agreed, "though it's generally the other way around. People generally come out in black and white first of all, and then begin to tone 'em down, and mix one in with the other, as they think things over and get qualms. But not Miss Saunders. It was yesterday she was careful. Didn't want to come down hard on any statement as it were. But this morning everything was sharp and clear. No more 'I thinks' nor 'to the best of my beliefs,' about her to-day. And I wonder why she won't stop at Riverview at night. ..."

"Fear," Pointer said briefly. "She's afraid. She wanted to accept that preposterous offer I made on your behalf, but wouldn't."

"You think she's afraid of Tangye?" Wilmot asked.

"Queer!"

"Her being afraid of Tangye," Pointer went on thoughtfully, shows that he either is, or she thinks he is, at least connected with his wife's death."

"As a matter of fact," Haviland said slowly, "that's what I thought as I watched her. That she was afraid, I mean. And I should think that's another essential in the case?"

Haviland eyed Pointer.

"Not if she's wrong. And she may be. Only time—and Tangye—will show. As Miss Saunders' evidence is so strongly on his side, it looks as though they might have made a bargain with each other. If so, in some way, the lost keys are mixed up in it. He and she both jib at those keys. Neither has made any effort to have them found. The maids were unaware of their loss."

"They both claim the keys are unimportant," Haviland reminded him.

"They do. And they both look uneasy when they're mentioned. At least Tangye does, always. And Miss Saunders was more than uneasy that time when I made her think Tangye had connected her with their loss."

"Well! Well! Well!" murmured Wilmot with gusto. "I still don't see any sign of a crime materialising, but you do give a glimpse into a very intriguing little family circle. But speaking about that visitor, how did she get out? That still remains as great a puzzle as ever."

Haviland promptly solved it for him.

"There's a cupboard in Mr. Tangye's room where overcoats and golf-clubs and such things hang. The back of it is really a door we found just now, leading out by the tradesman's gate. I didn't notice it yesterday, for I didn't search the house. I'm afraid I took her leaving a bit for granted in fact."

"You think she got out that way?" Wilmot asked. "If so, that would show?"

Pointer answered for Haviland, who was not quite certain what it ought to reveal by Scotland Yard standards of divination.

"For one thing that the caller who was mistaken for Mrs. Cranbourn, knew the house."

"Whew-w-w!" whistled Wilmot, "bloweth the wind that way?"

"Which way, Mr. Wilmot?" Haviland asked with a furrowed brow.

"Secret passages—vanishing ladies—gent's smoke-room—Sultan's favourite—that way. The way of the film vamp. Are you going in for the mysteries of Udolpho, Pointer? If so, I get off here and now. Architectural details always bore me to tears. There's no scope for the brain in that sort of thing."

"There's plenty of scope for any brains in this," Pointer reassured him. "For all of ours. Even for yours, Wilmot."

But the newspaper man shook his head.

"I ought to've refused the job. It's quite out of my line. This hunting for clues. . . . The Insurance Company ought to've sent down a retriever dog, not me!"

Pointer burst out laughing, so did Haviland, and so, after a moment's gloom, did Wilmot himself.

"Think so? Could Fido tell me why Miss Saunders gave no thought as to how that visitor got out? I think her bewilderment was genuine. What has been occupying her mind so intently that there was neither time nor room in it to spare? What's she been so busy over? I really think that's more in your line than Fido's, Wilmot. So, don't let them exchange you for him yet awhile."

"But I'm no good at this game," Wilmot protested. "You, as becomes a C.I.D. man, can't be happy without a crime to unearth. While I, for the life of me, am unable to even see the possibility of one here." He, too, spoke very seriously now. Seriously and thoughtfully. "I see odd trifles such as must generally accompany accidents or sudden deaths one would imagine. When the roof's torn off a man's house. But no more. For one thing, to me that revolver having been fired by Mrs. Tangye's left hand seems conclusive."

"It's the Insurance Company's best trump, I agree," Pointer said handsomely. "Yes, it's odd. Very."

"I don't call it odd. I call it an impossibility unless her death was either self-inflicted or due to an accident. For it clearly marks emotion. And as such is of great weight in proving a suicide, and not out of place in asserting an accident. But it couldn't exist—*couldn't*—in a murder. For I should like to remind you, Pointer, that there are such things as genuine suicides, and genuine accidents. Though they don't seem to've come your way. That Charteris tangle coming on top of the Eames Erskine Case has put your eye out."

"Very possibly. But your clever criminal always stages the effect of either accident or suicide. Preferably the former. Don't forget that either. You know as well as we do that not every case is docketed at the Yard under the label which the coroner's verdict hangs on it."

Wilmot did know.

"And that's a fact," murmured Haviland fervently. "Speaking of doors, Mr. Wilmot, that door found leading out of Tangye's smoking-room. . . . Well, what leads out of a thing, leads into it too!"

"And that's a fact," Wilmot quoted gravely.

"Of course it may mean nothing. In fact, I still don't see how there's a crime here, for Mrs. Tangye would have rung that bell quick as light if any unauthorised person had come into the morning-room."

Wilmot sighed.

"Entrances—exits—butter on fingers—Fido's job!" he murmured disconsolately. "But supposing this were a crime —which I'm perfectly satisfied it's not—on the evidence so far, that is to say—"

"Perfectly satisfied? Is that the Insurance Company speaking?" Pointer imitated a telephone call.

Wilmot grinned.

"Fairly satisfied then. A nice look-out for us it would be! Not the ghost of a hope of catching the criminal."

"I wouldn't bank on that," Pointer said tranquilly.

"Do you really mean that you believe we could catch a criminal with nothing more to start on than the little we've got hold of so far?" Wilmot's tone showed his incredulity. Yet he was a firm believer in New Scotland Yard. In the will to win of the quiet men trained there. And among these men Pointer had risen high and swiftly. Wilmot wondered if more had reached the ears of the C.I.D. than of the police.

"Routine does a lot," Pointer murmured placidly.

Wilmot laughed outright.

"I feel like Watson's youngest baby in the arms of the mighty Sherlock. Do you mean to tell me, seriously, that without the person who killed Mrs. Tangye—you quite understand that my acceptance of his, or her, existence is purely academic, and solely for the purposes of discussion—without his making one false step, you could hope to bring home this crime? I'd be willing to bet a thousand pounds it couldn't be done."

"You'd lose, Mr. Wilmot," Haviland said loyally. But he, too, had his doubts. He knew Pointer's record. But every man makes mistakes sometimes. The Chief Inspector was a favourite with those who worked under him. He was probity itself, unassuming, open-minded, quick, accurate, and absolutely untirable once he had set out on a trail. But he was no wizard. Haviland wondered uneasily if this case might not be going to be one of the Yard's few blunders. Somehow, Haviland could not say how, he felt that Wilmot might have less science, less determination, but more luck. It was not the way by which Wilmot considered that his past triumphs had been won. But allowance must be made for *esprit de corps*.

"If I'm right, then it's the one false step he's already taken which ought to do the trick," Pointer said grimly. "He's killed. And unless it's an entirely motiveless crime, a homicidal impulse—killed for a reason. In the case of a lunatic, I grant you, the best detective outside of a book, might not be able to do his duty. But if a motive once existed, it can be found again. It exists as much as a lump of concrete exists. It's better evidence. For it's indestructible.

"Of course," Wilmot mused. "I agree that once a man commits a crime, he sets machinery in motion which he can't stop without showing himself in the effort. For he's part of it. But what if he's too clever to make any move?"

He shook his head at the prospect of the law in such a case. So did Haviland.

Pointer's face hardened. "Murderers always think that if they can plan their crimes cleverly enough, they can get away with it. My whole life is based on the conviction that you *can't* have a premeditated crime with a motive so clever that it can't be found out, and traced home. Unless there's a slip in the handling of the investigations. The murderer gambles on that slip, that's all."

"I wonder!" Wilmot weighed the thought in his mental balance, then shook his head.

"Speaking of facts," Haviland suggested, "if we could find a few more. That cleaned-off safe door was odd. That smoking-room exit very handy. Still, they don't prove anything. Mr. Tangye's alibi seems very sound."

Pointer shook out the dottle from his pipe.

"Time's up. We had better return to the house. After that, I, or rather you, Wilmot, have an appointment with Stewart, he's the Tangyes' family solicitor as well as the Coroner, you know. And then you got Miss Eden to give you an appointment over the telephone for later in the afternoon."

"Miss Eden?"

"The friend with whom Mrs. Tangye spent the greater part of Sunday at Tunbridge Wells. She's up for the inquest and the funeral. I doubt though, if it will be easy to learn anything fresh from her—judging by her deposition."

"Sorry," Wilmot said apologetically, "but you'll have to deputise for me. I seem to've made double engagements for this afternoon. So, unless you would like to write my next article, and send in half a column of your opinion on the new Opera—"

Pointer declined with a laugh.

CHAPTER FOUR

POINTER stepped in for a moment with Haviland at the police station. He wanted the photographs of the revolver. They were ready for him. An Inspector hurried in. "Mr. Tangye's been telephoning, sir. He says he's gone over his wife's papers, and finds there's a large sum of money missing from the house. Fifteen hundred pounds. Says it must have been at Riverview yesterday."

"This does alter things for a fact!" Haviland jumped up with the eyes of a good watch dog who hears some one on the step. Was it possible that facts, real facts, facts which you could marshal and exhibit, were going to bear out the Chief Inspector's fantastic idea?

They telephoned the news on to Wilmot, and walked quickly up to Riverview. Tangye was waiting for them. He looked both angry and uneasy. Taking them into his study he closed the door, and rapidly amplified his message.

It seemed that Mrs. Tangye had employed a separate firm of solicitors for the management of her property. Sladen and Sladen of Baker Street. Tangye said that he himself knew nothing of her estate. Had always refused to know. But on going over the papers which the firm had sent him, he had found that half of a sum paid her during the past fortnight was missing.

"Like her keys," Pointer reflected aloud, and Tangye turned a swift, wary, glance on him. But he answered impatiently:

"The keys are of no importance. A sum of money is a different thing. It seems she sold a farm over a week ago for three thousand pounds. The money was paid in at her solicitor's office, and remained there till yesterday. But just after two, Mrs. Tangye drove up in a taxi, without an appointment, and took the whole amount away with her. She was paid in bank-notes. Half of those notes are missing."

"Bank-notes? Why not a cheque, sir?"

Tangye explained that his wife had had an invincible dislike to cheques. A bank had once failed, leaving her with an uncashed, worthless cheque. Since then, all her transactions had been strictly in notes.

"Well, of course," Haviland repeated, taking down the numbers of the notes, "this does alter things, for a fact."

"Not in the essentials. Mrs. Tangye's death was an accident. Couldn't of course have been anything else," Tangye said shortly, "but that missing sum may have been stolen."

"She would keep the money in her safe, I suppose?" Pointer suggested.

"She might have."

"You think the loss was unconnected with her death?"

"Obviously. But how many people would you trust in a house with the mistress dead, and a wad of notes like that?"

Pointer and Haviland nodded their agreement with the only possible answer to this question.

"But what makes you think your wife had not invested the money in some way? She might have posted that fifteen hundred off at any time between two and the hour she returned to Riverview—about four."

"I've always seen to her investments. Why should she pay a stockbroker's charges when she could get it done for nothing?"

"Perhaps she wanted a bit of a flutter with it, and did not like to you know. There's a tremendous boom in cotton just starting."

"Don't you suppose Sladen and I have 'phoned to every inside and outside man, every bucket-shop in the kingdom, before turning to you?" Tangye asked impatiently. "No offence, Chief Inspector, but I'm afraid you're only losing time with your questions. The best thing for you to do is—"

"For me to decide, sir," Pointer finished very quietly.

Tangye mumbled what was meant for an apology.

"I don't see how you can be sure that Mrs. Tangye might not have gambled in another name," the Scotland Yard official went on.

"No point in that. She was absolutely her own mistress."

"The exact halving of the money looks as though she had some definite purpose in view," Pointer went on unruffled.

"And how do you know that none was spent yesterday, sir? A lady can get rid of a lot of coin in a couple of hours, for a fact," Haviland said with the gloom of a husband and father, as he went off to the library to telephone the numbers of the missing banknotes to his inspector at the police station, with instructions as to where to try to-night.

"Fifteen hundred pounds!" Tangye repeated the sum under his breath as though the figures loomed large to him. "It's not the money in itself. But I don't like to be done. No man does. I won't be done!"

"It seems quite simple to me," Pointer said mendaciously. "Those lost keys and the lost money will be found to belong together. Find who has taken the one, and you'll find who has taken the other."

He was watching Tangye in the mirror, as he seemed engrossed in getting his pipe to draw better.

Tangye stiffened in his chair.

"Damned nonsense. You must excuse me, Chief Inspector. But that cock won't fight. Can't. I know those keys are somewhere in the house, as I told you. On thinking it over, I remember now quite clearly seeing them myself lying about the place after the police left. I can't recollect where— but I know I saw them."

Pointer dropped the subject of the keys.

"Mr. Tangye," he said instead in a low voice. "You

know more than you're telling us. About this missing money. Or, at least, you suspect more. You have some reason for feeling so certain it was stolen."

Tangye's face paled a little. He detached a cigar-band with extreme care, and laid it on the exact centre of a log, as though it were a votive offering, and as such had to be presented with strict conformity to rule.

"Not at all. But my knowledge of my wife's habits makes me feel sure that Mrs. Tangye had done none of the things with the money you suggest. I believe it was in the house when she had that fatal accident. I believe that some one, knowing it was there, stole it."

Pointer bent forward.

"Whom do you suspect?"

Tangye, got up and walked to the window. Drew up the blind with a snap, and let it down again with a crash. That done, he helped himself to a stiff drink. Then only did he reply.

"No one. That's what I want you to find out. You're so extraordinarily interested in Mrs. Tangye's death, which is no mystery, and perfectly simple—though God knows it's terrible enough—yet, when I hand over to you a genuine inquiry, you seem to want me to do the work, the investigation."

Tangye's nerves were evidently strained.

"It's the idea of being done, I can't stand," he said himself, as though in excuse.

They sat in silence for a few minutes.

"By the way, while the Superintendent is putting one of his men on to trying the railway stations and other open-all-night places, I'd like another word with you about Mrs. Tangye's cousin. We want to be sure he wasn't in touch with her just before her death."

"You can be sure. They were on anything but a friendly footing. Naturally. Oliver is a thoroughgoing blackguard. My wife usually refused to even speak of him. He would hardly venture to write to her— "

"But he might have come."

"Here? To Riverview? I should like to see him dare to show his face here. I should have had him kicked out inside of ten seconds, and as for Mrs. Tangye—! I suppose you know something of his record?"

Pointer only confessed to an extreme interest to learn it.

"He was sent down from Oxford. Cheating at cards. He's been auctioneer's clerk, sailor, orchid-hunter, and rum-runner since then."

"You feel quite certain that he had not written to Mrs. Tangye in all these years? She was his only relative."

Tangye sat, apparently thinking back.

"' Pon my word! I wonder if he could have had the collossal nerve! She used to say that he could blarney a cannibal. You know that he once got Branscombe to give him some money for a fresh start? Oliver started all right— drug-smuggling to the Bantus. Mrs. Tangye stopped the supplies as soon as she learnt of it."

"Was there anything odd about his appearance? I mean anything that would attract attention? Stick in the memory? Been easily recognised again?"

"Yes to all the list. Unforgettable sort of face. Bird of prey, yet clever! Then he was immensely tall and thin."

"Had he a limp?"

"He hadn't when I saw him, but if the rumour's true I heard some years back that he was gun-running for the Riffs, I should think it probable that he has one by now."

Pointer got as detailed an account of the missing man as Tangye's remembrance could supply. He asked if Miss Saunders might join them for a moment.

She came in with her quick, silent step, which yet conveyed no suggestion of lightness.

Pointer watched her in the mirror, his back to the door, as she entered. She flashed a swift glance first at him and then at Tangye. That glance was unmistakable to the eyes on her. It was a confederate's glance.

"Anything wrong?" was telegraphed as clearly as though ticked out in Morse. So these two were partners, at least for the time being. At any rate in something. Tangye's eyes avoided hers.

Turning, Pointer explained the circumstances of the missing money to her. He noticed that Tangye waited for him to do this. She looked startled and uneasy, and something else that even Pointer could not decipher, it was so quickly repressed. Pointer thought that she seemed inclined to doubt the whole story until she heard of the solicitor from whose offices Mrs. Tangye had taken the money only yesterday. She then said that Mrs. Tangye must have banked it, or used it in some way. Tangye retorted that that was what they all thought. He looked at the woman with a lowering stare.

"Do you want us to list the money under 'missing or stolen,' or only under 'stolen'?" Haviland asked returning to the room.

Tangye started a little.

"Under 'missing or stolen!" he said after moment's thought. It was the most natural form where a doubt existed. But it was also the only form which would let Tangye stop the inquiries should he later find, or pretend to find the money. Once entered as *Stolen*, only an order from the Home Office could check the search being carried through to the bitter end.

Did Tangye know this?

Pointer let Haviland do the talking, while he sat apparently listening. In reality observing. He noticed again how little the stockbroker turned to him. He made Tangye uneasy in some way. What way? And he made him more uneasy now that he was talking of the missing money. Why? And again why did Tangye try so hard to pull himself together during this talk. Each time that he was on the point of being natural, would come some evident effort.

Evident to Pointer's observant eyes, that he was anxious to make no slip. What sort of a slip? But he seemed genuinely eager that the money should be traced. Eager, and yet cautious. Who was he shielding or prepared to shield? The Chief Inspector speculated on the new turn the case had taken. Was it an honest turn? Fifteen hundred pounds in the house Tuesday afternoon. Was that connected with the death of Mrs. Tangye or was it but a coincidence? Certainly his idea of a crime was not weakened by this new piece of intelligence. There came another thought. This lost money fitted in so well with his theory of an outsider, •was it possible that that was Tangye's aim? What if he too knew of the unknown's existence, was in league with him, feared lest the police had learnt of his visit, and with the guilty man's haste to cover even non-existent tracks—had invented the lost money as a pretext for the stranger's visit?

But the longer Pointer studied the man talking to the keenly interested Haviland, the more he decided that Tangye's emotion about the loss was genuine. That Tangye was trying to repress, not to force, the note on this point. He acted to the very keen, trained eye of the detective officer like a man much more concerned in the matter than he cared to show. On this came the reflection that possibly Tangye had wanted the whole £3,000 so badly that he had had a hand in his wife's death. A hand so carefully concealed that now, little by little, he could venture to direct the search towards it. Was it a case of a criminal having been "done" by his accomplice, and trying to get that accomplice caught? Tangye's frequent use of the word suggested this. So did his manner. By what he did not say, as much as by what he did. Pointer believed that for some reason he dared not be more explicit. Yet Tangye was emphatically not a man to be frightened of shadows. A stockbroker must have good nerves.

Rising, Pointer asked Miss Saunders to come into the drawing-room. He closed the door with ostentatious care. It gave a confidential suggestion.

"Miss Saunders," Pointer spoke very low, "there seems to me, quite frankly to be something rather—well—odd, about this claim of Mr. Tangye to that fifteen hundred pounds. What do you think yourself?"

"Of course it isn't lost," she spoke shortly, and with a note of anger in her thin voice. "Mrs. Tangye's invested it somewhere that they haven't found yet. That's all."

"It's very perplexing," he said a little dismally, "very perplexing, indeed. Did you make any arrangements on Monday as to where you intended to go from here?" he asked in the same breath.

She had not expected that question. She all but jumped.

"I don't understand. Going from here? Monday? It was only Mrs. Tangye's death yesterday that made me decide to go to my sister's."

"You had your trunk brought down in the morning?"

"I thought Mrs. Tangye's idea of sending some clothes to the poor an excellent one," she said sweetly. "I intended to do the same."

"I see. Now, do you mind telling me where you were last Sunday? This lost money puts the case in our hands, and we've a regular routine to work through."

"Where was I last Sunday?" She turned a watchful eye on him. "At church, part of the time."

"It's the remaining part I want to hear about," he said lightly, "you left here, at what hour?"

"In time for the eleven o'clock service. After that I stayed with a friend. And we took the children to one of the museums by way of a treat."

"Could I have the name of the friend?"

"I couldn't think of dragging her into this sad business."

"And in the evening?"

"I spent helping her. She put me up."

"And Monday?"

"We spent shopping."

"For the children too, I suppose?" he said gravely.

A light flickered in her eyes. It looked like amusement.

"You might be a family man yourself," she murmured ironically. The door opened. But why had Tangye stopped outside to listen first? He glanced in airily. "Oh! Sorry to interrupt. I was afraid you had gone, Chief Inspector."

"No, I was saying to Miss Saunders that with such a sum in the house why of course we have to ask a number of fresh questions."

"But who would steal bank-notes?" Miss Saunders asked pertinently.

"When did you last see Mrs. Tangye at her safe?"

"Many months ago I saw her lay some books in it. She used it as a sort of cupboard at times. It was always unlocked."

"Could it be locked?"

"I don't know." She turned to Tangye, whose jaw shot forward.

"Of course it could be," the master of the house said briefly.

"And the key was on her key-ring, I suppose?" Pointer, continued.

"Possibly."

"Then the missing keys might be important, after all."

Tangye said nothing. Miss Saunders brushed the top of the marble mantelpiece with her hand. She, too, said nothing.

"Florence saw them at four on her mistress's desk," Pointer went on.

"So she says." Miss Saunders' tone was contemptuous. "You seem to attach great weight to a maid-servant's word— almost as great as to a reporter's!"

"As a rule, neither have anything to gain by mis-statements in a case of this kind," he said blandly. "You didn't happen to notice them in the room on your return from the library? I mean, before Florence came in?"

Tangye started. He cast a quick, furtive, look at Pointer and then at the woman.

"No," Miss Saunders said very composedly. "I do not think they were there then."

Pointer was apparently bending over a table near him, but he saw the hard, suspicious stare that Tangye gave the speaker. She returned it with something of defiance. There was a silence which the detective officer did not break. Here was no love affair, he thought. Whatever had been in the past, these two did not like, did not trust, each other now. He wondered why Tangye seemed so unwilling to link the lost keys with the lost money. The stockbroker did not strike him as a clever man outside of his own walk of life. If there. Though Pointer had a feeling, had had it from the first, that Tangye's path was beset—at least to the man's own thinking—with pitfalls. That he was afraid of saying one unweighed word, one hasty conclusion.

"She invested it, you may be sure," Regina Saunders said, turning towards the door, "but it's most distressing for every one until it's found. Olive's already given notice. Florence wants to leave when she does. Cook's looking out for a new post. I'm afraid, Mr. Tangye, that you won't be able to keep the house running many more days." She left them at that, with a cool nod apiece. Tangye looked after her without saying anything. There was a set to his full mouth which was not easy to read.

"I should like to see the maids, please—alone."

Olive came in first. She had told Pointer already that she had not seen the keys since just before lunch yesterday, and then in Mrs. Tangye's hands. Mrs. Tangye was in her bed-room at the time talking to Miss Saunders.

He had not asked for further details then. Now, he did. Olive was quite sure that she had heard the door of the safe shut and locked as she went on down the stairs, dusting the banisters. No other lock in the house sounded like a safe lock, she maintained, and Pointer privately agreed with her. Miss Saunders and Mrs. Tangye had passed her a moment later, going in to their lunch.

"Had they been quarrelling, do you think?"

"Oh, no, sir. Mrs. Tangye was looking quite calm. She was saying something like 'I can't help that, Miss Saunders. By this evening, if you please.' "

"And Miss Saunders?"

"Oh, she said nothing, sir. But she gave her a look as she stepped behind her for to pass. It was a look that said 'Just you wait; my lady!' if ever one did."

"Mustn't make too much out of a glance, Olive," Pointer said lightly.

"But you see, sir, Miss Saunders—she has a way of getting even with you. You can't tell yourself how she does it. If the mistress had lived—but there!" Olive stopped herself or tried to, then she burst out, "If Mrs. Tangye had lived, Miss Saunders wouldn't be acting as if she was mistress here. But there!" Again she pulled herself up. "We're leaving. It won't matter to Flo and me."

"Why are you leaving?"

Her voice faltered.

"I can't stand it, sir. I'm not so sure as I was that it was an accident. The more I thinks it over the more I feel as though there was something—something—not quite right about the mistress's end, sir. It's thinking about those foot-steps does it."

"You've no other reason for leaving?"

"I've nothing to complain of, sir. But how can I stay on in a house where there's a room I can't abear to enter, and a garden I can't pass through without it gives me a turn."

"The garden too?"

"Oh yes, sir! I never go through it without hearing those footsteps coming up behind me same as they come up behind the poor mistress. Seems as though they was after me too."

Looking at her pale face, Pointer thought it high time that she left.

"Have you any place in your mind?"

"Well, sir, Florence thinks—"

Pointer laughed.

"I'm quite sure she does. And so does Cook. But I want to know what you are going to do."

"I'm to go to Lady Ash, sir, and Flo is to come too,

later on. It was Miss Barbara as settled it. I'm glad to be going there. There won't be nothing to be frightened of in a house where Miss Barbara is."

"Ash? Wasn't that the name of the partner of Mr. Branscombe, Mrs. Tangye's first husband?"

"That's the lady, sir. They live just over the bridge in Kew. She's a friend of Mrs. Tangye's. But Miss Barbara, she never comes here. She's on the committee of the G.F.S. That's how I know her. She's a dear, Miss Barbara is! I'm going at the end of the week."

"Miss Saunders is leaving Riverview too, I understand?"

Olive looked surprised.

"Florence thinks– -" she caught herself up and laughed for the first time since Pointer had heard her.

"To think of not being allowed to speak of me own sister, sir! But that's Flo on the stairs now."

She really had quick ears. And accurate ones. Florence stepped in a moment later, and took her place.

"It's a dreadful idea about some money being missing, sir," she began earnestly, "I don't like to stay in a place where there's been a loss like that. None of us do. But what had we ought to do, sir?"

Pointer advised her to stay on until she could go to her next place.

"No one suspects you, or any of the servants," he reassured her, keeping the qualifying "so far" to himself. "But Florence, there's something that may have a bearing on this money, which you haven't told us."

"I, sir? Oh, I'm sure I've told you everything I could think of!"

Pointer hoped she had not been quite so thorough as that.

"It's about this quarrel between Mrs. and Mr. Tangye on Monday when he didn't stay to dinner."

"But there wasn't any quarrel, sir."

"Oh, yes, there was! Over—well, to be quite frank with you, I wouldn't say this to every one, mind, we heard it was over some one—a gentleman—whom Mrs. Tangye had known before, who used to write to her, and meet her now and then on the quiet."

Pointer looked inquiringly at Florence. She was shocked.

"Oh, sir! what a thing to say! And Mrs. Tangye not even buried yet!" Apparently there was a close time for scandal.

"We know she wasn't very fond of her husband," Pointer spoke as though half sorry for what he had said.

"Then you know more'n me, begging your pardon. Anyway, that's no reason for thinking *that* of her. She wasn't that sort. Not at all!"

"Yet there was a quarrel," Pointer spoke as though he knew what he was only guessing. "Was it connected with Miss Saunders, do you think? We've been told that Mrs. Tangye was sometimes a little jealous of her."

"My goodness! Whatever for?" Florence opened amazed eyes. "Why, Mrs. Tangye was twenty times handsomer! And whatever her faults, the mistress had a heart. Miss Saunders hasn't any heart. Cruel unkind she can be, if she thinks she dare."

"Oh, we were told that Mr. Tangye—"

"Don't you believe all you're told, sir," she said earnestly. Pointer kept his grave face. "There was nothing of that kind. At least I think so. I mean, I think not." Florence's tone showed that the idea was new to her.

"Then what did Mr. and Mrs. Tangye quarrel about on Monday afternoon? It was a very violent one. He struck her—" Pointer went on in a low voice. Florence jumped.

"Oh, no, sir! Never! The master wouldn't do such a thing. Besides, it was she who was so angry. He kept trying to pacify her." Florence put her hand to her mouth. Too late. Then she began to cry.

"Oh, I wouldn't do anything to make things worse for any one," she sobbed. "And it hadn't anything to do with her accident the next day, nor to do with this missing money, sir. It hadn't really!"

"Well, of course, if we knew that for certain—" Pointer said in an undecided tone, "of course if we could be sure it had nothing to do with the case why, that might be different. But you're certain it wasn't *he* who was in a rage?"

"Oh no, sir. That he wasn't! He never is!"

"But you told me that there was no quarrel at all between them? How can I believe you now?"

Pointer did not speak angrily. Florence was a gentle soul. She choked.

"I didn't want to make bad trouble worse, sir. But the mistress did go for the poor master last Monday. She seemed quite beside herself. Yet just before she spoke to me very quiet, as she'd been all day long."

Pointer still looked undecided.

"Well, of course, if we knew for certain what the quarrel was about, and it might not have to be entered at all," he repeated vaguely, "what exactly did Mrs. Tangye say? But be very careful, Florence, to only tell what you really heard. Not what you thought was said."

"I didn't hear anything worth repeating sir. Just half bits and ends. I wasn't listening, only putting something right on the tea-tray that had toppled over. I had to wait a moment before I could come in. The mistress—it's dreadful to say of her now she can't ever speak again— but she was raging wild. 'The house is mine and I insist on your leaving it' was the only sentence I heard. Complete that is. But she never meant it. Fond of the master she was, and he of her too, in his own way. But she kept on that he was to leave the house. A thing I shouldn't have thought she'd have said. He said he was going all right. But he stayed on for tea after all. So they must have made it up."

"But Mrs. Tangye must have said more than one sentence."

"Lots more, sir, but I couldn't give you her exact words. She said she had come to the limit. That she wasn't going to put up with things any more. That sort of talk, sir. Not meaning half, nor a quarter, of what she said."

"And he?"

"He kept his temper wonderful, sir. Kept hushing her. I heard him say once that she was making mountains out of molehills."

"Didn't he say anything more? I can't believe that there was no reference to money?"

"I didn't hear none, sir. Nothing but his trying to quiet her."

"You didn't hear any names? Such as Bligh, for instance?"

Florence shot him a shrewd look.

"No, sir. But I shouldn't have been surprised if I had."

"You don't think it could have been Mrs. Bligh who came to the house at six yesterday?"

"Oh, no, sir. I know Mrs. Bligh. She comes now and then to our best dinner parties. And I didn't make any mistake in the name, sir. The master read me that telegram, sir. But Cranbourn was the name the mistress gave. And, besides, she talked about her. Said as how she didn't want to be interrupted in her talk, as they hadn't met for so long, Mrs. Cranbourn living in Spain. I can't make out about that cable, sir. Seems to me most mysterious. It does indeed."

Pointer went off on another tack.

"And Mr. Tangye, now, did he ever have any friends in to tea for a chat in his smoking-room?"

"Many a time. Gentlemen only, of course."

"Ah, he'd find that way around to the back gate convenient, I dare say."

Florence looked puzzled for a moment.

"The master never uses that! The room was the house-keeper's when old Mrs. and Mr. Branscombe lived here, so I've heard."

"Didn't Mrs. Tangye sometimes use it? Or any friends others?"

Florence thought.

"I don't think so, sir. Though once she showed Miss Eden out that way the last time she stayed here. It is shorter if you're in a hurry to get to the telegraph office."

"When was this?"

"About a month ago."

There was another pause. Pointer seemed to have finished.

"By the way, who was it chose the room into which Mrs. Tangye's body was carried?" he asked conversationally.

"*She* did." This startling reply was explained by Florences' face of indignation.

"That's no way to treat a corpse, is it, sir? Disgraceful, I call it. Cook and Olive and me, we've put all the greenery around we can, but it's not a room fit for a corpse, is it, sir?"

Pointer thanked Florence and pausing for a second outside the den to hear the two voices within, slipped upstairs into Tangye's dressing-room. He gave it a quick, but sufficiently thorough search. In the clothes-basket he found a crumpled silk handkerchief, which still smelt of ether, and showed marks of dust. It was Tangye's own handkerchief. It had been used to wipe the safe. But was it he who had used it? Like everything else, it was inconclusive.

Pointer slipped downstairs once more, and let himself into the morning-room. He had "forgotten" to return the key.

He put all thought of the missing notes entirely on one side for the moment. The death was a fact. They were but a tale told him, and a tale with many perplexing features. Even granted moreover, that all was exactly as Tangye said, and even supposing them to be connected with Mrs. Tangye's death, they did not help to solve the immediate problem of how the woman had been killed, supposing the Chief Inspector to be right, and that she had been killed.

It certainly was going to be a stiff proposition to prove

a crime there; let alone solve it. Hitherto, even when they had first led the search astray, there had always been some clue, a match, a print of hand or foot, withered leaves, a smear of paint, to serve as a kick-off. To start the ball rolling. But if, as he believed, a murder had been committed here at Riverview, the criminal had done his work very neatly. No tags had been left lying about.

In an obvious murder a detective gets a certain amount of help from the general rule that an inmate of the house stages, or tries to stage, the effect of an outsider, an outsider that of a member of the household.

Clues in such cases read in the reverse direction as it were. But outsider and insider meet and merge in a well-set suicide scene.

The windows had been found latched by the Superintendent. That suggested some one in the house. Pointer and he had questioned Miss Saunders as well as Florence very closely, and both had no reason to think that the companion was holding anything back when she said that she had found them closed. If Pointer put a question mark beside her statement, it was merely because the woman had been in the room before the alarm was given. Was she an accomplice? The suicide effect made that doubtful. This was not a death by force, but by cunning. Mrs. Tangye had not been over-powered. That was certain. But out-witted in some way. So Pointer believed. Nor did the manner of death chosen suggest an accomplice.

Supposing she had been killed. How could it have been done? Swiftly he went over the room piece by piece. Still he found nothing suspicious. Finally he took out a couple of photographs which Rogers, the constable, had handed him at the police station. They were the enlargements of the marks on the revolver, and of Mrs. Tangye's finger-prints. He studied the latter first of all. They were certainly wonderfully clear. They had been made by Mrs. Tangye's left hand. There was no doubt of that. Her hand had been so greasy that it had left a perfect impression even of the palm. Yet there was a fitted basin with hot and cold water beside the morning-room. Was it likely that a woman—a lady— would sit still with fingers as buttery as a new cat's paws, and not wash them? Wilmot's suggestion of a slip and a hasty grab, did not explain this—supposing she intended to live. Of course if Wilmot and Haviland were right, Mrs. Tangye might have been so lost in brooding thoughts as to be inaccessible to material things. But the plate on the tea-table with its neat little lake of congealed butter did not bear out the idea of an accident.

The enlargements showed that his keen eyes had been right. The grip was a most singular one. The tips had clutched the revolver no harder than the palm of the hand. If as hard. But Pointer could not believe that such a shock as a bullet through the heart sends to every atom of the body, would not have contracted the hand sharply. Here, all had been even—flaccid. The only really strong pressure shown had been made by the palm and the bases of the fingers.

Pointer could think of but one explanation to that. An explanation so terrible that he must make sure that it really was the only one. Or at least, as sure as possible.

He looked long at his boot-tips. Then he studied the photographs again. But this time of the scratches on the revolver. They looked freshly made. Though in a weapon kept in a closed box that might not mean much. Apparently at some time or other the weapon had been bounced up and down among a lot of metal oddments. But that is not usually a Webley's fate, even unloaded. Nor did they look erratic enough for that. The enlargements showed him that two small marks were exactly duplicated on both sides. And the trigger had a central rake which did not extend to the bevelled edge. But for the finger-prints, it looked as though the trigger had been fired by some mechanical means. He thought of the missing key-ring. The mark on the trigger could well have been made by a ring snapped back.

But apart from probability, was there even the possibility of such a plan as that would mean, having been carried out here? The marks on the Webley puzzled Pointer, but not so much as the fact that it had been fired actually touching the woman's dress, pressed against her breast. This was the real kernel of the problem. How could a revolver have been got as near as that by any hand but her own, without alarming Mrs. Tangye? Haviland and Wilmot were one in saying that here lay the proof of accident, or suicide. And to crown all, as Haviland pointed out, the Webley must have been held very level. No hasty swing, or chance pointing of a weapon, this, if it were a crime. Full front, level with her heart, touching her dress.

And the bell beneath her nimble fingers had not even rung! It was a riddle. Granted that the firer was an intimate friend, companion, husband even, how could they have got that weapon so close against her? There had been no struggle. Pointer agreed with the upholders of the suicide, or accident theories on that.

He slipped out across the hall and stood a moment by the smoking-room door. Haviland had interpreted his glance correctly and was leading Tangye on to discuss past and present men to whom he had given odd jobs about the house and who might therefore, be labelled possible suspects. Pointer heard the gush of the soda water, and Haviland's "I don't mind if I do, sir," and returned to his own problem. He locked the door behind him and took a turn up and down the room. He felt as though he were faced by a stone wall, on the other side of which lay his goal. Somehow, or other he would get over or break through.

The fine poise of his head, the set of his jaw became more pronounced. Danger signals both with him.

It was the photograph of the dead woman herself, which he stood in front of him this time. Square and at her ease she sat in her light chair, feet together, one hand, fingers up, on her knee, the other extended limply down with the revolver on the floor below it. Why did she sit beside, not turned towards her tea-table?

Pointer did not believe that she had been moved after death. Yet there was something artificial about her pose which had struck him from the first. Something arranged. . . . Something set. . . . Set!

Pointer had an idea. She looked as though posed for her portrait. Suppose she had been!

Suppose the revolver had been hidden in a box-camera, and that Mrs. Tangye had been asked to sit for her picture. That would explain her position. Straight on her chair, facing into the room where the murderer would be pretending to focus her. The composed and yet stiff attitude of her body, especially of her feet. It would also explain the scratches on the revolver.

Pointer imagined an emptied box-camera, fitted with a few wires to hold the revolver. Its muzzle pressed against the hole in front where the lens would have been taken away. The click of the shutter at the side could be made to pull the trigger by the simplest of mechanical arrangements, such as a ring passed through a stout elastic band.

Pointer imagined the murderer asking for a portrait of the seated woman. Coming close and apparently focussing her in the "finder." Then suddenly advancing the box with a rush, and sending the bullet straight through her heart, almost noiselessly.

As he saw it, the murderer at once picked up Mrs. Tangye's left hand, rubbed it lightly with butter from the muffin dish, he had used his handkerchief probably, and then, pressed it around the weapon as much as possible as a living woman would have done, had she fired it. Then he had dropped the hand. It was a most artistic performance, but, as almost inevitable, just a shade over-acted. He had been a little too prodigal with the butter. He had pressed the palm a little too closely on the revolver.

Those footsteps in the garden, the "footsteps that

stopped". . . Pointer did not think the murderer would be late for his appointment. Rather the other way. Suppose he had been waiting in the garden till the exact time set. When Mrs. Tangye walked out into the darkness he might well have thought that a still better variant of the original idea was possible. The camera packed probably with asbestos shavings, would deaden the sound of any bullet—even if fired when all was still. There is always a certain risk in an indoors murder that some one may enter, and the crime be prevented, or suspicions aroused, or the murderer be caught red-handed. Pointer thought that those steps outside on the gravel path which the maids had heard coming closer, closer yet to Mrs. Tangye, might well have belonged to the murderer stalking his prey, until Florence's unexpected turning on of the light had stopped him, and told him that, after all, it would be best to proceed according to plan.

But whose steps were they? Whose? Man's or woman's? It was a devilishly ingenious idea. Who had thought it out, and carried it out? It could be any one, provided he, or she, had some excuse for taking Mrs. Tangye's photograph. There was Oliver Headly? He fitted many of the spaces very well indeed. Was he back in England? He had been an orchid-hunter at one time. It was to an orchid show that Mrs. Tangye had gone on Sunday. Had the cousins met at Tunbridge Wells? Had a reconciliation of sorts taken place?

There was Miss Saunders. . . . There was Tangye— Pointer thought of the glance which they had exchanged just now. Some understanding was between them. Her belief that Tangye had something to do with his wife's death must rest on some foundation, or Tangye would not be so reluctant to take a high hand about the money which he claimed was missing. For that Tangye suspected the woman of having stolen the money, Pointer was certain. His alibi was not what Pointer considered a good one. Like a middling hand at Bridge, it was neither bad enough to pass, nor good enough to bid on. All depended on what other cards might fit in with it.

And that quarrel with his wife. Her ordering of him out of the house which legally was hers. Tangye's face showed a temper that could, if let loose, be violent enough. He had used a Webley in the war. He reaped an immediate reward in the cessation of the double premiums, in the payment of the Insurance money, as well as in the control of his wife's invested funds.

Yes, Tangye stood to gain tremendously by his wife's death. In more ways than one, if gossip were true. One thing was certain. Whoever had killed Mrs. Tangye knew that the heralded visit of Mrs. Cranbourn was a bluff. The Chief Inspector did not believe that they would have chanced it otherwise.

Pointer heard the two men in the den go upstairs, Tangye saying something about showing Haviland a loose shutter.

Pointer stepped into Florence's pantry.

"Look here, I want to take a good photograph of the morning-room by flash-light. Just as part of the usual routine. Is there a camera in the house that I can borrow?"

"The master has one. He was talking of taking Mrs. Tangye's portrait only a few days ago."

"Mr. Tangye's just gone out, I think. But, anyway, his would hardly be large enough for a picture such as I want. I suppose it's one of the usual fold-up kodaks? Goes into a flat case like this?" He motioned a size.

He learnt that Tangye had just bought a new one, a large one, the kind of one that the Chief Inspector wanted, Florence thought.

"He took it down into the country on Saturday. I don't know if he brought it back or not."

Florence opened a press in the smoke-room. It was not there. Did any one else at Riverview photograph?

Miss Saunders did. The master had shown her how to use a camera that had been given her. It might do. It, too, was a box, though Florence thought not so large as

Pointer wanted.

Perhaps there was an old one of Mrs. Tangye's that he could have for the time being?

But Mrs. Tangye only had a very small vest pocket kodak. At that, to Pointer's apparent surprise, Tangye was heard descending the stairs. Thanking the maid, Pointer said he would be able to ask him about it, after all. But he took very good care to do no such thing, as leaving Haviland to follow, he walked on to the police station alone.

So Tangye photographed. Tangye had bought a new, large camera about a fortnight ago. Tangye had spoken of taking his wife's portrait. Humph. . . . And Miss Saunders photographed too. . . .

The lapping of the river no longer sounded to him like a whispered, threefold question. Rather it was like slipping footsteps with a catch in them. Slithering footsteps with a kink. They softly kept pace beside him till he reached the station, as if some Unseen were close at hand.

Here, as he had taken the longer way round, he found Haviland and Wilmot, who had cut his engagements and come down in a hurry.

"Of course, this is just some chance, some coincidence that has happened at the same time as Mrs. Tangye's death," Wilmot began at once. Wilmot's determination to be biased amused Pointer.

"Tangye may be quite right in saying that the loss of the money is unconnected with her death," Pointer reminded him, "I think there was a murder. *He* says there was a theft. If that's true, it's quite possible that we have two distinct crimes here, with two distinct criminals, or sets of criminals."

"Kind Heaven above, bring me safe to shore!" prayed Wilmot. "Fortunately, I have suicide to cling to or I should be drowned. Still, it's all vastly interesting. All this seeing an investigation in the raw, as it were. I confess I never realised how difficult it is to strike the right trail. How easy to get lost along the wrong one."

"There's one thing fairly certain," Pointer spoke with decision. "*If* the man who planned and carried out the murder also took the notes, then he will either have some paper exonerating him, purporting to be written by Mrs. Tangye, or really written by her, or it is Tangye himself. Tangye or a tool of Tangye's. He alone could have disposed of the notes without any questions being asked; without the numbers being traced. They are his property on the death of his wife. He may possibly have expected the whole sum to have been in the house. Certainly he had been let down over them in some job or deal. Nothing else explains his temper at their loss."

"Luckily, I'm not asked to do more than investigate any claim Tangye may make in proper form by a fortnight from yesterday. It's a fascinating cross-word puzzle. Though, mind you, suicide's the right word, and all these others are only duds that Dame Fortune insists on slipping into the spaces." The newspaper man spoke, as usual, with certainty.

"It's a funny show for a fact." Haviland's voice marked but little enthusiasm for the humour of it, but a great deal of determination to find the right word. "I thought at first that this money alters the whole case. So it would, in fact, but for the way she died." Haviland ran over the whole array of beloved facts.

Pointer unfolded his idea of a portrait—of a camera.

Haviland gasped. Wilmot actually let his eye-glass drop from a distended eye. He stared at Pointer with something like awe.

"By Jove! You really . . .? By Jove! I wonder! But, of course, it was suicide. Yet— If by some miracle it weren't!" He paused for a moment. "That criminal you're supposing has brains, Pointer!"

"So have we!" Pointer retorted briskly. "Better brains. Just because we're not criminals. They may commit clever crimes, but those gentry are never really clever, or they wouldn't commit them at all."

"That's not been my experience," Wilmot said sadly. "No. On the whole I'm afraid I think a criminal brain can be a very clever one. Too clever to be caught sometimes."

"You can't compare a crooked thing with a straight thing. Their minds must be warped." Pointer, apart from being one of the heads of the finest detective force in the world, was by nature of that "deep goodness given to men of real intelligence." He would never permit a crime to be invested with any aureole of genius, if he could help it. Wilmot shook his head, after another long "think."

"And how far does this new idea waft you? Mind, I don't for a moment think you're right, Pointer. But I like to have the novel read to me chapter by chapter."

Pointer clasped his hands behind his head, and looked up at the ceiling, his pipe between his teeth.

"Keeping my belief in a secret visitor—whether cousin or not—out of it, for safer reasoning, speaking offhand, going merely by the camera, not trying to fit it in with any other idea, I should say that it looks as if the murderer, if a man, was not a big man. Not a crack shot. Or hadn't good sight. He's very careful not to be able to miss. He's quick and deft with his hands. Those scratches on the revolver aren't fumbling ones. I should say his little machinery worked well. Quick and deft with his brains too, I should say. Neat and careful in all his ways. He makes no real blunder. Not one. I think, to be fair, we can't count the trifling over-doing of the butter a fault. Except for the machinery part, the whole has an almost feminine touch."

"I'm bound to say you're half persuading me there's something in your theory," Wilmot spoke grudgingly. "But no, no! That's the primrose path of fancy. I stick to the hum-drum,—the proven. The more I think it over, the more I doubt that camera idea of yours. It's too brilliant. It does too much credit to your imagination. Yet it's most alluring! Of course there is that cousin—but no! no!" He seemed to pull himself up on the brink of a swerve.

"Then you think her finger-prints were made for her?

That she was dead at the time?" Haviland could add two and two together as quickly as any man, provided they dealt with facts.

Pointer nodded.

"Haviland, farewell!" Wilmot declaimed dramatically. "I see that thou art lost to me. From now on, 'I am even as it were the sparrow that sitteth alone upon the house-tops.' I grant that it's a seductive theory " Wilmot looked as though greatly tempted to come over to the official camp too, "but there's too much of a revelation from Sinai about it for me. I'm a slow-going chap. I plod. I stumble. I grope."

Pointer and Haviland burst out laughing. For Wilmot's lightning deductions were famous. Though, as he truly said, they had hitherto always been made after the facts had been clarified and sifted, and the possibly relevant set aside from the provenly irrelevant.

"The strange thing is that use of the left hand," Pointer ruminated. "For—unless a blunder, of course—it dates the murderer. And as, so far, we've found no other blunder, it's possible that it was unavoidable. That he didn't— couldn't—know that she had educated herself out of it. That would mean that he belongs to an early part of her life. Before she went to France. Before her first marriage.'"

"In fact, it looks as if that left hand pointed directly to her cousin; first met again after long years, on Sunday," Haviland suggested. "Do you think he took Mrs. Tangye's keys off with him?"

"Possibly."

"If so, then it looks as though Mrs. Tangye had something he wanted to get hold of. Something more than the money, supposing he took that. I've tried banks and safe deposit vaults, and so on. I can't think of any other lockable place. . . ." Haviland sat turning over in his mind possible misses.

"You know," Wilmot thoughtfully swung his glass of light beer to and fro, "if I thought this a crime. If I were you in fact, Pointer, or you either now, Haviland, I should remember that it's quite possible that neither the cousin nor Miss Saunders, are connected with the murder, and yet that Tangye is. He seems to've been hard up for ready cash on Tuesday. Cheale's going to wire me in code if he learns of anything definite over in Dublin about that Irish failure that's expected to be announced next Saturday." And on that the party broke up.

CHAPTER FIVE

THE first name on the list which Pointer had drawn up before coming down to Twickenham was that of Mr. Stewart, the solicitor to the Tangyes, and also the Twickenham Coroner.

The Chief Inspector was shown in without any delay on sending in his card, and at once explained that he was acting for Wilmot, who was unavoidably prevented from coming. Stewart put the tips of his thin white hands together and waited. He was a very punctilious, elderly man, who did not look over pleased at Wilmot's substitute.

"Did Mrs. Tangye withdraw her will even temporarily from your keeping?" Pointer asked.

"She did not, Chief Inspector."

"Then I take it that she wrote to your firm suggesting altering her will, or at least asking for it back."

"And why do you 'take it' that way?" Stewart asked bleakly.

"Because of the character of the very searching questions you put at the inquest."

Stewart was drumming on the table before him.

"The point—about her having possibly asked for her will back—will have to be cleared up," Pointer spoke as though regretting the necessity. "Since Wilmot inclines to the belief that Mrs. Tangye's death was suicide. And you know his standing. The Company has given him carte blanche. He did think of applying formally for the handing over of any papers, or letters, in your possession, but I think we can arrange it between ourselves. After all, it's only just a matter of routine. She did write you on the point. We feel sure of that."

Stewart pressed a bell, and a moment later handed

Pointer a docketed letter.

It was from Mrs. Tangye, and was dated the night before she died.

> "*DEAR MR. STEWART,—Please send me my will at your*
> *earliest convenience for some alterations I wish to make. And*
> *please treat this request as strictly confidential.*
> "*Sincerely yours,*
> "*MABLE TANGYE.*"

"Did you send her the will?"

"It would have been posted to her Tuesday night, but for hearing of the terrible accident," Stewart stressed the word, "that happened to her."

"I think Mr. Wilmot would like to keep this. I'll give you the usual receipt." Pointer folded the letter away in his pocket book. Stewart said nothing.

"Had she ever asked for her will back before?"

"Never."

"Have you any idea as to the nature of the change she wished to make?"

"None whatever. I doubt if she would have made any—perhaps a small bequest to Miss Saunders. A very faithful, conscientious woman that. Otherwise I feel sure that the principal beneficiary would have remained Mr. Tangye."

"Yet you didn't mention the letter at the inquest."

"Mentioning it, which means producing it, would have served no useful purpose except to arouse painful and most unfounded gossip. And would have been contrary to her own written request."

Stewart looked sharply at the man in front of him. "I, too, take it that you are not satisfied with the finding of this morning?"

Had Stewart asked before that verdict was given he would have had a full reply, but now he was a dethroned monarch. Pointer said briefly:

"I am helping the Insurance Company, or rather Mr. Wilmot, to get a few facts together for his final judgment, and unfortunately I was not at the inquest myself. I've only read the reports."

"To some purpose," Stewart said acidly.

"You knew the dead woman for many years?" Pointer asked.

"I drew up her first marriage settlement. Or rather Branscombe's. She had nothing to settle. Her father had a small annuity. Her mother left nothing."

"What about her cousin Oliver?"

Stewart looked an inquiry.

"I understand that he is her only relative."

Stewart smiled faintly.

"I've had the pleasure of being on a case with you before, Mr. Chief Inspector. You understand a good deal more than that about Oliver Headly, I'll go bail. I shouldn't be surprised if you know where that unmitigated scallywag is at the present moment."

Pointer assured him that as yet he only knew of his existence, and the most outstanding features of his murky career.

Stewart added a few more. Among them that as he was a penniless orphan, his uncle, the Hampshire rector, had practically adopted him, had lavished a small income and a great love on the lad, and had died after a very painful interview •with his bank manager. The parson, white and haggard, had told the only big lie of his life. He accepted as his a signature on a cheque which the cashier had refused to pay out to the nephew. The old man had collapsed before he reached his home. Dying from a literally broken heart. Greatly to the relief of all who knew Oliver, that young man had left England about twelve years ago, and since then, as far as Stewart knew, had not been heard of.

Pointer asked if there had been anything of a love affair between the cousins.

Stewart did not know. But in the early days the rector had hoped they would marry. Stewart went on to say that he doubted if the wish would have come to anything, even without Oliver's putting himself outside the pale, for he understood that Mrs. Tangye had always disliked her cousin intensely.

Stewart was a man of scrupulous honesty. He would hold back what facts he could which would tell against his client, but nothing, not the wealth of Golconda, would have made him deviate from the truth. He now leant forward and tapped Pointer's knee with his glasses.

"There never was a more respectable, creditable past than Mrs. Tangye's, I should say."

He ran over the points of her uneventful life again, and of her first husband's settlements.

"You never came upon any trace of any one who might have a claim on her? Who might bear a grudge against her?"

Stewart made a gesture of definite negation.

Pointer looked at his boot-tips.

"She didn't also write about withdrawing her money from her husband's firm? She is bound to give him six months notice of any such action."

Stewart looked at the clock.

"Sorry to cut you short, Chief Inspector, but I have a client waiting."

"I should like that letter too, please," Pointer said placidly.

Stewart smiled.

"There is none such in existence."

Pointer felt fairly certain that in that case, it was Tangye who had destroyed it. Your family solicitor never destroys a paper, which may yet be wanted.

"Would you be prepared to swear that it had never reached you?"

"My time is up, Chief Inspector," Stewart said firmly, rising, and opening the door politely.

Pointer drove on to see Miss Eden, the next name on

his mental list, with plenty to occupy his mind.

So Mrs. Tangye had asked for her will back. After that —presumed—quarrel on Monday afternoon. If it had taken place at all, it must have been a serious one. And she had apparently either given notice, or been about to give notice of withdrawing her money, ten thousand, from Tangye's firm.

Mrs. Tangye seemed to have done some quick work on her return from Tunbridge Wells. Monday must have been a full day. Items:

Trunk packed, and sent off.

Husband quarrelled with, and apparently sent off too. Temporarily at least.

Will sent for.

There was a precipitancy, an urgency, about her actions which had struck him from the first.

He found Mary Eden, the friend with whom Mrs. Tangye seemed to have spent this last Sunday afternoon which the Chief Inspector thought so important, to be a quiet young woman of around thirty. She looked very self-possessed. He also thought that she looked as though she were steeling herself for an ordeal, as she turned towards him when he •was shown into the drawing-room of her flat.

As for Miss Eden, the Chief Inspector was a surprise to her. In his quiet manner. In the kind of good looks which nature had given him. He did not resemble in the least the Scotland Yard detectives of fiction, she thought. He reminded her a little of her brother, the finest amateur cricketer in England. Such splendid physical fitness generally meant a brain to match in her opinion, and always meant tireless energy.

Something in her glance made Pointer think—and rightly —that she regretted having given him the interview at all.

"I hope you won't think me troublesome when I ask— in Mr. Wilmot's stead—to see the letter that Mrs. Tangye wrote you after her return from Tunbridge," was Pointer's opening.

The hazel eyes fixed on his did not waver. Rather they steadied.

"Letter?" Pointer had an impression that Miss Eden would have liked to tell a lie, but either dared not, or would not.

"Just so. We know she sent you one," bluffed Pointer.

There was a pause. Miss Eden turned her face still more away from him.

"I'm afraid I didn't keep it. But I'll look for it afterwards, if you like, and send it on to Mr. Wilmot. I see his address is here—"

Pointer had used Wilmot's card with a pencilled line introducing himself only by name.

"Why does he wish to see it?"

"I believe the Insurance Company want to be sure of the hour when it was posted." He explained vaguely. "When did you receive it?"

"By the first post Monday morning," she said, after a slight pause.

That was what Pointer would have expected had any such shock taken place at Tunbridge as would adequately explain Mrs. Tangye's action of Monday and Tuesday. Judging by her appearance, she was not a woman to take counsel about her actions, he thought. He would expect her to make up her mind as to what she would do on the way back from Kent, write about it to her friend—for Miss Eden was a very close friend, all the reports showed—and then act on her own initiative.

He looked at Miss Eden with that quiet, pleasant glance of his that seemed to see so little, and saw so much.

She was on the alert now for questions about that letter. He knew as well as though he could read her mind that every defence was up, plenty of rounds ready, and no possibility of getting past her unnoticed. She had been taken by surprise when he had opened with the letter. But she was ready now. So that, throughout the rest of the interview he learnt nothing but the barest of facts. That Mrs. Tangye had arrived for lunch. That the two had gone to the orchid-show about three and left at five.

"Did you meet any one you knew down there?"

"Mrs. Tangye has no friends down there, and I know very few people in Tunbridge," was the evasive reply.

"But Mrs. Tangye was seen with—" Pointer spoke hesitatingly. "Perhaps she wasn't with you all the time," he added as a bright afterthought.

"All the time," Miss Eden said in a low voice. She was an exceedingly poor liar.

There was a short silence.

"Did she enjoy the show?"

"Not very much," Miss Eden spoke slowly, "it gave her a headache. Glasshouses are stuffy things at best, aren't they? Perhaps she got overtired." Her lip quivered as she finished.

"Oh? Wilmot thought you walked to the station afterwards?"

Again there came a little pause, then, "Mrs. Tangye fancied the air would do her headache good. So I told the car to go on to the station and wait for me there."

"Enclosed car?"

Miss Eden nodded.

"Partition between the driver and the other seats?"

Miss Eden's eyes darkened. After a second she said briefly, "No. But really these questions seem to me rather wide of the mark. . . ."

"Just part of the regular routine. Mr. Wilmot wants me to cover as large an amount of obvious ground as possible," Pointer reassured her. Asked about Oliver Headly, she relaxed for the first time. She grew natural. She had never liked Oliver, she said at once. His was one of those rare natures which, even when quite young, showed no trace of softness, of any thing but self-seeking.

She thought that his cousin had not heard from him since he left England years ago. She agreed, however, that, in spite of everything, a certain amount of family feeling for her only relative might have remained in Mrs. Tangye's heart.

Pointer seemed very interested in getting a description of Oliver. He listened closely though apparently casually.

"Striking appearance? Easy to recognise again if one met him suddenly?"

"Oh, unmistakable. But we think he must have died abroad—after all these years without a sign of life."

Miss Eden looked at the clock.

"What would you say was the most outstanding characteristic of Mrs. Tangye? Of her attitude to life I mean?" Pointer asked thoughtfully.

Miss Eden pondered.

"She had so many all about equal qualities," she murmured.

"There was pride—the right kind of pride which one might call self-respect. And there was directness—she was a very direct woman. There was a way she had of dwelling on the past. . . . Once she had lost a thing, she valued it higher than anything she owned; but, otherwise her's was a strong character."

And on that the interview ended.

Pointer had a most useful, though bulky, stud on one of the gloves which he never wore. Properly handled, it yielded a roll of tiny films the size of a pea, which could be enlarged into very useful portraits. Armed with these one of his detective-inspectors would be able to comb the show early to-morrow, and also the town. On Tuesday afternoon Mrs. Bligh was supposed to have been at her club. A woman detective was sent to try that out, by means of a bribe, and a substituted waitress.

Pointer drove off, feeling that to-morrow should bring some useful facts to light. But facts alone never solved any puzzle.

He ran over the events chronologically as he made for his rooms.

Friday night, Mr. and Mrs. Tangye had been at a dinner and a dance. Both apparently on the best of terms with the world and each other. Saturday morning all went as usual. In the afternoon Mrs. Tangye had attended a matinee with friends and gone on to a cheerful tea. Tangye had left about ten in the morning for his Norfolk week-end.

Pointer had called up his host over the telephone, and had been told that the stockbroker had spent all the time shooting wildfowl, until he left after lunch on Monday. Yet Tangye only owned two suitable guns, and neither of them had been taken down from their rack in his den. The dust on them had told Pointer as much, and the answers by the maids to a casually put question of his had proved it.

The Chief Inspector considered the visit to Norfolk as very hypothetical. Yet Tangye's friends were standing behind him solidly. And they were all men of good position. Here was no criminal clique. Pointer thought that if they backed his story up as they had done, it was because they knew quite well that he had spent the week-end, or at least, some of it, in company with a lady. With Mrs. Bligh probably. With the writer of that note—possibly—that Olive had seen Mrs. Tangye reading.

And Mrs. Tangye's interest in orchid-shows at Tunbridge, which had arisen so suddenly, was very likely connected with that letter too, as Haviland had thought.

Last Sunday! What had occurred, presumably down in Kent, that had so altered all Mrs. Tangye's quiet, well-ordered existence? That had—so Pointer expected to find—led to her death two days later?

He did not think that here was a crime dropped accidentally into events which were already stirring before it happened. The flight of Mrs. Tangye from her home, which he believed had been pending, and the death of Mrs. Tangye, were, he thought, linked. Though whether closely or loosely, time alone could show. Time and routine-work.

That night an undetected burglary was committed in London. The victim of the crime never knew of it. Tangye's offices in the city were entered by a tall, quick-moving figure, wearing rubber soles, and with the arm torch and adjustable keys of his craft. The burglar seemed to be an original. Everything that was not in the safe—a burglar-proof safe— was looked at, but the only things taken were oddments such as blotting paper, and the contents of the waste-paper baskets.

Pointer, for it was he, paused longingly on his way home, outside the flat over a shop where Miss Saunders lived with her sister, but the yapping of a small Pom sent him reluctantly off. Back in his own rooms he examined his haul, which did not include the keys as he had hoped. An hour's work piecing, reading, deciphering, made him certain that he had drawn a blank. And on that he turned in, and slept the sleep of the hard worker.

Next morning Pointer sent in his card to the particular Sladen who had acted for Mrs. Tangye in all estate matters. The solicitor was a cheery young man who looked on life as a great joke. He substantiated Tangye's story of the purchase of Clerkhill farm for three thousand pounds by a Mr. Philpotts, a farmer living near Rugby.

The money when paid over had been left in his safe by Mrs. Tangye who had discussed the merits of various Funding loans without deciding which appealed to her most.

Sladen, too, had heard from his late client herself about the bank that had failed, and knew of her unconquerable aversion to cheques.

"Pleasant lady, I understand?" Pointer asked.

"Very. Terrible shock to hear of such a death having come to her." Sladen actually looked grave for a moment.

"Of course, we're only concerned with tracing this money, but the Insurance Company is trying to decide whether accident or suicide was the more likely explanation." Pointer seemed in doubt himself.

"Not suicide," Sladen said positively. "Oh, dear, no! Not suicide! Very shrewd eye for a bargain. Very keen on having a *quid* for her *quo*."

"That's a help," Pointer looked grateful for any assistance. It was his most useful mask when he had to go in his own person to make inquiries.

"Now, this Mr. Philpotts.—he might be able to confirm that too?"

"Rather!" Sladen laughed again. "Not much doubt but that he'll agree with me. Would you like his address in town? He's staying for over the funeral. He used to know Mrs. Tangye years ago in her father's parish, when she was quite a little girl, so he told me."

"Keen amateur photographer, isn't he? I seem to recollect his name as exhibiting now and then. I go in for a bit of that sort of thing myself."

"Ah? Dare say. I know nothing of him personally."

"Then how did you come to suggest him as a purchaser?"

Pointer seemed bewildered. Sladen decided that the low amount of serious crime in London compared with that in other capitals is due to the natural goodness of the Londoner, rather than to any fear of detection.

"I didn't suggest him," he explained, "we advertised the farm in the usual way. Mr. Philpotts answered, and as his money was there in the bank, and Mrs. Tangye very much favoured him as a purchaser after she'd learnt that he used to be one of her father's church-wardens, why the deal went through."

"Had they met since those early days?"

"Not as far as I know. Mr. Philpotts liked everything in writing. So did Mrs. Tangye. We forwarded the papers to her and put the thing through for her."

Pointer had asked last night at Riverview whether Philpotts had ever been to the house. As far as was known he had not.

Next, the Chief Inspector wanted a detailed list of the papers sent by Sladen to Tangye. He read it through—once, and then·asked about a green cash book, and a brown account book of Mrs. Tangye's. Sladen had never had either in his care. Yet Pointer had found them in a locked drawer in Tangye's desk at his office, together with various other papers of Mrs. Tangye's which the Chief Inspector had duly listed, and which also, he now saw, were not on Sladen's list.

How had they got into Tangye's possession? When Haviland had seized on the absence of all personal papers from his wife's desk as a proof of suicide, Tangye, though indignant, had had to fall back on the explanation that his wife had destroyed them as a preliminary to her tour abroad with him. All the papers which he had seen in Tangye's drawer had been folded into trim slips, neatly and very fully docketed in the dead woman's writing. They looked as though they had been compressed into the smallest possible space. They looked, in fact, to Pointer, as though Mrs. Tangye had selected them as essential and sufficient for her purposes before destroying the others. Pointer had spent some time last night ,with them spread around him, and had noticed that every necessary item and note and receipt was included. But no more.

Yet he had found them in Tangye's drawer. Though the presence of them in his wife's desk would have taken away one of the two main props of the suicide theory which he fought so persistently, and which it was so much to his interest to disprove.

There had been nothing in the papers kept which gave any reason for his objecting to their being found and read.

Pointer questioned Sladen about the withdrawal of the money yesterday.

He was told that the whole transaction occupied a bare five minutes. A cab had driven up just after two; Sladen was busy with a client. His head clerk had taken the sum in question, three thousand pounds, from the safe, and obtained the usual receipt. He had ventured to expostulate on the danger of carrying large sums in handbags. Mrs. Tangye had assured him that it was to be immediately invested. She declined his offer of sending an escort; that was all Sladen knew.

Pointer learnt nothing more from his head clerk except his opinion of such unorthodox proceedings, and his belief that in some dim way they were connected with the entry of women into the law courts. When it came to facts, Johnston could not even say whether Mrs. Tangye had walked away from the offices, or taken a taxi, or whether she had a friend with her waiting outside. Pointer gathered that the old head clerk had been thrown into a state bordering on coma by the speed, and irregularity of Mrs. Tangye's actions. Neither the clerk, nor Sladen had ever heard her mention her will, or will-making. Nor had she ever referred to the money invested in her husband's firm.

Pointer asked for a specimen of Philpotts's writing and the number of every note paid for Clerkhill farm. He knew already that Tangye had not drawn out nor paid in, any large sums to his, or his wife's banking accounts during the past month.

The stockbroker had only given him the numbers of the missing notes, but since the dead woman had removed them all from the solicitor's care only a few hours before her end, the Chief Inspector felt a keen interest in each.

Accordingly he next had a brief interview with a young Jew of his acquaintance. Hyam was a rising financier, and his moments were precious. But, for the sake of a time when Pointer had saved him from a very nasty position, he could always spare a few for the Chief Inspector. Pointer only needed one. He wished to trace any possible activities of Tangye on the cotton market and learn what had become of the notes which the stockbroker had taken over on his wife's death. Would Hyam use any private means of finding out both points? The investigation would be greatly hampered, and incidentally a quite possibly blameless man harmed by inquiries, however discreet, undertaken officially. Hyam said "Trust him!" And Pointer hurried off to the largest orchid importer in the world, Jaffinsky, near the China Docks.

Jaffinsky was asked whether any well-known orchid-hunters were in England, just now. Pointer thought that these intrepid men, few in number, who face deaths tragic and solitary, as part of their daily work, would be sure to know one another, and might keep touch in that loose, yet sufficient way common to men whose task needs very special training and special gifts.

"There's Smith; he's looking after our plants at the Tunbridge show. His beat's Burma and the Himalayas. Then there's van Dam—we could get hold of him for you, I dare say. Sumatra's the same to him as his back garden. Or what about Filon, the Frenchman? What he can't tell you of Madagascar, or North Africa—but I forgot, he went back last week. And if you're interested in the Congo, Bielefeld's a marvel. He—"

"I'll try Smith," Pointer said. "It's only a toss-up. I want to inquire about a man, a one-time orchid-hunter too, so I was told."

Smith and the Chief Inspector were soon seated in a quiet little back room littered with moss and bamboo. Smith was a strange-looking fellow. The colour of mahogany, with a face apparently carved out of red stone, wide-apart eyes, gray in colour, very still and rarely blinking, a mouth like a slit, a chin like a grocer's scoop, and a body like a whip-thong.

Pointer explained in a few words what he wanted. Had Smith ever chanced to come across a man called in England, Oliver Headly? An Oxford undergraduate?

He was about to give a description, but Smith did not need more than the name.

"Headly? Oh yes, I knew him. About ten years ago. Afghan border. But he was no good."

"Why not?"

"Oh-h, many reasons. A good hunter of any kind of game—your kind, Chief Inspector, or my kind—is born, not made. Well, Headly wasn't born. Also he had too many irons in the fire. That border is rather tempting to a certain kind of man. Gun-running, opium smuggling, doped whisky, are all lucrative by-paths."

"And the kind of by-paths to appeal to Headly?"

"Anything with money in it would appeal to Headly. Especially if it was off the true. And if it had a spice of cruelty in it, so much the better. But why this interest in a chap who's dead?"

"Sure he's dead?"

"Filon told me a year ago that he saw him shot in Fez. Been gun-running for the Riffs. Shot under another name. Called himself Olivier, and refused to state his nationality. I'll give him that credit."

Pointer expressed a doubt as to Filon's information.

"I think you can depend on it. Our eyes are our bread-winners, you know. You learn to see accurately, if you're hunting orchids. Don't want to risk your neck to bring home something that grows on Wandsworth common. Besides, Headly wasn't a man to forget in a hurry. Filon told me he recognised him, waved to him, and that Headly waved back. They were going to blindfold him but he refused, and faced them smoking a cigarette."

Pointer obtained a few more details which would enable him to tap the French authorities at Fez, and get into touch with Mr. Filon, then he asked casually, "Was Oliver Headly a good shot?"

"Rotten. Luckily he knew it."

And with that, the inspector took his leave.

CHAPTER SIX

THE pace of an investigation is a variable tempo. Impossible to foresee. Some little detail, unimportant, never "mentioned in despatches," may take days. Some great step be covered in one stride.

Pointer had hardly finished making a few arrangements for trailing some of the characters in the little circle concerned so far, however vaguely, with Mrs. Tangye's death, when Haviland rang up.

"We've located one of the missing bank-notes, sir. It was paid in as part of a first-class ticket on a Royal Mail boat going to South America. Paid in by a young man of the name of Vardon."

"Vardon? Christian name?"

"Philip. Never heard of him before."

Pointer had. He opened a stand in one corner. Ran a finger over the cards, and presently drew out some papers. From these he extricated one, and glanced at it. It was a sort of genealogical tree of the Tangyes, the Branscombes, and the Headlys, as far as concerned the present generation. Philip Vardon was marked as the only living relative, bar the sister, of Mrs. Tangye's first husband, Clive Branscombe. He was the architect's cousin, and would now be about thirty-four. Apparently he was unmarried.

"That makes him a sort of cousin to Mrs. Tangye, in fact," Haviland noted at the other end. "The address the shipping office gives us is in Fulham."

"You'd better go there at once. I'm due at the Home Office. There can be no question of telephoning to me there. You'll have to handle Vardon yourself. Act on your own responsibility. Meanwhile, not a word to Tangye. There's something twisted about that money—and those keys."

Pointer reached for another telephone, and was connected at once.

The steamship company repeated what Haviland had just told him along the private wire from his station, but in more detail. Before they had closed last Tuesday about a quarter to seven, a first-class ticket to Puntas Arenas in Patagonia, had been sold to a Mr. Vardon, on a boat due to sail next Saturday. Two days off yet. He had crossed with them before, he said, nearly a year ago, on his coming to England from the same port.

"What class had he gone then?"

After some time Pointer got the reply that Vardon had come home second-class. Did they know his profession? He was an artist.

The Chief Inspector's further questions drew out the fact that Vardon had been in only a week ago, talking of going back steerage. Also that when he had dashed in late on Tuesday evening, he had seemed tremendously excited. The clerk at first thought that he had been drinking.

Haviland, with his Inspector, rushed up to the dingy apartments in Fulham. Only to learn that Vardon had left there late Tuesday night. He had come home about eleven, packed in a great hurry, and taxied his luggage to an hotel nearer the docks. The manageress was not surprised at the haste. Her lodger's month was just up, and as the rooms would have had to be taken for another four weeks, she had quite agreed with Vardon that there was no need for that expense, seeing that he had made up his mind to return to South America by the next boat.

She gave the young man an excellent character in every way. He had had two garrets called a suite for nearly a year now. Evidently his means were narrow, but she had no complaint about unpaid or dilatory bills.

As Haviland represented himself as a business man who had an appointment with Vardon, and might be coming in with him on a venture, he asked, and got, the name of the hotel to which the young man had gone.

Here again, Haviland was just too late. A Mr. Vardon had arrived last Tuesday, or rather early yesterday morning, it was past midnight—but he had not liked the room assigned him, and had gone to another hotel.

Which one? The hall porter could not say. As Haviland learnt that the man had taken his own luggage, and done without a cab, he tried the nearest. There was a certain brevity and ascerbity in the porter's tone that made Haviland wonder just what had happened, but he had no time to waste. In the second hotel he was told that a man of that name was stopping there till Saturday, when he was leaving by one of the Royal Mail steamers. Haviland sent up his card, an unofficial card. Could Mr. Vardon spare him a few minutes in private?

A slender, dark-eyed young man with a pleasant, rather gentle face, looking much under his real age, came down into the empty smoking-room at once.

"It's about Mrs. Tangye—" began Haviland.

Vardon stared. "She's not here."

The two police officers in plain clothes stared in their turn.

"Mrs. Tangye's dead. She was buried an hour ago," Haviland said after a pause.

"What?" Vardon certainly looked horrified, incredulous, amazement. "Mrs. Tangye buried—"

"Didn't you read of the case in the papers, sir?" Haviland asked. He pointed to one lying on the couch beside him. "Here's the whole story, and a bit more—for about the third time in *The Flashlight*."

Vardon snatched at it, and seemed to read it through breathlessly from beginning to end. It was an account of the funeral, and a last dishing up of the manner of her death.

"What an awful thing!" he dropped it to the floor and faced them with his eyes still distended. "I never even glanced at a sheet yesterday or to-day. Been too busy. And to think I heard the newsboys calling out

'Twickenham Inquest' yesterday, and never even stopped to buy a copy."

"Too busy?" Haviland repeated questioningly.

"I'm off to Patagonia day after to-morrow. Decided rather suddenly to return. Takes some work to get your things on board at such short notice."

Vardon picked up the paper again, and again seemed to read the column through, shaking his head here and there.

"What a shocking fatality! I must telephone at once--" he began. Then he seemed to really see the two strangers for the first time since one of them had handed him the paper.

"And may I ask to whom I'm talking? To what I owe this call?"

"It's about your ticket, sir." Haviland said slowly, "about one of the notes you paid for it. Where did you get them?"

"Is there something wrong with the notes? Do you mean that they're bad?" Vardon's face whitened. "Then I can't —what *do* you mean?" he finished hurriedly.

"Do you mind telling us where you got them? I'm afraid it's rather a serious business."

"In what way? Mrs. Tangye, the lady whose dreadful death is in that paper, gave me them last Tuesday afternoon—day before yesterday in my rooms at Fulham. The very afternoon on which it seems that she shot herself. She's backing me in a new venture of mine. But for God's sake, don't tell me these notes are no good! Why, I've cabled my partner! If I've let him in for—"

"They're genuine enough, as far as we know, sir. There's nothing of that kind the matter, I believe. Mrs. Tangye's executors couldn't account for their whereabouts, and we've been asked to trace them. I suppose you have some agreement, something in writing?"

"Naturally I have. I should rather think so! It's upstairs. I'll fetch it. I take it you are from her solicitors?"

"That's it, sir," Haviland nodded.

Left alone, the two police officers relaxed their tension. Vardon had made a good impression. Five minutes went by.

"Better go on up and lend a hand, Brown," Haviland suggested to the Inspector. "He looks to me like a chap who would need help with his packing."

A moment later a stony-faced Brown slipped in again, and holding the door shut behind him, gasped: "He's bolted!"

"Impossible!" Haviland sprinted up beside the other as though he had some infallible recipe for collecting the absent.

But Vardon had gone. He had walked out of the hotel immediately with his suitcase, nodded rather breathlessly to the hall porter, turned a corner, and vanished. As all room? were pre-paid no one had spoken to him.

The two police officers said little. There are some things for which speech is too limited.

"He fits everything!" Haviland said tensely, as very white about the gills, he reported what had happened to Pointer later in the afternoon. Haviland had cause to look pale. Scotland Yard does not tolerate many blunders. But Pointer knew only one unpardonable offence. That was untrustworthiness.

"Yes, sir! He fits in right enough."

Haviland waited miserably for compliments on his brilliant handling of the case. None came.

"Shall I get out a warrant for his arrest?" he ventured to ask, very much doubting whether he would be entrusted with it. "Though he's sure to make for abroad. An artist must know many a port where he can lie hid. South America, too!"

There was still another painful point for Haviland to trot out.

"He owns some sort of a box-camera. So they told me at his rooms in Fulham. It isn't with the suitcase, nor yet with the luggage he's sent to the boat."

Pointer sat awhile thinking.

"Got your car below? Good. I'll speak to Wilmot over the 'phone," he did so, telling him briefly of what had happened, and asking him to wait for Haviland who would bring him back to the Yard in his police "non-stoppable."

When Wilmot arrived, Pointer suggested a line of action on the part of the newspaper man, to which Wilmot consented after a little pressing.

Then Pointer turned to Haviland, and sketched to that slowly-reviving officer, how and where, the next step should be taken.

Pointer himself was just back not only from the "breakfast" but from Mrs. Tangye's funeral. It had been a more than usually melancholy affair. The knowledge that Scotland Yard was in some way concerning itself with her death made the wildest rumours run.

While there, however he had met a lady who had travelled up with Mrs. Tangye on her return from Tunbridge Wells. By chance getting into the same compartment at Ashford. She had found Mrs. Tangye suffering from a bad headache. Mrs. Tangye had referred to the orchids, and said that the heat had been too much for her. She had sat with closed eyes apparently suffering very much, till they reached town, where she had refused her companion's offer of a lift in her car, and bad taken a taxi.

So Pointer's doubts were solved as to whether whatever it was that had caused what he called the cleavage in Mrs. Tangye's life, had taken place at or after Tunbridge

If it had taken place on Sunday at all, it had apparently been while with Miss Eden.

Pointer's eyes were on that young woman a good deal during the funeral. She avoided Tangye. He avoided her.

At the funeral too, Pointer had met Philpotts the Rugby farmer. He looked an honest, elderly man.

Philpotts scoffed at the idea of Mrs. Tangye having had any intention of going where pounds, shillings, or even pence, mean nothing.

"She gave way on the fences, but she stuck to her point about the timber," he repeated several times, half admiringly, half grudgingly. Pointer had brought the talk around again to Mrs. Tangye. The farmer's knowledge of her early days added nothing new, any more than did his few recollections of her cousin. Philpotts's own alibi of Sunday, Monday and Tuesday, which Pointer obtained by many indirect turns of the talk, was unverifiable.

Sunday afternoon he claimed to have spent with his wife in Westminster Abbey. The same time on Monday had been earmarked for the National Gallery, and Tuesday, after four, had seen them either gazing at the shops, or in one of the large tea-rooms where identification is impossible.

"It's queer," Pointer said now, when talking him over with Haviland and Wilmot, after he had finished detailing his plan about Vardon, "how few of the people connected with Mrs. Tangye can be located last Tuesday between four and six. Mrs. Bligh, is so far, the sole person who is definitely vouched for by several, unbiased, witnesses. She really did play bridge at her club from before four until after six."

"What would you have?" Wilmot asked raising an eyebrow. "How many more points do you want to prove that there's no crime here? By the way, how about the man you sent down to Tunbridge with the family portrait-album?"

"Which unfortunately did not contain a picture of Oliver Headly. There seems to be none extant of him. But Watts has just reported. No one in the show itself can identify any of the faces. There was a huge crowd on Sunday. Some minor royalty present. But outside, just by the gates, he found a tobacconist who recognised Tangye as having bought a box of vestas from him in the early after-noon last Sunday. That's our only haul."

"Vardon fits everything," Haviland repeated sombrely. He refused to be either comforted, or diverted. "When he said he had an agreement in writing, I ought to've suspected something. After what you said! But he seemed so straightforward. Yet, I shouldn't wonder—"

And Haviland proceeded gaily to sketch a long-ago flirtation, a meeting after many years, a planned elopement, the sale of the farm, and a murder when he found that the woman insisted on accompanying her funds.

Wilmot listened. Now blowing hot, now cold, as was his way. He called it the impartial poise.

"You may be right all along the line, Haviland," Pointer said finally when appealed to as umpire, "but—so far—there's no reason known to us why Vardon shouldn't have come to the front door. In other words, he fits the preparations, but Oliver fits the French window."

"Front door! Back door!" Wilmot suppressed a yawn; "wouldn't any murderer have come to the French window?"

"My point is that Mrs. Tangye wouldn't have expected him to come that way," Pointer said rather dryly. "It's not a case of a house-breaker's murder, but of a carefully prepared plan, and of some one whom Mrs. Tangye invites —expects—that way."

"There's a door into and out of the smoking-room, we've just learnt. Wouldn't that be a more usual way of unnoticed entry than by a window? Your whole theory hangs on those windows, which were found closed remember."

"That Miss Saunders *said* she found closed. The smoking-room cupboard door has a Yale lock. Tangye has the only known key. Any one using it would have have had to cross the central hall to get at Mrs. Tangye. And Florence was on the alert."

There was a pause.

"The fact is, I've had another thought," Haviland said so impressively that his two hearers smiled, "of the man who bought the farm. Philpotts. He's an old acquaintance. He would know about the money. What about Philpotts as the gent of the footsteps the two girls heard? The farmer's sure to walk stiff with rheumatism."

"Why should he go to the French window rather than to the front door?"

"My dear chap, don't let a little thing like that stump you," Wilmot begged. "I repeat that obviously a man, or woman, with a criminal intent, would prefer to come, and above all to go, as unobtrusively as possible."

"Yes, but I repeat my question. The answer to which is the answer, I believe, to our whole riddle. Why should Mrs. Tangye aid him by lending herself to that entrance? It's not the coming of in the murderer by the window, but Mrs. Tangye's apparent preference for that way, that strikes such an odd note. On the other hand, if it could have been her cousin. ... If Filon was mistaken. . . ."

Late that same afternoon a young man was in the act of following his luggage on to the Harwich boat, when a hand touched his shoulder.

"Mr. Vardon? Don't go on. There's an officer from Scotland Yard waiting to arrest you by the gangway. Come with me. I'm a friend."

The man to whom these words were hurriedly whispered, jumped, and swung round on his heel.

"Let your gear go, and follow me. I've a taxi. Been waiting for you before they should nab you," Wilmot urged. Vardon followed the other to a cab. Once they were in, he loosened his muffler which hid the lower part of his face.

"Who on earth are you?"

Wilmot gave his name. To his surprise, it apparently conveyed nothing to Vardon.

"Newspaper man, you say? But how are you mixed up in this?"

"I travelled down in the same compartment with a C.I.D. man, and he talked a bit," Wilmot said. Truthfully enough. Pointer had talked—to him. "I learnt that you had been shadowed when you bought your ticket. Your passport gave you away. You had to have it renewed, didn't you? Hard luck! Well, I determined to get in first and whisk you off."

"But—why?"

"I'm acting as claims' investigator for the company in which Mrs. Tangye was insured. The policies excluded suicides. We believe her death to have been self-inflicted."

"Mrs. Tangye's death? But what on earth has that to do with me?" Vardon asked in seeming stupefaction. "I thought it was the notes that were in question."

Wilmot looked at him for a moment in silence.

"The police believe that death to have been a murder. Or at least they're trying to believe it," he said finally.

"What hour did she die?" Vardon asked feverishly. He certainly was either innocent, or a good actor.

"Between four and six on Tuesday afternoon at her house in Twickenham." There was absolute silence in the cab.

"Stop!" the artist suddenly rose. "Drive to the police station. I must face this thing. It's worse even than I thought. Infinitely worse. And that was bad enough!"

"I shouldn't go to the police, if I were you," Wilmot suggested, "better let me take you to a house I know of where you can have time to think things over."

"I'm innocent!" Vardon declared almost defiantly.

"My dear fellow, there is no criminal here in my belief. No fact has been laid before me—as yet—of a nature to change my opinion that Mrs. Tangye's death was a suicide, if not an accident. Apart altogether from acting for the Insurance Company, I—so far—believe that she shot herself because of domestic trouble."

"So do I!" came from the man beside him. "I'm absolutely certain that she killed herself. That was why she let me have that money. She wanted to make a gift of it. I've understood the whole strange episode since reading of her end."

Wilmot turned to him eagerly.

"Good. You can prove that?"

"Prove nothing. It's only my firm belief. Looking back on what she said, and how she said it."

There was another silence.

"Look here," Wilmot said, "I'm a newspaper man, as I told you, Special Correspondent to the *Daily Courier*, but not a syllable gets into the press of what you tell me. My word on that."

"Where are you taking me?" was Vardon's reply. He seemed wrestling with his own thoughts.

"To the rooms of a friend of a friend of mine." Again Wilmot spoke the literal truth. The rooms belonged to a friend of Pointer's. "You can stay quietly there till we can think of the best thing to do. How about changing your name?"

"I'd rather not. The police can't have anything worth while against me."

"Then, why did you run away?" Wilmot's glance asked.

Vardon flushed.

"It's awfully good of you to take me on trust, this way," he said awkwardly, as they drew up in a quiet street of Sloane Square.

The door was opened by a man who, though Vardon could not know it, was of the greatest service to the Yard. He, and his neatly kept house in which Pointer had installed him.

Going upstairs—the rooms were on the first floor, Bates never had any rooms on the ground floor "empty." It was too easy to get into and out of them—Vardon tripped. He recovered himself instantly.

"My leg gives out at times. Broke my knee-cap when I first got to Patagonia."

Wilmot was very thoughtful for some time after that little mishap.

The rooms were all that could be asked. The terms amazingly moderate.

But Wilmot explained that they belonged to an

"explorer" who sub-let them during his long absences. He did not add that the gentleman was now exploring Dartmoor prison.

Vardon heaved a quick sigh, as he heard the door close.

"Ever hunted?" he asked Wilmot.

"Rather! Why?"

"I used to love it. Used to think November marked the beginning of the real year. But never again! By Jove, no! Now that I know what it feels like to have the hounds after you."

There was a silence. Wilmot was patiently waiting.

Vardon leant on the mantelpiece.

"I wonder if you'll think me a fraud? After all your trouble and risk to get me here. But I must talk things over with my solicitor first. D'you mind coming in later on? Say, after dinner? About nine?"

Wilmot said he quite understood, and would come again at about ten.

Vardon held out his hand.

"I'm more grateful than I can say. Just at present I'm a bit stunned. You must make allowances."

They shook hands and Wilmot went back to Pointer.

The Chief Inspector sat thinking for a moment after Wilmot left him. A bell rang. He had a telephone extension which connected with Bates's instrument. Picking up that receiver, the Chief Inspector heard a voice asking for a number. A glance at the Yard's telephone directory gave him the name that fitted it as Dorset Steele, Solicitor, Bedford Row.

"Mr. Dorset Steele wanted on the telephone at once, please. No name," the voice went on. There was a pause. Then Pointer heard a gruff: "Well? Well? What is it? What is it?"

"Can you come and see me? You recognise the voice, don't you?"

"I do. Well? Well?" snapped the solicitor.

"I'm in a quandary. I can't come myself, but I'd like to

see you as soon as possible," Vardon gave his address.

"Coming at once," barked Dorset Steele, and hung up. Apparently Vardon was not the apple of the legal man's eye, yet in a very few minutes, Bates showed Dorset Steele up. A tall, thin, rather untidy looking man who carried his head a foot in advance of his rounded shoulders. The "lost golf-ball" look, Barbara Ash called it.

"Now, what's wrong?" he snapped by way of greeting, looking at the young man under his eyebrows like an old poodle of uncertain temper.

"I'm in a nasty hole. So much so that I didn't venture to clamber out by myself, until I had talked things over with you. The police all but arrested me to-day for the murder, or a share in the murder, of Mrs. Tangye."

"Ah!" Dorset Steele tossed his soft hat into a chair as though it were the ring. Then he promptly sat down on it. He stretched out his muddy boots—his boots seemed to find mud as a water diviner does springs—subconsciously. Then he nodded to himself, as though this were what he had long expected, and on the whole, hoped would happen.

"Your story?" he asked curtly, squinting at the other around a collar that suggested a liking for comfort.

"I haven't much of a one. Mrs. Tangye came to my rooms last Tuesday about—well shortly before three as nearly as I can now recollect. She said she knew that I had some sort of a land proposition in the Argentine in which I was trying to interest people over here. And that she had decided that as I was Clive's only relative, and he had left everything to her —Clive Branscombe was her first husband, you know—she wanted to take an interest in it with me. She pulled out one thousand five hundred pounds from an envelope in her bag as casually as though they had been a pair of gloves. She handed me the roll and said that another fifteen hundred should follow at the end of a twelvemonth. Would that do? I told her two thousand in all would be ample. I wanted to go into the question of percentages, and into the affair itself —which isn't in the Argentine really—but she wouldn't wait. Told me to write it all very fully, and send it to her at her bank. Obviously, in the light of what has happened that was just an excuse. She didn't even trouble to pretend an interest in what I was going to do with the money. I suggested three per cent for the first year, five the second, ten the third, and twenty-five after that. I don't mind telling you in confidence that it's an untouched quinine grove, and there's a fortune in it. The difficulty is to keep its location from being guessed at."

"Have you this promise of Mrs. Tangye's in writing?"

"That's the trouble. I insisted on her sitting down and writing a line to say that the fifteen hundred now, and the same amount to come after twelve months, was a loan. She scribbled off a few words to that effect while I wrote out a duplicate. We signed both. I wanted witnesses but though I nearly broke the bell, no one came. I rushed downstairs but there wasn't a soul in the office. There never is; I asked her to wait, but she wouldn't. Finally I had to let her go. She didn't even let me finish telling her that at Puntas Arenas, Maunde would have a proper agreement drawn up, signed, and witnessed, if she would do the same in town. She was out, and down the stairs before I had got the words out."

"Taxi waiting?"

"I don't think so. The Tube is next door."

"Well? Well? What about the line you say she did write?"

"I packed up and went to a hotel in the city, you know. Smith's hotel near the docks. And there my bag was lost or stolen. Her note about the money was in it as well as some other things that I need, too. I kicked up a row, but the bag was gone. They insisted that I had left it in the cab. I know better. I moved my remaining suitcase to a hotel opposite and there, this morning, two men, police officers from Twickenham, came to interview me. When they asked me to show them the paper I was in a tight place. They had just told me of Mrs. Tangye's suicide. I hadn't opened a paper for days. The news stunned me. And then this question about the money! I had cabled Maunde to go ahead. To sign the necessary papers. But I hadn't sent the money. I thought I'd take that out myself. I intended to sail Saturday, you know. It was on me. The positon was ghastly. That paper of Mrs. Tangye's was gone. She had tossed mine on the fire when I handed it to her. I decided that I must at least get the money off to Maunde at once. So I skipped. Whatever happens I'm glad I did. He's got the money by now. I cabled it over. As for me, I thought I could get aboard unnoticed if I went at once. But no such luck! And the end would have been the same if I'd told those two chaps that I couldn't find the bag."

"The effect on the jury wouldn't have been the same," snapped Dorset Steele.

"No. I'm afraid not. But it won't come to that. Of course, I've lost this *chukker*, I quite understand that. But give them time, and the police are sure to find out that she killed herself."

"Why didn't you come to the funeral? Barbara couldn't understand it."

"I hadn't an idea Mrs. Tangye was anything but in the best of health. Not an idea!"

"And why didn't you write to Barbara to tell her the news?"

"Mrs. Tangye asked me to say nothing about the loan."

"Eh?" Dorset Steele shot the young man a sharp glance.

"Yes. She told me to say nothing about her coming with me into the venture. I said, 'Certainly not, if you don't wish it,' and she nodded as though to imply that she most certainly did not wish it. But naturally that promise doesn't hold good under these circumstances."

"And now, where are you? Whose rooms are these?"

Vardon told him of what had happened down at the docks.

"You don't know your landlord then?"

"You mean the man downstairs? Not in the least. Why?"

"He was in Scotland Yard. If you're here, you're under observation." Pointer gave a laugh at the other solicitor's acumen, when, next morning, he heard this part of the conversation wound off the microphone in the "clock" on the mantelpiece which was recording every word the two men spoke. "The case is in the hands of Chief Inspector Pointer, I've learnt. They're keeping it dark about the death. They claim to be investigating only the loss of the money. But that's not the sort of a job he takes on. He's as unscrupulous in getting his evidence as any criminal in the land," Dorset Steele said savagely. There was a by no means forgotten incident in which one of his most carefully coached witnesses, and a bottle of whisky, and Pointer had all played a part, that still rankled. "He'll leave no stone unturned to hang you if you're guilty. But he's fair. He's as straight as that poker and about as easy to bend."

Vardon turned red. "So, I'm under observation! And I thanked that chap who stopped me going on the boat. . . . He'll get something other than thanks when I see him again!"

"Wilmot! A moment." Dorset Steele went to the telephone. He was soon in touch with a man he knew on the *Courier*. He laid down the tube with a grunt.

"That part is true. He is acting as claims' investigator for the moment to the Insurance Company. In place of Cheale. ..." Steele sat down again and fell into deep thought.

"He's on our side, therefore."

"Are you taking my case?" Vardon asked suddenly and bluntly.

Dorset Steele hesitated. He shot the young man a sour glance.

"Yes," he said at last. "But it's going to be stiffer than you think. Pointer's name in it means that. Suppose this turns into a murder case. Do you know the facts against you? There's the money traced to you which was last paid Mrs. Tangye. There's your slipping away. Where were you Tuesday afternoon around five?"

"I was strolling through the Army and Navy stores pricing things and making out a rough list."

"Speak to any salesmen?"

"Not one."

"Meet any one you knew?"

"By Jove, I did! Lift man who took me up to the bun floor used to be a chap—" his face fell. "Perhaps I'd better leave him out."

"Who is he?"

"He was one of the under-stewards on the boat I went out on. Got into trouble."

"What kind of trouble?"

"Some ass dropped his pocket-book literally at the chap's feet one night without noticing it. Poor Pike has a family who seem to specialise in expensive illnesses, so he picked it up, and I'm sorry to say, kept it. That was bad enough. But the worst of it was the Head steward saw him. End of Pike. He'd have been jailed only the passenger refused to prosecute."

"Were you the passenger?"

Vardon gave an awkward laugh.

"Holed it in one," he acknowledged.

"Help him afterwards?"

"Well—yes, I had to. The chap turned up by chance at a ranch where I was painting the barns. He was half starving. Winter was coming on. Winter on a Patagonian plain! He'd have died with those lungs of his. I got the R.M. to give him another chance on one of their fruiters. He's done quite well since then."

Dorset Steele looked at him.

"And that's the best you can do as an alibi? Nice witness for the jury to hear pulled to pieces. Nice motive to put him in your debt, so that he'd swear to anything to help you. That's what they'd say."

"I know the outlook's pretty poor." Vardon thrust his hands deeper into his trouser pockets, "but I didn't kill my one time cousin-in-law, Mr. Dorset Steele, even supposing she was killed. Anc that's something to go on, isn't it?"

Grudgingly the solicitor admitted that it might be. But apparently he would have vastly preferred guilt and a solid alibi.

There was another silence.

"Have you any explanation," Dorset Steele said suddenly, "any that we can make the jury, if it comes to that, I mean, as to why Mrs. Tangye suddenly paid you that money? I leave your story of an additional fifteen hundred out of it."

Vardon did not answer for a minute. "I can't explain it either," he said lamely. "We'd never met before. She said she wanted to settle up all her outstanding debts, and she thought I had a claim on Branscombe's estate. A moral claim. She talked a lot about wiping the slate clean before another start elsewhere, and so on. Oh, she meant to kill herself. Not a doubt about it! At the time I was too flustered to have my wits about me. She said that money could be a fetter under some circumstances, or at least of no use. And as I had written to her several times for a loan from her first husband's estate—"

"Tut! Tut!" barked Dorset Steele, "you had not! but go on in your own way for the moment."

"That was all there was. I thought I was in a dream, I assure you. I've lived in a dream till that man Wilmot touched me on the arm and, as I thought, saved me. By Jove, when he calls around later he'll hear what I think of him. I'm a quiet chap as a rule, but I won't answer for what I shall say to him."

Dorset Steele pursed his lips. Obviously he was considering the effect of a possible black eye on the jury as a consequence of the interview.

"Better not see him." He got up. "I must be off. I'll have a talk with the police and see if they're keeping anything important up their sleeves." He shot a glance at Vardon. There was no answer.

"You've nothing more to tell me?"

"I've told you all I know."

Dorset Steele looked savagely at him.

"And you expect a jury to swallow it?"

"Why not? It's the truth," there was a flash in Vardon's eyes.

"They'll certainly call it stranger than fiction," the solicitor promised grimly.

He got up off his hat, tossed it on his head, thrust his arms into his top-coat which he had taken into the room with him, and made for the door.

"See no one—if you can avoid it. Say as little as possible. And—keep cheerful."

He finished with an unexpected smile.

While Dorset Steele was talking to Vardon, Pointer was going through the artist's luggage. He found no camera, box or otherwise, but he came on a ring of keys beneath everything else in the suitcase which looked like household keys. The number of the Yale key tallied with that on the Riverview front door. So did the number of the safe key. Clearly these were the missing keys of Mrs. Tangye. The keys which Tangye refused to have connected with the missing notes. Which he said he had seen at Riverview on Tuesday, after the police had left.

CHAPTER SEVEN

HAVILAND was greatly cheered by the news of the keys.

"A clue at last!" he chortled.

"To what?" was Pointer's question. "To whom?"

Haviland stared.

"Why, to the whole affair. It's a direct link with Mrs. Tangye. In fact, it's a direct link with her murder, I should say."

Still Pointer did not reply.

"Well, it's a fact anyway!" Haviland said desperately, "just as his having two of those notes in his possession was a fact."

"Yes, but the sole importance of a fact lies in the way we look at it."

"A most true remark, oh, worthy sir!" chimed in Wilmot who had driven down with Pointer, and was now breakfasting at the Twickenham police station. "And let me also remind you two bloodhounds on the trail, that Vardon may have a perfectly satisfactory explanation of those keys being found in his possession."

"He's sure to have! In fact, when you see him, Mr. Wilmot, you'll find he'll explain everything so nicely that you'll think what a pleasure it is to meet such a candid young gentleman." Haviland was still sore.

"Insurance Company's dropping behind, I fear," Wilmot murmured. "I wonder, if after all, it was a crime? I wonder! This case certainly has unexpected light and dark places."

"The fact is, they always have," Haviland announced despondently.

"It's the charm of the word, of course," mused Wilmot,

"that's why people read detective stories. For that and—
the love of the chase."

"The love of justice," Pointer spoke for once with real
warmth, "it's because they satisfy that—I suppose the
deepest passion of every one's heart, but a criminal's—
that people read, and write, detective novels."

"I read 'em for facts, helpful facts," Haviland
volunteered. "Really, some of the dodges these writers get
hold of "

"You're wrong. Both of you." Wilmot, as usual, spoke
with certainty. "The same thing makes people read, that
makes you, Haviland, a policeman, and you, Pointer, a
detective. And that is for the sake of the thrill. Of the
manhunt. There's nothing else in the world quite like it.
Why, even I begin to get the whiff of it in my nostrils."

Pointer was silent. Only his friends knew the Chief
Inspector's dislike of that common phrase, and point of
view. To himself, Pointer was but a keen, impartial
keeper of the open road, the path of law and order. The
only path by which civilisation, to his mind, could march
on.

"I suppose Vardon'll be allowed to give his
explanation?" Wilmot asked a little curiously.

"In due time." It was Pointer speaking. "But as
Tangye's leaving town for a week-end, we'll go to
Riverview first. He's kept in the house with a cold, so he
told me. Are you coming with us, Haviland?"

But a dull affair of a burgled boot-shop deprived the
Superintendent of that pleasure.

"As a matter of fact, perhaps Vardon was the person
Tangye suspected all along," he said, hopefully, trying to
cheer himself by the suggestion that he was not about to
miss much.

Pointer and Wilmot walked to the house. The sun was
shining. A rather apologetic sun, as though begging
spectators not to ask too much. To remember that this
was November—and England. His rays, faint and pale,
seemed to cool rather than warm. Yet their touch spelled

beauty. They brought out the thrushes' song. They lifted the lark. They set free the strain of wren and robin in a clump of evergreen beside Richmond Bridge. Plaintive and sweet notes. Joyous and pearly. A blind man might have thought it spring, so mild was the day. But the trees knew better. They were only waiting for the coming of a wind with which to wrestle. Like giants stripped for a fight, their old clothes, the withered leaves, lying in tumbled heaps below them, they could now give back as good as they got.

Beautiful to look at, fine and firm, they swayed aloft. Concerned solely with their own affairs, till the burden of giving shade and shelter should be theirs once more.

Pointer's and Wilmot's arrival evidently roused Tangye from a revery in an armchair. He looked very haggard. Very unhappy. He turned an alert eye, none the less, on them when they were ushered in.

"What I have to say is in strict confidence," Pointer began. Tangye nodded. Looking an almost savage interest.

"One of the missing notes has been traced. To a Mr. Vardon."

"Var-don! Philip Vardon?" There was stupefaction in the other's voice. And something that sounded very like chagrin.

"You know him, sir? Who is he?"

"Why, a cousin of my late wife's first husband. A cousin of Clive Branscombe's. There's a mistake been made somewhere, Chief Inspector."

"Not unless the mistake was in the number of the notes given us." Pointer lobbed that ball back very swiftly.

"Is he with you now?" Tangye half rose.

"Unfortunately he tricked us by a tale of a document, and got away."

"Well—I'm—damned," Tangye repeated under his breath, his eyes goggling. Pointer gave him the outlines of what had happened.

Tangye listened with at least every appearance of breathless interest. "He says Mrs. Tangye gave him the money on Tuesday afternoon," he repeated thoughtfully. He was the business man now, weighing both sides. "In that case he's sure to have that paper he spoke of. It wouldn't be like her not to have the agreement in writing—nor like any woman—" a sudden passion rang in the grudging tone, "perhaps he merely rushed away to find it. Remembered he'd left it behind him in his lodgings. Hasty thing to do, but I think you'll find everything's all right when you get into touch with him again." Tangye strode over to his tantalus. Things were unlocked, tumblers clinked. As before, Pointer, and this time Wilmot, declined a drink. Tangye stood eyeing his cocktail with a bitterly disappointed air, as though his favourite recipe had gone back on him. As though the mixture were anything but what he had expected to see.

"But that would hardly explain how he came to have her keys packed away in his suitcase," Pointer continued.

Tangye's glass gave a postman's knock against the table.

"Let me see. . . ." Pointer seemed to ruminate, "isn't he a crack shot? Bisley prize-winner, or something of that kind?"

"I never heard so. He's quite fair with a gun. Can be trusted out with a keeper, at any rate."

"Has he ever spoken to you about this proposition of his?"

"Once. But I don't go in for that sort of thing. Never touch a speculation. Apparently my wife decided after all to have a try with him."

"I suppose he called here frequently on the subject," Pointer suggested.

"He's never been to the house."

"But a friend of your wife's, I suppose?"

"They had never met."

"Of yours, then?"

"Not especially. I've known him off and on since we

were boys. He, too, was at Haileybury, though after my time. Of course you'll stop all proceedings. Naturally he'll have a perfectly understandable explanation of both keys and money."

Pointer said nothing.

Tangye looked at him sharply. "*I* lodged the complaint, or information, or whatever the official name is, and now I withdraw it—until we hear from Vardon."

"Very good," Pointer was unperturbed. "Personally I'm only interested in the missing money, and the keys, in so far as they may concern a theory regarding Mrs. Tangye's death."

"Regarding it as what?" Tangye stopped his glass midway to his lips.

Pointer looked very official. Wilmot's face showed nothing. He had been listening and watching with equal keenness.

"It looks as though Vardon's capture might end the inquiry that we've been making—as a matter of routine— into Mrs. Tangye's death. In other words, sir, I fancy the charge against Mr. Vardon may have to be murder. I'm sorry to use the word about your wife's death, but that's what it looks like at present. You understand that this is entirely confidential. Is not to go any further."

"What—on—earth—do—you—mean, Chief Inspector?" Tangye seemed unable to believe his ears. His hand shook so that he replaced the glass hastily on the table. "Wilmot here claims that Mrs. Tangye's death was a suicide. I have maintained, and the Coroner has maintained, that it was due to an accident."

"But we at Scotland Yard are wondering if it mayn't be due to a crime," Pointer said concisely.

"Things look very black against Mr. Vardon," the Chief Inspector went on in his level, unemotional tones, "other things than I am at liberty to speak of."

"How black?" burst from Tangye. It was an odd question.

"Black enough to dangle him at a rope's end," was

Pointer's reply. Made with calculated brutality. "Those notes together with those keys in his luggage will do the trick alone."

"You forget I saw the keys here at the house long after Mrs. Tangye was dead," Tangye said instantly. He evidently was not too rattled to think swiftly.

"So if Mr. Vardon says Mrs. Tangye handed them to him, or dropped them in his room by accident, as she gave him the money, he's lying?" pounced the Chief Inspector.

Tangye splashed the soda water that he was pouring out, in a fine fireman's spray over himself. He set the tumbler down hastily, and mopped. Then he picked up the glass again. He hesitated. Finally he almost threw it on a side-table and poked the fire. Very much to its detriment.

"I must have mistaken some other bunch of keys for my wife's. Obviously that's what I did. Miss Saunders' probably. But in any case there's no question of murder, nor of foul play of any kind here. As a matter of fact, solid fact," he glanced at Wilmot and flushed, "Mrs. Tangye shot herself. That's the honest truth. She *did* commit suicide. I meant to keep it to myself. But of course I can't let a man be arrested for what never happened. And that's why I believe she let him have the money. It would be all of one piece."

"You're sure Mrs. Tangye's death was suicide?" Pointer asked.

"Haven't I just said so? I might as well be hung for a sheep as a lamb. She told me she was going to do it. Told me on Monday afternoon. I didn't believe her—then!"

Wilmot had hard work not to show how great was his triumph at this news. Even as it was, a good deal leaked through.

"And about those keys of Mrs. Tangye's found among Mr. Vardon's things. Have you any idea how they got in his possession?" Pointer asked thoughtfully.

"I? How should I have?"

"Just so." Pointer spoke regretfully. "I was afraid of

that. Doubtless there's no explanation possible that lets him out. Well, of course, they're pretty damning, and plain, evidence."

"Evidence of what? Why the devil do you harp on those keys? Ten to one as he says, Mrs. Tangye dropped them in his rooms when she sat talking over the business deal."

"But they were seen here at Riverview after she returned. At four."

"Who saw them? I told you I wasn't sure of which bunch I saw."

"But Florence is sure."

"Florence! Florence has muddled them with other times. Florence!" Tangye repeated irritably. "I tell you Mrs. Tangye shot herself. And that sad fact makes your suspicions absurd."

Tangye turned to the soda water. He had replenished his glass.

Pointer had been standing playing with the lever, apparently idly. It seemed to be jammed. Tangye took out his penknife and with a few neat touches set it going again. He was talking as he worked.

"Thrown up my hand, haven't I? But damn it all, there is a limit to what one can do for filthy lucre. Mrs. Tangye," he pulled himself up. "But no matter. Where was I?"

"You were telling us about what she said on Monday."

"I got back from Norfolk about five. She—well—" He paused as though at a loss how to tell the facts, and yet not be lacking in decency to the dead. "We quarrelled. Badly. Finally she said that she was going to end it. To kill herself. I said something like 'don't do anything foolish,' and she turned on me saying that 'what she was going to do was wise—not foolish, whatever I might think.' I went up to town hoping that things would calm down of themselves. You know what happened next day before I saw her again. I think she delayed that shot till just about time for me to get to Riverview." He was very pale. "Life's a mad thing." He said after a pause, "Damned mad."

"I knew it was suicide all along," Wilmot said quietly. "I can send in the report of your statement to my Company, of course?"

"Of course."

"And exactly why did you say her death was due to an accident?" Pointer asked eyeing the repairs done to the lever with an apparently absent-minded gaze. They were quite up to the standard of the work necessary to arrange that camera.

"Why brand myself as a suicide's husband? Why broadcast our domestic unhappiness? No one guessed it. There was nothing overt. We got on each other's nerves from the first, that was all."

"The firm of Deakin and O'Malley was hammered on the Dublin Stock Exchange this morning. I am to understand then that your firm is not involved in its difficulties?" Pointer asked.

"You've been listening to idle rumours," Tangye said suavely. "My firm is in no difficulties. I can't say that the hammer may not be heard to-day over there—" he glanced from his windows toward where the city lay, "but not for me."

He spoke with conviction. His only mistake was to let a note of triumph creep into his voice. There was a village blacksmith's ring of "something accomplished, something done," about that, and his gaze, that told of strenuous effort and hard-won success.

"And you think that after a quarrel with her husband, of the kind you suggest on Monday, a wife would kill herself Tuesday, leaving everything to that husband?" Pointer asked again.

"It's what happened here. Mrs. Tangye was a very fair-minded woman, when there was no question of her temper leading her wrong. She was a splendid character at bottom. Possibly on the other hand, she may not have remembered her will, any more than I did at first." He spoke the last words very clearly.

"Naturally," Wilmot assured him pleasantly. Pointer shot him an amused look. He was sure that Wilmot would find anything "natural" which backed up Tangye's confession that his wife bad killed herself.

"And now to get down to facts," Pointer might have been Haviland, "would you be more explicit as to the trouble between yourself and your wife? What exactly did Mrs. Tangye say on Monday?"

Tangye gave a short laugh. Not of mirth.

"I can't tell you half nor a quarter of what she said. I don't think she could herself, if she were alive, poor girl. You know what a woman is when she's beside herself with some fancied grievance."

"Try and remember as much as you can," Pointer suggested prosaically. "For the fact that Mrs. Tangye wrote to Mr. Stewart, yours and her solicitor, asking him to notify your firm that she wished to withdraw the ten thousand pounds invested by her in it, makes the quarrel very important."

Tangye's lids drooped over his rather bold eyes. He stood silent for a moment. Then he wheeled smartly about. The very sound of his heels told that he had made up his mind. He walked to the door.

"Excuse me a moment." He was gone.

Wilmot looked at Pointer. His eyes waved the flag of victory. "I *knew* I couldn't be wrong!" he said softly. "I knew it *must be* suicide!" Pointer slipped out of the door like a shadow. Wilmot thought that there was something unpleasant in seeing such a big man move so silently. There was more here than mere absence of sound. Pointer's very body seemed to blur with the shadows of the dark day.

The Chief Inspector stood a second in the hall beside Rogers the constable, listening intently. Then he stole swiftly up the stairs to the first landing. He made for a little sitting-room taken over by Miss Saunders. There he heard a low murmur. In a second a police "stethescope" was pressed against the crack. The ends in his ears. "Very well," he heard Miss Saunders say. "I'm quite ready. I felt sure it would come."

There was a stir.

Pointer was sitting in the same chair as before and in the same attitude when Tangye opened the door again, this time for Miss Saunders to precede him. She was self-possessed as always. Very sure of herself, in her prim way.

"I think Miss Saunders should hear what I am obliged to say," Tangye said briskly. Shutting the door resolutely behind him. His manner was positively business-like.

"You asked me now, Chief Inspector, what my late wife and I quarrelled over on Monday when I returned from my week-end. I'm sorry to say it was over her having unexpectedly found out that Miss Saunders and I had gone for a spin in my car Sunday afternoon. We met at Tunbridge Wells. Lunched together at an hotel there, and drove around to the orchid-show. By bad luck my wife happened to be there, too, and caught sight of us. After all, there was nothing wrong in what we did. Injudicious, of course. We both see that now?" he finished.

"Quite so. Injudicious, but not wrong," Miss Saunders echoed letting her eyes for a second dart from face to face.

"If you would like to question Miss Saunders, I think she would be kind enough to answer you," Tangye went on.

"I don't think there's any need of anything so painful," Pointer said stolidly but with his eyes on the other man.

They were large eyes. Very quiet eyes. Very clear eyes.

"Well, then," Tangye went on, almost as though dictating a letter, "as I said, Mrs. Tangye saw us."

"And you didn't see her?"

"I didn't. Did you, Miss Saunders?" Tangye turned to her. She shook her head.

"Please say whether you did or not?" Tangye ordered, still with that indefinable tone of brisk command of the situation in his voice. He might have been sailing a yacht, with a breeze blowing that just suited him and his boat.

"No, I didn't see her," Miss Saunders spoke up briskly too.

"Yet we stayed in the show some time. How long would you think?" he went on.

"About two hours, I fancy."

"I put it about that too," he nodded. "I thought it better not to see Miss Saunders off in the train, so we said good-bye outside the station."

There was a pause. Tangye looked around on his hearers almost as though expecting applause. Obviously Pointer and Wilmot were being treated to a benefit performance. But whose benefit? Tangye's, or Miss Saunders', or the absent Vardon's. Miss Saunders rose and slipped quietly from the room.

"And now perhaps you'll be able to tell us some of the things your wife said to you on this Monday afternoon?" Pointer asked.

Tangye shook his head. "I'm afraid I don't remember much. She was absolutely unlike herself. We've had quarrels before, of course. But never one like that. I quite misunderstood the position. You see, I thought—I fancied she was bluffing. Mrs, Tangye, I mean. I had an idea—totally wrong as it turned out—that she was not nearly so angry as she chose to seem. I thought she was overdoing it. I see now that it was hysteria, and dangerous hysteria at that. But I give you my word that I only thought then she had decided to give me a bit of a scare so as to teach me not to do that sort of thing again."

"That's very interesting," Pointer said slowly. "She struck you as really not angry? You thought it acting?"

"I swear I did. Overdone acting at that. I thought she was forcing the note all the way along. More fool I!" Tangye sighed heavily. His brief air of triumph had entirely left him.

"Did she ask you to leave the house?" Pointer put in.

Tangye seemed to feel a sudden check. He hesitated

for a second. "Possibly. I think she did say that among the flood of other things."

"You weren't discussing money affairs then?"

Tangye stiffened. "I don't understand."

Pointer gave him no explanation, as rising, he made his way to the drawing-room where Miss Saunders sat reading.

"I suppose you know about Mr. Vardon," he began chattily.

She stared at him.

"Know what?"

"Well, strictly in confidence, it looks very much as though we might have to arrest him in connection with Mrs. Tangye's death."

Miss Saunders' face flamed a brick red. Her lips parted in a curious tense look, drawn away from her rather long teeth.

"Mr. Vardon? Mrs. Tangye's death? What are you talking about?" There was a spark in the depths of her bright, rat-like eyes.

Pointer repeated that certain facts had come to their knowledge which unless explained, looked very bad for Mr. Vardon. The presence of her keys in his luggage, for one thing.

Miss Saunders sat tapping the end of her thumb nail against her clenched teeth. It was the gesture of one uncertain what to do. What to say. "And of course, Mr. Tangye let you think it!" she said under her breath.

Pointer looked at her meaningly and nodded.

Miss Saunders gave a little sound as though she were choking.

"Why do you think Mrs. Tangye's death was a murder?" she asked. There was no hesitation about her use of that terrible word. No look of shrinking in her face. Yet she had lived three years with the woman about whom she was putting that grisly question. She might have been a collector inquiring, why an expert thought his Goya drawing to be a Mengs. There was intense, burning interest in the coming answer, but no personal emotion.

"Well, we do. The outlook for every one in the house is quite altered by the mere supposition. To come to the point of this interview, your own alibi is unsatisfactory."

That got home. She bit her lip.

"It's not genuine. Miss Martins, as I believe the manageress of the tea-room is called, mistook you evidently for another customer. In any case the fact that she is your sister would discount her evidence. There's no use your denying what we know, Miss Saunders," as she opened her lips, "the matter is too serious for that. Where were you really between four and six Tuesday?" His voice came sharp and stern. She licked her thin lips with a tongue that shot out like a snake's, swift and furtive.

"At the library and then in the tea-room. My alibi is quite good. As to its having been substantiated by my sister—why not? She's in charge at the tea-room. Others may have seen me there if you've frightened her into some mistake. I won't pretend to misunderstand you, you know. But what possible cause should *I* have had for harming Mrs, Tangye?"

Pointer bent forward and stared hard at her. She blinked.

"Why, you yourself have been trying to force the note of your—understanding—with Mr. Tangye."

This time she turned a genuine and ghastly gray.

"It's a lie!" she rose to her feet and her eyes widened. "Blundering idiots! If I had killed her, wouldn't I be the first to snatch at the chance of accusing Mr. Vardon? But I tell you he didn't do it! Oh, you fool! You damned fool!" She shivered with fury. Pointer thought for a second that she would actually fly at him. Her small eyes, set close together like those of a bird, seemed to snap fire, so fierce was their glare.

The door opened. But why had Tangye paused once again outside to listen?

Miss Saunders passed him with one contemptuous,

yet menacing glance.

"What in the world—" Tangye began. "I stepped in to ask if you would be a witness to my statement, which Wilmot is taking down. My formal renouncement of the Insurance claim on my wife."

Pointer followed him back into his den.

"Bit previous," Pointer glanced down at the paper. "It may not be Vardon, but it may not be suicide, either."

Wilmot looked put out. The case was as good as over as far as he was concerned. He was mentally drafting a cable to his little Galician village, at the same time as this letter of Tangye's.

"You mean you *will* make a murder out of it?"

Tangye's last whisky had been nearly neat.

"I assure you," Pointer said gently, as he had to say so often, "that Scotland Yard is not Moloch, to be fed with human sacrifices, innocent or guilty, no matter which, so long as the supply doesn't run short. If Mrs. Tangye's death was a suicide, you may be sure that that will end the inquiry, and we shall turn our attention elsewhere. But we must get the thing clearly worked out. That's part of the routine."

Pointer left the two alone at that, and took a turn in the garden. The robin, whose preserve this was, eyed him hopefully. Pointer looked energetic. He might be going to use a spade. But the Chief Inspector was oblivious of fluting call or confident bright eyes. He was thinking. So it was to be suicide. According to Tangye. But according to Pointer? That was what really mattered.

It was a very sudden right-about-turn, this of Tangye's. Neatly executed, but very sudden. Was it the peril in which Tangye learnt for the first time that a man stood whom he considered innocent? Or was it something else, deeper? Was what seemed disinterestedness self-interest? Did Tangye suddenly realise that the question of murder was in the air? Did he want to scotch, not so much a present, unfounded accusation, as a possibly well-founded one in the future? Did he see himself as Vardon's

successor in the list of suspects, and decided to block that
eventuality? Or was the widower merely a belatedly
honest man? Was Wilmot right? Had Haviland been right
in the beginning? Was Mrs. Tangye's death, after all, self-
inflicted, in spite of smoky room and scratched revolver?
Or were Tangye and Vardon in collusion? Those keys. . . .

Returning to the house he and Wilmot took their
leave.

"My field day, I think!" the newspaper man stepped
out cheerily; "we've got the motive. You were right about
it having been that Sunday down at Tunbridge that
practically fired the shot. The husband throws up his
claim—"

"The investigator packs his trunks, sends in his bill,
and flits to sunnier climes," Pointer finished the picture.

Wilmot chortled.

"Of course you, as the representative of the law, tried
to spoil it all. But nothing will undo the fact that Tangye
confesses he was only trying it on with the Insurance
society. He's obviously however, not the man to hang an
innocent chap. I think Tangye's genuinely shocked to find
that by trying to swindle the Company out of that
insurance payment, he's tying the noose around the neck
of another. He comes forward and says very honestly that
his wife told him in so many words that she intended to
kill herself."

"But she didn't!"

"Didn't kill herself? I think—in spite of many
difficulties, perplexities—that she did."

"Of course you do. No offence, Wilmot, but that's what
the Company expects you to do until actually convinced.
That's your brief."

Wilmot looked at him with surprise on his face. "Do
you mean to say that you suspect this double confession
or confidence, of just now? In Heaven's name, why?"

"Why should I believe it? That's more to the point."

" 'Pon my word, it's too bad!" Wilmot's voice was
frankly peevish. Here was the case, his case, settled, and

here was this obstinate policeman still holding up the traffic.

"There are two sides to every question," Pointer reminded him.

"Not to a circle. A never-ending circle, which this case seems to be in your eyes," was Wilmot's tart rejoinder.

"Indeed? What about inside and outside?"

Wilmot laughed, almost against his will. "What makes you doubt what we've just heard?" he asked finally.

"My dear fellow! If Tangye had carried a banner inscribed, 'I'm doing a neat bit of acting. What price a brain-wave?' It couldn't have been clearer. Miss Saunders too, was very pleased with her star-turn. In the beginning."

They reached the station. Haviland had returned. He now listened eagerly.

"Ah, I thought Tangye wouldn't be able to explain away the fact of those keys!" Haviland said gleefully. "Funny he should try to. I wonder what really did happen to them?"

"I wonder too," Pointer said. "Certain it is that Tangye could tell us if he wished to."

"Looks as though Vardon and Tangye have an understanding of some sort, in fact," Haviland thought. "And that's why Miss Saunders wanted to help him as well as Tangye—at least, I suppose that's why. . . ."

"She's the owner of a 'one-good-turn-a-day' nature, you think? You two chaps make me tired. Forgive my frankness," Wilmot stifled a yawn, "but why cudgel your brains for some recondite solution? Miss Saunders and Tangye went off on Sunday. She's quite willing to snatch at any alleviation on the sly. Like most of her sex. Tangye's right; there's no murder here. There's suicide. And there's possibly, but only possibly, a theft."

"Suicide? Because Mrs. Tangye saw her husband and her companion looking at orchids together? Her sense of proportion must have been out of action. Come, Wilmot, you don't believe that yourself!"

"I believe," Wilmot said earnestly, "that Mrs. Tangye had far more ground than that. Far more reason. That she had fought a losing battle well and long. That finding she was steadily being driven back, in spite of all her efforts, she got tired of the useless struggle, and ended it. That has, up to now, been my theory, unless it really was an accident. Failing either of those, my own mind turns more and more to that missing cousin of hers. The man with the love of money and the streak of cruelty in his character. I suppose you're getting into touch with the Frenchman, Filon?"

"Trying to. Also with Fez. There, of course, we shall have no difficulty. They will doubtless be able to furnish us with photographs and finger-prints of the man they shot. The man who called himself Olivier."

CHAPTER EIGHT

POINTER had found one other thing among Vardon's effects which might have a bearing on the case. This was a packet of four letters tied with a shoe-lace. They were all from an address which he had seen already given in the police reports as the home of Sir Richard Ash, the partner of the late Branscombe.

The notes were short ones. Beginning "Dear Philip," and ending "Sincerely yours, Barbara Ash."

And sincere enough the writer seemed to have been. Phrases such as "you're sleeping life away," varied with, "can't you wake up, and show what's really in you?" Once came the surprising aphorism, "There's no use your saying that content's a jewel. It isn't. It's awfully cheap paste."

Pointer had sat awhile thinking, after he read them. All but one were undated. The envelopes were missing, but the shortness, the absence of general news, the thick linen paper suggested that the notes had been sent to some one in England. They were the kind of letters that might be expected to have some effect. Had they stirred a man up to commit a crime? It was possible. It would depend on the man, and on whether they came as a final touch on the dipping scales of right and wrong. The keys were a different matter.

These damning keys. Seen in the morning-room at Riverview just before the end—if Florence was right—and found lying among a lot of oddments in the bottom of Vardon's valise marked for the hold. Pointer did not think that they had been slipped in after the things on top had been packed. Apart from how Vardon had got hold of them, why had he kept them? Were they to be used again? If so, why pack them in the bottom, and in a bag not intended for the voyage?

"A gentleman from New Scotland Yard to see you, sir," Bates announced immediately after the interview with Tangye, laying Pointer's card down beside the young man who sat reading the *Araucana*. In spirit back in the New World, listening to a war-chief's song.

Fiery and fresh, the lines still hummed in his head.

"No—I—eh " Before he could collect his thoughts sufficiently to finish his protest, Pointer was bowing to him. Vardon did not ask what the Chief Inspector wanted. He waited. Pointer explained himself at once.

"I'm in charge of the investigations about that missing money. Would you mind telling me how the note which has been traced to you, came into your possession? I ought to tell you that a criminal charge may follow, and that, if so, what you say may be used against you. You are quite at liberty to refuse to answer—if you think it wise."

Vardon looked as though greatly tempted to avail himself of the freedom. But after a moment, he told Pointer the same story as he had the solicitor.

"And how do you explain the fact that her keys have been found in your luggage?" the Chief Inspector asked when the artist was silent.

"Her keys? Impossible! Mrs. Tangye's keys!" Vardon sat open-mouthed.

Pointer said that it was true, nevertheless.

Vardon, after staring at him, as though he might be joking, finally suggested that Mrs. Tangye must have dropped them unnoticed on his table when she was in his room. The artist went on to say that he had started his packing, by shaking the tablecloth into his valise, and then throwing in other things on top. The valise bore out this simple method.

"What hour did Mrs. Tangye come to your room?"

"About three."

"And what hour did you start packing?"

Vardon thought that he had begun about a quarter past eleven, when he came in from a musical play to which he had gone.

"Did you have any other visitors in your rooms on Tuesday?"

Vardon said that, as far as he knew, nobody had come to see him.

"And now, why did you—well—decamp, when Superintendent Haviland and an inspector of his called on you yesterday morning?"

Vardon flushed hotly. Up and up, the crimson surged, until his very ears burned a brick red against his fair hair.

"I lost my head," he said bitterly. "I wanted time to think things over."

"And to get rid of the remainder of the notes," Pointer finished to himself.

"Few people care to be caught in a tight corner by the police," Vardon went on. "That note I got Mrs. Tangye to write was in my bag. My bag had gone. Not that it's of any value except for that precious bit of paper. You must confess the outlook was pretty bad for me."

Naturally, since a man cannot be both hare and hound, Pointer never considered any outlook so bad that jockeying the police would better it.

"May I ask—by the way, we're verifying the whereabouts of every one, of course—merely a matter of routine—where you were this last Sunday?"

"Sunday?" Vardon seemed puzzled. "At a concert in the Albert Hall."

"Meet any friends?"

"No."

"Did you go alone?"

"Yes."

"And Monday afternoon?"

"Writing letters in my diggings."

"And Tuesday afternoon, from four to six?"

Vardon waited a moment as though to be quite sure.

"I did a lot of strolling through shops generally," he said vaguely.

"You were seen near Twickenham on a motor-bicycle about five," Pointer said suddenly. "Can you explain that?"

"I was thinking of calling on a friend who lives out that way. Then I changed my mind. Half decided to call on Mrs. Tangye and ask a question about the sending off the rest of the money. Thought better of that, too. Decided that I was too wrought up to think clearly, and roamed the shops instead, chiefly the Army and Navy stores."

"Just so. But may I ask why you didn't mention this trip across the river just now? Why you didn't tell it me voluntarily?"

The worm turned.

"Does any one ever tell anything voluntarily to the police?" Yardon asked, and Pointer's eye acknowledged the hit.

"You didn't go to Riverview itself last Tuesday?"

"I only wish I had." Vardon leant forward. "I looked at my watch as I crossed Richmond Bridge. It was a little before five. Had I gone on, it might have made all the difference. A chat sometimes does."

"Were you on friendly terms with Mrs. Tangye?"

"I'd never met her before. She came up last Tuesday unannounced. As she came in she introduced herself."

"I see. You never went to see your cousin after his marriage?"

Vardon played with the covers of the book beside him. He had the true artist's hands. Small-boned, slender.

"Once. Our parents had not been on good terms. He was much older than I. By chance Mrs. Branscombe was out that day. Just as, by chance, I was in South America when they married, and at sea the day he died."

"Mrs. Tangye was different, you say, from what you expected?"

"Rather!"

"And how was it that you had so clear an idea of what

she would be like? Since you had never met her?"

"Oh—well—I had heard of her, you know. Got an impression of a rather masterful character—"

"I see." Pointer looked at his boot tips as he sat resting his head on one hand. "Have you written to Mrs. Tangye lately?" Pointer asked next.

Vardon hesitated. Palpably.

"I think I've said all on the subject that I care to say, for the present," he said finally.

"So you *did* write? You did ask her for money? You see, I've no intention of being unnecessarily prying, but we know that you came home from South America some ten months ago now, and approached various people in the city with a view to interesting them in some proposition of yours. Now it seems likely that you would have mentioned the matter to the woman who had inherited all your cousin's money. Was the proposition a gold mine, as they say?"

"In a way. I'm afraid I can't discuss it with you." There was a silence. "Don't think I'm keeping anything back that can help you." Vardon went on quickly, "to my mind, what will help you best, would be to make you realise Mrs. Tangye's whole manner on Tuesday. She struck me as being in a most extraordinary—I don't know what to call it—mood— state of mind? She was paying me one thousand five hundred pounds in ready money. Not being a rich woman, that must have meant something to her. It did to me, by Jove. Yet she gave me a feeling that she wanted to get it over, and be at something else. I doubt if ever such a large sum was given to a totally unexpecting person with such casual speed." For the first time Vardon smiled a little. "She tugged the envelope out of her handbag and handed it to me. . . ."

"One moment! Was it already in an envelope? I mean didn't she have to separate it from any other notes?"

"No. She had two envelopes. The other looked about the same size. She handed me the one without looking at it. She asked me to count the money. I could hardly see. I had to count it four times, and each time it added up to something different. So I let it go at that, and pretended to find it correct. I had to almost hold on to her to get her to sit down and write that note saying that it was a loan, before she was out of the room in a sort of whirl of hurry and flurry. *I* felt that way, of course. *I* had a hundred things to do. But I should have expected Mrs. Tangye, or any

woman, to talk a lot. Give me some good advice. Ask questions as to how it would be first applied. But no. All the business part of the interview I had to force on her. She acted as though she had handed me a ticket for Peter Pan. I can't explain it except by her intending to kill herself."

"What makes you so sure?"

"This gift of the money, for one thing. I didn't see it at the time in that light, naturally, but above all, her manner, her air of being done with things. Finished with them. I can't express clearly what made me think that. For, after that loan of the money, the rest was a confused jumble, but the impression was made very clearly.

"One thing I'm certain of. If it wasn't suicide, then it was accident. Mrs. Tangye struck me as just the kind of woman to have an accident with a weapon. She was very hasty in her movements. Very impatient. I can imagine her snatching at something that caught in her laces, and giving a pull. Thank God, if the shot had to be fatal, at least, it was instantaneous." And at that Varden walked to the window to raise it.

As he did so, he all but tripped. It was but a second's catch in his step, but Pointer, like Wilmot, thought of those words of the maid.

"And what exactly was it that made you change your mind on Tuesday about going on to see her? When you were so near Riverview."

"I thought it seemed rather ridiculous. Like an interchange of state visits. She had been to see me at three. I to run in to see her at five. I didn't want her to think that I was going to sit in her pocket."

"You didn't pass the house?"

"No."

"Do you know the companion at Riverview?"

Vardon started. Whether because of the question, or be cause his mind was on something else, it was impossible to tell.

"No."

"May I ask the name of the friend who lives out Twickenham way?"

"You may not. Sorry."

Pointer was fairly certain that it was Barbara Ash.

"Mr. Vardon, we want nothing in the world, nothing," Pointer spoke very convincingly, "but to get at the truth about the death of Mrs. Tangye. That's the only reason, I assure you, why I ask unpleasant questions, dig up uncomfortable things, and generally make myself a confounded nuisance. The only things I'm interested in, the only things I remember, are what help on the search. A search for truth, remember. Truth and justice. Nothing else.

"You say you think Mrs. Tangye's death was a suicide. I don't. But if you could convince yourself that we don't want you, or any man, unless he's guilty, we might be able to help each other.

"If you're guilty, of course you must do the best for yourself you can. I think I should get you in the end," Pointer gave the other a knife-like look. "But if you're innocent, I assure you that no one—not even the girl you were going to see Tuesday 'out Twickenham way,' can want more earnestly to prove you so. For that means a step nearer to the right man, the guilty man."

It was a long speech for Pointer. But it had done its work—apparently. Vardon seemed in a more friendly mood.

"You mean I'm as suspect as all that?"

"Frankly, things look very black against you."

"But how could there be a murder here? Why? Mrs.

Tangye wasn't the kind of a woman to stir people to violent emotion either way, I should have thought. She seemed a nice, warm-hearted, hot-tempered, high-spirited woman."

Why hot-tempered and high-spirited, Pointer wondered.

"You say, she wasn't the kind of woman to stir people deeply," the Chief Inspector repeated. "I'm afraid the fact that she very likely had some fifteen hundred pounds, on, or near her, last Tuesday afternoon, and that they may have thought she had three thousand with her, would stir some hearts to their very foundations."

Vardon showed an aghast face. He asked about the money. Pointer told him the outlines of the land sale, and then questioned him about his work.

Vardon spoke interestingly of it. He had started out as a painter of portraits in Buenos Aires. Come down to barns, fences, and signposts in Argentina, then, so he told Pointer—drifted to Patagonia, taken up photography when he had a frozen right wrist that refused to limber up—and now was working as a film photographer of wild animals. Of the creatures that live lives so like, yet so unlike our own.

Pointer asked him whether he could change his own film camera into one that would carry plates, and the two discussed mechanical means. Vardon showed an expert's skill in taking a kodak to pieces that he drew out of his pocket, and re-assembling it.

Finally Pointer questioned him about the lost bag. Vardon did not seem in a hurry to let him have the details.

"I'm afraid it's gone for good. Left in the taxi probably. Fortunately, except for that paper of Mrs. Tangye's, there was nothing of value in it."

"Rather an important exception," Pointer said dryly. He had ascertained that the young man had not acted as though there was nothing of any value in the bag when he first learned of its disappearance.

"Very much so," Vardon agreed. "I thought I gave it to the page-boy when I drove up. But they deny that. I was paying the cabby at the time, who was slow about making the right change. Then in the lounge, after a room had been given me, I stayed down looking up time-tables and comparing routes. It must have been nearly half an hour later that I finally went upstairs. Even then I didn't miss the bag at once. When I did, I ran downstairs but the hotel denied all knowledge of it. We got a bit warm, and I went off to another hotel."

"Did you go back to the first one afterwards to inquire?"

"I did, naturally. I asked for the manager. And the band played the same tune as before. Hall porter, lift-boy, chamber-maid, and reception-clerk. I think on the whole, now I'm cooler, that they're doubtless right. I must have left it in the cab or at my old diggings. Or on the pavement outside while I waited for the taxi to come up."

Pointer knew that on Wednesday morning, Vardon had made every effort to get the bag traced. He had telephoned Scotland Yard about its loss, describing its contents as chiefly papers of no value except to the owner but offering a reward of five pounds for its return. He had sent a similar announcement to be inserted in the personals of the *Morning Post*. His message to the "Lost" department had been very urgent. He had spoken as though greatly concerned to recover the bag. Now he professed himself quite prepared to accept its loss as a definite fact. Yet, in it, so he claimed, was this important paper. Pointer thought that Vardon on the whole, would prefer the bag not to be found. And the Chief Inspector wondered why. Was the paper, the important half-sheet, with Mrs. Tangye's words on it, really in the bag? If so, was it accompanied by other papers of which he wished the police to remain in ignorance?"

Had there been a bag at all, or had there not?

Pointer's last questions were about Tangye. Vardon said he knew him fairly well. Had he approached him about this "gold mine" of his in South America? Vardon at once said that he had written to ask if the subject would interest him, and had received a pleasant but definite letter saying that Tangye never speculated or went in for possibly risky investments. As to Riverview itself, Vardon had spent many a week there as a lad. It had belonged to his grandparents.

Pointer spoke of Oliver Headly. Vardon had met him once by chance on a boat crossing to South America about eight years ago, and taken a great dislike to the man whom he spoke of as a disgrace to his race.

Did he know what had become of him? Vardon said that save for•the fact that he had made Latin America too hot to hold him, he had heard nothing of him.

Pointer found Haviland waiting for him at the Yard. Ostensibly with some housebreaker's finger-prints to be verified, but in reality to hear how the interview had gone. He had no doubt as to the guilty man. Vardon's flight, he thought, meant just that. And his explanations, he considered very poor.

"In fact, I never saw a poorer case," he repeated now for the third time. "The money traced to him. He confesses to having the whole of the missing sum, and he takes good care to get it into the hands of a confederate. Keys of her safe and doors found in his possession. Proof that he knows the dead woman's companion. Proof that he was seen hanging around the house at the time of the death. Why, it's a cert,

for a fact!"

"Dorset Steele's a good man," Pointer murmured, "no better criminal solictor in town." The wording was ambiguous, but Haviland agreed.

"Still, not all the lawyers' brains in the Kingdom can talk away facts. But it's odd he doesn't seem to give a damn for the bag now. It should be all important to him, and that's a fact. But with, or without it, his solicitor'll have his work cut out to get him off, if you choose to have him arrested."

"That's just it." Pointer seemed finally convinced that his boot tips had nothing more to tell him. "That's just it, Haviland. Send Vardon up for trial, and accuse him of Mrs. Tangye's murder, and I doubt if he'd have a dog's chance of getting off without at least penal servitude for life."

"You don't think he's guilty, sir? Not after those keys?" It was not so much a question as an exclamation.

"I don't know yet."

"Well, I can't see what answer he could make to such a charge, in fact," Haviland said in a distinctly disappointed tone. Visions of returning with Vardon handcuffed fading from his mind. He bore the young man a grudge. He had all but cost Henry Haviland his official life.

Dorset Steele was thinking very much what Haviland was saying as he ordered his lunch. He sat staring at his meat with such a suspicious air, that the waiter hovered near anxiously.

"Tough job!" muttered the solicitor, stabbing at the plate with his fork.

"Tough chop?" repeated Smithers horrified. "Indeed, sir?" and whisking it off, he retired in person to the grill. Dorset Steele gulped down a glass of port, followed it with boiled potatoes, and rising, under the impression that he had had his usual meal, passed out.

"Miss Barbara waiting to see you, sir," he was told at his office. A young girl who looked about twenty—she was six years older—light of foot as Atalanta ran up to him.

"I couldn't get to you before, grandfather, how did it go? Will he be all right?"

"Nice muddle you've got the firm into," he said testily. "The young man is guilty."

"Guilty of stealing that money? Oh, no! No!"

"If he can't find the bag, supposing he's definitely arrested, that's what the jury will say, and that's all that matters!"

Barbara pulled a chair up, stood on it, and laid her

cheek against his wild, gray hair.

"How you frightened me till I remembered it was only you! Now tell me all—everything."

He told her, peering at her every now and then over his glasses. She was a pleasant sight. A pretty girl, if the term be not taken too strictly. She was tall, slender, erect; with bright brown eyes, bright brown hair, a bright pink and white complexion, bright rose-red lips, a bright smile, and one beauty. A laugh of rare charm. Like silver bells ringing in the sunlight. But she was not laughing now. Dorset Steele had been to see Pointer. The Chief Inspector had been frank as to the larger charge that hovered as yet dimly in the background, but which was to move slowly, inexorably, to the foreground of its own weight as it were, Barbara listened in silence. She was breathing fast and tense when the solicitor had finished.

"You think his having been seen near Riverview at that hour so bad? Grandfather? *We* live near there, you know," her voice quivered, "wouldn't it explain matters if people knew that Phil and I had just got engaged—secretly? Suppose Mrs. Tangye had guessed that, and for that reason wanted to help him—and me. Philip only asked for the money so as to marry me, you know."

"Eh?" Dorset Steele wheeled, and stood looking at her like a rook inspecting a Jenny Wren. Then he took a turn up and down, his hands under his coat-tails that napped in time to his tread.

"You'll break down when you're cross-questioned. For this case may yet go before a jury. You'll break down, and then where will we be? Worse off than ever! The jury—"

"I shan't break down. Phil asked me to marry him many times. And I—I—" she hung her head. Two bright drops rolled slowly over her soft young cheeks. "I don't want to tell a lie, but I must, oh, I must save him! In my heart I said yes. Surely I can truthfully say I accepted him. I did in my heart. Where's my bag, my hanky's in it—"

"M-m,," mumbled the solicitor gruffly, but wiping the

tears off with a very tender touch. "Yes—that might be a help. He was hovering around Twickenham on Tuesday to see you? I guessed as much."

"Oh, yes! That's quite true."

"It's all quite true, or it's of no use," snapped Dorset Steele. "And that about Mrs. Tangye—yes—yes—that might help. But what about yourself?" he shot the question at her savagely. "What about yourself, heigh? All the notoriety? All the ordeal? Though you've grit in you. What about yourself, child?"

"Oh, grandfather," the girl, quite undismayed by his glare, caught hold of his coat with both hands and buried her face between them, "if you save him you save all of me. I was such a pig to him! I thought he was too easy-going, too contented. I thought he needed waking up. I only talked to him about money—money—money, every time he asked me to marry him. The last time I jeered at him because he was poor."

"Are you going to tell that to any jury?" stormed Dorset Steele, apparently beside himself with indignation, but patting the back of one brown little hand. "Because, if you are, it's all up with him. There's the motive. Don't you see?" This time he released himself resolutely. "Barbara, my dear, are you sure he's innocent?"

She did not raise her head. "Grandfather, you know he's innocent!" And even the keen old lawyer did not notice that she had not answered his question.

"M-m, well, perhaps I think so—but you see his father and I were old friends—" then the solicitor shook off his momentary weakness, "but the only question that concerns us, is what will the jury think? Now put your bonnet on, and I'll take you to see him. If you've thought it over. Weighed the consequences. Heaven knows what your mother will say when she hears of it!"

"Put my what on? What do you suppose this is?" Barbara touched the velvet tam o'shanter she wore. "I'm ready. As to mother—she's still in Yorkshire."

According to all novelists, Barbara ought to have stopped to use her powder-puff before starting off. She did not own that apparently inevitable adjunct to every woman. Certainly Philip Vardon noticed nothing amiss as the door swung open and Dorset Steele barking: "I've brought some one to see you," shut it, and walked the landing outside.

Vardon started up. Pointer had only just left him. He leapt forward; then he took a step back.

"You oughtn't to've come, Barby. But, how like you! How like you!"

"Phil, dear Phil!" It was she who ran to him and put both arms around his neck. "Ybu poor dear boy! You poor darling!"

And after that Vardon took the goods the gods provide but once in a life, and the two were tragically happy. Sensing danger, yet content for the moment, till a harsh, irascible, cough sounded outside.

"It's my grandfather. I must go. Now, remember, we got engaged last Saturday on the links. I asked you not to tell any one."

"It was to see you I biked down to Kew, Tuesday afternoon. I wanted to tell you what had happened!" He stood looking into the face he thought so lovely.

"I wish you had come to the house," she sighed.

"Unfortunately I remembered that you had said that on Tuesday you were going to your aunt's at Hampton Court, so I didn't ring. I didn't want to meet your mother. Not after the last interview I had with her."

"Mother's a darling. But she knows so little of life. She doesn't know how to judge," explained her aged daughter. There fell a dead silence. Barbara wished that she had not used that last word. The door opened with considerable difficulty.

"Ready?" growled Dorset Steele, and started ahead down the passage.

Barbara took a 'bus back to her home. With every turn of the wheels her heart grew heavier. She had told her grandfather that Vardon was innocent, but she felt a sickening doubt as she thought over the whole position. Now that she was alone by herself. Away from that atmosphere of suspense, and pity, and dread. The doubt came first when her thoughts again ran over their talk last Saturday. It had been on the Richmond links.

Vardon had asked her to marry him. There was another; young man in the offing, and he was jealous. Very jealous. Barbara had thought this just as well then. Every detail came back to her now, and added its mite to the growing pile of fear deep down within her.

"Why don't you get some money?" she had asked impatiently. "Others get it. Why can't you? Nobody cares how nowadays."

"That's the sort of speech to make a man commit a crime," Vardon had said thoughtfully, rather than indignantly.

His words had startled her even then. She had looked at him half laughing, half impatient. She had been thinking of business. As she looked round at him his face seemed to her to have changed. The desire for money exudes a poison gas of its own, necessary though our modern life has made the shekel. Its blight lay on Vardon at that moment. It had taken something from his face, leaving it, even to her eyes, less attractive.

"It's no use asking me if I love you, when you haven't enough to marry on. Mind you, I don't promise that I should marry you under any circumstances. What about playing on? Some one else may possibly want that bunker where your ball has been resting this half-hour."

Vardon had picked up his niblick. He was the sort of man, she reflected, who would always use a niblick in a bunker. Barbara watched him slogging away. The lie was certainly bad. But was he one to make the best of it? Five explosions clouded the air with sand and stones before the ball was shot out—to lie very close to the pin she had to own. Half the bunker seemed to have accompanied it.

Barbara gave her own ball a neat little undercut and

holed it. Philip promptly went on with the talk.

"I asked you to marry me just now," he said rather sternly, "and you pointed out that a poor devil of an artist—or photographer, worse yet—living in Patagonia has no right to a wife. As Spiers wants to marry you, and is well off, am I to understand that he will be the lucky man?"

Barbara had known both the men in question since her early teens. She was not in the least nervous.

"I told you the strict truth, Phil." Voice and face were alike kind at that moment. "You're letting every opportunity drift past you. I don't believe you've ever exerted yourself in your life! What have you to share with a girl? Nothing except fat content."

"Fat content!" the words stung her as she remembered them to-day. There had been no fat content in the face she had just held so close to her own. His laugh even then had exasperated her. Why could she not let him go? But there were times when Vardon seemed to have Barbara under a reluctant spell. It was his good looks, she had told herself last Saturday, not the good qualities she believed underlay his gentleness. She despised man or woman who was led by the outside of things. Surely she would not be so disinclined to part, if Phil had a broken nose, and turned his feet in? She even gifted him with a pair of outstanding ears in her effort to be honest with herself.

Vardon, quite unconscious of these devastating changes in his appearance, played on moodily.

"Money is a test nowadays. Of course it's horrid. But you can't get away from it. Father would like to see the old Mandarin idea of knowledge the only nobility, but" she shook her head. "So, until you have enough for two to live on, you're not in the running."

"And dear Spiers passes the post with ease?"

There was no doubt about Vardon having lost his usually sweet temper. His drive nearly swiped the tee-box off its foundation. His ball rocketed up to heaven like a

Saint Catherine's wheel surrounded with tufts of grass and debris.

Barbara had eyed him coldly.

She intended to turn away in silence. But at twenty-six it is still hard to be dignified with an old playfellow.

"Edgar's money would have nothing to do with it in any case," she replied loftily. "I don't care any more for him than I do for you, but at least he can ask a girl to marry without being ridiculous. And you can't. Not as things stand. Sorry not to finish the round, but I'm tired."

She meant that she was cross.

"Look here!" he said hotly. "You quote your father. I wonder what he would say to giving up the round in a fit of sulks?"

Privately Barbara wondered too. But she had an answer ready. What woman ever runs completely out of that ammunition?

"After your language when you sliced into those briars, I think he would advise it," she said primly. The very hedge itself fell back a foot.

Suddenly she laughed. After all youth is youth. Vardon joined in, and they finished the round in at least neutrality. When it was over he held a gate shut that led to the high road.

"If I had money, Barby, should I be in the running? If I were prosperous, and all that, would you marry me?"

"It isn't the money, though it does take that to live nowadays. It's all that not having money stands for."

"There's that pamphlet of mine on South American lizards . . ." he began.

"Finished?" She turned on him with an eager light in her dark eyes. At the look on his face Barbara flushed in vexation. She would have liked to shake him. Shake him till the cloak of take-things-as-they-came should drop off him.

"I see," she said in a low tone. "Not finished, still!"

"Hang it all, writing isn't like hurdy-gurdy, that you turn the handle."

"I think a hurdy-gurdy more to be respected. It would mean effort. You don't make any. You never have! If we married, people would say that it was *I* who married you!"

Barbara thought again of her last glimpse of him. His face had not looked easy-going at that moment. Vaguely even then, the girl had felt that instead of doing good she had done harm.

She had meant to prod Philip's better nature awake. Had she prodded the other side of him instead? It was Barbara's first qualm on that score. Her first lesson gainst improving her fellow-mortals. But she had felt so sure that deep within careless, easy-going Philip Vardon lay a man, generally fast asleep, who sometimes, at rare intervals, had walked and talked with her. It was that seldom seen, other Vardon, who had captured her. He was not in the least like the lazy casual fellow with whom she generally had to be content. She began to realise that there are at least three sides to everybody. The best, the worst, and that serviceable mixture of both, the everyday. In striving to rouse the best had she stirred up the worst? Even last Saturday she had been vaguely uneasy.

Barbara trembled as she stared out of the window. Did she love Vardon? She was not sure. Not at this moment. A little while ago, talking to her grandfather of his peril, in the room with him, seeing his worn face, an overwhelming rush of feeling, such as she had never dreamt of, had swept her away, in spite of herself as it were. But now? Now that she could lose sight of his danger, her thoughts swung around to herself. Had she been quite honest on Saturday with her talk of money as the test of character? She sat thinking awhile. Barbara had a shrewd inner vision. There was good stuff in her. Her mother wanted her to marry Edgar Spiers. Edgar was well off. She had thought that she wanted to follow her heart, and marry Vardon, provided she could wake him up to work harder. What she had really wanted, she saw it now, was to marry both a man with money, and the man she—if not loved —was attracted to. It was not him whom she had tried to help, but herself. Yes, herself. She wanted to marry him, and at the same time marry well. She did not spare her feelings. And what was the result of her efforts? With cold terror she realised that Philip Vardon, who, if left to himself would never have hurt a fellow creature, would possibly, probably, be shortly accused of murder. Accused of it. Could he be guilty? She did not think so. But in this sudden white honesty that flamed through her, she knew that whatever she might appear before man, before God she felt a doubt. A doubt which would prevent her marrying him. She would fight for him till he got out from under this awful cloud, but then—she would have to take stock of where she stood. All the passionate side of her nature he touched. All that side, that has to do with self-sacrifice, with pity, he now called towards him. But Barbara knew she would need more than this. She would not marry Philip until she was absolutely certain that he was innocent. But no one should know that.

CHAPTER NINE

POINTER too, was making for Kew, also for the home of Sir Richard Ash, in his quality as one-time partner of Vardon's cousin.

The house inside showed the unmistakable signs of a large family, and small means. But the comfortable, untidy, drawing-room struck a pleasanter note than many a prettier one.

It rang of happy hours.

Sir Richard was a small, dapper man, with eyes alert and bright.

"I suppose your call has to do with my late partner's unfortunate cousin," he began without preamble, once the greetings were over and Pointer seated, "Mr. Dorset Steele telephoned us of his trouble."

The door opened, and Barbara came in. She had just got back.

She was about to leave the two alone with a murmured word of apology, when her eyes fell on the stranger's card that Sir Richard Ash had laid on a table near the door.

"Oh!" she came closer, "are you—is that—"

"I'm from New Scotland Yard," Pointer said with a bow.

He thought that she had one of the most taking faces that he had ever seen. Her eyes, at once fearless and penetrating, rested on his in a mute question.

"Oh, Mr. Chief Inspector, have you found out yet if it was—an accident?"

"My dear!" her father said gently, but she kept her eyes on the detective officer.

Pointer was moved by that look.

"Perhaps I could tell you something—" she began, "something about Mr. Vardon. You know, we're engaged?"

"My dear!" her father said again gently.

Pointer looked at her very kindly. Nothing short of absolute necessity would have made him question her. He, who knew so well what snares his questions often held! Not willingly would he lay the burden on her young heart of wondering afterwards if it had been something that she had said, or failed to say, which had led her lover to his death. For, it might yet come to that.

"I think I shan't need to trouble you," Pointer said easily, "but thank you for the offer."

Her father looked relieved. She only watched the more intently, trying to read what lay behind the words. A little of the truth she guessed, and went very white.

"There's nothing like routine-work in a case of this kind," Pointer assured her. "And perhaps if I might speak to Sir Richard—"

"Alone," chirped Sir Richard in great relief, "my dear— the Chief Inspector's time—"

"But daddy, you can't tell him as much as I can."

Pointer saw that there was nothing for it but the truth.

"It's this way. Suppose you wished afterwards you'd put things differently, mightn't it worry you? I don't think it would be quite fair to you, just because you and Mr. Vardon are engaged."

She said no more, and left them. It might seem a dreadful thing of which to suspect a nice girl, but the Chief Inspector would have been unwilling to bet on the point, so certain did it seem to him, that outside, with her ear against the door jamb, Miss Ash would have been found.

"How long has Miss Ash been engaged?"

Now that was just the question at issue between Barbara and her parents. Sir Richard always attributed it to the wonderful intuition of woman that Barbara hugged him quite especially that night. He replied:

"She tells us that they became engaged about a week ago. They intended to keep it to themselves till the young man should have a more assured future."

"You have no objections to the match?"

"Apart from his lack of means, none at all. I like Philip Vardon. He's been very unfairly treated in the past, to my thinking, and taken it splendidly."

"You mean?"

"His Cousin Branscombe's will. Philip Vardon should have had the land left him. Every foot of it was Vardon. It came to Clive Branscombe through his mother. But he was one of those men whom a handsome, imperious woman can twist around her little ringer. And Mrs. Tangye, poor soul, was both those things."

"Otherwise a nice woman?"

"Most certainly."

"Ever anything against her? Hint of scandal, or that sort of thing?"

"Not a breath."

"Did she strike you as a very, how shall I put it—law-abiding woman? I mean, do you think she would ever lend herself to anything illegal in any way?'

Pointer was thinking of blackmail.

"The last woman in the world," Sir Richard assured him with a smile, and very definitely.

"Or to be mixed up in anything illegal?"

"Or to be mixed up in anything not strictly above-board, and most respectable. In fact her respectability—I should say—was a shield and buckler nothing could get past."

He tried Ash on another tack, but Sir Richard knew personally nothing of Mrs. Tangye's cousin, nor of her inner life since she had married her present husband.

Pointer thanked him and had risen to go. Turning to him again he said civilly:

"Miss Ash has a bad cold, I see. I'm afraid it's a legacy from the funeral yesterday."

"No. She's getting over an old one. Though I always

say that I don't know about weddings, but one funeral is sure to make another. Yet in her case, it seems to've done no harm."

Pointer hoped that the architect's saw would come true in this case. He certainly intended to do his best to see that Mrs. Tangye's funeral should be followed by another—that of her murderer.

The Chief Inspector found Wilmot at the police station, chatting to Haviland.

"Vardon's alibi is rotten." Haviland spoke cheerfully. "As for his box-camera he says he sold it to a man he met in the train a month ago for a fiver. Hard up for an excuse! In fact, he fits the theory we now have of the murder to a T, sir."

"All but the preparations on Mrs. Tangye's part for his unseen arrival," Pointer said in his unmoved way. "A most important 'but,' Haviland. Otherwise, I agree that he fits, supposing his story to be false. For obviously Mrs. Tangye wouldn't have gone openly to the man's room who, a couple of hours later, was to come so secretly to Riverview, in order to hand him a sum of money she could just as easily have given him at her own house."

"Hence the yarn, you think?" Haviland asked.

"Possibly. But on the other hand, if Vardon's telling the truth, and she did go to Fulham, did give him the money to use for them both, the account he gives of her fits in with what we know of the rest of Mrs. Tangye's actions last Tuesday. Her rush would be not to be too late for that most important appointment in the Riverview morning-room. An appointment for which she had prepared so well. The distrait manner which Vardon mentions would be due to it. So on the whole, until we learn of something that shakes his story, or that would explain why he should be expected to come by the French windows, and not by the front door, I accept it."

"What he told you fits in most of all with suicide," Wilmot reminded him.

Pointer shot him an ironic glance.

"I don't see the Insurance Company's advocate seeing it, if it didn't."

"Any more than I can see a crime here—yet," Wilmot said seriously. "That little point he told you about Mrs. Tangye picking up her pen with her left hand shows what happened. She fired that shot too with her left hand. Or she had an accident while holding it in her left hand. Vardon's no criminal. Apart from every moral consideration, he hasn't the brains for such a crime as you're postulating."

And here Pointer rather agreed. Though with reservations. Criminals have odd pockets of cunning, which even a trained eye may overlook in a first summing up of their character.

Haviland glanced up from his papers.

"I tried that speech of yours on the tea-room manageress. She crumpled."

"What rune was this?" Wilmot asked. "Does Pointer go in for incantations? Pray lend it to me. I'm off to see my tailor."

But Pointer, it seemed, had only told Haviland to ask if it were true, as Miss Saunders maintained, that she had been wearing a purple cloak on Tuesday. The manageress had fallen into the trap, and said that she had been.

"The more I seemed to doubt Miss Saunders having really worn that cloak—she hasn't such a thing in her wardrobe, of course—the more the woman remembered it. Well, of course, that does for the alibi. Once a liar always a liar. And that's a fact. The two women have put their heads together, and concocted it. That's what happened. As a matter of fact, I don't believe now that Miss Saunders was either at the tea-rooms or in the library last Tuesday afternoon between four and six."

Haviland looked half-uneasy at the boldness of his own thoughts, but Wilmot and Pointer only nodded, as though each had already reached that point some time ago.

Barbara meanwhile was discussing the man in charge of the case with her grandfather.

"Looks to be a bit off-colour," Dorset Steele said moodily. He was sitting with his latest stamp between his fingers. The solicitor collected.

"Does he?" in tones of horror.

"Don't you think so?" He held out a Sandwich Island gem. Barbara covered it promptly with the ash tray. A present from herself, which the solicitor regularly produced during her visits, and which he as regularly forgot to use.

"I'm speaking of the Chief Inspector from Scotland Yard. He seems so tied by what he calls routine."

"Huh!" snorted Dorset Steele, almost blowing the stamp off the table. "Routine, indeed! that's what he called his work in that Mailing affair last year. Would Mailing have come out with the truth and ruined our whole defence if Pointer hadn't—" Dorset Steele broke off too indignant to continue, though Barbara heard a muttered "Bottle of ginger-beer indeed! Our best witness!" Snatching up a lens, the solicitor examined a purchase viciously.

"He's a good man," he admitted finally, grudgingly. "His evidence always carries tremendous weight with any judge and jury."

"I'm going to go to the hotel in the city where Phil went, and I'm going to hunt there for that bag of his," Barbara said suddenly. "Of course it's there. He says he saw it taken in by one of the lift-boys. I'm sure I can find it. He pretends now that he doesn't want me to bother. That it's not worth finding, but that's only to save me worrying."

Dorset Steele was sure she could not find it. Pointer had telephoned to him only a little while ago, that two of Scotland Yard's men had failed to trace it. He knew, though Pointer had rung off, that the Yard were searching taxis and left-luggage places. But he thought any diversion good for Barbara.

"I never heard of a madder idea!" he said crossly, and Barbara only smiled. She sped down to the hotel. To the booking-clerk, a pretty girl with a sympathetic eye, she explained that she was Vardon's fiancee and, as he couldn't come for the bag himself, she wanted to make quite sure that it hadn't been overlooked in some odd corner. It contained some important papers.

The girl was friendly. But though she summoned porters and lift-boys, the bag was denied by all and sundry as resolutely as a pain by a Christian Scientist.

Barbara halted disconsolately in the lounge, loath to go. The feeling that though right, she was impotent, that something more should be done, but she did not know what, made her desperate. So much hung on the bag. Had it been stolen? Had some honest mischance happened to it?

"Good morning, Miss Ash," said a voice she had heard for the first time yesterday. A voice that sounded wonderfully pleasant just now. It suggested resource. It suggested power. She shook hands with the Chief Inspector.

"Come about the bag? Not found it yet, I see. What do you say to some tea and toast while I carry on?"

He piloted her into the coffee-room. It was a cold day and a chilly room but his mere presence was comforting. He was so thoroughly on his own ground. Mentally, if not actually.

Barbara handed over the reins gladly.

Pointer started in with asking for the lift-boy, who by this time considered himself the hotel's most interesting inmate. The lad told his side of the story fluently enough.

"There was a lot of luggage come in. Party of Americans arrived. I took it all up in the service lift, and then carried it down, storey by storey. The hall porter had seen to its being chalked with the numbers of the rooms. The gentleman never had a bag with him at all. That's flat."

"Did you take any more luggage up afterwards?"

"No. It was my last trip."

Pointer went up in the lift. He was shown over the hotel willingly enough. The management wanted the thing settled. Pointer represented himself as coming on behalf of the luggage insurance company from whom Vardon was claiming the value of the bag.

Nothing was to be seen that even distantly resembled the article in question. The lift-boy who had taken over after the first one went off duty was next summoned. His answer to Pointer's question, as to what he would do if he found any overlooked luggage left on the top floor landing, was that he would bring it down.

"I'd place it in the lift, like I always do if it's there, and either come down with it if I'd the time, or the night porter 'd haul it down when the lift was next wanted. Either way, nothing couldn't get lost. You can't lose luggage in this hotel, sir, not if you tried!"

"There's no light by the lift on the top floor."

"The lamp in the corridor is enough. You don't need light to get in or take out luggage. All you want is to see the number on 'em. And the corridor lamp is good enough for that."

Pointer nodded. He had done with the boy. He now asked for the lift's mechanician, and a ladder. Together the two mounted on top of the cage. The workman flashed a repairer's lamp around. There, hidden from view by a deep ornamental border, lay a brown kit-bag, marked P.V.

"That's what I'm after!" Pointer picked it up, and gave a receipt—on a luggage insurance company's paper—to the hall porter.

What had happened must have been that the first boy left the bag on the top landing by an oversight. The second boy, seeing the number of a room on a lower floor chalked on it, had heaved it into the lift as he thought, but on to the lift as it turned out, which had already been sent down. The dim light, and dark shaft had at once suggested this to Pointer.

No man but an absolutely fearless one rises high, either at Scotland Yard, or in the Force. Yet Pointer held his very breath as he tiptoed past the coffee-room door, at which Barbara was casting constant glances.

His footsteps would not have disturbed a tigress with a wounded cub. But Barbara heard them. She darted out into the hall just as he was arranging a message to be delivered to her later—much later.

"You've got the bag? Phil's bag? Oh, well done."

Pointer made the best of what he considered a very bad job, and let her accompany him back to his car. Nothing but actual violence would have torn her from his find. He span out the tale of his discovery to the utmost as they drove along.

"You're taking it to Mr. Vardon, of course?"

"Of course!" Pointer echoed loftily as though nothing in the world could ever induce him to trifle with, or detain, another's property. "But I think we'll just call in and tell Mr. Dorset Steele its found. He's on our way."

"I want to be there when it's opened." Barbara's fine little nostrils were quivering like a filly's with eagerness.

Pointer was very official.

"I'm afraid this kind of thing—routine work—must be done as routine," he said stiffly. "I think you can trust Mr. Dorset Steele to state the case accurately to you afterwards."

Barbara seemed duly crushed as he had hoped.

"Where would you like me to put you down?" he asked as they came in sight of the solicitor's office.

"My bank is quite close," she suggested pleasantly. It was next door. Pointer glanced sharply at her, but Barbara was counting some change in her purse with the look of incredulous and pained surprise which that operation generally calls forth on a woman's face. Her whole air was business-like. Absorbed.

She shook hands with him and tripped into the lobby. To run swiftly through a passage, out the other side, up a back stair and into the office of Dorset Steele. She tried the knob of his private office. It was locked.

"No one can come in!" snapped Dorset Steele's voice.

"It's me, grandfather," she said meekly. He made no reply.

The head clerk who had witnessed her mad swoop upon the inner room, proffered a paper. Barbara wrapt herself in it haughtily, blinking to keep back the tears.

"Phil's bag! I know they're opening it without waiting for him!" So, she was not to be there. To see his vindication. She wanted to read that piece of paper more than any of them could. It would be balm to her quivering, doubt-tormented spirit.

The door was finally unbolted. Barbara was in like a wind-driven bird.

"Well?" she asked, "well?" For there stood the bag in the centre of the table. "Have you opened it? Without Philip?"

"A pretty state of things!" fumed Dorset Steele, putting an arm around her. "My private door practically forced open like—"

"Did you find it?" she asked in quivering suspense.

"A paper signed Mable Tangye giving Mr. Vardon the money to invest for her, is here all right, Miss Ash," Pointer reassured her.

"Then, what's wrong?" she asked her grandfather, looking searchingly into his face, "what's wrong?"

"Nothing!" he snapped, dropping his arm, and turning away.

Barbara's gaze grew more agonised.

"I think you'd better explain, sir," Pointer said quietly. He opened the bag again; he lifted out an envelope.

"There's the paper giving him the use of the money. But would you say that was written by Mrs. Tangye?" he asked Barbara reluctantly.

Barbara stared at it. Her eyes blurred.

"I—I don't know her writing well enough to say."

"It's not like any specimens which Mr. Dorset Steele and I have," Pointer explained. "And it's written with Mr.

Vardon's stylograph. And on his paper. The last is natural of course. So is the pen, perhaps, but that writing—?" He eyed it very hard.

"I know you'll take his word—" she began. It was a silly sentence. But she was speaking as much to her own heart as to Pointer. She turned to him, confident of being met half-way. Then she stared. He had altered. She had thought his eyes kind; they were steel. For the first time Barbara sensed that the man beside her was by nature a close-in fighter. The cut of his nostrils, the set of his lips, the very bone formation of his good-looking face, would have told a skilled observer as much at a glance. But for the first time in her knowledge of him, the invincible, fiery, essence of the spirit was flaming through the calm exterior of the man.

Instinct told her that nothing would move the Chief Inspector to alter the course which he thought the true one, by the breadth of an atom. She was right, nothing would.

He seemed to her suddenly very awful. Very terrible. She would not be the first who had had cause to think him so.

She looked dumbly at her grandfather.

"The Chief Inspector believes it's a forgery," he said curtly.

Pointer did not go as far as that, he only considered a forgery as possible.

Barbara sat down. She felt faint. What was this law that never seemed satisfied? She thought of the gulls that she had fed only this morning on the Embankment. Their stretched necks and greedy eyes intent on more, always more. Cruel and insatiable by some law of their very being. Remorseless.

"Philip's clever with his pen," she said swiftly, "if he had wanted to copy Mrs. Tangye's writing, he'd have done it better than that."

Her grandfather's eyes stopped her. Dorset Steele looked as though he were going to bite.

"We maintain that it was written with Mrs. Tangye's left hand, and as such would naturally show great differences," the solicitor said at once.

"Leaving that on one side for the moment. As we three are together, and since Mr. Vardon hasn't got here yet—we telephoned to him to come on," Pointer explained to Barbara—"there's another point I'd like to ask you about, Miss Ash."

"You don't need to answer, mind!" Dorset Steele threw in.

"A man came to Twickenham police station this morning. To see the Superintendent. He spends his free afternoons going over the fields close to Richmond golf links with his dog picking lost balls. It seems he heard you and Mr. Vardon together last Saturday afternoon. He was out of sight, he says, behind a thicket at the time. According to him, Mr. Vardon was speaking as though he hadn't any certainty that you would marry him. Yet you told us that you had become engaged some days before then."

Pointer stopped Barbara with a gesture as cautionary as her grandfather's might have been.

"I don't want you to answer without thinking very carefully over your reply. According to this man, Mr. Vardon spoke unwillingly of a screw that he could turn—if need be— which would let him make a good deal of money. According to this man, you called over your shoulder as you moved away, out of earshot, that if so, he had better turn it, and turn it hard. Now, if you care to explain this conversation when you've thought over your answers—they are very important, Miss Ash—I would like to hear what you have to say. You're not bound in any way to reply, as Mr. Dorset Steele, here says, but if you should care to clear the points up—that about the date of your engagement, as to whether Mr. Vardon did make any such remark, and you such a rejoinder–"

"The man misunderstood the whole thing," Barbara said quickly. "Mr. Vardon and I had—well—had a quarrel. I was in a horrid temper. Things had been rubbing it in to me what marrying a poor man meant—"

Lady Ash would not have cared to hear herself alluded to as "things." "Philip has the sweetest, kindest temper in the world. I was a perfect little beast to him. Oh, a perfect toad. Simply too loathsome for words. I goaded him into saying those words. Of course, he didn't mean anything. And, of course, I knew he didn't mean anything!"

"The man heard incorrectly. No such words in fact, were spoken," interrupted Dorset Steele in such stentorian tones that his clerk in the next room jumped. "*Will* you hold your tongue, Barbara!"

Barbara shook her head.

"If this story is going about, it had better be faced. It's just luck that the only time such a phrase was ever used, was when there was an eavesdroppr. It was Banks, wasn't it?" she asked. "Father of Bobby Banks, whom we had to discharge. He was one of the caddies." Barbara was honorary secretary of the golf club run by the G.F.S.

"Exactly. The man had a grudge, and magnified some trifle," Dorset Steele nodded energetically.

"Mr. Vardon refused to see me this morning," Pointer said after a pause.

"On my instructions," snapped the solicitor.

"Pity. He might be able to straighten this little tangle out by one word."

"My experience is that one word only ties tangles tighter." In his irritation Dorset Steele was getting as alliterative as a Skald.

"You still think it's safer not to let him talk to me?" Pointer asked.

"Safer? You mean wiser. Certainly. Look at this whole conversation—" the solicitor evidently considered it a sorry sight. "The case is going to the dogs."

Pointer, without glancing at Barbara, rose.

"If you'll excuse me, I'll smoke a pipe outside."

He thought that the girl needed a respite.

In silence Barbara stretched a hand up to her grandfather's shoulder and side by side the two stood looking into the fire.

She saw a dark enough picture. He saw a worse one still.

"Did I—did I bungle things?" she asked at last, under her breath. "The truth seemed best."

"Truth!" the solicitor snorted. "This conversation on the links—"

"If only it hadn't happened," she said sadly.

"If only it hadn't been overheard, it could have been kept from the jury!" he muttered. "Well, when you see your Philip next, try to din a few elementary facts into his head. Truth is what it's best for the other side to believe," he repeated forcefully.

"You'll never din that into his head. Nor into mine either, I'm afraid."

Pointer came in again. He still had the bag with him. Now he placed it on a table behind the door.

"Nothing is to be said about that, until the door is closed."

He took up a place at the window, Steps were heard outside. Coming up the stairs. They were on the first floor. Suddenly there came a little halt in them. A sort of catch. Then they went on again. The door opened. Vardon came in. He looked older, leaner. Barbara felt with a sudden pang that she would give all that she possessed to see again that sunny, all's-well-with-the-world look on his face. She watched him with misty eyes. Had she turned an innocent man into a criminal? Was it possible that she had egged him on, talked him on, nagged him on to— She hated herself for the terrible doubt but it was there. Not of the man as he would have been had she let him alone, but of the man whose nerves she might have worn down with her constant reproachings, exhortations for many months now. Had he—the stranger—done this thing?

Vardon's eyebrows lifted as he shook hands with the

two of them.

"We've found the bag that went astray," Pointer said cheerfully. "Just look through it, and see if everything's there. It's unlocked, as you said."

Vardon started. He looked swiftly, not at the bag, but first at Pointer and then at the solicitor. The bag came third. Then he opened it, and bent over the things inside. Pointer had put the paper nearly on top.

"Ah, here it is! Now, you see!" Vardon drew it out. But the paper had been under his fingers for fully a second. True, he looked as though a load had fallen from him, but he also looked a little bewildered. Pointer thought that he looked as though not quite able to believe his own luck.

The Chief Inspector took the sheet and asked if he identified it as the one that Mrs. Tangye had written in his rooms. If so, the Scotland Yard man would take it with him, giving Dorset Steele a receipt for it. The solicitor initialled it. He had every confidence in Pointer but he took nothing on trust. Like Pointer himself.

"Mr. Vardon, what screw did you have that you could turn to order to get money?" Pointer asked as the paper changed hands finally.

Vardon's face darkened. He looked narrowly at the two men. He did not glance towards Barbara.

"Just a silly phrase," he said earnestly. "Just a silly, empty phrase."

And to this explanation he stuck. Barbara said nothing. She sat wrapt in suffering. Had Philip only meant that? His face came back to her. Lowering. Tainted by their talk—her talk—of money as the only goal. She felt certain that he had meant something more.

Pointer left the three to a dreary silence, and drove off.

"So he really had a real bag and a real paper from Mrs. Tangye," Wilmot murmured when he dropped in at the Yard in answer to a telephone message from Pointer.

"And the latter fact interested him far less than his

uncertainty as to whether something else was, or was not in the bag."

"Perhaps he was acting?"

"He was far too absorbed in finding out what was in the bag—and what was not. So am I therefore."

"Pretty wide field." Wilmot gave his little smile, "I mean, what might have been in the bag, and wasn't."

"Pretty wide, but not illimitable."

"Well, of course, as a matter of fact, it would have to be something the bag would contain." Haviland had managed to make time to be present at the interview too.

Wilmot at once agreed that that would shut out certain articles.

"And I can see the objections to it being a live animal, or a gas, or a liquid," the newspaper man went on suavely. "But even so, the field seems pretty wide for guesswork. Pray, how do you start, Pointer?"

"Something like this: Vardon expected to find something in that bag that wasn't there. He did not look in the least worried, or regretful at its absence, and was on the whole, thankful not to find it.

"So, evidently it was something that would have made his position worse. That is to say, that would have thrown a deeper suspicion on him.

"While his fingers actually passed by the sheet of paper we all wanted to see, the one he claims Mrs. Tangye wrote when she gave him the money, they kept searching the pockets in the bag's lining. Pockets that would only admit of papers. He stared first and hardest at a long envelope—which proved to contain his cheque-book. He pulled it half out while he thought we were all busy with the paper. As soon as he had a clear view of its top, he thrust it back. The address was away from him. It was an unopened envelope evidently, but of the same long, narrow shape, that's the danger. He eyed the remaining papers and books but he didn't take any up."

"Securities?" asked Wilmot, "do you think he is missing anything of that kind?"

"I don't think it's money. Vardon didn't look as he would have done if anything on which he had counted were missing, let alone anything for the sake of which he might be supposed to've committed a crime. And the oddest thing is he didn't know whether it was there or not. It's not a case of something missing in the ordinary sense. There aren't many things which would fit the facts. He doesn't seem to be nervy of it turning up anywhere else, whatever 'it' is. At least, he has made no efforts to go back on his tracks in any way."

"That's his cunning!" came from Haviland.

Pointer rose. His minutes were valuable.

He himself was off to Vardon's late lodgings in Fulham. An Inspector of his had been there and found nothing. Watts could be trusted, yet Pointer felt that something had escaped his eye, as it must have Haviland's. But he came down to the ground floor in the draughty house with nothing scored. The rooms, still empty, were detective proof.

"Mr. Vardon can't come himself," he explained to the frowsy manageress, who seemed to think that a pearl necklace, which would have staggered a Romanoff, went particularly well with a woollen pullover. "But he's afraid he's left something behind. I couldn't quite make out what, over the telephone. Something about a paper. . . ."

She shook her head.

"Not here. He's lost it somewhere else. Mislaid it like as not. He reely was too rushed to notice what he was doing last Tuesday."

"Yes, he took all his luggage with him," she went on in answer to a question of the Chief Inspector's. "A new cabin trunk; old trunk for the hold, a suit case and a bag."

That was the tally. Pointer tried again.

"Still he misses something, and thinks it was left here. I couldn't make out over the 'phone just what as I say. How about an overcoat, or a hat, or a cane even, left in the hall stand?"

She made a motion with her hand and ran down to a

semi-basement, negotiating the holes in the carpet with the skill of a pilot among familiar buoys. A moment later she called up:

"Here's his top-coat. His old one. He was wearing a new one when he left. He must have forgotten this. It's his, all right. I mended those pockets for him once myself."

Pointer laid it over his arm and thanked her. Then he stayed on chatting. He learnt nothing about the artist from the woman. Vardon's had been a quiet, unobtrusive figure in the house, liked, but hardly noticed.

He switched the talk to Mrs. Tangye's accidental death. The manageress remembered reading the case in the papers. She had had no idea that her late lodger knew the lady.

"He more than knew her. He was a relation. There's a regular family row raging just now because he says he wasn't told of her death till he saw it in the papers. The family say that one of 'em came here that same evening— last Tuesday —and left a message for him."

Pointer wanted to find out whether the keys found in Vardon's luggage might have been left on his table, as he alleged, though not necessarily by Mrs. Tangye. Florence was still as certain as ever that she had noticed them on the desk at Riverview at four—after Mrs. Tangye's last outing.

"I didn't hear of any message. But, of course, in a house like this. . . ."

"Under a management like this," Pointer amended mentally.

"Still, if any one at all called last Tuesday evening, it would likely have been about the death. I expect it was a lady," he hazarded.

"A lady did call here last Tuesday for Vardon"—a young man lounged in for some change for the telephone. "She waited in a car outside for him. As I came up the steps she bent forward and asked me, if by chance, I knew whether Mr. Vardon were in. I glanced up at his windows, saw a light, and told her he was. She sat back with a grunt—but without a thankee."

"Pretty woman? Young? Fair-haired?"

"Look here! I'm off!" the stranger backed out laughing.

"No, no! It's all right. She's a rising cinema star. Is she as pretty as they say?"

"If she's a star, she belongs to the Milky Way. The face I had a glimpse of wasn't one to fill the stalls."

"About twenty?" persisted Pointer.

"Times two!"

The Chief Inspector looked disappointed.

"Oh, you mean his cousin! Thin, hatched-faced type, with small dark eyes?" Pointer went on to describe Miss Saunders very accurately though apparently casually.

"That's her!"

"Well, of course then he's right. And he wasn't told. She—his cousin.—wouldn't know either. Not at that hour. I take it it was about eight?"

"About."

"I wonder she waited for him. I wouldn't. Vardon's such a careless chap. I dare say she had to sit on for another hour."

"No. I heard him come running down only a few minutes later and the car buzz off. My rooms are below his."

"I'll bet he was still wrestling with his tie as they drove away," laughed Pointer. But the other had not looked out of his window.

The manageress knew nothing more. No one in the house knew more. Pointer shook the patently expectant hand, raised his hat, pressed the starter, and let in the clutch in one co-ordinated action. There was a paper in the inner pocket of the coat. It felt like a letter.

In a quiet square he examined his find. It was a long, official-looking envelope addressed to, "The Registrar of Wills, Somerset House, London."

With his penkife he raised the flap which was stuck down but not sealed. He drew out a will. By it Mable

Tangye left everything of which she should die possessed, to Philip Vardon, cousin of the late Clive Branscombe, and appointed him sole executor.

The will was on a form obtainable at any stationer's. Below the printed matter was written in Mable Tangye's writing, but a singularly uneven writing—that she requested Philip Vardon, if possible, not to withdraw the ten thousand pounds invested in Harold Tangye's firm for at least two years, unless the stockbroker had pre-deceased him.

Pointer tapped the paper thoughtfully.

It was witnessed by one, Edmund Stone, stationer, of 10 River Road, Twickenham, and Robert Murray, assistant, at the same address.

The date was last Monday. Monday! The day before the one on which Mrs. Tangye had a fatal accident, said the coroner. Committed suicide, said Tangye and Wilmot. Been murdered, said Pointer.

The Chief Inspector replaced the envelope, and sat on, staring at his patent tips that winked back at him as though they could tell him a great joke if they would. But what Pointer already knew was sufficient to keep his thoughts occupied.

No wonder the artist was nervous lest this paper should fall into the hands of the police. Here was motive, and motive sufficient some might say. Vardon, the sole legatee —fitted every step of the way now, if his story of Mrs. Tangye's visit were false—except the entrance by the French windows.

There, like some cabalistic Sign of Protection, stood the big question mark, raised by Pointer's own theory of the crime.

So long as he could not be linked with that, so long as no reason showed itself why Mrs. Tangye should have arranged for him to come secretly, Vardon could not be considered more suspect than Miss Saunders, nor than Tangye, supposing the husband to have used another man as his tool.

It was possible, quite possible, that Haviland was right, that Mrs. Tangye had been preparing to go to Patagonia with Philip Vardon, but if so, if Vardon were the criminal, then some strange reason lay behind the murder which had not been even guessed at yet. Of that the Chief Inspector felt assured. Before arresting the artist, Pointer intended to be absolutely certain of his guilt. The odds were too enormously against Vardon to permit of any other course. Here was no case of a man refusing to explain. Whether true ones, or false ones, he had a reply to every question.

Pointer gave his head an impatient shake. He wanted something that could connect up with those footsteps heard in the garden, walking stealthily behind Mrs. Tangye, stopped by, fearful of, the light.

Those footsteps still belonged to no one. Disembodied, Pointer heard them day and night. Whose were they? Vardon's? The husband's? Oliver Headly's? Or those of some still unknown, unsuspected person, some tremendously important person in Mrs. Tangye's life? They might still be anybody's. They still lay in the no-man's land between all the events.

Pointer's thoughts turned back to the will itself. The absolute deletion of her husband's name as a beneficiary, and yet the request at the foot about not withdrawing the money from his firm immediately. That little note was stranger than the will itself, Pointer thought. Supposing the latter to be genuine. He could imagine a woman leaving her fortune away from a husband with whom she had cause to be angry, with whom she was about to have a furious quarrel, but in that case, why the apparent unwillingness to inconvenience him unduly? That did not look like blind rage.

A new thought stirred in the great detective's mind. He put it on one side for the moment, and concentrated on Vardon, and Vardon's rooms last Tuesday evening.

What of him and Miss Saunders? Supposing that the evidence Pointer had just gleaned had been accurate, she had been at Fulham about eight last Tuesday evening. In other words, as soon as she could get there after the police had left Riverview. She had apparently not gone upstairs, but some one had run down and driven off with her.

Pointer called in his thoughts, which were racing too far away on a breast-high scent, and turned his car towards the stationer's, where the will form had been possibly bought, where at all events, it appeared to have been witnessed.

CHAPTER TEN

POINTER stopped his car at the stationer's in Victoria Road. He produced his official card. Mr. Stone showed him into a little back parlour with outward calm and some inward trepidation.

He was thinking of sundry half-crowns on "certs" that came and went—chiefly went, on most days of the racing year. But Pointer was affability itself. Did Stone remember any one calling at his shop last Monday, and buying a will-form?

Stone heaved a sigh of relief. He remembered the lady perfectly. Mrs. Tangye it was, "as shot herself by accident the day afterwards." She had come in to ask where the nearest agent for Carter Patterson's could be found. He had pointed out the shop further down.

Looking around her, with the patently amiable intention of buying something, she had picked up a will-form from a pile by the door.

"Will-forms! , . ." The idea had seemed to go home. She had read the printed paper through, and stood a moment, as though thinking. Stone had been called to another part of the shop to help his assistant hold his own in a wordy dispute about some weekly payment, and forgot the lady. The argument was a long one, necessitating much searching of ledgers. When it was over, he saw the lady seated on a chair writing on the bottom of one of the forms. She covered what she had written with a sheet of blotting-paper and asked him and his assistant, now alone in the shop, to witness her signature, saying that what she was signing was her last will and testament. They witnessed for her, and received what Mr. Stone considered a very handsome payment for the trouble. He saw her slip the will into an envelope which she bought from him, and, after a moment's hesitation, address it to the Registrar of Wills, Somerset House, before folding it up unfastened, and putting it into her hand-bag.

His identification of the lady as Mrs. Tangye was fairly satisfactory. He had only seen her in a dusky shop, in her hat, but he remembered her name perfectly. He had remembered it when he read of her death in the paper.

"Some people say it's all nonsense about being bad luck to make your will. I dunno. My brother made his will and died the same year. And look at this case! Still of course if you mess about with loaded firearms—will or no will—you're likely to end up sudden."

Pointer saw that the man was under the honest impression, as was his assistant, that it was this will which had been referred to at the inquest. The Chief Inspector drove on his way again with another little brick added to his pile.

" 'Unless Charles Tangye should pre-decease Philip Vardon,'" Wilmot read aloud again. "M-m."

"Just so," Pointer agreed, "not so much look of suicide about that proviso as there might be, eh?"

Wilmot re-fixed his eye-glass.

"Why so? My Company claims that Mrs. Tangye was staging an accident effect. This was part of the pasteboard scenery. To make a will, and then shoot herself, would look a bit obvious. That proviso is merely a stage-direction. Nothing more. And there's another thing," Wilmot went on in a thoughtful tone, "this paper knocks your idea of a romantic visitor on the head. Where's any mention in it of the chap with whom you thought she was about to decamp? Of the 'footsteps that stopped,' in other words?"

"Why, he's the only one mentioned!" Haviland struck in, "Vardon, in fact. He's deluded her into leaving him all her money, and he gets rid of her before she can spoil his plan of marrying Miss Ash."

Wilmot had to allow that this was possible.

"I wonder where Tangye comes into this." Wilmot screwed up his eyes, thinking hard. "If a crime, *if*, mark you both! mark you both! I have a strong inward feeling that in some way he and that woman—" he broke off and finished his cigarette in silence. "I should think this will may be a blow to him," he began again. "Cheale writes me that Tangye's hard hit by the Irish failure. That there were large commitments left on his hands."

"Tangye—Vardon. Vardon—Tangye," Haviland murmured. "And just a bit of Oliver Headly thrown in. They sort of swing to and fro. And Miss Saunders now with one, now with the other." Haviland had been puffing finger-print powder over the will. He shook it off, and then compared the result with his photographs of prints belonging to the "circle."

"Lot's of men's prints. Vague ones we haven't got. Shop fingers, I take it. Several smallish ones in gloves. Mrs. Tangye's, in fact. But here are Vardon's clear enough. Here at the corners. Though you found the flap of the envelope gummed down, he must have opened it and read it through before he shut it up again."

"Do you still go by finger-prints?" Wilmot spoke as though to a user of bows and arrows, but Haviland refused to be drawn. He knew the most modern suspicion of that form of proof, but he himself swore by it.

"Obviously Vardon knew the contents of the will or he wouldn't have worried about it's possibly being in his bag," Pointer spoke a little dryly. "If Mrs. Tangye had left her money to the hospitals, Vardon would have told us of it, you may be sure."

Pointer's constable-clerk brought in a set of papers, and his two visitors left. They had been talking in his room at the Yard. In the plainly furnished but airy inner den where the Chief Inspector worked alone with his many knee-hole tables. One to every case, in which he was concerned. The reports brought him were from Hyam, and they helped to fill in a few more of the blanks still vacant in the puzzle.

On Wednesday morning, as soon as the banks in Manchester opened, those notes to the value of fifteen hundred pounds which Tangye said were safe, that half the Clerkhill farm price in other words, in which Pointer was most keenly interested—had among others, been handed in by a clerk from William Merchant and Son, Cotton brokers. The men who were most concerned in the great cotton boom now sky-rocketing. Tangye's hosts during at least part of his last week-end.

The notes could obviously not have been posted later than Tuesday night from town to reach Manchester by Wednesday morning. Pointer thought it even possible that Tangye had sent them off by the six-thirty collection.

Certain it was that Haviland had not found any of them in the morning-room, nor in the open safe on his arrival at Riverview ten minutes past the hour. But they might have been reposing in some other room, or even in the pockets of either Tangye or Miss Saunders.

The Chief Inspector had thought for some time that Tangye must have been at his home during the hours of suspicion, or the woman's hold over him could not have been what Pointer believed it was, a strangle-hold. He felt sure that she had seen the stockbroker there between the death of Mrs. Tangye and the arrival of the police.

Had she caught him red-handed, and helped him to erase any traces he might have left? Or had the companion only found a dead woman, drawn her own grim conclusions, and made her bargain with that knowledge, and the ready money she had found. It was a sum, which coming just when it did, might have meant salvation to Tangye, allowing him to carry on his margins until the stock soared next day.

Tangye's manner, his suppressed fury when he believed that probably double that sum had been there. His hope that the thief would be caught while he did not dare to speak clearer as to the thief's possible identity, all looked to Pointer as though Tangye had linked Miss

Saunders with that loss with a promptness and a certainty that seemed difficult to understand unless Miss Saunders had been the provider of the one half, and was therefore suspected of being the thief of the other half. But if so, what had she received in exchange? She was not a woman to give up as much as a bent sixpence without some equivalent. What •would she accept in return? Not money, for she was handing that over. Then, if not money, what would tempt her? Pointer knew of one thing that would. A promise of marriage. And, if he knew anything of Regina Saunders, it •would have been a promise in writing. Had Tangye given her this? It would explain that air of having secretly, not as yet to be openly shown, the upper hand, the whip-hand, which had struck all three men interested in the investigation.

It would explain, too, Tangye's tone, as he had ground out between his teeth that if Mrs. Tangye had given Vardon the money, as was claimed, there would be something in writing to show for it.

Pointer pushed in the little pigeon-hole in his brain where this new item was now laid, and turned to the task immediately before him. An interview with Miss Eden, which he thought might be rather difficult. He had asked for it over the telephone, and learnt that she was down at her settlement in Bethnal Green.

He found her in a tiny private room looking very tired.

"Is there anything wrong?" she asked. A poor opening move.

"Mr. Tangye now states that his wife committed suicide and withdraws all claim to the insurance money.

"We have learnt that while at the orchid-show with you, Mrs. Tangye saw her husband and—and—" Pointer looked mysterious, "jumping to conclusions—doubtless wrong ones, she first told him on Monday of her intention to kill herself, and on Tuesday carried it out."

Pointer might have been a father in an early Victorian drama.

Miss Eden waited.

"No! No!" she murmured brokenly, "oh, no!" She covered her face with her hands. "How could she let it drive her to such a dreadful act!"

After a second she recovered herself.

"Suppose you tell me, though it's rather late in the day," Pointer was very grave, "just what did happen. We know it from other sources, but I would like to hear your side."

"How could she have let it drive her to do that?" Miss Eden murmured half to herself. Pointer felt that she had asked herself that question many times.

"Just what did she see?" he spoke less sternly now.

"It all seems so utterly inadequate," she answered wearily. "We were walking through the Brazilian Garden they made there, when suddenly Mrs. Tangye—" Mary Eden hesitated for her words, "I've heard of people starting back as though they saw an abyss opening before them, but I never saw it done before. It really was as though Mrs. Tangye felt the ground give under her. She jumped back with a sort of gasp. Her face was as white as that—" Mary touched a paper beside her, "I had been looking somewhere else, but following her eyes I saw—I just caught sight of—well, of Mr. Tangye and some woman's sleeve—turning the next corner ahead of us."

There was a short silence.

"That was all. Absolutely all. Of course—I know—Mrs. Tangye had some previous knowledge, and recognised the sleeve. But why should she have looked like that? She let me lead her away as though she were in a sort of dream, but as soon as we sat down she jumped up, and said she wanted to go back for a moment, would I mind waiting for her? She was only gone ten minutes at most, if as long. When she joined me again, she wanted to leave at once. Would I stay on without her? She thought fresh air might do her good. I insisted on going to the station with her. Walking up and down the platform, waiting for the train to come in, she told me about a letter, which had brought her down to the show. I had not heard of it before, or I should not have gone with her."

"Can you recall the exact words in which she spoke of the letter?" Pointer asked.

Miss Eden thought for a moment.

"As nearly as I can recollect her words, they were, 'To think that I only came down because of that woman's silly letter.' Then she was silent until the train came in."

"Was Mrs. Tangye angry?"

"I think she was too stunned to be angry. She seemed really quite dazed. I think—" Miss Eden showed her perplexity in her face, "I think Mrs. Tangye must have been brooding over her troubles until she lost her mental balance. What was there in all this to give such a terrible shock as she had had? I think there must be more behind, than we shall ever know. Some family tendency to suicide. Some morbid strain."

"And the letter she wrote you?"

"I kept it." She flushed scarlet. "But I couldn't bear—when there was no need—for you to see that last note of hers. But now that there's a question of some innocent person being implicated in quite a wrong idea of Mrs. Tangye's death, you ought to read it. Here it is." She held it out to him.

"DEAR MARY,—I know you will be shocked by what I am
about to do. But it is too late to enter into all that leads me to
take the step you will soon learn of. I know your kind heart
will not judge me harshly. I cannot think of yesterday calmly.
Suppose I had not gone! I am taking the only possible way
out of the trouble for all of us. I am not thinking only of
myself, believe me.
"And so, till we meet again dear, dear friend, in some

future
   where all will be understood—good-bye.
   "Your affectionate,
   "MABLE."

Pointer handed the letter back to Miss Eden.

"I do not think it will be needed. But please keep it carefully."

Mary hastened to slip it into a locked drawer as though she could not bear to look at it. There was a pause.

"Was Mrs. Tangye an impulsive woman?" Pointer asked.

"Very. To me she was always kindness itself. But there's no use saying she was an easy woman to live with. She wasn't."

"Would she be likely to take a strained view of anything not in itself wrong?"

Miss Eden looked surprised.

"It's odd your saying that. For Mrs. Tangye was most sensitive about what she considered deception. If she thought that things were being kept from her, she could be utterly deaf to reason, or even justice."

"Was she a frank woman herself?"

Mary Eden considered.

"She was a truthful woman," she said finally. "I don't know that I should call her a frank woman. She was too reserved for that."

Pointer asked a number of questions as to the person seen with Tangye at the flower-show.

Miss Eden could only repeat that she had barely glimpsed the sleeve of a very smart squirrel coat. Now Miss Saunders had a squirrel coat. Pointer had noticed her wearing it. Miss Eden went on to say that she seemed tallish. That, too, fitted the companion, as well as Mrs. Bligh.

Miss Eden felt quite sure that Tangye had not seen his wife. He and his companion had turned off at right angles, or rather, were already turning, when Mrs. Tangye had given her start and backward step.

Pointer left time for a little pause, then he said:

"You heard from Mr. Tangye, I see, about our visit?"

"No."

"Then how did you know that an innocent person was 'implicated in quite a wrong idea of Mrs. Tangye's death'?"

Miss Eden made a little motion with her hand.

"That slipped out. I heard from Miss Ash about Philip Vardon. She often works down here. She's here now. And I've something to tell you about Mr. Vardon—and Mrs. Tangye"—she hesitated, evidently with little liking for the task.

"In a way, it seems like betraying the confidence of the dead. But she had a very keen sense of justice. I think it would grieve her now—where she is—if I kept silence. I heard what I'm going to tell you from Mrs. Tangye herself. I haven't spoken of it to Miss Ash. I thought of writing to Mr. Vardon, but I've decided that the quickest way, in the interests of justice would be to tell you.

"The day before Mr. Branscombe died, Mr. Vardon dropped in to see his cousin. From what followed, Mrs. Branscombe—as she was then, of course—thought that his call had been artfully planned. I don't see why it wasn't mere chance. She herself was out, getting a breath of air. She nursed her husband splendidly. He died of pneumonia, you know. Well, in the night she came in and found him working away on a new will. A will leaving that money to her, but the land and houses to Philip Vardon. When she asked her husband what it meant— the paper had slipped

from under his pillow—he told her of Philip's call. Mr. Branscombe was too ill to be questioned much and towards morning he grew worse and died.

"Mable imagined a sort of conspiracy between her husband and his cousin. She thought they were trying to do something behind her back which should have been done openly. I understand that she flung the paper into the fire—it was only a draft, not even finished—and wrote Mr. Vardon a letter. It must have been a terrible one if it was anything like what she told me she said. I believe Mr. Vardon consulted a solicitor with a view to taking action. But he decided to do nothing. Mrs. Tangye kept the story to herself except for telling me, and Philip Vardon has a very forgiving nature. A very sweet temper. But, though Barbara doesn't know it, I feel sure that the screw he threatened to turn—she told me how important you think that speech—was that burnt paper. It was Mr. Branscombe's intention to alter his will. And in common justice, Mable should have carried out his wishes.

"Please don't misunderstand her," Mary Eden bent forward earnestly, "she was anything but a mean woman, but she thought poor Philip had tried by underhand scheming to trick her husband when he was too ill to be quite sure what he was doing. Philip Vardon! Who never had a scheming thought in his life? You can quite see now why she would give him that money, that fifteen hundred, can't you, and promise him the remainder of what the house fetched?"

Wilmot at any rate would be able to, Pointer thought a little ruefully.

"I quite expected she would have mentioned him in her will," Miss Eden went on, "I think she would have done so, if it hadn't been made at the time of her second marriage. While she still felt resentful."

"I've heard a rumour that another will's been found, leaving everything lock, stock, and barrel, to Mr. Vardon."

"Oh, no! That's quite out of the question. She never would have done that. It wouldn't have been fair to her husband. We were talking of wills only a little while ago—two or three months at most—and she said that she looked on the money invested in Mr. Tangye's firm as his absolutely. That she had told him so when they were married. But that she felt free to do what she liked with the rest."

The Chief Inspector left Mary Eden without telling her that she had done just as much harm as good to Vardon's case. Some might say she had given the prosecution a splendid motive; evidence of resentment or vengeance on Vardon's part.

Pointer imagined that the artist saw it in that light too. Hence his silence. Though Mrs. Tangye might have made it a condition of the handing over to him of the money. Might have accompanied it by some speech such as: "If I give you this, will you let bygones be bygones?"

Pointer did not drive himself this time. He sat back, lost in thought. He was trying to keep the whole series of loose facts in his grasp. Miss Eden's account had disappointed the Chief Inspector greatly. It had been of no help whatever as far as the incidents of the orchid-show were concerned. That letter did not sound like a meeting with Oliver Headly. Even Tangye and Miss Saunders, or Tangye and Mrs. Bligh could not account for it, he thought, could not have changed Mrs. Tangye's whole outlook on life. What had really happened down there? Whom had she seen, whom met when she had slipped away for those few minutes from her friend? Pointer felt that there must be far more here than he had yet learnt. Must be. Was Miss Eden's story true? Was that letter genuinely written after Mrs. Tangye's return Sunday night? The envelope was. And the letter matched its writing. Jerky, dashed off with quivering fingers.

The idea, born in Pointer's mind when he read that will —the will leaving everything to Vardon, and nothing to Tangye—was stirring now.

He found, on his return to Scotland Yard, that two cables had come from Fez with a portrait—also cabled—of Olivier, gun-runner to the Riffs. Pointer had the portrait at once sent out to Oliver Headly's college at Oxford. No one was able to definitely recognise in the ragged, gaunt, man with the week's growth of beard, and the hard lines around his mouth and eyes, the young man who had had to leave sooner than he had intended. All agreed that it could very possibly be Oliver Headly after the sort of life he seemed to have led. Smith, the orchid-hunter, had also a copy shown him. He, too, could not be sure. He thought it was a picture of Headly, but he was not certain. It was the best that Pointer could do on that score, so he put it aside.

Mrs. Tangye might have kept more watch on her cousin's career than was thought. She might have believed him dead, and have met him suddenly in the flesh. More, she might well have known that for some law-breaking exploit of his, his life, or at least, his liberty, was forfeit if he were recognised. Yes, that might explain some, but not all the actions of the next days.

His thoughts passed on to Vardon. Hastily his mind ran over the reports gathered about the artist.

As a boy, at Haileybury he had not been distinguished for games, nor yet for study, but in that most important field on which only the English public school sets its proper value, in character, he was a favourite with men and boys.

CHAPTER ELEVEN

THE Chief Inspector went on to see Vardon again. As he climbed the stairs to the first floor a very sweet tenor reached him. Vardon could sing.

The Chief Inspector opened skilfully, but Vardon either was, or professed to be, in ignorance, as to any callers at his flat last Tuesday evening, or of any object which could have attracted them during his absence.

True, Pointer learned that about a fortnight ago Tangye had been met by chance in the street, and had come on up to see a Patagonian iguana, since presented to the Zoo. But he had stayed a bare fifteen minutes, and had not been alone in the room.

"Did any one telephone to you last Tuesday close on eight?"

"Yes," Vardon said, some one had. So, at least, one of the chambermaids had told him, but, on hearing that he was out, the voice, a man's voice, had said that another time would do as well, and had left no message.

That, at any rate, fitted. Tangye, if not an invited guest, would have wanted to know that Vardon was out, before running up stairs. Even if the artist's rooms had been locked, the key, as Pointer himself had found just now, had doubtless hung below his number on the indicator board, and, in that ill-kept house, any stray passer-by could have taken it.

And if those keys were not taken by Philip Vardon, if they really had been left in his rooms unknown to him, then, since Regina Saunders was below, Pointer believed that the only other person worried by any mention of them, Tangye—was connected with their puzzling re-appearance among the artist's effects.

Pointer, after learning the exact date of Tangye's call at the rooms, which told him nothing, passed on immediately to another important point.

"Why did Mrs. Tangye make a will in your favour?" The question came in exactly the same tones as the preceding ones.

Vardon paled. He said nothing. Pointer repeated the question. Vardon fingered the Spanish book which he had been reading when the Chief Inspector had first come to see him. Pointer was wont to say that as a rule, the less mind a man possessed, the greater difficuty he had in knowing it, but the Chief Inspector did not think that that was the trouble here. Vardon, like Tangye when he had heard of the discovery of the keys, was rather weighing alternatives, neither of which he liked.

"I don't know," he said undecidedly.

"Equally unaware of why you didn't mention the fact to us?"

"Naturally I didn't volunteer information which has no bearing on the case. Things look black enough, in all conscience, without my touching 'em up."

"You know," Pointer said after a second, "if you're innocent, I really think you would do best for yourself to tell us everything. Short of an actual confession on your part, I don't see how the case could look worse—"

Vardon went to his telephone, and tried to reach Dorset Steele, but the solicitor was out of town.

He came back, and again his foot gave a sort of queer little jerk as he crossed the carpet.

"Very well," he said finally, "I'll trust to your being honest. And not trying to trap me into some talk that can be twisted afterwards. You asked me why Mrs. Tangye made that will. I told you I don't know, and you've as good as called me a liar. I don't know, but I can guess. She had evidently, patently, had a definite rupture with Tangye. Hence the gift of the money, and the change in her will. She told me, I've forgotten to mention that, to send the properly drawn-up contract to her bank, not to

Riverview."

Pointer nodded.

"She handed you the will fastened up, I suppose?"

"Any one would suppose so. But it wasn't even gummed down. Just as she was rushing out of the room she picked it up from the table, where she had laid it on entering, and said, 'Glance this through and then post it for me, please.' With that she was gone. I took it for granted it was to do with the money lent me, until I read it. And that was really why I nearly went in to see her later in the afternoon.

"That, and to ask her if I mightn't speak, to one particular friend, of her backing our venture. But the will was most in my mind. It didn't seem playing the game. There was no reason for her to swing from one extreme to another." Vardon looked as though he would have taken back that last sentence if he could; "That is—er—it seemed unfair to Tangye. At any rate, I decided not to post the will until I had talked the matter over with her, or written about it to her."

Pointer stared at his boots. Then he looked up.

"Was there any question of a silence as to something that had happened in the past—implied or not—on your part, in return for the loan, or for the will?"

Vardon ran his finger along some of the Castilian words as though spelling them out.

"I consider such a question rather an insult," he said finally, in a low voice.

"It isn't meant in that way." Pointer spoke very earnestly. "You surely don't wish Mrs. Tangye's murderer to escape justice?"

"But she wasn't murdered!" Vardon said shortly.

"She was," Pointer was quite frank now. "To the best of my belief, she was. And a peculiarly cruel, dastardly, murder, too. Surely you're not against me in my hunt for the criminal?"

Vardon seemed stirred by the ring in the other's voice.

"You're one of the brass-hats at Scotland Yard, they

tell me," he spoke uneasily, "you chaps take crimes rather for granted. Crimes and criminals."

"Not in this case. Unless I miss my guess, we've here as clever a criminal as I've yet encountered. I need every particle of help that can be given me. If I waste my time over innocent people the real culprit may get away. Now I read—well—many things into that will. And I ask you again, was there nothing known to you in her past which Mrs. Tangye wished kept a secret?"

Vardon hesitated.

Pointer went on, "I never met her alive, but if I know anything of faces, the last thing Mrs. Tangye would have wanted would be for her murderer to get off."

"And the last thing I or any one would want. But you *must* be mistaken for once, Chief Inspector. You must be! Who would murder Mrs. Tangye? Tangye has been here— as you, of course, know. He tells me there's nothing missing. With the fifteen hundred pounds loaned me, every farthing's accounted for. Then why on earth should any one kill her?"

"We have our own ideas on that." At least Pointer was beginning to have the glimmering of one since reading that will. "Then at most, Mrs. Tangye only referred to that draft of a will made by her former husband,—by Branscombe,—in his last night? The draft which she burnt?"

Vardon's look of bewilderment was almost comic.

"How the dickens—how the dickens did you learn of that?"

"Routine work. But, frankly, was that the screw you intended to turn—on Mrs. Tangye?"

Vardon's face flamed.

"Ghastly expression to've used. But—well, it was. You see, my grandmother—Clive Branscombe's grandmother, too—was a Vardon. She used to always say that the land she had brought the Branscombes was to come back to us Vardons ultimately. Sir Richard Ash, Branscombe's partner, nearly got my cousin to make a will to that effect once. But Clive put it off—until he tried to draft it again, too late. As you've learnt in some miraculous way. I thought there was no one alive now who knew of that incident."

"And didn't she ask you on Tuesday not to speak of it?"

"Yes. She asked me to forgive and forget what had happened after Clive's death, and she said something which is rather terrible. In the light of what happened. 'You'll find it'll all come right—and very speedily.'"

That last was one to Wilmot, Pointer thought as he hurried off. His next interview was with Tangye. He wondered how the stockbroker would take the news of a later, altered will.

Tangye almost leaped to his feet when Pointer told him briefly that in the course of some routine work, a will of Mrs. Tangye's had been found, dated last Tuesday, leaving everything of which she should die possessed to Vardon.

"Vardon! Impossible!" he said again, as he had said before, but with a very different intonation. "Preposterous! I shall fight it! I deny its genuiness. Mrs. Tangye repeatedly told me that the money invested in the firm was to be mine on her death."

But the surprise he tried to put into his voice did not carry conviction to Pointer.

Pointer had only handed him a photographic copy. The photograph itself had been carefully locked up at Scotland Yard.

Tangye flung it on the table.

"I don't take back a word of what I said. Truth is truth. My wife told me she intended to commit suicide. You find her shot, with the revolver beneath her hand that fired the bullet. No struggle. No hint of foul play. . . ."

"There are hints of it," Pointer put in quietly, "only hints, it's true."

"Because I don't think he killed my wife, doesn't mean

that I intend to sit still and see Vardon sweep the board clean. Right's right. But one man's wrong is no man's right." Tangye was getting incoherent. "The land yes. If my wife sold a farm, and chose to let him have the money, that's nothing to me, once I know where the money was, but it was agreed, when we married, that her ten thousand—" he was off again.

Pointer had to interrupt the tenth rendering of the same motive to take his leave.

He slipped into the morning-room where Miss Saunders was generally to be found. Just now she was standing looking up at a large portrait of Mrs. Tangye on the wall. A very recent addition to the room.

"I had the enlargement done in Bond Street. Rather good, don't you think?" she asked Pointer. Without waiting for a reply she went on, "I think her picture should be about the house. I like to see it."

Anything smugger than her tone could not be imagined. Finally she took her eyes away with an almost visible effort.

"Has anything fresh turned up, Mr. Chief Inspector?"

"Yes. We've found another will of Mrs. Tangye's. Later than the one read at the inquest. Leaving everything to Mr. Vardon."

She stared at him a moment in silence. Then, compressing her lips, she swept the mantelpiece with the edge of her cupped hand.

"Leaving everything?" she finally asked.

He nodded.

"Genuine?"

"Mr. Tangye thinks not."

"But you?" she gave him a piercing look.

"We see no reason to doubt it, so far."

She made no comment. Turning, she left the room, apparently lost in thought.

Pointer went for a walk in the old Deer Park. It was a sunny afternoon; the elms and larches showing gold under a cloudless sky. There was a buoyant pulse in the wind and sun. The air on his face brought with it smells of frost, of oak leaves, of wet soil under some southern wall, of a belt of spruce to windward.

Blue was the sky overhead, blue the wet ruts underfoot, against the yellow litter of leaves on the ground. Pointer smoked and meditated. His thoughts on Tangye and Vardon first of all.

Miss Saunders, judging from her question to the stranger entering the chambers, had seemed to think that the stockbroker was having a talk with Vardon, but Tangye and Miss Saunders were by no means in each other's complete confidence.

But supposing that Mrs. Tangye's husband had been in the artist's rooms last Tuesday, what would have taken him there? Within an hour or two of his wife's terrible death.

Did Tangye know of that gift of the money—or of the will? Had he come to search the artist's rooms for them? A few discreet questions had told Pointer that Vardon was quite unaware of any search among his effects, and nothing is harder, to an amateur, than to hunt through another person's belongings and leave them as they were.

Still it was possible that the motive which had brought Tangye to the rooms, supposing him to have come, was connected with his wife's visit only a few hours before. But he had apparently taken Miss Saunders there. It might be therefore, that what he had wanted was a necessity, was a step, in something which he and she were to proceed to do together.

It was, of course, quite easy to disbelieve Vardon's story, and see in him the man who had joined the waiting woman and driven off. But though Pointer did not distrust simple explanations, he generally tried to make sure that no other ones were possible, before accepting them.

One thing was certain. If Tangye had left the keys on Vardon's table, he had done so unintentionally. His quick confession, or at any rate, his effort to exculpate Vardon as soon as he heard that one of the notes had been traced to the artist, showed that he was not trying to fasten any guilt on the other man. That, too, was evidently the last thing desired by Miss Saunders, but in her case, if she had made a bargain with Tangye, naturally she would not want her purchased help to seem unneeded.

Vardon's room—Mrs. Tangye's keys—Tangye—Pointer's thoughts passed on to the will. And to the new and startling idea it had given him.

Suddenly he came upon Barbara, a couple of irons under her arm, on her way home from the links. She looked careworn, he thought.

"Suppose we exchange news." He fell into step beside her in obedience to a gesture.

"Do you give a fair exchange-rate?" She spoke a little wistfully.

He acknowledged the hit with a laugh. A laugh of sympathy; he was very sorry for Barbara.

"I'll give you full value. Speaking plainly, Miss Ash, I want to find out something definite from Mrs. Tangye's past. Nothing in the least to her discredit, but I want to reconstruct her life. Before she married Branscombe."

Barbara's eyes widened. But she was one of the very few people who, when they have nothing to say, say nothing.

"You see," he was not looking at her, but at a fine old stag who paced towards them with ideas of apples, "some people might think there was a good, sound, probable motive for a murder already to hand. But I want to make sure that there isn't a better, sounder, more probable one still, to be got. It's tremendously true that the strongest motive wins, you know."

There was a long silence. The stag walked huffily off. Pointer felt that something was stirring in Barbara, was welling up within her. But after a moment she said quietly, "Surely you know everything there is to know about Mrs. Tangye's past. I've just been talking to my grandfather. He says that the worst thing against Mr.

Vardon is that he was seen near Riverview late on Tuesday afternoon. Is that the case? I mean, is that a very important thing against him?"

"Very," Pointer admitted, still not looking at her.

"Of course, if any one else had been seen on Tuesday near Riverview between four and six, it would make a great deal of difference. But as it is Mr. Vardon seems the only one. That—taken into consideration with other things —does look very serious."

They were across Richmond Bridge by now. Barbara said good-bye abruptly. The short winter day was almost over when Pointer turned back. Stray leaves touched his cheek with cold little fingers as they fell. The lights of a barge drawn up to be mended shone red like the eyes of the Great Sea Serpent, who had found a refuge at last. Pale winter moths floated past. The moths that some old folk say are the spirits of the dead. They vanished, or were palely seen, as they drifted now through darkness, now through the rays of a lamp. They were too much like the underlying facts of Mrs. Tangye's death, he thought, to be pleasant company for a detective officer.

Pointer had purposely given himself plenty of time before turning in at Twickenham police court. He was not surprised to find Barbara Ash being politely entertained by Haviland. The Superintendent was showing her his stamp collection, knowing that her grandfather owned a notable one.

"There's something very fascinating about stamps," Haviland was saying as Pointer hung up his hat. "Nothing uncertain about them. I always liked geography at school. History no. There's no proving half of what they tell you in history. But in geography, if they say a town or river is in a certain place, you can go and find out for yourself. You can prove it, as a matter of fact. Even if you don't do it, you know you could go and look. Or dig ..."

Pointer seemed just sufficiently surprised to see Barbara again so soon. She flinched a little, as she looked up at him. Then she took a seat further from the light.

"I've something very important to say," Barbara was pale beneath her tan, "I suppose I should have told you before, but I didn't realise—things—until our talk just now. My grandfather doesn't know I'm here," she added, with a quaintly reassuring voice.

"And that's a good thing, too," Haviland thought. Barbara paused for a moment.

"I—I was afraid he might think it unwise—what I am going to say."

Pointer thought this highly likely. Only tell the police what they already know, was Dorset Steele's motto.

Barbara drew a deep breath. She went paler yet.

"Mr. Tangye is supposed to've been in town until after six. At least so my grandfather tells me—"

The two officials nodded.

"Yet I saw him coming out of Riverview's side gate, the tradesman's gate, just a few minutes after the churches around struck half past five."

"Where exactly were you?"

"I was at the corner before you get to the house, coming up from the river. It's a place where some hollies hang far over the road."

"What did Mr. Tangye do?"

"He opened the gate very carefully, and very slowly, and closed it, after standing as though listening for a second, very quickly behind him. Then he jumped into his car, and was off. I don't think he saw me."

"Was the engine running?"

"I think so."

"Had he anything in his hand?"

"Yes; a package of some sort."

Pointer nodded towards some shelves.

"Could you pick out a book of about the size of the package you saw in his hand?"

Barbara picked up an A.B.C. and a Continental Bradshaw. She thought that the box in Tangye's hand was about the thickness of the latter and the general size

of the former. Could it have been a camera? Pointer
asked. Barbara thought that it looked not unlike a large
box-camera.

"He came out so oddly. So noiselessly," she repeated,
"He opened the gate without making a sound. And he
looked up and down the garden path before closing it."

"He looked towards the house?"

Barbara nodded. There was a short silence.

"And you yourself, Miss Ash, how did you come to be
so close to Riverview?"

"Oh, I merely happened to be passing," she said
awkwardly. "You can go to our house from the Richmond
links either around by Riverview or through the Deer
Park."

Pointer sat quite still. His eyes on his pen point for
once. He had not expected this. He really had thought
this girl a fine, honest, creature. Was she too to come
within the circle of those tainted suspects of his? Oh, the
pity of it!

Barbara spoke again. Impulsively, in a rush. This
time in her natural voice. A voice that suggested all
things young, and frank, and fair. "I—I take that back. I
mean, that wasn't truthful," she broke off in great
distress.

Pointer came to her aid.

"You're trying to tell us, aren't you," he said very
kindly, "that you were the visitor whom the maid mistook
for Mrs. Cranburn? At least that's what we've thought for
some time."

Pointer had at least suspected as much since his visit
to her father. Barbara fitted in with so many points of the
case. Florence might easily have mistaken a bundled-up
figure for that of a stout woman. And the voice of a girl
with a cold for a wheezy voice. Barbara looked both
relieved, and a little appalled.

"I'm glad you know," she said quietly, "I would have
spoken at once only I was afraid—after you detained Mr.
Vardon, that you might think there was some connection

—on his part— I mean, because it was me. Florence didn't recognise me. She had only seen me once."

So Barbara, too, thought that Vardon might be guilty. Or else she would have come forward at once. Her explanation held good for the time since Vardon was under police observation, but from the first she must have suspected him.

"You were calling on Mrs. Tangye?" Pointer asked pleasantly. "I think you can depend on us, Miss Ash, not to misunderstand."

Wilmot, who had dropped in to ask a question of Haviland, took a seat after a glance of permission from Barbara.

"Just a friendly call, I suppose?" Wilmot asked.

"No," she sat with her eyes on her gloved hands, obviously suffering. "No; not quite that. Not unfriendly, of course. I wanted to see if I couldn't get Mrs. Tangye to do something for Mr. Vardon. After that talk on the links," she glanced at Pointer, "I, too, was rather stirred up, and wondered whether she, a comparatively wealthy woman, might not be induced to give Mr. Vardon at least a hearing. He has a perfectly sound proposition to lay before any one. But she wouldn't let him even tell her of it."

"Had you ever broached the subject with Mrs. Tangye before?" Pointer asked.

"Never. But I telephoned Sunday afternoon and asked if I might come in early about three on Monday afternoon as there was something I wanted to talk over with her. She said that she would be at her dressmaker's at that hour. I suggested the next day, Tuesday, about five. She said that would suit her excellently, especially if I would come to tea. On Monday evening she rang me up to put off my coming indefinitely, saying she would write and make another appointment, but I was out, and the maid forgot to give me her message; so I went on Tuesday, expecting to see her."

"Do you remember just what she told the maid

Monday evening over the 'phone?"

"Norton says that Mrs. Tangye said, 'Ask Miss Barbara not to come to-morrow as we arranged. I have a most urgent engagement that I can't put off. Tell her I'm so sorry. I'll write and explain.' But, as I say, the message wasn't given me until Tuesday night when Norton read of Mrs. Tangye's death in the evening papers. Meantime I started rather late for Riverview from Hampton Court Palace, where a relative lives." She gave the name. "I was driving our car myself; something went wrong. It's always leaving you in the lurch when you want to bustle along. There's a good garage not far from Riverview, you have to pass the house coming from Hampton Court." She gave its address. "That's when I saw Mr. Tangye leaving by the side gate. I went on to the garage and had a long wait there until some one came to whom I cared to hand over the car. Then I hurried on to Riverview, though it was nearly six. As I came to the tradesmen's gate I found Mr. Tangye had left it open. It cuts off a corner of the little drive, so I took it too. I walked around the clump of laurels this side of the morning-room to look in. I wondered if Mrs. Tangye had given me up. But through the curtains I saw that the light was on, and hurried back around to the front door. As I stepped away the curtain was pulled aside for a second, and some one—a woman—peered out between them. Perhaps she heard me on the path."

Barbara paused for half a second.

"It was Miss Saunders—I suppose," she added slowly.

"Why suppose?" Wilmot asked.

"It was the most dreadful face I've ever seen," the girl said in a low voice. "The face of a ghoul. Malignant. Horrible. Gloating." She shuddered as it seemed to rise again before her.

"Did she see you?"

Barbara shook her head.

"She was looking in the opposite direction, after one glance around. As though after Mr. Tangye. I only saw

her for a second. I hurried to the front door and rang the
bell. You know what happened then."

"What made you choose the morning-room?" Pointer
asked. He wanted to give her time, and began with the
least important question.

"Mrs. Tangye had said over the 'phone, 'five will suit
me perfectly. You won't mind having tea with me in the
morning-room, I know.'"

"You knew the house?"

"Oh, yes. In dear old Mrs. Branscombe's days I used to
be there a lot."

"And now, tell us what happened after you rang the
bell. Just as though we knew nothing."

Barbara recounted the story with which they were all
so familiar by now. She had nothing new to add to the
scene in the morning-room.

"Did you see the revolver?"

She nodded. "Underneath her left hand. The next
thing I remember was hearing a man's voice saying,
outside the room, 'I don't think I can do much harm if you
and the maid have both been in.' And I thought I should
only be in the doctor's way. I took it for granted it was a
doctor. I thought a caller was certainly not wanted in the
house at such a moment. There were plenty of women to
help. I crossed the hall into what used to be the
housekeeper's room in the old days. It's evidently a
smoking-room now. A moment later I heard people in the
hall, and the same voice, it was the reporter's I learnt at
the inquest, asking if that was the room. I let myself out
by the tradesmen's door."

"And why did you say nothing at your home of having
been to Riverview?" Pointer asked.

"I'm not by way of visiting Mrs. Tangye. Every one
knows that. I should have had to explain why I suddenly
called at Riverview after having refused to go with
mother times out of number."

"The coroner remarked on your absence at the
inquest."

"Yes. But he said my evidence could not have made any difference as I had not seen Mrs. Tangye alive. I should have come forward in spite of everything, if he hadn't added that. But you see, I hoped to keep it from my own people—and from strangers—that I was going to ask Mrs. Tangye to help Philip Vardon. It's only now--"

"Now that dear Philip is involved," Pointer finished to himself, rather grimly.

"Now that I am bringing a sort of accusation against Mr. Tangye, that I see I must tell everything against myself as well. I owe the truth, all of it, to Mr. Tangye and to you." Barbara's eyes would have softened a Chinese executioner.

"Did you notice her keys lying on her desk?" Pointer asked.

"Yes. I instinctively looked around for a glass of water, and they were lying beside a glass. I almost touched them before I noticed that hole just over poor Mrs. Tangye's heart."

"And can you swear that you had not been to Riverview before your arrival at six last Tuesday?"

She looked surprised.

"Certainly, I can. We discussed the time when I left the Palace at five, after having been there from before four. And at the garage both the girl who was there to take telephone orders, and I kept our eyes on the clock till a mechanic finally arrived just before six."

When she had left they looked at one another.

"To think I dropped in to tell you two that Tangye has sent in a formal renunciation of his wife's insurance money. Alas! I know full well what wild hopes this last little bit of tittle-tattle will rouse in any policeman's bosom." Wilmot groaned. "I don't say that my own is quite unperturbed."

"Well, I dunno. . . ." Haviland lit a cigar. "Her story may seem to let Vardon out, but the fact of her having been at Riverview at all last Tuesday, just at that hour too, lets him in deeper than ever to my thinking. And

even if she's telling us the truth—we can easily verify it—
it goes to show how much he needed that leg-up. The fact
is that both he and Tangye were evidently desperate for
funds just at that time." Haviland glanced questioningly,
however, at the Chief Inspector.

"Her story sounded truthful," was the brief reply.

"So it did. But the fact is, all tales told us police sound
that," Haviland commented shrewdly, "when, like Miss
Ash, they take time to think them over. A gal and her
young man! I dunno!"

"We always knew Miss Saunders was putting the
screw on Tangye. The only screw that would make him
knuckle under, something connected with Mrs. Tangye's
death." Wilmot had been thinking over Barbara's story.
He, too, thought it had a truthful ring.

"That part of it's just what the Chief Inspector and me
have maintained from the first," the unblushing Haviland
said with quite a patronising smile.

"What you, or any one else, maintains from the first,
doesn't count," Wilmot retorted, "it's only what you
maintain at the end, that does. I confess—I confess— "

He sat obviously considering the new light thrown by
the girl on the case.

"It certainly is very disturbing for my Company," he
finally decided aloud. But further than that he would not
go.

CHAPTER TWELVE

POINTER got through to the stockbroker over the telephone. He told the answering clerk that he—Mr. Wright, the name had been agreed on with Tangye, wanted to speak to Tangye at once. Tangye promptly suggested that Wright should come on to see him in about two hours' time. Until then, every minute was already engaged.

Pointer agreed, and put in some hours, hard work at his own rooms in the Yard, wading through the papers waiting for him. Among them were reports on the purchasers of Lux cameras. In all England, only three of them had been sold from any known photographic dealers during the last six months. And all to men. One had been in the Haymarket to a man identified from his portrait at once by manager and salesman as Tangye. That had been close on a fortnight before his wife's death. One had been in Exmouth, and had been bought by a deeply bronzed, very big, youngish man, who looked as though he had lived an uncommonly hard life. One had been sold in Folkestone, only last Monday morning as soon as the shop opened. In this case the buyer had, by chance, been recognized by the salesman as Professor Orison, guest of honour of the local P.S.A. the evening before.

Like the other two, Professor Orison had carried the camera away with him.

So it was a Lux that Tangye had bought. What had become of it? Pointer had already sent a man down with careful instructions to Norfolk, to the house where Tangye had week-ended. He had learnt that the stockbroker had only been absent from the shooting-party from early on Sunday till the evening.

He knew too, that Tangye had arrived at North

Walsingham with a camera, because the railway porter had identified his portrait as that of one of Mr. Riddell's guests who had brought one with him on his arrival on Saturday, and refused to let him, the porter, carry it even as far as the car. When the same man left for town, Monday noon, he had no camera with him. A footman at the house, too, was quite sure that Mr. Tangye had left on Sunday morning with his camera in the car beside him, and had not brought it back on his return in the late afternoon. He said that Tangye had spoken as though he intended making a present of it to a lady, and was only testing it first, he supposed that the stockbroker had done so on the Sunday.

Detective Inspector Watts represented himself as sent from the photographic dealers to whom Tangye had complained of a faulty lens. They maintained that the camera must have had a bad fall after it left their hands, and he, Watts, wanted to trace the camera's movements very carefully. Pointer sat a moment gazing across the river running beneath his windows.

That youngish, sunburnt-looking man at Exmouth— Vaguely the description would have passed for Oliver Headly —supposing Oliver to be alive. He took up his pen. It seemed a hopeless quest, but instructions were sent to the Exmouth constabulary to do their best. They were furnished with portraits of the man as he had been twenty years ago. The photographs from Fez were no good here, for that man had undoubtedly been stood against a wall by a firing-party. Then came the last of the three purchasers—Professor Orison.

Pointer had heard of him as one of the smart lads of the moment. A lecturer in duchesses' drawing-rooms on the Power of the Mind. For all that, his erudition, like his degree, was laughed at by scholars.

Pointer had seen him a couple of times. At a royal garden party. At a ducal wedding. Orison was a striking figure. Thin, elderly, bent, with a face like a wrinkled glove in which burned two dark, keen eyes beneath tufted white brows. He claimed to be of noble Polish descent on his mother's side, and wore a long drooping Polish moustache, and a Paderewski-like mop of fine silvery hair. He even spoke with a Polish accent.

Pointer turned to *Who's Who*, and learnt that Drummond Orison, Ph.D. of Palmyra, U. S. A., the son of a physician, had been born in Brussels some seventy years ago. That he had travelled a great deal, especially in the East. That he had, never married. That he now lived in Hampstead, and that his recreations were "Thinking and butterfly catching." That his publications included two volumes on "The Quantum Theory as applied to Mind," and other books of a like ilk. All of them fairly recent publications.

To any one but Pointer it would have seemed a blameless record. Even a Lux camera might have passed as innocent in such hands, but the Professor had bought it last Monday, and in Folkstone—Folkestone, the end of the railway line on which Tunbridge Wells lies!

Pointer marked his report with a sign that meant that the thinker's home was to be the object of special, but very discreet attention by the policemen who passed it, and that the passing of it should be included in their programme as often as possible.

He added in his neat legible writing that the Folkestone salesman should be skilfully tapped for possible further details of last Sunday evening. Then he wrote out some instructions for his own C.I.D. and wound up by cabling to his confreres in Brussels for particulars of Orison's life while there.

Pointer's man had already learnt that the Professor had apparently spent last Sunday afternoon travelling to Folkestone, and Monday and Tuesday in his study at Hampstead. All seemed quite as it should be, bar that untimely purchase of a camera. But Pointer took no one at his face value. Or at least very few people.

It was now high time to drive off for Tangye's office. Pointer was shown in at once. Tangye met him with some impatience.

"Some important development, I suppose? Since you've asked me to lose a week-end in town."

"The case is developing," Pointer assured him a little grimly, "but do you think it's quite fair to your old clerk to let him in for perjury? For a criminal prosecution? We have a very reliable witness who saw you during five to six last Tuesday—not here in your office."

"Impossible!" Tangye said fiercely, "a damned lie!"

"What was in that package, sir, that you were seen carrying out of the tradesmen's gate at Riverview about half-past five?"

Tangye seemed to shrink into his clothes. His knuckles whitened as he gripped the edge of the writing-table.

"I tell you I wasn't near the place," he began to bluster. "Mistaken identity!"

"Independent witnesses," Pointer bluffed back.

Tangye rose, and Pointer had to take his leave; to find Haviland waiting for him in his room at the Yard. The Superintendent had had a chat with Mrs. Bligh's maid.

Tangye had brought the camera in question with him when he came to lunch at Tunbridge on Sunday. The maid explained that her mistress then expected to be invited on a certain yachting cruise to Egypt, and since her hostess-to-be was a keen photographer, she had asked Tangye to buy her the best camera for temples and indoor work, and to show her how to use it.

"But she either lost it, or it didn't please her, or something. Anyway, she didn't have it with her when she came home. Nor he neither. I know, for I went out to the car. There wasn't any camera in it," the maid explained.

In the course of further conversation she let it drop that at the best of times Mrs. Bligh was not a lady who permitted questions, and that since she had not received the invitation in question, it would be as much as the maid's life was worth to speak of photography in any form.

Pointer had already had a private note issued to all photographic dealers, second-hand shops, and even to all dustmen in town, asking them to watch out for a large box-camera which might have been left for repairs, or been thrown out, broken up. So far nothing had resulted. He had not thought that it would.

What had become of Tangye's—or Mrs. Bligh's—camera? Duly entering its absence in his notes of the case, he turned to some other work, but within an hour there came another message over the 'phone from the stockbroker. Would Pointer make it convenient to see him again at his office?

It was a very chastened Tangye who was speaking.

Pointer dropped everything and hurried into the city.

Tangye shook hands almost eagerly.

"So glad I could catch you. I wanted to see you again at once. I want to—er—modify—er In fact, I've a damned unpleasant statement to make." He spoke as though it were the fault of the detective-officer, then he got himself in hand again. "It's about my alibi. There's no use trying to throw dust in your eyes, I find."

Pointer thought that bricks rather than dust had been used, but he only bowed.

"As a matter of fact," Tangye avoided Pointer's placid gaze, "I spent part of those two hours which interest you so much with Miss Saunders, in the Old Deer Park."

Tangye went on to tell of an appeal to him on Tuesday from his wife's companion after she had received notice to leave Riverview at once. They had met in the Park, talked it over until at half-past five, he had driven back to his office to see what could be done.

"Miss Saunders, of course, will bear out every word of this," he finished.

"Of course," Pointer echoed politely.

Tangye shot him a glance, but the Chief Inspector took his leave without further comment. He was due in the Assistant Commissioner's room.

Pointer and his superiors at New Scotland Yard did

not see eye to eye about Mrs. Tangye's death. The Assistant Commissioner agreed with Wilmot that only a very active fancy could find a crime in it. Barbara Ash's little story gave Captain Pelham food for thought, however, and he sat awhile digesting it.

"Looks as though you were going to be right once again, Pointer, in that it was a murder, but mistaken in your theory of how it happened."

"I don't think that's possible," Pointer was never conceited, but he spoke very firmly. "In many cases, my theory might be wrong or right, and yet the case would stand. But not here. Either Mrs. Tangye was murdered as I imagine, or she wasn't murdered at all. It's that cousin of her's, Oliver, that complicates all the reasoning."

"You mean that if he dove-tailed with the murderer by chance, or intention, your idea of an appointment in the Riverview morning-room loses all its force? That's one of the things I want to talk to you about.

"We've had a private report from a man whom, even to you, I can only call Captain X. He's been doing some secret service work in Morocco. Personally, from what he told me, I haven't the shadow of a doubt that the Olivier whom the French shot was Oliver Headly. In any case, Oliver was a doomed man from the time the French and Spaniards joined forces. He knew too much. And he knew it too accurately. When they caught him, he got a note through to Captain X, giving him some very important information. Unfortunately he had clearly sent a previous note which never reached its billet. The Riffs caught the carrier, X thinks. In this second note he winds up with 'Don't forget the message to my cousin.' He signs his note, as he always did, merely with a circle. X says he met Olivier and is absolutely sure that he was an Englishman, a man of education, a bad hat, and a plucky devil. His age he puts at the age Headly would be now, and he once saw a book in his possession with the initials O. H. inside it. I think all this rules Mrs. Tangye's cousin out. Of course there's just a chance that he wasn't Olivier, and therefore, may still be alive, but I think it's hardly worth considering. Meanwhile, there's another point.

"Vardon's uncle, he's an M.P. for God knows where, has been writing to us," Pelham went on pensively. He was a long, loose-limbed, clever-looking man "A nasty note. Wants to know if we are armed with *lettres de cachet*, and threatens to set the press on to asking if *Habeas Corpus* is dead or not. We've got to let Vardon go. Or arrest him. That's an order from on high. Now, what shall it be?"

Pointer had expected this.

"Very good, sir. Vardon shall be told at once that he can go where he likes. Fortunately where he likes will be Patagonia."

"I'm glad that's your idea of good fortune. I suppose you chatter Patagonian too, like a native, and will be off there before we know where you are?"

Pointer laughed.

"No, sir, I'm not interested in Patagonia—so far. What I mean is that he'll be practically under observation all the time. I shall tell him that we have no objection to his leaving, and ask the captain of whatever ship he chooses to keep an eye on him. If I may, I'll telephone the good news to him at once."

"So Oliver Headly, the cousin, is out of it. Well, as a matter of fact, he never was really in it," came from Haviland, as he and Wilmot lunched with Pointer.

"I'm not concerned with Oliver. He's beyond our powers to investigate or locate," Pointer agreed. "At any rate, Tangye doesn't fulfil the necessary conditions. Even without Miss Saunders' support of his latest alibi. I think he's merely a frightened man, though frightened for very good reasons."

"All the facts we've been able to discover, I still consider only accidental, not incidental—from the point of view of a crime," Wilmot mused, "but had there been a crime here, I should have thought Tangye—"

"Vardon, Mr. Wilmot!" Haviland struck in, "Vardon's in the very middle of things. The keys in his luggage. That will—"

"Ah, that will!" the newspaper man frowned thoughtfully, "that will!"

"That will suggests a new thought to me," Pointer said after a moment's pause.

"A quarrel with her husband?" Wilmot finished.

"I don't call it the will of an angry woman," Pointer continued. "No, I think—I think—there's but one explanation that fits that will. Easily. And that is that Mrs. Tangye felt that Tangye had no right to the money."

"Forfeited it, in fact, by his treatment of her?" Haviland looked a little doubtful. Wilmot only waited.

"Suppose Mrs. Tangye had been married before she met Branscombe? Married secretly. Thought her husband dead. Say he was some one—possibly a criminal—of whom she was bitterly ashamed as soon as she had married him. There are three years of her life of which we have no record, you remember. Suppose she saw down at Tunbridge last Sunday, not Tangye and anybody, but this first husband, this only legal husband whom she had thought long dead and buried—I think, that would explain everything. And that alone.

"Tangye is away Sunday. She sees to it that he's away Monday as well. He may have been speaking the truth when he tells us that that quarrel had a forced, theatrical air. She may have snatched at the pretext afforded her by his having been down at the show, just as she would have jumped at any other excuse. Her one thought, if my idea is correct, would be to get the man out of the house who isn't her husband, who never was her husband, and have a reasonable motive in the eyes of her circle, for leaving him. By the same argument, Branscombe's money reverts to his heir. She halves the sale of the farm, her only loose money, and calls in the sum invested in Tangye's firm which I think she intended to halve too."

There was a silence as he finished.

"You think that Vardon was really her husband!" Haviland ejaculated under his breath.

"Where does this lead to—?" Wilmot asked slowly, "I don't see—?"

"Vardon. That's where it leads to, Mr. Wilmot, and that's a fact."

"Vardon?" Pointer spoke meditatively—. "Maybe, but at any rate it leads, apparently, directly away from Tangye. At any rate I shall work from along a different line, and we shall see where we fetch up. Of course, it's a mere guess. But it's a guess that might account for Mrs. Tangye's wish not to have her visitor come to the front door. She would naturally be nervous about any one seeing the man who was really her husband:—and, if I'm right, her only husband. It was a position which would make any woman get rattled."

"But why should he kill her?" asked Wilmot, perplexity in his voice, "this is all very interesting, very exciting even, but where does it lead to? Why the deuce should he kill her? She, him—yes. But there's no sense in his doing away with her!"

"Suppose he were a convicted felon? A sentence still hanging over him? Or, married? Has a family? Or on the eve of another marriage? He, too, may have believed her dead. Since he seems to've made no effort to come across her before. There might be reasons, many reasons, which would fit in here."

"Vardon fits in, right enough in fact," Haviland murmured. "He's in love with that pretty Miss Ash."

"Would fit! Might be reasons!" Wilmot shook his head. "Pointer, your suspicion is like the sun which only circles, but never sets."

"Still, it would fit the facts," Haviland said with enthusiasm, "and—"

"You mean it fits Vardon," Wilmot retorted tartly. "I think we're only getting more and more at sea. You're going too far and too fast, Pointer, when you take to inventing a third husband for that poor lady, or rather only one."

Pointer merely nodded a pleasant good-bye as he hurried off. Three years of Mrs. Tangye's life were unexplored. The years from twenty to twenty-three. Her father was dead by that time. She had gone away with a relative of her mother's, a highly respectable lady, who had died two years before Miss Headly reappeared to teach in a high school in town. She had always been a poor correspondent. Her friends had believed that she had meanwhile been somewhere in the north of England. The Headmistress of the school in London thought that she had gone as governess to some family connection, but as she knew Mable Headly of old, she had not looked the matter up.

It was quite possible that those three years would not explain the mystery, but Pointer could see no other chance of clearing it up. But how to get on the track of them? He had been trying in vain all this week to get into touch with any one who could supply him with a clue, a jumping-off board. None had been found. Possibly there was no mystery. If so, this last effort, too, would end in vague ripples. If the guilty man were Vardon, the investigations would come back to the artist. Slowly possibly, but surely. Those footsteps that stopped in the garden last Tuesday. . . .

They still were on the wrong side of the circle which, as he reminded Wilmot, had two sides. Would they resist his efforts much longer to trace the person to whom they belonged?

It was barely possible, of course, that Mable Headly had got actively entangled with criminals, not merely by a hypothetical marriage to one. She might have dipped down into the underworld herself. But a criminal for three years and before, and after, those years never to fall below the line of highest respectability? Pointer had never come across such a case, for Mrs. Tangye had not struck any one as a two-sided woman. All that Pointer could learn of her was of a piece.

What did fit his theory, was what he had heard about her throwing a halo over the past. Over what she had lost.

Pointer thought this explained her actions when, or if, she had met a first husband whom she had supposed dead, last Sunday. Suppose that husband in need of money? Suppose he had ingratiated himself with her? Suppose he had talked of starting life again together? Mrs. Tangye had shown herself a woman very easily affected by men. Mrs. Tangye collects her papers bearing on her money affairs, gives away her clothes which would only remind her of what must shock her deeply—life with a man to whom she finds she is not married. That letter to Miss Eden becomes intelligible under this light. After receiving this rediscovered husband on Monday, they arrange that on Tuesday she shall leave Riverview, either with him, or more likely far, after him. Pointer thought that she was obviously planning her escape from her old life to look like a separation from Tangye because of Tangye's flirtations. Pointer could imagine more than one reason why Mrs. Tangye —to give her the name she bore, but which he had begun to think might not have been hers legally—should decide not to reveal the truth till later, if ever.

Seeing her husband's infatuation with Mrs. Bligh, Pointer thought that she was the type to haye never told the real truth, to have never set free the man and woman she thought had deceived her. She had looked a very jealous woman to Pointer. He recalled Miss Eden's words about her being capable under provocation, of acting very unjustly.

Pointer's men had not been able to trace any marriage earlier than that to Branscombe. But she might have married abroad. Or even under another name. But the point was, how to get into touch with her past?

He went for one of his short, brisk, walks in the pouring rain that slanted down like silver threads sewing earth to heaven.

How to get into touch with that buried past of Mrs. Tangye's? With that unknown bit that extended from fifteen years ago, from the time when the late Lady Susan Dawlish, her mother's aunt, took her away on her father's death, till she reappeared in the London high school, three years later.

The last time he had seen Tangye in Riverview, the stock-broker had been taking down his wife's fishing-gear from the wall. Her basket had been a roomy, Welsh osier creel. How about the flies in an old book that Pointer had borrowed on his first visit to the den, a fly-book evidently home-made, bearing the initials M. H. on the coarse flannelette cover? He had taken is as an additional proof that Mrs. Tangye had really been left-handed in her girlhood, since it dated from then, so Tangye had told him, when he let him keep it temporarily.

They were not Scottish flies, that Pointer knew. Each locality has its own variants of the regular standbys, and these were different from those he had himself used in Scottish rivers. Apart from whence they came, they had told him several things.

They had been made by a left-handed person, and, though very neatly done, the cheapest materials alone had been used. And they were copies of cheap flies, too, so Pointer thought. Now, neither Over nor Nether Wallop lies by a river, yet these flies had seen much usage. They were salmon flies moreover, and such a complete set would hardly have been made for a mere visit to relations. Nor could Pointer trace any such visits, and he had tried hard. These flies therefore, he thought, might belong to that uncharted bit of Mable Headly's life.

Pointer drove to an angler's shop in Jermyn Street which he himself often patronised.

"Welsh flies these," the salesman said, pouring over the lot, "old-fashioned. Twenty years old, I should say, or copies of flies twenty years old. That's an Usk Canary. But whipped to a string of gut! Tut, tut! Home-made evidently. But neatly done. And neatly used too. You can always tell if they've been jerked. Hullo. That's one of Father William's old Parsons. He's given up those hackles years ago. But that's no copy."

"Sure? It may be important."

"Certain. If I found the Grand Lama using it in Thibet, I'd be certain."

"And who is Father William?"

"He's a character, that's what he is, sir. And the best rod south of the Tweed, amateur or pro. He never leaves the Usk. Not he! To see him cast a fly—oh, it's a beautiful sight! He's always out with his rod as soon as they take the nets off. Began life as a gillie. Used to sell his flies to the gentlemen who employed him, and so started in the business. Those Durham Rangers and Jock Scotts over there are his work. They look a bit light, but Lord, they make the right ripples. And that's the whole secret, ain't it, sir? It's not so much the fly you use, though that counts, of course, it's the way he 'lights. But it takes Father William to get the right kick out of 'em. He has a way!"

Pointer asked for the address of this pattern.

"William Morgan is his name. His cottage is TyCerrigllwydian. It's just outside the town of Usk. But you'll never find him there, sir. He's out fishing all day, and at the Inn of an evening. He loves to talk, does Father William. Age? Getting on for seventy, I should say, and good for another seventy again."

Usk? Now Usk is not far from Cardiff. And Pointer had just been reading that name in connection with the dead woman, though not a close connection. Remembering Tangye's and Sladen's words about Mrs. Tangye having told each of them that she had once had something to do with a bank that had failed, Pointer had had a list of all such failures in the last twenty years sent him. Her name had not figured among the depositors, but that meant little. There had been a big smash fourteen years ago in Cardiff.

And also—oddly enough about that time—he was very

vague as to dates, said he never could be sure within a couple of years, Vardon claimed to have had his headquarters at Cardiff for some eighteen months while working partly on some local stage scenery, partly on sketches of the country around. His dates were so elastic, and his localities so vague, that Pointer again wondered whether this were accident or design. He had wrung a few names out of him finally, and turned them over to Watts of the C.I.D. to investigate.

Pointer drove first to New Scotland Yard, and arranged matters with the Assistant Commissioner. Then he dropped in to see Wilmot.

"I'm leaving the affair in Haviland's hands for a while," he explained.

"Who's he to lose this time?" Wilmot asked with great interest.

Pointer had to laugh.

"He can turn to you for advice if he gets hung up in too many facts, and the Yard'll throw cold water on any schemes, which are over-desperate with regard to Vardon. I want to be free to do a bit of routine work."

"In the wilds of Upper, or Nether Wallop?"

"Neither. I'm off to hobnob by the banks of the swift-flowing Usk with a gentleman yclept Father William."

"It sounds a pleasant change from the hurly-burly of town," Wilmot murmured enviously, "a big detectve has a tremendous pull over a newspaper man. We can't suddenly feel that our work demands a dash to the forests of Malay, or a fortnight in the best hotel of a smart winter resort. You can. You don't have to keep a list of the relations who've already died; nor check up your attacks of the flu. What's your excuse?"

Pointer told him. Wilmot was thoroughly interested, but expressed himself as very sceptical of any good results.

"Seems a blind alley to me."

"That's to find out. Merely as part of the regular routine it has to be tried."

"The Insurance Company has just sent me a little reminder that things seem to be hanging fire."

"Why not come along with me on your own? The nets are being left off the Usk a month late this year. Come and help me fish."

"*Me*? My dear chap, I shall prepare to receive you when you return in silence and tears, and I promise you here and voluntarily, to ask no questions, nor, except under severest provocation, to mention the word Wales in your presence for the next five years."

"That ought to suffice."

There was a ring on the telephone. It was from Watts. Was the Chief Inspector in Wilmot's rooms by chance? Pointer assured him that he was.

"I haven't been able to check up Vardon in Cardiff, sir. The address he gave you was pulled down some eight years ago. The company for which he claimed to've painted that scenery, failed about two years before that. None of the inns about remember him. I couldn't come on any trace of him at all."

Pointer turned away thoughtfully.

CHAPTER THIRTEEN

VARDON had barely laid down the telephone before he dashed into a taxi and drove to Dorset Steele's office with news that he was now a free men. The lawyer hummed, and hawed, and threw—not so much cold water as vinegar, on the other's apparent optimism. He refused to see the daylight at the end of the tunnel.

Oddly enough, Barbara, too, was not so radiant as Vardon seemed to be. She was more concerned with what Pointer had said than with the mere fact of Philip being allowed to go where he pleased.

"Did he say that he thought you innocent?" she asked more than once. Vardon put her off with pointing out that deeds spoke louder than words. But Barbara was not satisfied.

She went to see the Chief Inspector herself.

"Does this mean that you think he's innocent?" she asked bluntly.

"Do you know what would happen to me if I let him go, and he were guilty?" Pointer asked with apparent candour. "We're not allowed to make blunders like that, Miss Ash. We're expected to go down with the ship."

"Grandfather says he'll be watched in Sweden where he has to go first—about some timber, and afterwards on the ship to Patagonia. Closer even than on land. He'll be watched in every port. He'll be watched between every port."

Pointer did not reply. Grandfather was a wise old bird. Barbara left him, but little comforted.

A ring came at the door of the little studio where she worked at her china painting. Barbara was not pleased. Visitors meant dust, and dust meant specks.

It was Mary Eden. Barbara liked Mary. Though one was older than the other, they were both of them Cheltenham girls. That counted. Mary was looking ill.

"I was passing, and felt that I must drop in and see you. Do I disturb you?"

Barbara told her that she did not, and by way of proving the statement, began putting her things away in a cupboard.

"Is it true that Philip Vardon is leaving for Patagonia?" Mary asked suddenly.

Barbara said that it was true. Mary Eden shivered, and drew closer to the fire. There was silence for a few minutes.

"I'm glad he's free from suspicion. But oh, Barby! Barby!" and with that, to her own, and Barbara's, boundless surprise, Mary Eden began to cry. Terribly. Heart-

brokenly.

It was over in a moment. But it was not forgotten, and it left its traces on the elder girl's face. These were the kind of tears that relieve.

"Since you've seen so much, I might as well tell you all," Mary said brokenly. "It's Charlie Tangye. He thinks he's going to be arrested—for his wife's murder. Murder!" Mary Eden shivered. "It's no use pretending that things aren't very suspicious. You see, he was in a frightfully tight place financially, it seems, and—well, of course, it was his own money—but he seems to've sent off some hundreds that same evening that she died. I couldn't make out about the money. Apparently Chief Inspector Pointer thinks it was taken before the police got to Riverview, and of course, that looks bad. So do—other things. Some one saw him come out of the house about five." Barbara winced. "He went back for some papers to do with his, and her insurance. Intending to raise money on them. And, of course, that looks terrible. His having kept silence, as well as his having been there, and the reason for his going. It's all terrible. Miss Saunders is standing by him splendidly. I wouldn't have thought she had it in her. But he's desperately afraid that the police intend to arrest him. He thinks Pointer doesn't believe her."

Barbara felt appallingly guilty. Had she bought Vardon's release with the torture of another man? Like Mary Eden, she felt sure of easy-going Mr. Tangye's innocence.

"I don't suppose you can help," Mary went on forlornly, "but if you can think of some trifle? I—" she spoke wistfully. "I did help to clear Philip, you know, and by something that told frightfully against Mr. Tangye. He says the Superintendent spoke as though I might be called as a witness against him." She bent forward again.

"Barbara, I helped to clear Philip," she repeated, "can't you help to clear Charlie Tangye? You're so quick-witted. Can't you think of anything we can do?"

Barbara had no help to give, and Mary kissed her as she left.

"Forget this scene, Barby," she said, holding her hand. "Forget it entirely. What I've said, and what I haven't said."

Barbara let her go with a remorseful heart. How could she have acted otherwise? Yet what had she done? It was ridiculous to suppose that Tangye was guilty, but if his wife's death was a murder, as the police maintained, then some one had done it. Some one, but surely not, oh surely not. . . .

She broke the cup on which she was working, and merely pushed the bits on one side with her foot, as she sat thinking.

Chief Inspector Pointer had said that the best motive would win. Barbara felt afraid of the detective-officer since that one glimpse of the inner man. But his words carried weight. Could she find another motive than the obvious one of the will, the money. That was what he was trying to do she knew. He had questioned her about Mrs. Tangye's past, but the Ashes had only known the dead woman since her marriage to Branscombe. Barbara had been of no help, nor had Lady Ash, to whom her daughter had written at once, been able to remember anything that would serve.

But she had sent a letter to her husband saying that Barbara ought to go away for a while. Sir Richard agreed most emphatically. Barbara had refused. Now she reconsidered that refusal. There would be no rest for her anywhere till she knew who really had killed Mrs. Tangye. She shivered. Up till now her intervention had only made things worse for everybody in turn. But she must try again and again.

Barbara knew that Mrs. Tangye's early life in her father's parish till she was nineteen had been searched by Scotland Yard without any result, so her grandfather had told her. But what about France? As a true Briton, the girl had a feeling that if anything odd, or out of the way, had happened in Mrs. Tangye's past, it would be abroad. But there was no use in her going to France. Her command of that tricky but charming language was such as a high-school education generally leaves with its pupils. It was all right in England, but seemed all wrong in France. The replies of the natives even to the simplest of statements, failed to restrict themselves to a vocabulary, which surely was voluminous enough, judging by the years that it had taken to acquire.

Barbara reluctantly decided that she was foredoomed to failure, since she must clearly confine herself to her home land. But where to begin? How to begin?

Common sense told her that everything had been already sifted. Yet the Chief Inspector had questioned her as though he were not entirely satisfied. If she had a chance, Barbara decided that it would be found in some unnoticed corner. But how to find that corner? She sat cleaning her brushes and thinking. Had she any knowledge, any forgotten, overlaid, scrap of information which would help?"

It was when she had given it up as hopeless, and started on her work again, that she remembered some old songs.

When Mr. Branscombe died, now four years ago, Mrs. Branscombe, as she then was, had sent his Broadwood piano to Sir Richard Ash, saying that Cecil Branscombe had wanted his old partner to have it as a souvenir of their friendship. A music bench had accompanied the gift. In it the Ashes had found an armful of old songs. They were still lying somewhere in the attic. Lady Ash had spoken at once of sending them back. But the widow had said, with obvious sincerity, that though she had no idea of their presence in the bench, she never sang them, and had no use for them.

Barbara seemed to remember an inscription of some sort on one of them.

She disinterred the tattered bundle at home after a considerable hunt. One only was marked, and that with a round rubber stamp, "W. Griffith, Cathedral Road, Newport."

It was a little Welsh song, very dog-eared. At one time or other It had been a favourite. It was a man's song. Set for a tenor voice.

Still it suggested to her a possible starting point. Newport itself seemed too commercial to figure on any girl's itinerary, but Caerlean was close by, the home of the Round Table Knights. Close, too, was beautiful Llandaff Cathedral of which her father had often spoke to her. Tintern Abbey was not far off. Raglan Castle was within reach. Yes, to Newport Barbara would go, and since whatever it may be for the man, this world emphatically holds that still less is it good for a girl to be alone, she decided to take her mother's advice in yet another respect, and let Olive come with her. Poor Olive was still badly in need of bracing up.

Dorset Steele was out of town, she was rather glad of that. The critic on the hearth is apt to be avoided in times of doubt.

As to funds, she had just sold a dinner service for eighteen guineas. Eighteen and five are twenty-three. With that in hand, Barbara felt sure that she and Olive could stay a fortnight in some quiet spot.

Not even November can take the beauty out of South Wales. And through that land of dingle and dell, glen and mountain torrent, waterfall and wooded hill, ferny dale, and sweeping uplands runs the Usk; broad and winding. The river, beloved alike by Welshman, and artist, historian, salmon and trout.

The Wye may equal it, but nothing in the wide world can surpass—in its own way—the sweep between two rivers. Just now the only colours were soft aquamarine and gray, but in its proper season all would be bright with orchards and hop fields, drooping willows and golden wheatfields set among the shimmering green of fragrant meadows belted by hills, and ringed by distant mountains. And all down the valley other little rippling streams branch out, each with its waterfalls, and bending arms of ferns. The Country of Castles, and of Arthur's Knights this. Of tales that circle every hillock and sit on every stone. Wealhas Tales; tales of fairies. Tales of fighting by the score. The very dust is the dust of bards, of sweet singers to the harp.

The Usk runs between curving banks, and broadens here and there into dusky pools with gay, one-storeyed homesteads set at intervals along it; their thatched roofs a joy to the eye.

Pointer thought of the reams of paper covered by rhapsodies about the beauties of other lands, beauties far below those of this little corner of Britain.

The town of Usk is a charming nook in summer, but it looked rather forlorn on a wet November day. Fishermen by trade, or inclination, seemed to be its only male inhabitants.

Pointer went first to the police station. No one of the name of Headly was remembered there. No photograph of the Riverview circle awoke any recollection in Inspector or constable. Remained Father William.

The day was fine, yet not too fine. A perfect angler's day. Pointer followed his gillie down to the hurrying river, where he speedily put his rod together. It had not been used for over a year now. He tested it, limbering his wrists, and snapping them to get the right flip, the little flip which would send the fly dancing up again when almost on the water, to alight as though by its own volition.

He took out his book of flies. The gillie pointed to one, and mumbled something about its being from Father William, oh, yes.

Pointer knotted on one of the local celebrity's masterpieces and set to work. It was over an hour later when he got his chance. There came a surging plunge, a tug, the line flew screaming off the reel. Pointer was fast in a salmon. Whir-r-r went the line as the fish tore in a mad rush down the stream. Then up he came. A mighty form that rose with a swirl. One of those strange, mysterious creatures who live in an element, a world of their own, where men die, and who die where men live. He shot clear of the water in a great leap. More beautiful than anything that breathes in the open air. Beautiful as a fairy's dream. His whole splendid length one curve of glistening silver with mauve shadows, a twirling, splashing, like a living water-wheel. Almost translucent he looked, showing purple and azure, and green, and always that molten, living silver.

Again and again he leaped, sending the water high into the air. Each time Pointer dropped the tip of his rod, and so saved the cast. This salmon knew the game. There was a last year's spawning ring marked on those bright flanks. He struck a smashing blow with his tail to free himself. Another scream from the reel, and off he flew. Pointer had to race to keep below him as he made downstream with what seemed the speed of an express train.

From slippery rock to mossy stone Pointer jumped, and scrambled.

Then the salmon took a breather. He burrowed, trying to free his lip from the barb. He sulked. He circled heavily round and round this new pool with a vigour that told the rage in his heart.

Again came the flash of silver lightning, swirling, diving, leaping, shaking, in a frantic effort to get free, then came another rush that bent the rod like a bow, that cut a feather of spray as the line ripped through the water.

Skilfully Pointer parried each stroke, his finger on the snapping reel to check the play. At every turn, and tumble, and toss, Pointer's rod held him, played him, wound him in or reeled him out. Then came a rest, Pointer wiped the sweat from his eyes. The fish was not sulking now. The line was too taut for that. Like a cross thoroughbred in a dull stable, he was thinking out some fresh devilment for the next round. It came suddenly. The salmon rose like a whirlwind. The water seemed lifeless compared to the beautiful lights and shadows of him. Living light, and living shadow.

With a break that was like a punch he was off. This time there was even more method. He was trying to catch the gut between two sharp stones. He gave another wonderful exhibition of a silver Catherine's wheel on the churned and broken surface of the water. The very sun came out to watch, and turned him to gold. The rod quivered under the strain. Pointer stood, or ran, or leaped, calm-eyed, watchful, alert, trying to think with the fish below. Then came the last round. Pointer was keeping him in rough water to tire him out. The fish realised this, and came upstream at such a rate that he all but shot past. The rod was bent down, and down, and down still more in a mighty pull. But the strain told on the salmon. Shorter and shorter grew his rushes. Less and less wonderful his leaps and whirls. At last he rose on his side. Spent. Done.

Pointer towed him to the side. The gillie drove the gaff home, and lifted him ashore.

"Well done, sir!" came a voice—not unexpected by Pointer. He had played for it more than for the fish. "A fine, fresh run, twenty-pounder."

Pointer looked at the fish on the bank. The sight was not pretty. Sunken and glassy those bright eyes, open that close-clipped jaw. Gone was the wonderful iridescence of the scales. The wild and savage creature, an Apollo's bow of energy, was straight and still now. He was, to what he had been, as a two-days' cut flower it to its growing sister. Pointer was no sportsman in the sense of slayer. He had to hunt men. He did so with the certainty that he was doing the best work possible for the world, and even, in reality, for them. But to lift this beautiful thing out of its element, to kill it, gave him no pleasure. He had landed what he was after, however, and that was Father William's attention.

"Twenty pounds, you think? He looked the size of a motor-bus to me awhile back, and pulled like one."

"You've made a wonderful beginning," the man on the bank went on approvingly, "and if that ain't one of my flies —I'm William Morgan, Father William, they call me—why, I'm prepared to eat it."

Pointer assured him that there was no necessity for such an extreme measure. He added that he would not dream of beginning his first fishing in Wales with any other cast. Father William, plump as a ball of butter, smiled, well-pleased.

"It was a fine fight. Newcomer to these waters, you say, sir? But done a good bit of salmon fishing, I can see."

Pointer mentioned his name, only his name.

"A woman taught me to cast my first fly. Came from near here, I believe."

"Came from around here? What name, might I ask, sir! I know all the rods O Gaergybi i Gaerdydd, as we say. These years and old years back. Sixty years back."

"She was a Miss Headly when I knew her. I believe she married afterwards. I don't know what the name of her husband was."

"Miss Headly? Not a name I've ever heard. No." Father William shook his head.

"But she used to buy her flies off you, when she could afford it. Big, tall, handsome woman. Carried herself well. Used to fish hereabouts fifteen years ago, or a little less. Left-handed."

"Left-handed! Oh, you mean, Mrs. Hart! Only left-handed person I've ever known. She was a wonder, she was. And tall, and handsome, as you say. Dark, too. Dark as one of us. Yes, Mrs. Hart is who you mean, sir."

"Very likely. I knew her before her marriage. Does she still live here?"

"Drowned, sir. Drowned with her husband off Newport. Caught in a tempest. Boat upset. Neither of them ever heard of again. Silent sort of lady, but her rod could talk. Being left-handed was no bar to her. Let me see, she must have been drowned going for ten years ago. Or more still. More like thirteen it would be. Yes, the years go past like the water in the river, and mean no more. They always were, they always are. Well, I've had plenty for my share. Seems one of the few things you can have your fill of, without doing other people out of their share. Years, I mean. Yes." And Father William led his companion to the Angler's Rest, for the day was over. Here the fish was weighed, and the tale of his killing told to the little knot of the fraternity sitting around the fire, their clothes steaming like the mist in the valley when the sun shines, their long glasses steaming too.

It was a wonderful old kitchen. Six feet up, around the mighty hearth with its ingle-nook seats, and well away from the blazing logs, ran a large brass half-hoop on which a red curtain hung. The curtain in many divisions was only pulled shut when all the "club" had assembled. Then it was not only pulled close, but tucked under the cushioned seats of the semi-circle of chairs, shutting out all the world except fishermen and their tales.

Father William was the presiding chairman. From him a little pathway led by the side of the billowing curtain to the rest of the tiled kitchen. Through this passage came the maid with the drinks. Toddy, as brewed by Father William, was the usual call, and Pointer echoed it. Talk became general. Pointer was accepted.

He let the flood of misses, and catches, and weights and measures flow on for an hour by the great clock above his head. Then he introduced the object of his presence. Some solicitors in town wanted to trace Miss Headly, he said. Question of a bit of money left her on her sister's death.

"As I was coming here for some fishing, I said I would ask around. Miss Headly of hereabouts taught me to fish years ago, before she married. This is a portrait of her sister. Is this at all like the lady you call Mrs. Hart? The two sisters as girls were said to resemble each other closely."

Only two men besides Father William had known Mrs. Hart. They all three thought that the portrait of Mrs. Tangye—taken only a few months ago—might well have passed as a picture of Mrs. Hart, supposing that poor woman to have lived on.

"She was a younger woman then, you see," one of the men said handing back the portrait, "twenty, and a bit. No more. Too young to've come to such an end. But it's the young ones as are the rash ones."

None of the three had known her intimately.

"Mrs. Hart was a hard woman," one of them said.

"Hardly treated, I thought," another corrected; "her husband drank, I heard. She had to sell her catches to keep her body and soul together."

"What was her husband?" Pointer asked.

"Used to swank about an estate of his, but after he was drowned, it came out that he was a little peddling grocer's manager down in Newport."

Pointer could collect no facts from the talk. Even the tragedy was but a vague memory. The broken boat had been found one morning after a sudden storm, on Peterstone Flats, just outside Newport, at the mouth of the Usk.

No trace of either body had ever been found, but the tide, and the rocks, and the storm would account for that. Pointer let the talk swing round to fishing again. He did not want to arouse curiosity. He had better means of learning the truth now than from idle gossip.

He sent off a telegram to the Yard to look up the marriage records of all H's with even greater care than had been done. Then Pointer caught the train into noisy Newport.

CHAPTER FOURTEEN

NEXT morning Pointer awoke from a dream in which he had been playing a weird game of golf. He had not been able to hit a ball, let alone drive one! Worn out, he had just clambered over a hazard to find Wilmot on the eighteenth green holing a magnificent putt, and saying affably, "Try my pet club Intuition; it's more flexible than that old-fashioned iron Proof which I see you still use."

The dream haunted Pointer, but half an hour later saw him at the chief police office in Newport, turning over the records of thirteen years ago. He found the tragedy reported in full. The brief description of the couple fitted Mrs. Tangye for the woman, and for the husband might have fitted Vardon, or many another man.

Irving Hart, described as a grocery shop manager, was the same age as his wife: twenty-two.

The boat used by the husband for salt-water fishing was a small yacht of three tons, partially covered, yawl-rigged, which he had himself skilfully fitted up. The kind of little craft a man could be out in all night if need be. A shore loafer came forward to testify that he helped Hart himself launch it rather late in the afternoon. Mrs. Hart came down at the last moment and got in. He, the witness, had warned them that a change of weather was coming, but Hart had only laughed at him.

Within two hours there were wild sea manes tossing as far as the eye could see. By nightfall no boat could have hoped to put in. Many a one went to pieces in that storm. Many a fisherman failed to return.

The loafer in question had long disappeared. His evidence at the time had been believed, partly because it was considered unbiased, partly because none of the Harts' effects were missing from their rooms. A couple of very respectable women, too, bore out that they had seen Mrs. Hart about the time mentioned walking fast to the cove where the boat lay. Creel and rod in hand, oilskin on arm.

As to the shop—the only address entered in the newspaper accounts or on the warrant—the great new docks had engulfed the street where it had stood. A police-sergeant, who remembered the inquest well, had a hazy notion that the Harts had lodged somewhere else, but he was not certain on the matter, far less could he remember any address. The Chief Inspector was unable to find any one who could settle this point. Water rates— gas companies—all had only the shop address.

One thing was curious, Hart seemed to have no background. Pointer could not learn of any parents, any home, from which he had come.

True, this was not unusual, supposing him to be ashamed of all three. He might even have none, in any but the literal sense of the word. He might have been an orphan— a foundling—an unwanted child.

On the other hand, if Hart were Vardon, then the lack was easily, obviously, explained. There was no mystery about Vardon's parentage and home. Vardon's whereabouts could not be traced during that summer nor for the year succeeding, nor for that matter, without the expenditure of a great deal of time and money, for still another couple of years, which he purported to have spent journeying round the world.

Certainly here in Wales, death, or other natural causes seemed to have removed every one with whom he claimed to have come in contact.

A reply telegram came from the Yard in cipher. The Somerset House register showed no sign of yielding any earlier marriage on Mable Headley's part than that to Branscombe.

Pointer looked hard at his boot-tips. Apart from his belief that the woman he had heard called Mrs. Tangye would not have stooped to such a position, the tale he had learnt sounded preposterous unless Mable Headly had been tied to Hart. Why should she, young, with many friends, and certificates that would enable her to teach in any school in the British Isles, have stayed to face such drudgery? Yet if she had been married, how to find the record of it?

In a moment he was on his feet, and at work on what he called routine.

He worked backwards, and forwards, and sideways, and all ways around his new idea of a marriage at sea, and as the result of three days and nights of incessant work, he learnt an interesting little tale which unravelled at least a part of the mystery that so perplexed him, the mystery of Mrs. Tangye's actions just before she was murdered.

The story, duly vouched for step by step, was as follows:

Lady Susan Dawlish had come to Bettws-y-coed one summer fifteen years ago with her great-niece, Mable Headly, then about twenty. They had stayed at the best hotel in that lovely spot. Mable played an uncommonly good game of tennis. So did a Mr. Hart, a visitor at the same hotel. Also he sang in a well-trained tenor, while Mable played charming accompaniments. He gave out that he belonged to a good family in Ireland. Talked of his hunters, and polo ponies, and passed for the younger son of a hard-up land-owner. Lady Susan disliked him intensely at first sight, and took the pretext of "doctor's advice" to go to Colwyn Bay. She had complained of the young man's unwanted attentions, mentioning that any such match would be preposterous, as her great-niece would be extremely well off, since she, Lady Susan, intended leaving her all her money. The old lady was wealthy, even by post-war standards.

At Colwyn Bay, Pointer found that Hart had followed the two women, taking up his quarters in another hotel, but one which used the same tennis courts. But after a fortnight Lady Susan received a telegram. Her maid had told the manageress that it was from some relatives who were starting for the Colonies, relatives of the older woman, whom Miss Headly did not even know. Lady Susan went on to Holyhead to see them off, taking her maid with her. They were only to be gone two days.

Miss Headly promptly utilised the first to go out with Hart on a little craft which plied up and down the coast.

They went out beyond the three-mile limit, upon which the skipper, and owner, married them. A perfectly valid marriage.

The two young people returned next morning, very pleased with themselves. Old Lady Susan would have to make the best of it now. But she never returned. That afternoon a telegram arrived to say that she had been knocked down by a motor, and killed instantly. That was all the manageress knew. She, and others in the hotel, still remembered the sea-marriage of the young couple. The woman identified the portrait of Mrs. Tangye as that of the gay, brisk, young woman of fifteen years ago.

As for Hart, like the hotel keeper at the inland resort, she had liked him immensely. "So gentlemanly," "such a sweet temper," "so romantic."

The description was still the same as Pointer had heard on the Usk. Apparently Hart had no distinguishing marks of any kind except his good tennis, and even better singing.

A solicitor's story came next. A solicitor in Chester where Lady Susan lived. She had made a will years before, leaving everything to the relatives whom she had gone to Holyhead to see that Saturday. Mable Headly was not even mentioned in it. The solicitor remembered a young whelp quite clearly who had come to splutter and bluster about the will.

He had also a vague recollection of a pale, silent, haughty-looking wife, the great-niece of his late client, who seemed only anxious for her husband to come away with her. The solicitor had wondered how on earth she had come to marry him. Again Pointer could not obtain

any definite description. The solicitor proved quite
unable, as well as unwilling to identify Vardon from his
portrait, but neither could he say that the photograph
might not be that of the man he had only seen once.

Pointer devoted himself to Hart's surroundings. With
great difficulty he unearthed some one who remembered
Hart in Newport. Hart at that time was an auctioneer's
assistant. This was just before his holiday in Bettws-y-
coed. Pointer's informant told him with a chuckle that
Hart always saved up, and took a holiday "regardless,"
hoping to meet some wealthy girl, or widow, preferably
the latter. "Not so long to wait," added his one-time
friend, "at least, that's what he used to say."

Here, too, the portrait of Vardon, a good one, was not
of much use. One moment, like the hotel manageress, the
man did not think it possible for Hart to have changed his
appearance so completely, but the next he weakened, and
murmured that fifteen years would make a difference.

Apart from identification, the sordid tale so far was
clear enough. Hart, at that time the young auctioneer's
clerk, just then out of a job, had cajoled what he doubtless
mistook for a wealthy girl of the upper classes into a
hurried marriage with him. It was easy to picture his
disgust when he found himself instead of better off,
saddled with a girl without a penny. Pointer too imagined
her desperate efforts to right things. He thought that the
woman whom he had only seen lying, as he believed,
murdered, would have put up a good fight to make and
keep a home.

This acquaintance of Hart's had no idea where Mr.
and Mrs. Hart lived. The shop of which Hart claimed to
be, and probably was, the manager, was the kind known
as a lock-up. The man had never met Mrs. Hart except in
the shop, where, according to him, she was a live wire
wasted. Hart had a way of shutting himself up for
hours—drinking, the man said, and the shop, already at
the bottom of the hill when the Harts had taken it over,
slid completely out of sight. Then came, after nearly two

years of married life, the finding of the boat, the tragedy, as it was assumed to be.

This was something learnt, but it left the kernel of the riddle—to Pointer—still unexplained. From many small things in the report of the inquest, he believed that-the wife had really gone out in that boat, but not so Hart. Yet his wife would know that he was not in the boat. His wife would surely have made some inquiries again later on. Especially would that be the case, if she were of such a character as "the murdered woman," so Pointer called her in his mind.

Finally Pointer got the real explanation. He got it from the Chaplain of a Sailors' Home at Cardiff, whither his search for Captain Todhunter, had led him. Todhunter was the master mariner who had married Irving Hart and Mable Headly in that swift fashion, nearly fifteen years ago.

Drunk when in charge of his old tub some four years later, he had lost her. And with his boat, lost his own means of livelihood. He had died in the Home about two years ago.

Before he died, he had made a statement on oath which was duly taken down and witnessed. It was still in the Chaplain's care. By it, Captain Todhunter revoked a statement which he and his mate had made to Mrs. Hart two years after her marriage to Hart. It seemed that the husband had tired of the tie and had arranged "for a consideration" with the needy captain to come and make a so-called confession to his wife. The confession being that the ship was *within* the statutory three-mile limit, not outside it when the marriage was solemnised, and that, therefore, Mable Headly and Irving Hart were not, and never had been, married. The captain said that the young woman had taken it quietly enough.

She had made inquiries, but as his mate stood in with the captain, these had only confirmed Todhunter's story. Miss Headly had not noticed the name of a ship off for Pernambuco, which had sighted them, and signalled them a message to take back to the owners in Cardiff just before the ceremony, which she was now told was worthless. Had she done so, she could have proved, as Pointer now did, that over four nautical miles, not three, separated them from the nearest shore. She had finally, after her interview with the mate, accepted the "confession" as genuine. And on the next day, had come the news of the fatal accident to both plotter, and plotted against.

All the parties were dead, said the Chaplain. There were no children. There seemed to be no living relatives. So, after communicating the paper to the Chief Constable the Chaplain had kept the matter to himself.

As to the accident to Mrs. Tangye, the only other name given in the papers had been that of her previous marriage. Headly had not been mentioned.

Captain Todhunter had always kept his log books, and Pointer verified the place of the marriage by them, and by the log of the signalling ship whose first mate, through his glasses, had seen the marriage actually performed, and would have signalled his good wishes to the young couple but for lack of time, and trouble with the crew.

Pointer further learned that his owners had received a letter only a little over a week ago on the matter. A letter signed M. H., and dated that last Sunday of Mrs. Tangye's life. It was in her writing, without any attempt at alteration, and was to the effect that the writer enclosed a five-pound note to pay for immediate inquiries to be made as to a ship which was off Colwyn Bay on a date fifteen years ago and at a given hour. The date and the hour of the marriage of Hart and Mable Headly. Had any such ship signalled to a little steamer called the *Seafoam*? The writer wanted to know whether the latter, the ship sighted, was within three miles from land or not. A great deal hung on the fact the letter added, and requested that the reply be sent with all possible speed to the initials at the foot, Paddington Post office. To be called for. Something in the note, more than the money, had hurried up the inquiry which was only a matter of a couple of hours.

On Monday night a reply had been posted as directed, giving the exact description of the *Sea-foam*, stating that the present captain, the then first officer of the passing steamer, had seen a marriage ceremony performed aboard her, beside a little garlanded rail. That the Captain's testimony, and the log book from which the information was taken, were open to inspection and verification at all times. The readers of the note had guessed M. H.'s reason for writing.

"Run to earth at last," Pointer said to himself. He meant the interpretation—the making clear, of Mrs. Tangye's last days, and at least some, if not all, of the motive for the murder. Mable Hart had either staged that boat accident, or had had a genuine one.

In either case, she had decided to cut the complicated hateful string that her life had become. Hart had probably believed that she had killed herself intentionally; but the thought had aroused no pity in him. Only suggested the idea of escaping himself by bribing the beach loafer to say that he had seen both husband and wife set sail in the ill-fated boat.

At any rate, Hart had doubtless believed her drowned, and continued in that belief. Until when?

If he were Vardon, until his cousin married Mable Headly. If he were not Vardon, then until they met at the orchid-show. If he were not Vardon, that meeting might well have been fortuitous. In either case, what followed would, Pointer thought, have run on similar lines. Hart had played a bold game. He had probably told the woman who considered herself Mrs. Tangye that, though he had snatched at the fact that by some strange mistake he was believed to have been drowned, and though he fully believed in her own death in that storm, yet he had never rested till he had sifted the matter of their marriage, and proved it to be genuine. Todhunter, Hart would claim, had been actuated by hopes of blackmail. Hart had then given Mrs. Tangye the name and address of the owners of the ship that had passed them during these fateful hours fifteen years ago.

He had evidently used every art to soften a woman's heart. And Mrs. Tangye? Remembering that tendency of hers to gild the past at the expense of the present, Pointer could see how she could have been beguiled by this apparently repentant man, who after all, would hold a place in her heart that no other man could ever fill. And who is not touched by the thought of fidelity? If Hart had told her of unhappy years of regret and remorse, of vain longings to have the past over again. . . .

Pointer walked his hotel room back and forwards. Every one of Mrs. Tangye's actions was explained by this completed story. Her agitation when she saw Hart. Her slipping away from Miss Eden to talk to him, her silence on the way to the station and the train up to town. Her prostration on her arrival at the house which she had considered hitherto her home. Her letter to Miss Eden showing that she had decided on at least the outlines of her flight even then. Though still, Pointer was by no means sure that Mrs. Tangye had decided to go with Hart.

On Monday came her preparations for the secret meeting in the early afternoon before Tangye should return, a meeting arranged at Tunbridge. During that talk, the man who was certainly planning her murder even as he sat looking about him, thinking of this, rejecting that, had won her trust completely.

He and she had mapped out exactly what each was to do, so at least Mrs. Tangye would imagine, little dreaming of just what terrible decision was being worked out in the heart of the man who seemed so touchingly anxious to start life afresh with her.

Then came the return of Tangye, the forced quarrel to ensure his going up to town, and to give her a pretext for leaving him, ostensibly an outraged wife. Apart from any quarrel, it was easy to understand that Mrs. Tangye would refuse the loan of money to Tangye from funds in which she believed that she, and therefore far less he, had no real rights. As to what would have come afterwards, Pointer could only guess, nor did it matter. On the whole he believed that Mrs. Tangye would have gone abroad. At any rate this Monday, she had written for her old will restoring Branscombe's money to Cecil Branscombe's heir.

That will! If Hart were Vardon, it, and the gift of the fifteen hundred pounds took on another light. In that case, it was a bad blunder.

Inevitable, perhaps, under the pressure of lack of funds. Pointer followed that thought all through its ramifications. If Hart were Vardon, then all his story of the gift of the money in his rooms, of the talk there was false. Nothing bore out his statement. But neither did any known facts contradict it.

But how about the will if Hart were *not* Vardon?

In that case it would be enormously to his interest not to have Mrs. Tangye die intestate, with always the possibility of her first marriage, her only legal marriage, cropping out.

Pointer imagined that Hart would have very much pressed the point about the will. It would create an atmosphere of disinterestedness on his side—supposing he were not Vardon. In the latter case it would have taken careful handling. But then the whole affair had been handled carefully.

At any rate, because of Hart's pressure, Mrs. Tangye had hurried out at once after his visit on Monday, bought the will form, and made her will. Pointer thought that looked as though she expected to be very busy, perhaps to be away on a journey, and was afraid of it slipping her memory. As to the notice of withdrawal of funds from Tangye's firm; Mrs. Tanyge might have been going to use it, or some of it, for herself. She could have justified the keeping back, at least temporarily, for her own use of a part of Clive Branscombe's money, by the certainty that if the dead man had known the facts, he would not have wished her to stand penniless in the world.

The rest of her actions on Monday, the Chief Inspector thought, was Mrs. Tangye's own doing.

On Tuesday she had dealt with her private papers, and requested Miss Saunders to be ready to leave Riverview that evening. Not in anger, nor from jealousy had this last been done, but merely as part of her plan.

But who was Hart? Hart, the murderer. Hart, who had been in such a hurry to wipe out the existence of the woman whose one crime was that she had listened to him that summer morning in Wales?

Pointer could find no portrait of the man; though he brought all his ingenuity to bear on the task of unearthing one. But he got the promise of the choirmaster who had trained Hart's voice that he would come to town immediately he should be summoned, to "take a look at some faces," among which Pointer intended to take care that Vardon's should be present. That young man was expected to return from Sweden to-morrow, and to be held up for two days in town before his boat sailed for South America. One thing was certain, Hart was not Tangye. Apart from crass improbability, Hart was fairish, Tangye was very dark. Fifteen years ago, Tangye was at Oxford and had just won his Blue. But was there some collusion? In detective work things are so rarely what they seem. True, by the discovery of a still living first husband, Tangye lost all claim to any money left by Branscombe, but, according to Hyam's latest confidential note, Tangye was to-day a very wealthy man. His gamble in cotton had turned out a magnificent success. He could well afford—now—to lose his late wife's capital.

There was always that key-ring, linking Tangye, and Miss Saunders, and Vardon.

And there was the belief expressed by Wilmot that supposing there were a crime here, then Tangye would be found in some way implicated. Pointer thought of the great crime-specialist's words more than once as he took the train back to town, every nerve tingling, as it would with him, when the end of a hard case was in sight.

CHAPTER FIFTEEN

WILMOT and Haviland met Pointer at the London Terminus. The Chief Inspector took them on with him to New Scotland Yard, where he told the tale to them and the Assistant Commissioner at the same time. Captain Pelham punctuated the telling with a few shrewd questions. When it was over he glanced at Wilmot.

"You and I will find it difficult to keep our feet, Wilmot, against this."

Wilmot refused to consider that all was lost.

"Though I grant you, Pointer, that your theory's wonderfully improved from the puny shade it was when you showed it last. But, as I see it, it immeasurably strengthens the idea of suicide. Immeasurably. Suppose every fact to be right, except the end. Have Mrs. Tangye hate—as she would, depend on it—the very thought of Hart! Just imagine her situation, her truly terrible situation. She's not married to Tangye. She never was married to Branscombe. She loathes her real husband. If she tells the world the truth, she places herself in a most pitiful position.

"Even if she takes Tangye into her confidence, she knows him well enough to feel sure that he won't be able to keep it to himself. He will be free to marry Mrs. Bligh, or possibly Miss Eden. Poor Mrs. Tangye! A wife and yet not a wife! Rather than face a life in hiding, a life of perpetual humiliation, of never-dying gossip, she picks up that revolver. . . . No wonder she fired it with the left hand! I don't see any need for a Hart in the final scene. I only see a broken heart. An agonised, tormented soul!"

Wilmot's voice had a ring of deep feeling in it for once.

"And I see Vardon," murmured Haviland, "though I see what you mean too, Mr. Wilmot. As a matter of fact, for the poor lady, it was just as well it all ended when it did."

"I still see no certain crime here," Wilmot spoke with a touch of reluctance that marked something approaching conversion in his attitude, "not yet. Though I confess, I'm a bit shaken—just a bit, by that legacy.

"Should it be a crime here, then I feel sure it will still turn out to be a Tangye-Saunders affair. You say Tangye wasn't Hart. Granted. But I say that the murderer—if he exists—doesn't need to be Hart either. What about Tangye in a disguise? What about Philpotts even? What about that cousin whose death we assume, but can't prove, therefore, can't be certain of? What about Miss Saunders slipping in through those open windows? What about Miss Eden even. . . . When you've had Vardon quite definitely not identified as Hart, perhaps you'll come over to my way of thinking."

"Perhaps we shall," Pointer said thoughtfully, as he went to an inner office. "But Tangye will still be available, if wanted. And so will the rest of your rather sweeping list."

Wilmot elaborated to his theory of some more subtle combinations of the Riverview persons.

Pelham listened, but only half in agreement.

"You may be right, that's what I've maintained myself up till now. But you know—well, Pointer is Pointer!" Mayor Pelham finished with a smile.

"Yes, but he's not God-Almighty! I don't deny that this story needs very careful weighing," Wilmot went on, "I don't pretend that it doesn't alter some things. But, don't forget that it opens the door to blackmail. Suppose some one else had stumbled on it, too?"

"Vardon?" Haviland asked again, almost in spite of himself.

Pointer entered: "I wired to the man who's shadowing Vardon to keep watch night and day, and above all make a note of every one who speaks to his charge."

"He'll find it difficult to give us the slip with Inspector

Watts on his heels," Haviland muttered in gratified tones.

"You think Vardon is in danger?" put in the quicker-witted newspaper man.

"If he's not Hart, we do," Pelham answered very seriously, "in that case, if Hart can do away with Vardon in some manner that prevents definite identification of the body— why, he'll think that he's hung up the case indefinitely."

"Then he doesn't know Pointer," Wilmot turned to the Chief Inspector in mock despair. "What's a body more or less to you? You'd merely think out some fresh tale of mystery, and sail on, with or without the corpse.

"No, no!" Wilmot made a gesture with his cigarette suggestive of dispersing smoke, or a crowd of tiny gnats, from in front of his eyes, "you postulate a murderer who not only left no trace of his presence at the scene of his supposed crime, but has given us no sign of life throughout the investigation. No effort has been made to mislead us. There has been no stir in the underwood of the case to mark the passage of a secret criminal, and we've all •been listening attentively. I can't think Vardon, or any other man, would have such iron nerve."

"The thing I'm afraid of," Pointer spoke very gravely, a little uneasily, "is that there may be still another murder. However, the only witness I found in Wales, who could identify Hart—possibly—is spending a couple of days in a nursing-home."

"Eh?" asked Pelham.

"I really hadn't the face to ask for any more men, sir. So I suggested a quiet retreat to him. It's only a matter of two or three days, and free of charge. I told him that he might get sandbagged outside. That idea made him skip under shelter like a lamb. The doctor's in the secret, but all the rest, even the Matron, think it's suicidal mania. He's never left alone, allowed no visitors, watched day and night, and the staff are laying themselves out to amuse him. His only complaint will be that the food is all cut up, and that he won't be allowed to shave himself, but that's not much. Once Vardon's ship is back from Sweden, it's due to-morrow, he'll be escorted up to town and taken over by us like royalty. I think we've done our best to safeguard him, as we have Vardon. . . ."

"I hope we shan't slip up on the question of identification," Pelham said, "it's absolutely vital here. If *only* we had been able to lay our hands on a photograph of this Hart!"

"As far as I could find out, he never had one taken," Pointer was not pleased with that fact.

"I can't see how you can doubt that Vardon's the murderer," Haviland said firmly, "it all seems of a piece. In fact, it's like one of these prehistoric monsters you hear of, where first you find a footprint—heard a pair of them in this case—and then you get a bit of a bone. Then comes along the spine, and finally you wind up with the skull, and there you are."

"Ah," Pointer said good-humouredly, "the great thing is not to link up one beast's snout with another creature's tail. It doesn't matter in a museum case, but it might in one of ours."

And with that small joke the men separated. Wilmot and Haviland going on with Pointer to see Tangye.

Pointer had sent the stockbroker a telegram before starting up to town.

It was a very jaded looking man who glanced up at the two tall figures, one in uniform, one in tweeds, as followed by Wilmot they were shown into his den by a servant who they knew, and Tangye knew, was a butler detective.

"Well?" Tangye said tersely, rather white about his tightening lips.

"Now, sir," Pointer took a chair unasked. "We haven't the man who murdered Mrs. Tangye but information has come to hand which tends to let you out. As you've seemed to feel yourself an object of suspicion—-"

"Seemed to feel!" Tangye flashed back, unlocking a tantalus and pouring out some whisky for himself which he merely waved beneath the siphon as a matter of form. He did not ask any of the three to drink with him. He had not forgotten the day when Pointer had refused. Nor a later day when even Wilmot had made some excuse.

"We've thought it the right thing to come and tell you that much. Naturally we'd like you to keep it to yourself for the present."

Pointer laid little stress on this last point. He thought it most unlikely that his researches into Hart's past were not known to the murderer.

"But I think you ought to be frank with us. Tell us the truth of the tangle that you've got yourself into."

"Indeed?" Tangye wheeled around. "You expect a full confession of the crime perhaps?"

"No," Pointer said equably, "we merely would like your own account of *why* you gave Miss Saunders that promise to marry her. Why you went to Vardon's rooms on the Tuesday your wife was found dead. *Why* you returned to Riverview about five on the same Tuesday afternoon. Of course, we have a tolerably complete idea of what happened, but if you could explain the various points satisfactorily, ·we would not expect to mention them at the trial. Nor to question Messrs. Merchant of Nottingham about the notes they received Wednesday morning. Notes known to have been in your late wife's possession yet posted by you before the police left the house Tuesday afternoon."

Tangye's teeth met with a click. He was very pale. He eyed the Chief Inspector as though sizing him up.

Wilmot bent forward.

"I should like to relieve you of my presence," he said earnestly, "but as I understand that the police maintain the idea of murder, my Company would expect me to be present."

"One more or less—" Tangye said, not over civilly. "Do I understand that, unless wanted, my statement will be kept private?"

Pointer explained that that was what he hoped,

though he could not give an absolute promise.

Tangye had another drink.

"You seem to know an amazing lot already," he said grudgingly.

"Oh, like most people, we know a good deal more than we say," Pointer agreed pleasantly.

Tangye looked him over with a most unloving eye.

"Well, here goes! Mrs. Tangye and I had a quarrel on Monday afternoon. It was started by her. It entirely concerned her having caught sight of another lady and me at Tunbridge orchid-show. I told you that much. Only the lady was not Miss Saunders. Her name doesn't matter "

"One moment. You mean Miss Eden?" Pointer nodded his head as though this much he knew already.

Tangye's cheeks flamed.

"I mean nothing of the kind. Do you mean to tell me that you're dragging even Miss Eden's name into this unsavoury mess? A woman who's an angel of goodness and innocence? A girl who—"

"Well, we know that she was there. And that she talked to you. At the orchid-show." Pointer said urbanely.

"The lady I was with was Mrs. Bligh," Tangye snapped out. "Her address is—" he gave it. "And now I trust that information has laid those monstrous suspicions of yours about another person."

"It has," Pointer assured him, "but you see, sir, half an explanation is no good to us, and only tends to drag in innocent people."

Tangye gulped.

"All that I told you about Mrs. Tangye's manner take as repeated," he said after a moment. "Everything was exactly as I told you, except that Miss Saunders' name was never mentioned. I stayed on—" he hesitated, "I stayed on to tea," he repeated. After a pause he began again, "Well, I stayed on because there was something I wanted to speak about. Something I wanted to say." Again he stopped.

"We know about that Irish firm having let you down," Pointer put in. The going was very hard for Tangye just here evidently. "We know that on Monday at noon Mr. O'Malley sent you a wire in code to say that he couldn't meet his liabilities and was off for abroad. We know that no blame whatever attaches to your firm for the position in which it found itself."

"Ah, you know that?" this time Tangye looked relieved, "Well, you've guessed why I stayed on. I had come back home intending to ask my wife to help me out. A damned unpleasant errand. And you can imagine my feelings when the interview started in as it did. But I thought I might talk her into a better temper. She was quick-tempered, but placable—as a rule. I found her adamant. I didn't even mention money. It was impossible. And yet I needed it as I've never needed it before in my life. I went back to town, and on Tuesday morning tried to see if I could raise some. But credit in the city is an odd thing. The whisper of O'Malley's difficulties had got about, and no bank would lend. It would have been suicide to borrow privately. My liabilities, since Dublin had let me in, were too high. Now my insurance papers were in my desk at home. I could raise something on them. My wife's policy was there too. In her own writing-table. I decided to raise money on mine, and if I could manage it, on my wife's as well. I paid the premiums on both.

"I drove home without any thought of slipping away unnoticed, but as it happened the commissionaire was busy with a messenger boy as I came out of the alley and never saw me. I decided to leave the car at a turning near Riverview, and let myself into the house quietly. I had no desire to meet Mrs. Tangye. ... I got the documents I wanted. Then I remembered my wife's insurance papers. She kept them in the safe. I ran upstairs, made sure that no one was in our bed-room, and tried the knob. But for once the safe was locked. I went downstairs again. There was no sound in the morning-room. Mrs. Tangye might be out. I slipped into the garden through a side door in my study. Going around to the morning-room, I saw that no light was lit, and that one of the windows was ajar. I felt sure from that that Mrs. Tangye was out. So, switching on the lamp by her desk. I opened it. It was unlocked. The keys were lying on top. The desk was empty except that in the pigeon-hole where she usually kept her policy, was a small pile of account books and papers neatly tied together. Just as I caught sight of one end of the paper I was after, I heard a sound outside the door. I thought it was Mrs. Tangye, and snatching up the packet, I slipped out into the garden again. It was, of course, Miss Saunders who opened the door as I left by the window. She watched me go."—Tangye's hand shook as he lit a cigar.

"There's no doubt about it that my wife must have been sitting dead in that alcove all the time. Florence says she didn't leave the room after four she thinks. It's a horrible thought, but I think it's a true one."

"I think so, too," Pointer agreed soberly. "What did you do then?"

"I slipped out by the tradesmen's gate, and into my car which I'd left at the first turning. Drove to the city and raised in five minutes a little money, though nothing like what I needed. But I had made up my mind what I was going to do with it. I have an acquaintance— Merchant of Merchant Bros., as you seem to know. He's in cotton. We had talked things over on Saturday in Norfolk. He had urged me for once to come in on a speculation. The biggest thing of the last fifty years he called it, and rightly. A few fivers margined at the beginning of this cotton boom might mean thousands at the end. It has. I got the loan, telephoned to Manchester and posted him the cheque. Then I got my car out, took my wife's books back with me, and drove home intending to make things up with her. When I got to Riverview the Superintendent was here, and I was told that Mrs. Tangye was dead.

"The moment you, Superintendent, went upstairs to look over the bedroom, Miss Saunders came into my den." Tangye paused and shot out his lower lip. "She had an envelope in her hands with fifteen hundred pounds in it in bank notes. In a whisper she told me that she had found this envelope lying in Mrs. Tangye's safe. I knew my wife had just sold a farm. I had no idea for how much. There was still time to post the money to Manchester. I thanked her, and decided to pass over her having unlocked the safe without authority. Slipped out of the house and round to the post office. There I telephoned to Merchant's son in the City. He passed my message on to his father, and I posted the notes. On that I returned to the house, to find Miss Saunders sitting here waiting for me. The police had gone. She sat in the chair you're in now, Superintendent." Tangye fixed a meditative eye on the piece of furniture in question.

"It certainly was an unexpected interview. Miss Saunders accused me of shooting my wife. In a way it makes it infinitely more ghastly that I believe she really and truly believes I did fire that shot. Though how she thinks Mrs. Tangye would let herself be picked off like a half-frozen bee! All that stuff she told you was, of course, invention on her part, but I think she believes I murdered Mrs. Tangye, and then lost my head, and left the notes behind me. Well, I saw pretty quickly what a position I was in. I'm bound to say she helped me to see it. There were the insurance policies on which I had raised money. There was the fifteen hundred which I had just posted; by the six-thirty post, too! There was my presence at Riverview—I had no idea then that I hadn't been seen leaving my office. That was pure luck. There was the visit on Sunday to the orchid-show with a lady. There was the quarrel on Monday! It made an ugly story. Miss Saunders didn't slur anything over. She told me that she had cleaned up all marks of my coming in to the morning-room, and closed the windows which I had left, as I found them open. Miss Saunders made me an offer. To back up any story I should tell. To substitute her name for that of the lady who really was with me on Sunday, if I would marry her—Miss Saunders—and give her the promise in writing; at once.

"Otherwise she intended to denounce me. She told me that she would say that she had seen me actually with the pistol in my hand. I'm bound to say she put the wind up me all right. The more I thought it over, the worse it looked. I couldn't make up my mind what to do. Marry that octopus! Penal servitude didn't seem much better, barring of course the disgrace. Then there flashed into my mind a bottle of vanishing ink I'd seen in Vardon's rooms only a fortnight before. It looked just like the regular stuff, only it wouldn't last a fortnight. He had won it on shipboard as a booby prize, he told me. It's common stuff in every South American stationer's."

Pointer thought of his wasted efforts.

"I 'phoned up to find if he was in. He wasn't. But I decided to try for that ink all the same. It meant salvation to me.

"I told Miss Saunders I would pick her up just over Richmond Bridge, and take her along to my office where my head clerk was still busy, I told her he could be depended on not to talk, and that I would write her a marriage promise there. I took my wife's papers off with me again—I couldn't put them back in her desk after, the police had been over it—and drove around to Vardon's, then I made an excuse that I must run up and tell him of the accident. But the ink was gone. He'd given it to a friend only a couple of days before, I've since learnt. There was no help for it. We went on to my office. There I wrote out an agreement which she read through and tightened up. She put it inside her dress and went back alone to Riverview. She told me, by the way, with that engaging frankness which is one of her most amiable characteristics, that the paper would be kept in its sealed envelope by her legal advisor, whoever that exalted personage may be. This was evidently a warning that it would be no use for me to murder her to get it back. I noticed, as possibly you did, that she refused to spend any night at Riverview?"

"We noticed it," Pointer said with a faint smile. There was a pause.

"Thank you, sir, for being so frank. If all goes well, you'll be able to snap your fingers at that paper. It was practically blackmail. Now at the orchid-show did you see Mrs. Tangye?"

"Not I! I hadn't the shadow of an idea that she was there until I ran into Miss Eden by chance. She told me of Mrs. Tangye's having seen me and my companion. And of her having looked terribly upset. I pooh-poohed the idea that she should mind. Naturally it wasn't what I should have chosen. But a flower-show! After all a flower-show! Second to being seen at a picture gallery I should have thought. Miss Eden, however, warned me that my wife was terribly upset. I didn't believe her. But I decided it might be as well not to linger. A meeting might have been most awkward. So the lady and I left. Next day came the quarrel. I think that's the circle complete!"

Pointer thought a moment.

"And how did you get hold of Mrs. Tangye's keys?"

"Miss Saunders handed them to me. While we were in the car driving to Vardon's. I must have been ass enough to drop them in his rooms when I tried to open a bookcase. I don't remember what became of them, so I suppose I left them lying on his table. You see, at the time I thought them of no importance. Then came the discovery of that missing, or rather unentered-money. I confess I thought that Miss Saunders had taken it, and only handed me the half. 'Pon my word, I hoped as much. I wish to Heaven she could be jailed, but I suppose there's no chance of that?"

Pointer did not enter into that pious hope. There was a little silence.

"I want to say one thing more." Tangye spoke very earnestly. "I want to say it solemnly; you're making a mistake, Chief Inspector. There's no crime here. Mrs. Tangye fired that shot herself. That I swear."

"And that I believe," Wilmot said simply.

"Firmly?" asked Haviland.

"I have intervals of doubt," Wilmot confessed, "but I find myself always swinging back to my original, and your original, belief."

"You found the French windows open?" Pointer asked their host.

"Ajar. Since learning of your suspicions of foul play I've searched my mind most anxiously, and there wasn't a footprint or any sign of disturbance as of any one else having been in the room," Tangye said, very thoughtfully. "My wife's chair was out of sight, back in the alcove hidden by that screen, but the other chair was in full view. Even the cushion on it was all plump and smooth. No sign of any one having sat in it."

There was a pause.

"Miss Saunders cleaned the door of the safe after opening it, I suppose?"

"Trust her!"

"And, since we are clearing up these various details, what became of the Lux camera you took with you to Tunbridge on Sunday?"

Tangye seemed bewildered.

"Lux camera? Oh—h—? I left it at the orchid show. Lost it. It was a present to the lady who was with me. I was carrying it for her and showing her how to use it, when she caught sight of some friends and went off to speak to them; I stayed behind trying it on some plants. That was when Miss Eden ran into me. I put it down beside us on the rustic bench we sat on to talk, and forgot the damned thing. It was never wanted again. Mrs. Bligh seemed to have lost all her interest in photography when I saw her next, and told her that I had just discovered what I must have done. I was thankful to be spared making any inquiries down at the show. Naturally, after Mrs. Tangye's death, the very name sickened me."

Pointer had had his own inquiries made since learning from Mrs. Bligh's maid of the camera's disappearance. It had not been seen. If Tangye's story was true, some one had "annexed" it.

"There's one other thing I wish to say," Tangye said as his guests rose to go. "I have withdrawn all opposition to the probating of that will that Mrs. Tangye signed the Monday before she died."

"You think it's genuine?" Haviland frowned. He did not.

"I always held that Vardon had a right to the land. As to the money—I have no wish to hand over the sum in question to the lawyers. Vardon agrees to leave it in my firm. They would not," was the laconic reply.

"And your wife's notice of withdrawal of her funds?"

Tangye's face darkened. "A cursed unfair and vindictive thing of her to want to do. I can't understand it. Except that the poor girl really was off her head."

"You knew of the notice?"

"Stewart gave me the note when you telephoned him for an interview. Lest you should ask. ... I destroyed it."

Tangye still looked black. Evidently he had not forgiven his wife for that letter. Pointer thought that its existence had gone far to make Tangye take her death as he had done.

There was a short silence in the police car that Pointer was driving.

"Vardon's luck seems too good to last," Haviland spoke crossly. "And that's a fact! First he gets the fifteen hundred pounds handed him and no questions asked. Then a will is found on him giving him ten thousand in cash and close on that in land—and still no questions to be asked."

"It does make one wonder!"

"Whether he is Tangye's friend and accomplice?" mused Wilmot. "I've never had so fascinating a problem to ponder. No murder, I still think. Yes, in spite of the great Hart discovery. At least I think I think so. But there certainly is an intricate shadow-dance here, which is vastly interesting."

"Quite apart from the rest of his story, I shouldn't wonder if Mrs. Tangye might not have told Tangye the truth about meeting Hart on Sunday, if it hadn't been for seeing Mrs. Bligh with him down at Tunbridge." The Chief Inspector had been pursuing his own thoughts.

"You speak as though an assumption were the same as a fact," Wilmot's tone had something of bewilderment in it, "you assume Hart's still alive. Without a shred of evidence to back that assumption you go on to imagine him as having been at Tunbridge on Sunday, and at Riverview, Monday and Tuesday. My dear chap, you can't expect a logical mind to assume so much. You might equally well argue that Headly *pere* was not really dead, and that it was him she saw, and so on. . . ."

"But if Hart's Vardon, Mr. Wilmot, then he becomes a fact," Haviland pointed out, as he got down at his police station. He wondered why the other two laughed.

CHAPTER SIXTEEN

THE day after Pointer had searched Newport without finding a trace of the Hart's home-circle, Barbara arrived at that bustling town.

She had spent the time coming down in the train in thought.

There were only two things about Mrs. Tangye which marked her out from all the other women whom Barbara knew. Her salmon fishing, a little. Her love of duets, very decidedly. Mrs. Tangye had once spoken as though she had always played them, even as a little girl.

W. Griffith was the name of the best music shop in Newport, she was told at a stationer's where she inquired if such a firm still existed.

Leaving Olive to paddle along the sands, and try to swim in a foot of water, Barbara set off down Cathedral Street. How to begin? To enter a shop and merely ask if they had ever supplied music to a Miss Headly, might not lead far.

Barbara was very nervous when she finally decided on what to say. She entered the shop, therefore, with an air of defiant self-possession.

"I want to get hold of some duets that used to be popular years ago," she told the pleasant-faced, elderly man who came forward. "I'm a nurse"; she flushed to the brim of her hat, as though the profession were a blot on any family "and I have a patient," she forced herself to say, "who used to love playing duets. I think it might help her—it's a mental case—if she could get hold again of some of the very ones she used to play with a friend, a Miss Headly. I should of course, expect to pay specially for them. Have you been here long?"

"We've been established here since Naseby."

"She lived in this part of the world, and so did her friend. And she got some at least of her music from you."

"She would naturally," the man said with conscious pride. "You'd have to go to *Caer* to get a music-seller of the same class. If she went in for duets, you may be sure she got them from us. Here, at this very counter."

Barbara slipped a "refresher" across the said counter, and after the proper expostulation it vanished.

"Years ago, you think? I ought to be able to help you. My memory's a fine one, if I do say it. And we don't have many people asking for duets nowadays. We didn't then. I can't call to mind any one but Mrs. Hart. Not as a regular thing."

Barbara was disappointed.

"Hart? Headly, Miss Headly was the name of my patient's friend. It was she who used to do the music buying, I believe."

Headly conveyed nothing to the shopman, and he said so. "Beautiful player was Mrs. Hart," he rambled on, "knew about music. Kept abreast of things. Loss to the whole town when that sad accident happened. She was drowned just outside that sandbar over there. Handsome, young lady. Carried herself like a guardsman. Fine at salmon fishing too. I think she was good at anything she did. And quick with her wits as with her fingers. Looked like one of us, not like a foreigner—eh, I mean an Englishwoman."

"Dark?"

"Dark and dashing, I might say," the man spoke sentimentally.

"And drowned?"

"Drowned thirteen years ago. We none of us know what's ahead of us. I always say that if we did, half of us would go off our heads."

That seemed a nice, healthy way of looking at life to Barbara. This drowned woman could not possibly be Mrs. Tangye. Obviously. Yet, some things fitted. General age. Love of duets. Salmon fishing. Appearance. Could Mrs.

Tangye have had a sister after all? Or was this merely a chance resemblance?

Barbara listened to a long-winded account of the accident. To her it settled the matter. Then she pricked up her ears again.

"Both she and her husband had come down in the world. So he said. I don't know about him. Though he was the sort that's bound to sink. But it was true enough of her. She was a lady. Parson's daughter. Had an aunt a lady of title, so he used to brag."

Parson's daughter? Titled aunt? But drowned?

"Was she left-handed, by any chance?"

"I don't remember. I wouldn't notice that, you see, when she was playing."

Barbara got him to give her the address of a little dairy shop above which the Hart's had lived. The salesman had often spent an evening there. "In the beginning," he was careful to add.

The address in question turned out to be a small milk shop in a backwater. It was a neat affair, with a snowy marble counter, white new-laid eggs, jars of honey arranged in a golden pyramid, and a shining bowl of milk with a silver cover from which to serve customers.

All looked spotless. So did Mr. Pringle who was just about to serve a dirty urchin. The boy handed over a smutty jug. Pringle filled it casually with a funnel clean as a whistle. The surplus of milk ran cheerfully down the dirty handle just now held by the grimy fingers, and back into the gleaming bowl. By the time this would have been repeated many times, Barbara wondered what the last customer bought.

Courageously she asked for a glass from it, however, and sat down to chat. She was passing through Newport, she told the man, and wanted to learn some facts about friends of friends of hers. Called Hart. They used to live here fourteen or so so years ago. Could he tell her anything about them?

"I can, Miss," Pringle spoke with the pride of the local

bard, "they lodged here with us, being English like us. Niceish young couple. At least she was. He wasn't worthy of her. I hopes I'm not paining you, but if you know about him—why, you do! They was drowned in a terrible squall —as I suppose you've heard?"

Barbara said she had.

"It was very terrible," she added, "I believe she was quite young, and a very handsome girl."

"Very handsome. As to young—she would be only about twenty I suppose."

"Were they—was she married here in Newport?" Barbara did not know what to ask. Clearly the drowned Mrs. Hart could not be the alive and later married Miss Headly. But yet. . . .

"No, miss. They was married before they came. Only just married, and already unhappy. Incompatibles, that was what they were. And you can't expect two things that don't go together, to go together," Mr. Pringle said wisely. "Milk and vinegar now. It's no use saying prayers over milk and vinegar. They're bound to part sooner or later. Because people are joined in church don't make 'em one. My wife she don't hold with me, but I goes by what I sees. Not by what I hears."

"What was Mr. Hart like?"

"Black-tempered man. Dark blight was his way when things went wrong. Didn't speak out, only had a look in his eyes and a pinch of his lips that meant bitter words when they should be alone together. Some said he drank. He was always out of the shop and upstairs locked in his little room. I don't say she never brought trouble on herself. She had a high spirit. And quick with her tongue too. But the poor girl hadn't a dog's chance with him. Not a dog's chance. My wife she liked Hart. But I was sorry for her."

"I suppose she was the Mable Hart my friends knew? Was her name Headly before her marriage?"

"Her first name was Mable. We didn't know her family name. Never learnt it. She—well—she didn't dare trust herself to talk of her home. That's how it struck me. But there couldn't have been two Mable Harts living in Newport, and both drown the same night. Could there, miss?"

Barbara agreed. She thought the existence of one quite enough of an enigma.

"Irving Hart was his name. Some relation to Lord Irving, he told us. But I noticed she never said no such stuff."

Barbara wished that she had been prepared for this interview, and the one before it at the music-shop. She was fearful of blundering. Her mind in a whirl. She drew out a photograph of Mrs. Tangye.

"This is a cousin of Mrs. Hart's. She's very like the one you used to know, I believe. I'm going to leave the photograph to be enlarged at a shop near here, that's how I have it by me."

Barbara felt that she was growing into a frightful liar. And possibly—probably—no, certainly, all to no good.

"Like Mrs. Hart?" the man sniffed. "Why, this one might be t'other's mother." He checked himself and looked more carefully at it. "Of course, fifteen years— But Mrs. Hart was a slender, tall slip of a girl. . . . Still, of course, fifteen years— Mother!" he called to the rear of the shop. Mrs. Pringle appeared and looked curiously at the portrait.

"Why it's the very spit of Mrs. Hart! As she would be if she'd lived till now, poor soul. When they was both young girls, she must have been as like our Mrs. Hart as one pea's like another. I say 'our Mrs. Hart' but I ought to say your Mrs. Hart." She turned to her husband. "You always had a soft spot in your heart for her, Tom. I was sorrier for her husband. Nasty temper she had, when she thought things weren't as they should be. Oh, yes, she had, Tom. And just being drowned doesn't turn her into an angel. Or what's the use of having to go to church and keep oneself respectable here, if that's all there is to it? Not that we ever saw her at her best, poor dear." The woman's face softened as she handed the photograph of "the cousin" back to Barbara. "Things went from bad to worse with them. Her money too, it was. Born to better things she was, as her underwear showed clearly. A parson's daughter she was, and though Tom and I are Wesleyans, we're broad-minded. And played the piano something beautiful. She kept her piano as long as she could. Used to play duets with her husband at first. He could play as well as he could sing."

"Was *he* a parson's son?" Barbara asked by way of reaching this mysterious husband of the mysterious, inexplicable Mrs. Hart.

"Not much!" came from Pringle. "Common! No class at all!"

"You're all wrong, Tom," Mrs. Pringle was indignant. "I don't say as he behaved right. I mean about money-matters, but he was a gentleman—or better!" Mrs. Pringle lowered her voice mysteriously, "I think he was something better still. You don't seem to know about him, miss?"

Barbara said that her friends had only known Mrs. Hart before her marriage and knew nothing whatever of the husband.

"*I* think he didn't dare ask his father for help," Mrs. Pringle went on.

Pringle's sniff said what he thought.

"Poor thing! She did scrape, and save, and pinch," Mrs. Pringle spoke with real pity now. "And then to get drowned, both of 'em, like rats in a trap! It do seem hard! What might her name have been before she married, miss?"

"Headly. Mable Headly."

"There now! I said to Tom all her things was marked M. H., though I was sure they was older than her marriage. Changed her name and not her letter. Unlucky, isn't it, miss."

Again Barbara agreed. Still all at sea. Still half dazed as to where Mrs. Hart ended, and Mrs. Tangye began.

They must be one. But how could they be? Why should they be?"

"Have you a portrait of him? I should like to see one," Barbara asked after a little pause during which she sipped her milk.

"There now! If you'd only come last week, miss. My brother'd have shown you a fine one. Taking a family group of Tom and me and our daughter Nest we was, one day on the front step, when the door behind us opened, and Mr. Hart walked right into the middle of us. Just as we was all looking pleasant, and my brother was pressing the bulb. So he got took too and never knew it. The trouble came just then."

"Owed everybody right and left." Pringle explained. "We'd never have been paid up, neither, if it hadn't been for Mrs. Hart. The very last thing she did, miss, was to settle for everything. Paid it the evening of the storm. Just before she hurried down to the cove. And when I seed her little watch with the pearls around it hanging in Jones' window, I knew where she got the money from."

"Oh, don't, Tom!" broke in Mrs. Pringle in great distress. "I can't abide to hear you tell that. She loved that watch. Present from her auntie, she once let slip. I'm sure we wouldn't have cared if she'd let things run on a bit longer."

"They couldn't have run on, mother; not much longer. What would Mrs. Hart have done then? She'd have died of it."

"I wish I could see that photograph of Mr. Hart," Barbara said finally.

"I'll write and ask my brother to send me a copy. If you're staying on here, and like to drop in some time next week. . . ."

Barbara said that would be very kind, and promptly asked Mr. and Mrs. Pringle to come to the theatre with her that night.

On her return from the play, Barbara got little sleep. Yet the whole story as she saw it, was simple. Mrs.

Tangye had escaped from the storm which had drowned her husband, and had taken up life again as Miss Headly. Doubtless Mr. Branscombe and Mr. Tangye knew the truth. Barbara's interest in Hart was merely curiosity and a vague hope that the Chief Inspector might be able to make some use of the fact of his existence. She had not learnt anything that mattered, so she thought.

She even felt very ashamed of having listened to so much gossip. After all, whether Mrs. Tangye had been married twice, or three times, could only concern herself and her own circle.

Barbara found it impossible next day to learn more of the Harts. The only people she could hear of who had known the young couple remained the Pringles, and the salesman at the music-shop. It had not been worth coming for. Hart's picture, she would, of course, hand on at once to Pointer, but what good would that do? When two more days passed with no result, she decided not even to wait for it, though Mrs. Pringle had asked her brother to print Barbara an enlargement of his copy, and had promised to send it to her hotel on this, the third day. Saddened, bitterly disappointed, she and Olive returned to town. She decided, however, on the way up to tell at once what she had learnt, and what she had failed to learn, to the man in charge of the investigations. She was surprised to find how much reliance she placed on Pointer. Though she remained a little afraid of him since that interview in her grandfather's office. But she felt sure that he would never let the truth down. And she must—she must learn the truth! The sooner her tale was told the Chief Inspector the sooner she could tackle some other point in Mrs. Tangye's life. Some point which would perhaps yield something worth learning.

Her grandfather was down in the country, as he called Wimbledon, drawing up an old lady's monthly will. Pointer was not at New Scotland Yard she was told in reply to a telephoned inquiry. As a matter of fact, Pointer was just then on his way to meet Vardon's train, and conduct him to the buffet where the choirmaster from Newport sat drinking endless cups of coffee out of his own thermos flask, and within arms' length of three waitresses who had been duly propitiated.

She tried for Haviland. Haviland was not in his police station. But she finally found Wilmot in. He told her that he would be pleased to either see her at his flat, or meet her anywhere she wished.

Barbara chose his rooms, and hustling Olive into a taxi drove to them.

She ran up the stairs, and was hardly in Wilmot's spacious, beautifully reticent rooms, before she poured out what she had found and what she so tremendously regretted not having found in Wales.

Wilmot listened with breathless interest.

"You've done splendidly!" he told her warmly. Somewhat to her surprise. "And the photograph?" Even he looked keenly interested as he held out his hand.

"It's to be posted on to me from the hotel. I left my address. It'll be here to-night, or to-morrow morning." She branched off to again ask whether that first marriage would in any way help to orient the inquiry into the dead woman's past.

But Wilmot considered the portrait the greatest stride which the case had yet made towards a solution.

"We must get into touch with the Chief Inspector," he reached for his telephone under a beautiful old lacquer bell. Barbara told him that she had asked in vain for Pointer at Scotland Yard or at his own home. None the less Wilmot tried his luck too.

"Out. They don't know when he'll be back. This is awkward!"

He stood with pursed lips. What steps ought he to take? How to act quickly and yet most efficaciously? He did not want Pointer to come upon some ill-considered, hastily carried out decision. Wilmot prided himself on always making the best possible use of any information which he received.

"The Assistant Commissioner has just rung me up to ask if by chance he were here. It seems that the Yard have traced a Hart, a brother of Irving Hart's. He seems to be a sort of secretary, or assistant to a Professor Orison. I don't know if you've ever heard the name?"

"Professor Orison? Oh yes. I heard a lecture of his once, in what I suppose he called English. But this brother —you think he may be of help?"

Barbara thought Wilmot was attaching undue importance to what was, after all, an old, finished item of Mrs. Tangye's past.

Wilmot did not care to explain just what the photograph might really mean.

"The trouble is this brother is off for Berlin to-night. And the Yard doesn't know whether Pointer wants him stopped or not. An awkward thing to blunder just now. It's Pointer's case, you see." Wilmot stood a second looking irresolutely at the girl.

"Can't I help? Oh, Mr. Wilmot, please don't shunt me! For Phil's sake—for the sake of bringing Mrs. Tangye's murderer to justice, I'd do anything! Anything!"

He came closer and looked at her keenly.

"I believe you would I" he said encouragingly. "Splendid!" He thought for half a second. "Yes, that's the best thing to do. You go to Professor Orison's house. This man Hart isn't there. We've just telephoned to the Professor to ask. He says he's doing some home work, and that he doesn't expect to see him till to-morrow. But should Hart suddenly go there while I'm looking him up down where he lives in Bloomsbury, you'll be on hand. You might get some facts from him. You'll be safe in speaking quite openly to him."

"And what about Olive? She's down below in the taxi."

Again Wilmot reflected for a second.

"We'll take her along in my car! She might come in useful for sending a message, or whatever maids do come in for." He finished vaguely. He was in a tearing hurry, and Barbara caught his spirit of rush. Of things drawing to a climax. But he made time for two things.

"I must leave a line to tell Pointer what we're after. And send a message to the same effect to the Yard."

And, in spite of her impatience, he scribbled a note, slipped it in an envelope, addressed it to Pointer, and left it conspicuously on his table. Then he turned to his 'phone, and Barbara heard the code word for the C.I.D. of Scotland Yard.

"Tell Chief Inspector Pointer that Miss Ash and I are going to see this Hart at once. She to Professor Orison's house, and I to his lodgings in Bloomsbury. Leave this message at every place where Inspector Pointer may call."

A moment more and he was running beside her down the stairs.

In his car he rattled on in the highest spirits. Barbara had never seen Wilmot on the war-path before. This was Wilmot, the great reporter. Wilmot of the War.

"I'll come with you to Professor Orison's to make sure Hart isn't in the house. Then I'll taxi on to him, and wait till Pointer joins me. He wont be long. If you, meanwhile will be kind enough to stay at the Professor's till I 'phone you—half an hour should settle everything. The lower rooms in his house are a sort of Polish museum, you know. Ever been there?"

Barbara never had.

"I've heard it's jolly good. Scotland Yard, in its note, said that Hart, when he's there, acts as showman; when he's away, the Professor sometimes takes a hand himself. If he does, try to get him to talk about Hart. You may pick up something about the family. Where Hart came from, and so on. Say you think you knew a sister-in-law of his."

Barbara bit her lip. She felt that she only understood a very small part of the real story, and yet would have to act as though she knew all. Few positions are more hobbling to an intelligent person.

"Can't you explain a little more about why Mr. Hart

matters?"

"I know that you won't mind if I say that that's for Chief Inspector Pointer to do. It's his case. I don't know how much he wants suppressed, how much told."

Barbara nodded. She quite understood. Handicapped though she would be, if she got a chance, she would do her best.

Wilmot stopped in front of a narrow, black and white house. A tall, repellent-faced woman answered the bell.

"Is Mr. Hart—Professor Orison's secretary—in?" Wilmot inquired.

"No, sir. The Professor is in though."

"Oh, thank you—no need to trouble him. The collection is on view, isn't it?" Wilmot asked pleasantly.

"Till seven o'clock, sir." The woman stood aside.

Wilmot hurried back to the cab, and was off round the nearest corner. Just as the woman was closing the door, Olive shivered violently.

"I'm cold, that's all, miss. Must have caught a chill," she answered to Barbara's inquiring look as they followed the woman into a large, panelled room filled chiefly with weapons more or less interesting, running from Batory to Langiewicz. They were left alone. The next room had a press of Zainer incunabula, some interesting *siiletcsiki* cartoons, and a complete set of Polish stamps.

Barbara roamed the rooms restlessly, seeing nothing. Why was Hart thrust so much in the foreground? Wilmot evidently knew of him as Mrs. Tangye's first husband, and of his death. Why was the photograph of a man drowned thirteen years ago so important?"

Suddenly Olive gave a low cry. It was not loud, but it brought Barbara to her feet with prickling skin.

"What's the matter?" she asked tensely.

"The steps!" Olive was on her feet too. Listening in a strange attitude that seemed to flinch back even as it bent forward.

"The footsteps! The footsteps that stopped! They've stopped again on the landing above us. I knew! I smelled death! They're coming in! They're coming in! They won't stop this time. Oh, Miss Barbara, run—run! They're coming for us!"

The girl fell on to a seat in what Barbara thought was a faint. But it was something deeper than that. She herself was entirely unaffected by the girl's mad words, though the tone of horror had startled her. Had she had a clue to them, it might have been different.

The door opened, and an old man, with thick white hair and eyebrows, and a skin so wrinkled that he looked like a deflated balloon, came into the room, bowing politely.

"Did I hear some one call? I am Professor Orison and—is your young friend ill?" He broke off. "The air is somewhat stuffy in here, I am afraid. It is impossible to open a window without admitting smuts."

Barbara would have recognised the Professor again without having heard his name. His was neither an appearance nor an accent to be mistaken.

He rang the bell.

"Let me assist you and my housekeeper to carry her upstairs into an airier room."

Olive was taken up to a neat, simple bedroom on the floor above. It was a warm, prepossessing room, and on his advice they laid the girl down on the bed without making further efforts to revive her.

"Leave that to nature." The professor felt the girl's pulse. "I have some trifling knowledge of medicine. Enough to know a case of fatigue, and a chill after insufficient food. She will be better if left alone—in perfect quiet. There is such a thing as mental noise and rush," he added, smiling gently, as Barbara lingered. "Thoughts can disturb."

Barbara told him that Olive had had a great shock recently.

"Just so. Deranged nerves. Let her be by herself in this darkened room, and I guarantee that when you look in again in half an hour's time, she will be sleeping quietly, and can then be wakened without any danger. Wakened to have a cup of tea, I should suggest, which my housekeeper prepares very well. Now, if you like to come back with me to the rooms below I think I may be able to make them a little more interesting than they were without explanations. My secretary unfortunately is not here for another hour or so. He has a better command of English than I."

Barbara followed him out of the room and down below. She liked Professor Orison, and was keen to question him about Hart.

CHAPTER SEVENTEEN

OLIVE woke up as the door shut behind Barbara and the Professor. She woke up absolutely clear in her mind, not as one coming out of a faint. It was more as though her spirit had been away receiving definite instructions, given a certain part to carry through.

She flung aside the down quilt, and got up noiselessly.

The voices of Barbara and the Professor could be heard chatting pleasantly together as they went down the stairs, and then stopped as they shut the door behind them.

Olive leant against the wall in a sudden access, not of fear, but of knowledge. Knowledge of evil. Certainty of danger. Whether from the Professor, or his housekeeper, or from some other source, this house was no place for herself or for Barbara Ash. Some imminent peril menaced both. She even felt certain of the extent of the danger.

It was death by violence that was so close to them.

She slipped, bareheaded as she was, for they had taken off her hat, down to the floor below. She was just stealthily turning the Yale lock of the front door when the room beside it opened, and the housekeeper put out her head.

"Sh-h!" Olive whispered. "I'm off to the pub for a drink. My young lady's temperance, so mum's the word. I'll bring back a bottle of sommat warming for you too."

The woman leered at her.

"I thought that faint of yours was a bit deep. Mind you don't stay out too long."

"Trust me!" Olive whispered.

"Better let me turn that knob for you. There's a trick to it. I'll leave it on the latch for you. Mind you don't forget the bottle. Make it gin, dearie, make it gin."

Down the little path to the gate Olive hurried. Leaving it open she raced headlong to the corner; a mongrel in the next garden was barking his envy, he was so tired of his own little patch of lawn.

At the corner a constable stood talking to two men in tweeds. One tall, one medium. Olive put all her strength into a last spurt.

"Inspector Pointer! Help! Miss Barbara. . . . Oh, you're too late! Too late!"

Pointer had wheeled at the first sight of the flying figure. He had run to meet the girl, "The end house?"

Olive nodded.

The end house was Professor Orison's. It was the only gate that stood open. Pointer did not wait to hear more. Nor did Vardon.

The Chief Inspector had played for all England. The first forward of his time. But he had never run as he ran now. Vardon was close at his heels. The constable brought up the rear helping Olive along.

Pointer jumped the steps, and thundered out a true policeman's knock with the wrought iron knocker before he flung the door open. He wanted all within the house to know that the Law was at hand. It was a knock to make any evil-doer pause.

From far above him he heard another kind of pounding as though some one were beating on the door of a locked room.

As Pointer rushed into the hall, the housekeeper shrank back fearfully into a doorway.

"Whatever is the matter?" she quavered. "First the maid runs off. Then the young lady runs out into the garden and clambers over the wall, and the master after her. Giving me a blow on the chest in passing that knocked the breath out of me."

Far overhead, the sound of knocking and banging continued.

Pointer, a hand on her arm, ran her out to the back. He did not intend to leave her alone, and the constable with Olive were still in the street. Vardon was flying up the stairs, three at a time, calling:

"Barbara! Where are you? It's me—Philip!"

There was a small garden, mostly paved with stone and with herbaceous borders. The three walls were covered with ivy. Pointer gave one swift look about him. A knowledgeable look, then he turned. No person, man or woman, had clambered over those plants or scrambled over those leaves. There was no way out except through the house.

He wasted no words on the woman. But dropped her with the constable who had now arrived with Olive. The young man was evidently not quite sure whether the girl was under arrest or not. Another policeman came hurrying up.

"Olive! Which room?" Pointer asked.

"I don't know! I don't know where she went to!"

Pointer had only waited for her first sentence.

"Watch this woman," he thrust the housekeeper into a chair. "Come on upstairs, one of you men."

He leaped up them himself, to find in a top bedroom an amazed Vardon staring at a bent old gentleman with a wild head of white hair. He was tied to his chair, and a towel made a very good gag. The noise they had heard was the legs of his chair which he had rocked violently to and fro on the wooden floor.

Pointer rushed into the next room. And into the ones beyond. Then he was back again. The second constable at his heels, while Vardon sawed at Professor Orison's gag.

"He may know something. Have you seen anything of a young lady? Quick! It's touch and go!" Vardon asked.

"Robbery! My collection!" yelled the Professor, thrusting him aside and trying to rise. "My Post Office Mauritius —the fourteenth of its kind—"

By this time Pointer was on the floor below. He sent the second constable up to look after Orison.

"Finish untying him, and stay with him till I call you."

Vardon joined Pointer, and began moving heavy

couches, peering into wardrobes, crawling under beds. He worked like a man possessed.

As for Pointer, one dart into each room, a glance in each object of a size to hide a body, and he was out again.

Running up from the basement to the ground floor, he found Olive staring blindly about her with distended eyes.

"The footsteps! I knew when they stopped! Oh, Miss Barby—dear Miss Barby! I heard them come into this room. . . ."

Vardon rushed down to them. He turned despairingly to Pointer.

"You say she didn't leave by the back door. We had the front one in sight from the corner. Then where is she? For God's sake find her! I can't I"

Vardon's face looked old, and white, and fallen in.

Never in all Pointer's life had so awful a responsibility been his. For Barbara was in the house—according to Olive, and he believed the girl—yet he could not find her. To really search that house, any house, to tap the walls, examine the floors, would take hours. Hours! And every second here was vital.

Vardon, in his own anguish—almost beyond bearing—thought the Chief Inspector looked unperturbed. But it was years before this late afternoon in November ceased to haunt Pointer.

Another man might have tried this—thought that—believed some other thing; but Pointer knew. He knew that Barbara Ash was beyond human aid. And, had things been different, Pointer could have loved Barbara.

The dog next door began to bark again furiously. The constable in charge of the housekeeper in the hall opened the front door to look out, his hand on the woman's arm. The dog's master had returned.

Even in his dash to the house Pointer had placed the mongrel as a lurcher. The gypsy's and the poacher's dog. Bred for the unbelievable quickness of its scenting powers, its skill in finding, its intelligence.

Pointer, using a chairback as a pole, hurled himself across the room, the hall, through the door and down the steps. He vaulted the railing between the two houses.

"There's a girl missing. She's in that house. Your dog . . . It's life or death."

The man, young and wiry, dashed back with him, the dog one streak beside him, his gray-hound blood to the fore.

"Here!" Pointer stopped him in the print-room, the one which Olive had heard Babara enter.

"We think she's been concealed somewhere. In the walls or a secret cupboard."

Like master, like dog; the lurcher was all eagerness.

"Find her, Pal! Seek! Seek! Find her!" said his master, setting his own mind intently to grip the dog's mind. Pointer and Vardon were doing the same. Every nerve in their bodies was with the dog, in some ways the cleverest beast that lives, who stood for the barest second with one paw lifted. Then he made straight for a wall, and stretching down between his front paws, nosed between them. In a second, Pointer, Vardon, and his master, had flung aside the five-foot broad bookcase which stood in no wise different from the other cases ranged at regular intervals around the room. Behind it the wall looked unbroken. But Pointer ran his finger nails along the panelling. Pulling, not pressing. Suddenly the whole panel moved towards him. As he hoped, some one had been in too great a hurry to dose the secret door absolutely true on to its invisible catch. One pressure of a clumsy hand, and all would have been lost.

Inside, hanging to a bracket, was something like a bag— something covered with a brown cloth—it was Barbara.

Olive fainted.

They cut Barbara down, and laid her on the floor. The dog whimpered unheeded as he licked one hand clenched in agony.

Every village constable is instructed in how to bring

people back to consciousness.

"Schaefer's method, I see. I'm in the R.A.F. Can I help?" The dog's master looked serviceable.

"You work that arm. You, that one, Vardon. Now, in time to my counts!" Pointer dug his fingers beneath Barbara's young ribs. Fortunately nowdays no time has to be lost in taking off bodices, and cutting laces.

Pointer, while he worked, called out some instructions to the constable in the hall. Among other orders, the man was to telephone for a doctor.

Rhythmically, quietly, they worked over the girl. Giles, the flying man, changing places with Pointer every five minutes. As for Olive, when she came to herself again, she crouched in a corner, huddled and shivering.

A quarter of an hour passed.

Pointer felt his very heart turning cold. The bloated mask that was Barbara's face was taking on a set look. The terrible purple colour seemed growing more fixed. The swollen lips had fallen still further apart. The whole body of the young girl seemed heavier, less flexible.

The other saw the change too. The R.A.F. man was biting his lips. Vardon's face was too agonised to look at. He was working quietly, obediently, desperately, but he was sobbing now under his whistling breath.

Pointer handed him the arm which he was flexing and turned away. He tore out one of the big, plain, silver, cufflinks he wore. Silver, so that no thief should be tempted to steal them. With a turn of the link he unscrewed one lozenge-shaped end. Inside it, was what looked like a compressed cocoon. Pointer ripped it open with a touch of his penknife. Within was something wrapped in a leaf. Still faintly green. Pointer unfolded it.

It was a fresh *Guru* nut in a tiny lotus leaf once wet with lotus dew. A slave's ransom among the Senussi. Five of them a princess's dower. A Sheik had given it to Pointer in gratitude for timely help. Pointer now crushed it with the handle of his knife. He laid the crumbs on the girl's black tongue and kept the mouth gently shut. Then it was his turn to relieve Giles.

Five minutes passed. Vardon gave a cry. The lips beneath his hand had trembled and tried to close. Another second and the colour of Barbara's face changed from blue-red to white which slowly turned creamy. The eyes, though bloodshot were back in their sockets now, and the lids covered them softly. Still another minute and they lifted again. Barbara looked at Vardon. A look that he never forgot, though he never quite fathomed it. Confidence and love were in it, and something humble. Something that mutely asked forgiveness. For Barbara came back to consciousness with the certainty as to Vardon's innocence of Mrs. Tangye's death shining like a great light within her heart. She knew at last, by some conviction of the soul, some telepathy of the spirit, that, whoever might be guilty, it was not he.

Vardon had got her into his arms, her head was lying against his breast. What he murmured to her, those around did not have to forget, they did not hear it, so disconnecting is great excitement.

They learnt afterwards that by chance the cord around her neck had been pulled tight in such a way that she had been garotted. The chief pressure had not come on her windpipe, or there would have been no chance of saving her.

Pointer called in the constable from the telephone. The man had been recording an unbroken series of blanks. A great medical congress was on, the Chief Inspector now remembered, and every qualified man would be at it.

Pointer took his place, called up Scotland Yard, and rattle off a code order. Then he slammed down the receiver, and hurried back into the room.

Barbara was sitting up and trying to speak. Pointer thought that she had better be given no stimulant after that nut, but he suggested that she should be carried into the next room, where there was a roaring fire, and where incidentally, the Professor had been trying to extract information from an imperturbable but dumbfounded constable. Barbara croaked out a refusal to be carried, and insisted on walking, though Vardon kept his arm around her and Giles crooked an elbow to be used if wanted. Pal barked his joy. He liked girls, and in some way he felt that this one belonged to him.

Pointer detained his master, and handed him his official card when they were alone.

"We owe you and your dog—" Pointer's voice shook. For once, the Chief Inspector could not finish a sentence. Another three minutes, and not all the *Guru* nuts in the world could have saved Barbara.

Giles whistled the lurcher to him. "He's not much to look at, or rather he's too much. But I've always been glad I stole him—saving your presence—as a pup from a drunken tinker, who was beating him to death. He gave his greyhound-collie-airedale-retriever-setter-spaniel a friendly smack.

"Thanks so much for asking us to your party," he said prettily, and the detective officer laughed, glad of the relief to the tension of the past few minutes, "but Pal and I mustn't stay longer. We promised mother to be back early."

"If ever you're in a tight place, Mr. Giles, you call on me!" Pointer showed him to the door. There was a fog outside, growing thicker every minute.

The meeting between Barbara and the Professor was almost amusing.

The Professor stared in feeble bewilderment, and listened to her story in something like a frenzy of weakness and excitement.

Her tale was brief.

She did not recollect what had happened to her beyond that, as she was bending over a tattered Zainer, something—it was a brown clothes bag from an upper room—had been pulled over her head from behind, its cord drawn tight by an unseen hand. She had felt first as though hit by a flash of light, and then, as though dropping through endless space into darkness. Unconsciousness had come at once.

"But when—what time?" Orison shrilled, "What hour was it when you came here? You say you saw Professor Orison. I'm Professor Orison. The only Professor Orison. I've never seen you before." He eyed Barbara with suspicion.

She told him the time. Barbara was feeling amazingly herself again. She was in no pain. Even her swollen neck did not hurt her unless she touched it. She felt as though she had been given a drink of some powerful elixir. It was Olive who looked as though she had been at the verge of death. Red-eyed, haggard, ghastly pale, she kept close to Pointer's side.

Once in crossing to the fire to stoke it, Vardon tripped a little. Olive flinched like a beaten dog who hears the whip.

Orison put a shaking, wrinkled hand to his head. "But I was upstairs at that time! Tied and gagged!"

His story was that, nearly half an hour before the time Barbara had got to the house, he had been in the house alone, as he thought, except for his housekeeper, and was stooping with his back to the door, fitting a key into the rather difficult lock of the press that housed his stamp collection, when something, or some one, had pressed his head on to the floor where a sponge lay, apparently dropped from space. When he next recollected anything, he was alone in an upper bedroom, bound and gagged. He could hear nothing of what passed in the house, for the towel over his mouth passed across his ears as well.

"But surely our stories can wait," Orison fumed shrilly, "I presume you are satisfied of this young lady's bona fides—" he looked as though he himself were not, "the essential is to get back my green Mauritius. 1847. Three thousand pounds! Not yet listed! I know it's been taken—" He tottered into the next room and gave a screech that sounded like a rusty siren.

"I knew it! Gone!"

Pointer led him gently, but firmly, back into the other room.

"You really need to rest yourself, sir," he warned him, "at your age--"

"My age!" piped the Professor indignantly, "my age, sir, is no more than your own. Mind, mind is what counts. And as long as the power of growth exists, so long——" his voice trailed off feebly. He looked a very old man as he sat mouthing at them.

Tea was brought in by one of the constables.

"The housekeeper was too upset to bring it herself, sir," he explained to Pointer, "says she isn't accustomed to seeing double. Or rather to having a gentleman be downstairs and upstairs at the same time."

"Now what did she mean by that?" mumbled Orison after a thirsty drink, "the female mind is apt to lack coherence."

"She means that some one impersonated you, sir, this afternoon. That the man whom Miss Ash here saw and talked to was made up to look like you, not a difficult feat, and evidently deceived your housekeeper as well. As to your stamp, we shall get the man who stole it, the man who passed himself off as you."

"Hart!" Barbara said suddenly. For the moment she had forgotten the talk with Wilmot.

"Hart? My secretary? Well—what of him?" Orison mumbled, groping for his spectacles, as though they would help him find the man.

There was a ring at the front door.

"That'll be Wilmot!" Pointer said eagerly rising, and going to it himself. But it was Haviland who came back with him a second later. Haviland, who brought in wisps of fog clinging to him. The Superintendent evidently had no clue to this little meeting, and rubbed his chin thoughtfully after the barest of greetings all around.

Pointer did not stop to tell him of what had just taken place. He wanted to hear as quickly as possible what

Barbara had to tell, since she seemed so able to talk. She poured out her tale of Newport, of the Harts who lived there, of the possible relationship with Professor Orison's secretary, as telephoned on from the C.I.D. "But does all this lead us to my Mauritius?" the Professor interrupted once irascibly. No one heeded him.

"So Wilmot has gone to this Hart's address in Bloomsbury." Pointer looked very uneasy. "Is there a telephone to your secretary's rooms, sir?"

Orison said there was not.

"Humph. The fog's too thick to try to leave the house—" Pointer peered behind the curtain at the solid black wall. "Wilmot's a good man, none better in his own line, but this is not his line. This is a policeman's job. He's an amateur. He may have no idea of the dangerous nature of the man he thinks is Hart's brother-in-law."

"Mr. Wilmot may be in trouble, that's a fact." Haviland too, looked worried.

"Mr. Wilmot? Do you mean Mr. Arthur Wilmot, the Japanese collector?" asked Orison, in the tone of a man trying to find some familiar landmark.

"Mr. Wilmot's a newspaper man. A special corresponddent. As a matter of fact, he's better known to you, sir, I dare say, as W. W.," Haviland explained.

"Oh!" the Professor's eyes lost their look of interest. "A journalist. A reporter, I suppose? Necessary, but degrading office."

Pointer sat staring at his boot-tips.

"Just as well that there's some one at the other end of this line, even though it is a position of danger. Nothing can be done until this pea-soup lifts, but I'll use your telephone, if I may, sir, and give the Yard an outline of what's up."

"Outline? Tell them the date. 1847. And the colour— green."

Haviland heard of the Professor's loss with a concern that seemed to placate him a little.

Pointer came back.

"They can't do anything either till this lifts. Let's hope Wilmot's wits will pull him through, and yet detain Hart. Now, sir, since we're all here as your guests would you like to hear the real reason for the attack this afternoon? An attack, not on your collection, but aimed solely at Miss Ash here?"

Orison blinked. He said that he certainly should like to hear the explanation of such an astounding statement.

"But that stamp has been taken!" he pointed out.

"Overlooked, sir, I think you'll find when you've time to go over your collection more at leisure. But do you remember hearing of the death of a Mrs. Tangye just over a week ago?"

As he expected, the Professor shook his head.

"No. I never read newspapers. The waves set up by their articles are not conducive to that calmness essential to the mental worker."

The Professor looked longingly at his desk. On a kneehole table lay the draft of a lecture on Minkowski. He was just making his argument clear that under certain aspects of space-time the triply extended, and the singly enduring can be one and the same attribute.

Pointer, who had looked at the open sheets thought that they could wait. He settled himself still more at ease in his chair, one hand fingering the pipe in his pocket, as the next best thing to smoking it, and began:

"It may help to pass the time for you, Miss Ash, and you, Olive, since you can't get away. Once upon a time, or literally, thirty-five years ago, a curate's daughter was born. Her name was Mable Headly."

Pointer ran through the story that he had just lately been piecing together.

"Apparently, Professor, this Hart who was believed to have been drowned and your secretary are one and the same person, not brothers-in-law," Pointer wound up, "you see our interest in him now? It looks as though he had been aware of Miss Ash's investigations down at Newport, and realising that if once she gets hold of his portrait, the only portrait perhaps that exists of him, it will be put in our hands and printed in every newspaper by us—he determines to put her out of the way. He himself writes a note to the Assistant Commissioner, so I think we shall find, telling him of your secretary's name and existence. Haviland and I don't get the news, because by chance we're out. But it reaches Wilmot, who acts as Hart thought he would. I think Hart expected Wilmot to come here with Miss Ash. In which case he doubtless would have separated them, and duplicated his murderous attempt."

"Then Hart—Hart killed Mrs. Tangye?" Barbara asked, no longer bewildered.

"That's what we think. And Hart chloroformed the Professor and tried to strangle you. We were just in time, or rather—but that must wait. The point is this? Who is Hart? Is he Oliver Headly? That's what it looks like to me. When you get that photograph which is to be sent on from your Newport hotel, we shall know."

Barbara had a momentary, dizzying realisation of the danger that had hovered—struck—and been parried.

"I fail to grasp entirely the validity of the reasons that make you think that my secretary—" the Professor joined his finger-tips wearily, "my secretary—is—this— wanted— man " his voice trailed off. His mouth remained half open. His eyes grew dull.

Pointer poured him out some brandy.

"All this has upset you, sir—"

"It would have upset any one!" snapped the Professor ungraciously, coughing as he drank off the thimbleful. "Any one! An irreparable loss! Even if you catch the thief—I mean, the murderer—" he hastily corrected, "I shall never see my Mauritius again! Never! And it was to figure in a drawing-room talk which I had promised the dowager Duchess of Kingsford to give this afternoon. I ought to go—the fog's lifting—she will expect me. I feel hardly able, but I suppose . . ."

He maundered on. Pointer drew the curtains. Some

one switched off the lights. Outside was only pale gray now. The little group of people so strangely brought together for one tremendous hour, began to break up. Barbara and Olive put on their hats; Vardon watching Barbara as though she might go to pieces any moment. Olive was hardly able to get her hands to her head. Barbara, who had not yet been told of the essential part she, too, had played in her escape from death, helping her, encouragingly.

Pointer and Haviland drifted to the hall outside, where the constable sat thinking out possible solutions to all that he had seen and heard this afternoon—and not seen and not heard.

"I'll stay on here in case Hart turns up " Pointer opened the door to look out, "he may play a bold part, knowing that neither victim saw him. Or Wilmot may telephone. Try to get to him, as soon as the house-party has gone. There's a taxi passing—" Pointer turned to the constable who was listening eagerly, "get it for us. And a second as well, if you can."

The Professor, very shaky about the knees, came out and began to fumble for his top-coat.

Haviland buttoned him up.

"Would you allow us to remain for a little while?" Pointer asked, "your housekeeper is below. We want to question her. Also, I think it possible that your secretary may play the part of innocence, and come on here."

The Professor gave the permission with alacrity.

"I should be glad for you to wait, at least until that young lady has left. I must say I consider the part she and her maid have played in this strange affair very obscure. And that man who came with you? He, I understand, is not a member of your admirable Force?"

"No. He's here by chance. But he's engaged to Miss Ash."

"Exactly!" the suspicion in the Professor's voice became more acute. "I consider the whole affair needs a great deal more investigation than it has had—"

The taxi drew in.

"You take this one, sir," Pointer advised, "there's another behind there for the ladies. Let me put you in, you look pretty well done."

Pointer lifted the bent figure like a child down the steps to the taxi. Haviland, grinning, opened the door.

A couple of men were passing. Another, on the other side of the road, lingered.

Pointer turned to the nearest.

"Here is Professor Orison," he said, literally laying his burden in the other's arms, and slipping, as he did so, a respirator over the man's mouth. At least it looked like a respirator, but it fitted uncommonly closely. "Take him to the station, Watts. Wash him well, and you'll find Mr. Wilmot. Put Mr. Wilmot through the mangle, and you'll find Hart. Irving Hart. Wanted for the murder of his wife, Mable Hart, and the attempted murder of Miss Ash. You have warrants made out in all three names?"

Detective Inspector Watts nodded.

"Yes, sir. Here, Miller, handcuff the left hand to yours. I'll do the same with his right. We'll see he doesn't get a chance to lift either to his mouth, sir."

Pointer and Haviland retraced their steps. A dog barked from a neighbouring window. Some one hastily shut him up. Evidently Pal and his master were interested spectators.

"He'll read about it to-night. I wouldn't arrest Wilmot in the room for fear of a scene. Those two girls have had enough of horrors. You got my message too, I see, Newnes. I suppose Inspector Watts has been bringing you up to date as you came along?"

"Rather! Back in a minute!" Newnes started off at a run to the nearest telephone.

Haviland closed the front door. The spare constable was dismissed from extra duty, the other had been sent to the police station with the housekeeper long go. Haviland held the knob a second in his hand and stood staring at Pointer. He had kept his face absolutely wooden outside, but it had paled.

"Wilmot! Mr. Wilmot! Well, I'm—I'm—I *am!* And that's a fact! Oh, well played, sir! But Mr. Wilmot!"

It spoke volumes for Pointer's standing, that Haviland did not, even for a second, question the facts.

"You've known it all along?" he asked with deep respect.

"Not a bit of it. Never suspected it till an hour ago. Let's clear the house, and I'll explain."

Meanwhile Barbara would have followed the Professor into the hall, but Olive had stopped her.

"Don't go near him, miss! He's been meaning murder every second since they brought us into the room. He's been sitting there longing to wring both our necks, and only putting it off." Olive's cheeks had colour in them now. "I wasn't ill. I was terrified. Afraid lest he should get the better of the Inspector in some way."

Pointer and Haviland returned.

"Right you are, Olive," Haviland nodded. "But, as a matter of fact, you don't get the better of Chief Inspector Pointer easily. He's–-"

"I'll call and see you to-morrow, if I may, Miss Ash," Pointer broke in hurriedly, "if only to thank you for what you've done. That Pringle family, and above all, that photograph of Hart. . . . But we mustn't start explanations now. You may not think it, but you need quiet. And so does Olive. I'll answer every question to-morrow, and ask just a few myself."

Barbara did not move.

"Is Philip cleared, Mr. Chief Inspector? Absolutely? I know he's innocent—" her eyes met her fiance's for one magic moment, "but is he cleared?"

"Absolutely and definitely."

"But how do you—" began Vardon.

"Ah, here's your cab," was his only answer. "Mr. Vardon will see you both safely home," and Pointer most inhospitably opened the door. But this time it was Olive, who stopped.

"Miss Barbara! That photograph! I'm sure I have it here in my bag. The hall-porter at the hotel gave me at the last minute what I thought was only some price lists I'd asked about, never thinking we was going to leave Newport so suddenly. He said they were for me, and I dropped them into my bag.

"There wasn't any letter amongst them. And in the train I read the papers you bought, Miss. But while I was waiting for you outside Mr. Wilmot's rooms, I looked through them. One envelope is for you, and you can feel there's a picture inside it. I'd have given it you immediate, only Mr. Wilmot was talking so hard after we got into his car and you both seemed in such a rush. Just now I didn't say nothing. Not in front of that Professor! Here it is, miss."

Pointer laid a hand on it.

"I'm asking an awful lot. But will you let me have this—without looking at it yourself? I think, thanks to you that the—" he was going to say "prosecution" but changed the word to "case, has got a tremendous lift."

"Since Hart is Mrs. Tangye's murderer, I don't want to see his portrait." Barbara shivered. "But how did you catch him? I thought he had got away from here?"

"You let Mr. Vardon take you home now," was Pointer's soothing answer. "And we'll have a long talk to-morrow, but just one question first. How did you get out of the house, Olive? You saved Miss Barbara's life by that plucky run."

Olive explained, while Barbara for the first time learnt the sequence of events in her rescue.

The two girls clung to each other. Olive was crying, Barbara was beginning to feel exhausted. The powerful stimulant of the nut was passing off. She was glad to let Vardon close the taxi door on the three of them.

Pointer drew out the photograph, a cabinet-sized enlargement of a family group. There in the centre, out of the shadows, looked a face. The face of Wilmot. Practically unaltered, except for the haziness of a beard just beginning to show.

A ring came on the telephone. Pointer leapt for the instrument. Listened; and turned away with a smile.

"He's safely searched and locked up. All rings and personal belongings have been taken from him. Haviland, we've won!" He drew a deep breath.

"This last hour I've been like Olive—terrified. But lest he should guess, we, or rather, I, knew the truth. Frightened for fear he should make some slip I should have to notice. That's why I talked such a lot when that confounded fog came down. That's why I sent his housekeeper off to be locked up as soon as possible. Wilmot would be sure to have poison handy. Ring, cigar-case, watch. A dozen possible places. Even before I knew who Hart would turn out to be, I expected I might have trouble to take him alive. So I kept that respirator of mine handy. No getting anything into his mouth with that on, even without Watts's added precautions.

"Death by his own hand would be too utterly inadequate. He's not to escape punishment like that."

"But what in the world made you link Wilmot with Professor Orison? You say you had no idea of it till this afternoon? I still don't understand it, sir. The fact is," Haviland confessed honestly, "the more I think it over, the less I see how you did it."

"It was a mistake on his part to tie his hands together, back to back. It looked very convincing, but it showed his palms. Interested in palmistry, Haviland?"

"Me? Not much! Why?"

"I pay great attention to palms. Ever since a crook detected me by mine. That over-rated villain, Peace, once said that policemen only looked at faces never at hands. They're one of the few things make-up doesn't change. I can recognise a hand now. Any one's. It's a mere matter of training—of routine. And Wilmot happens to have the most extraordinary lines, and absence of lines. Those palms turned towards me were Wilmot's, and no one else's in the world. That gave me a tremendous jar. Miss

Ash being missing could only be Hart's work. Obviously. And here in the house where she had last been seen alive, was Orison with Wilmot's hands. The chain made itself. Orison— Wilmot—Hart. And, well, if ever there was a moment to be quick off the mark, it was when I believed Miss Ash was in the house, and couldn't find her. For I knew then, or rather I feared, that those hands being Wilmot's meant that we should find her dead or dying." Pointer walked to the window, and stood there for a long minute before he turned round again. "Nothing but Olive's rush out of the house—nothing but the fact that by God's mercy, Vardon and I were at hand—we were asking the constable to point us out Orison's house— saved her.

"As for Miss Ash's story about Wilmot's sending her here post-haste—those messages he sent to the Yard, and the one from the Assistant Commissioner about Hart the secretary, and the letter left for me on his table, will all turn out to be dummies, of course. We may be sure that he had some very neat plan for throwing us off the scent mapped out in that dark brain of his. All I knew an hour ago was, that the delay before she saw the Professor would have been sufficient to let Wilmot get into Orison's things."

"He always was a lightning worker!" Newnes threw in. The reporter had returned, and was writing like a delirious hen scratching for food.

"And a cruel, ruthless venal beast under all his smooth manners. Every one on the staff loathed him. So he stole groceries for his shop, did he? Wilmot has always bragged about belonging to some pious Catholic mother too devout to send him to college. Educated by a tutor, and all that! And all the time he had been a drunken little manager in a filthy slum!"

Newnes had always had a thorough dislike of the special correspondent.

"I rather think he was writing, not drinking, in his locked room," Pointer thought, "he may have been getting into touch with editors even in those days. Oddly enough, there was a penny bazaar not far away, I studied the old ordnance map, called Wilmot's Bazaar. Very likely he took his pen- name from that."

"I'll find out when his articles were first heard of," Newnes promised himself.

"Well, as a matter of fact," Haviland confided slowly, "I thought his manner beside Mrs. Tangye's coffin very uncalled for. His joking and smoking—but I thought it just his way."

"His yarn about Hart being the Professor's secretary was rather thin," Newnes looked up long enough to hazard.

"Had it been cast-iron it would have made no difference. Wilmot didn't guess that we knew all about the Professor's household after hearing that he had bought a Lux camera. He has no secretary here. He has a room and a typist at Sentinel House. For added proof—if one can have such a thing—I puffed one of my fingerprint cigarettes over the papers on his desk. Wilmot's prints are there clear and plain."

"But when did you get Wilmot's prints?" Haviland puzzled. "I thought you didn't suspect him as a matter of fact till just now."

"I'm afraid I was remiss enough not to suspect you either, Haviland," Pointer acknowledged with a faint laugh. "There was no more reason to suspect Wilmot than any other man south of the Cheviots. But I took all our prints, so that if need should arise, I could sift out our three from any I might be interested in. Wilmot left his on a liqueur glass one night when we dined together."

"And how long has this been going on?" asked Newnes. "Why did Wilmot start being Orison in the first place?"

"Ah, why! I shouldn't be surprised—between ourselves— if this weren't the first crime that Wilmot has committed. Orison has only been known to be in existence about three years.

"You remember the steamboat murder as it was called, just three years ago? Norton had the case. It was never solved. Rajah's son found murdered and some thousands of pounds of Bearer bonds missing? Wilmot was one of the party I now remember. I shouldn't wonder if Norton will be able to make some connections when he hears of this. As to Orison's success, Wilmot is an uncommonly brainy chap. Also he chose a field where a flow of language does instead of facts, I take it. I mean metaphysics, and so on."

Pointer had never been able to master that subject.

"Yes, Orison—in case of need—would make a very useful second incarnation of Wilmot. Or third, if we call him Hart. He knew how to meet the right people, too," the Chief Inspector went on.

"And he knew how to advertise, none better," Newnes said contemptuously. "I wondered why the Polish Professor was so to the fore in every report of social things. Wilmot would be able to arrange that without any one being the wiser. But about just now—how did he manage to tie himself up like that? I never saw such a piece of work."

"A series of granny's hitches. A useful fisherman's knot, which you tie loosely and can pull tight. The loose end was fastened to the bedpost, so that the further he worked his chair away, the tighter everything went. That was part of what made him thump about so."

"But those wrinkles!" Newnes murmured when he had got the outlines down, "they really looked impossible to doubt."

"They're real enough—while they last. I've made them myself. But that, Newnes, isn't for publication. Just forget Orison's make-up."

"But how's it done. Between ourselves?"

"There's a very common substance, which, mixed with gelatine and allowed to harden into a jelly, can be liquefied in a second with hot water. You paint it on with a brush, or sponge it on. As it dries—it takes only a minute by an open window—it contracts the skin into a thousand puckers. It can only be washed off in very hot water. That was what I was on my way to do when Olive ran out."

Haviland stared. So did Newnes.

"Well, Orison's appearance so obviously lent itself to the idea of a disguise, once you thought of it in that light, and knew about that wrinkle-making dodge. I intended to call on him, have him ask me to tea, and then—well—I shouldn't wonder if he had found himself feeling suddenly rather faint. I should have got close enough to him to make sure whether that skin was natural or not. You can tell the manufactured article when you know what signs to look for. Vardon, who has been quite definitely not identified by the Newport choirmaster, was coming along to see if he could recognise the voice. I thought Orison might possibly be Oliver Headly. And Vardon knew Oliver. I think one of the reasons Orison wanted to be off, was that he had made himself up rather hurriedly. After all, Miss Ash would stare at him as you and I would."

Newnes got up, his wad of notes in his hand.

"Of all the tales to spin! You knew he was engaged to Lord Vibart's daughter, I suppose? *Secret de polichinelle.* It was to be announced at Christmas."

"So that was it," Pointer said thoughtfully. "A smart, and, I suppose, wealthy marriage?"

"Rather! She was left half shares in the paper by her grandfather who started it, you know. Her husband could become one of the most influential men in England if he had brains. That's why Lord Vibart is said to've finally given his consent. No one can deny that Wilmot has brains."

"High stakes!" Pointer was looking through the papers in the writing-table as he talked.

"No other kind would attract Wilmot in fact," Haviland thought.

"Yes," Pointer went on, "it must have been a blow when he met his wife. Undoubtedly he believed her drowned, and with her all record of those sordid early years."

"Miss Vibart is a beautiful girl," Newnes said. "She's supposed to be most frightfully in love with him. He's very successful with women, you know."

"Beautiful? Wilmot would like that too." Pointer was rapidly glancing at a pile of papers in front of him. Haviland was doing the same.

"Well, she's had an escape second only to Miss Ash's." Pointer lit his pipe. "But one can imagine the shock it must have been to Wilmot to discover that he was, after all, still tied to a penniless woman of no particular family or influence. Mr. Branscombe left everything he had to his 'wife.' I doubt if she could have kept a penny of his money. And I feel sure she wouldn't have, finally. Altogether the fact that she was alive meant the utter ruin of all Wilmot's plans. No wonder he had to work quickly."

"To think that when I pulled him out of the train at Victoria, he had just come away from a murder!" Newnes looked stirred. "He was a fine actor, and no mistake!"

"Every criminal must be, or go under at once," Pointer threw in with but little enthusiasm.

Newnes bustled off.

"What's much more thrilling—to me—" Pointer said grimly, "is the thought that if I had detected any make-up in the Professor's appearance on close inspection, I intended to tell you and Wilmot of him to-night. Nice little surprise it would have been for Wilmot!"

"In point of fact, sir," Haviland rubbed his chin appreciatively, "he didn't miss any of the surprise. Last glimpse I had of him his eyes were still popping out of their sockets. Neatest thing of its kind I ever saw done! So it was Wilmot whom Mrs. Tangye met at Tunbridge," Haviland was trying to get the facts clear.

"Must have been."

The trial that ended Wilmot's earthly career, showed this to have been the case. He had gone there idly, interested in the unhealthy flowers to be exhibited, as anything abnormal drew him, and come face to face with the wife whom he thought drowned long ago.

"And he probably started as Wilmot from town, though Professor Orison arrived at Folkestone in time for dinner that evening. Probably. At any rate, no Orison was noticed going down. And considering how empty the carriages were, that seems odd. Wilmot doubtless changed after the orchid-show, using an empty compartment, as I often do. His disguise would only take five minutes at most. I expect we shall find the Professor had some flat, or chambers, somewhere in town where little attention is paid to the tenants' doings, and that Wilmot will have had rooms or chambers adjoining, but with an entrance in another street. With a very carefully concealed communicating door made, Orison could come and Wilmot go, or vice versa." There was a little pause.

"I rather fancy," Pointer was meditating aloud, "that when Wilmot came to Riverview on Monday, he counselled that quarrel between the husband and wife, hoping that it would be a violent one. And would be overheard. Just in case things went crooked, and the suicide, or accident theories should stick a bit."

"As a matter of fact," Haviland ruminated, "it must have been ticklish work listening to you unrolling the crime, and not have been able to throw you off the track, Chief Inspector. And I see that you're right in saying that a man can't hide, or bury, or do away with clues that only exist in the mind." Haviland began to realise the possible advantages of reasoning over trailing.

"He would have liked to throw suspicion on Tangye, had it been safe. I think that was subconscious jealousy working."

Pointer was right in that idea. Just as it was subconscious jealousy on his own part which made him so determined that Vardon should have more than fair play, should only be arrested on over-whelming proof.

"No wonder Wilmot wouldn't come along to Usk," the

Chief Inspector said, thinking back. "Nor down to Tunbridge Wells. Nor meet Miss Eden. He was playing safety first."

"Nor attend the funeral even," Haviland added. "As a matter of fact, I don't envy his feelings when Miss Ash came in with the news of that portrait group."

"Oh, I think he rather enjoyed the excitement it gave him. He had still a good, a very good chance of suppressing the portrait, after getting rid of the two girls. And if there was any trouble, Orison could be *spurlos versenkt*. Though except for Wilmot there was no one to connect the Professor with the girls—once his housekeeper had been silenced. He drove them here himself.

"Oh, I think he meant to do things on the grand scale. It was his one chance. Then, if all went well, Orison would probably have faded away in time. He's been less and less before the public of late. I think Wilmot was tiring of him, and—if he was concerned in that steamboat murder— began to feel himself quite safe."

"Was his housekeeper in it all?"

"She was in his power, at any rate. I don't think there's much doubt of that. She would do, as well as say, whatever he told her. From the way she eyed the constable when he came in with Olive, I knew she had had trouble with the police before."

"Newnes was right in saying that he was an actor. Who ever would have guessed, without some reason for it, that the Professor was anything other than a weak, old gentleman. And his story about his double all so neat and pat!"

"Humph! I was very careful not to tackle that double. The last thing I wanted was a crack in his plating. As to the note of age, Orison forced that. It could be put down to shock. But it also let him hobble about. Wilmot has a catch in his step. Did you notice it when I was telling the Assistant Commissioner and you two about the Hart marriage? It only seems to come when he's greatly excited

—some sort of nerve spasm apparently. He stepped to the window to look out. I heard it then for the first time. This afternoon, he couldn't walk without it. And there's his poor sight. . . . That single eyeglass of his is for use, as much as for show. Nor have I ever heard of his being even a fair shot."

Pointer rose. Orison's writing-table had yielded nothing. He had done the arrested murderer the justice not to expect that it would.

"No wonder Wilmot was such an authority on criminals. No wonder he could enter so well into their minds. He was himself, that hero beloved of some fiction-writers, the super-criminal. Come, Haviland, we have all the proof we need without hunting for it. This second murder—attempted murder—proves the authorship of the first. If more proof were needed than we have already and can get elsewhere. Yes, Miss Ash has been of more help than I would have believed possible. Consciously and unconsciously. Yet I can truthfully say that I hope to Heaven no amateur will ever assist a case of mine in quite the same way again. After all, risk is what you and I are paid for. It's part of the routine. But to see that gentle girl hanging there—-" Pointer drew hard on his pipe.

"To think that the steps Olive heard were Wilmot's!" Haviland chose his fattest cigar as most sustaining. He felt that he needed support. "In fact, 'the footsteps that stopped' have been close beside us all the time. Walking along with us, and the case."

"They're stopped now," Pointer's face was ruthless, "or soon will be. They'll walk no more in any victim's garden."

"And that's a fact," Haviland said solemnly, as they shut the door behind them.

THE END

Other Resurrected Press Books in *The Chief Inspector Pointer Mystery* Series

Murder at Bridge

When an afternoon bridge party attended by some of Hamilton's leading citizens ends with the hostess being murdered in her boudoir, Special Investigator Dundee of the District Attorney's office is called in. But one of the attendees is guilty? There are plenty of suspects: the victim's former lover, her current suitor, the retired judge who is being blackmailed, the victim's maid who had been horribly disfigured accidentally by the murdered woman, or any of the women who's husbands had flirted with the victim. Or was she murdered by an outsider whose motive had nothing to do with the town of Hamilton. Find the answer in . . . **Murder at Bridge**

One Drop of Blood

When Dr. Koenig, head of Mayfield Sanitarium is murdered, the District Attorney's Special Investigator, "Bonnie" Dundee must go undercover to find the killer. Were any of the inmates of the asylum insane enough to have committed the crime? Or, was it one of the staff, motivated by jealousy? And what was is the secret in the murdered man's past. Find the answer in . . . **One Drop of Blood**

AVAILABLE FROM RESURRECTED PRESS!

THE EDWARDIAN DETECTIVES
LITERARY SLEUTHS OF THE EDWARDIAN ERA

The exploits of the great Victorian Detectives, Poe's C. Auguste Dupin, Gaboriau's Lecoq, and most famously, Arthur Conan Doyle's Sherlock Holmes, are well known. But what of those fictional detectives that came after, those of the Edwardian Age? The period between the death of Queen Victoria and the First World War had been called the Golden Age of the detective short story, but how familiar is the modern reader with the sleuths of this era? And such an extraordinary group they were, including in their numbers an unassuming English priest, a blind man, a master of disguises, a lecturer in medical jurisprudence, a noble woman working for Scotland Yard, and a savant so brilliant he was known as "The Thinking Machine."

To introduce readers to these detectives, Resurrected Press has assembled a collection of stories featuring these and other remarkable sleuths in The Edwardian Detectives.

- The Case of Laker, Absconded by Arthur Morrison
- The Fenchurch Street Mystery by Baroness Orczy
- The Crime of the French Café by Nick Carter
- The Man with Nailed Shoes by R Austin Freeman
- The Blue Cross by G. K. Chesterton
- The Case of the Pocket Diary Found in the Snow by Augusta Groner
- The Ninescore Mystery by Baroness Orczy
- The Riddle of the Ninth Finger by Thomas W. Hanshew
- The Knight's Cross Signal Problem by Ernest Bramah

- The Problem of Cell 13 by Jacques Futrelle
- The Conundrum of the Golf Links by Percy James Brebner
- The Silkworms of Florence by Clifford Ashdown
- The Gateway of the Monster by William Hope Hodgson
- The Affair at the Semiramis Hotel by A. E. W. Mason
- The Affair of the Avalanche Bicycle & Tyre Co., LTD by Arthur Morrison

RESURRECTED PRESS CLASSIC MYSTERY CATALOGUE

Journeys into Mystery
Travel and Mystery in a More Elegant Time

The Edwardian Detectives
Literary Sleuths of the Edwardian Era

Gems of Mystery
Lost Jewels from a More Elegant Age

E. C. Bentley
Trent's Last Case: The Woman in Black

Ernest Bramah
Max Carrados Resurrected:
The Detective Stories of Max Carrados

Agatha Christie
The Secret Adversary
The Mysterious Affair at Styles

Octavus Roy Cohen
Midnight

Freeman Wills Croft
The Ponson Case
The Pit Prop Syndicate

J. S. Fletcher
The Herapath Property
The Rayner-Slade Amalgamation
The Chestermarke Instinct
The Paradise Mystery
Dead Men's Money

The Middle of Things
Ravensdene Court
Scarhaven Keep
The Orange-Yellow Diamond
The Middle Temple Murder
The Tallyrand Maxim
The Borough Treasurer
In the Mayor's Parlour
The Saftey Pin

R. Austin Freeman
The Mystery of 31 New Inn from the Dr. Thorndyke Series
John Thorndyke's Cases from the Dr. Thorndyke Series
The Red Thumb Mark from The Dr. Thorndyke Series
The Eye of Osiris from The Dr. Thorndyke Series
A Silent Witness from the Dr. John Thorndyke Series
The Cat's Eye from the Dr. John Thorndyke Series
Helen Vardon's Confession: A Dr. John Thorndyke Story
As a Thief in the Night: A Dr. John Thorndyke Story
Mr. Pottermack's Oversight: A Dr. John Thorndyke Story
Dr. Thorndyke Intervenes: A Dr. John Thorndyke Story
The Singing Bone: The Adventures of Dr. Thorndyke
The Stoneware Monkey: A Dr. John Thorndyke Story
The Great Portrait Mystery, and Other Stories: A Collection of Dr. John Thorndyke and Other Stories
The Penrose Mystery: A Dr. John Thorndyke Story
The Uttermost Farthing: A Savant's Vendetta

Arthur Griffiths
The Passenger From Calais
The Rome Express

Fergus Hume
The Mystery of a Hansom Cab
The Green Mummy
The Silent House
The Secret Passage

Edgar Jepson
The Loudwater Mystery

A. E. W. Mason
At the Villa Rose

A. A. Milne
The Red House Mystery
Baroness Emma Orczy
The Old Man in the Corner

Edgar Allan Poe
The Detective Stories of Edgar Allan Poe

Arthur J. Rees
The Hampstead Mystery
The Shrieking Pit
The Hand In The Dark
The Moon Rock
The Mystery of the Downs

Mary Roberts Rinehart
Sight Unseen and The Confession

Dorothy L. Sayers
Whose Body?

Sir William Magnay
The Hunt Ball Mystery

Mabel and Paul Thorne
The Sheridan Road Mystery

Louis Tracy
The Strange Case of Mortimer Fenley
The Albert Gate Mystery
The Bartlett Mystery
The Postmaster's Daughter
The House of Peril
The Sandling Case: What Would You Have Done?
Charles Edmonds Walk
The Paternoster Ruby

John R. Watson
The Mystery of the Downs
The Hampstead Mystery

Edgar Wallace
The Daffodil Mystery
The Crimson Circle

Carolyn Wells
Vicky Van
The Man Who Fell Through the Earth
In the Onyx Lobby
Raspberry Jam
The Clue
The Room with the Tassels
The Vanishing of Betty Varian
The Mystery Girl
The White Alley
The Curved Blades
Anybody but Anne
The Bride of a Moment
Faulkner's Folly
The Diamond Pin
The Gold Bag
The Mystery of the Sycamore
The Come Backy

Raoul Whitfield
Death in a Bowl

And much more!
Visit ResurrectedPress.com
for our complete catalogue

About Resurrected Press

A division of Intrepid Ink, LLC, Resurrected Press is dedicated to bringing high quality, vintage books back into publication. See our entire catalogue and find out more at www.ResurrectedPress.com.

About Intrepid Ink, LLC

Intrepid Ink, LLC provides full publishing services to authors of fiction and non-fiction books, eBooks and websites. From editing to formatting, from publishing to marketing, Intrepid Ink gets your creative works into the hands of the people who want to read them. Find out more at www.IntrepidInk.com.

www.ingramcontent.com/pod-product-compliance
Lightning Source LLC
Chambersburg PA
CBHW071050250626
47159CB00002B/428

*9 7 8 1 9 3 7 0 2 2 7 5 4 *